ENSORCELLED

PRINCE OF THE DOOMED CITY:

BOOK 3

FIRE
WYRM
BOOKS

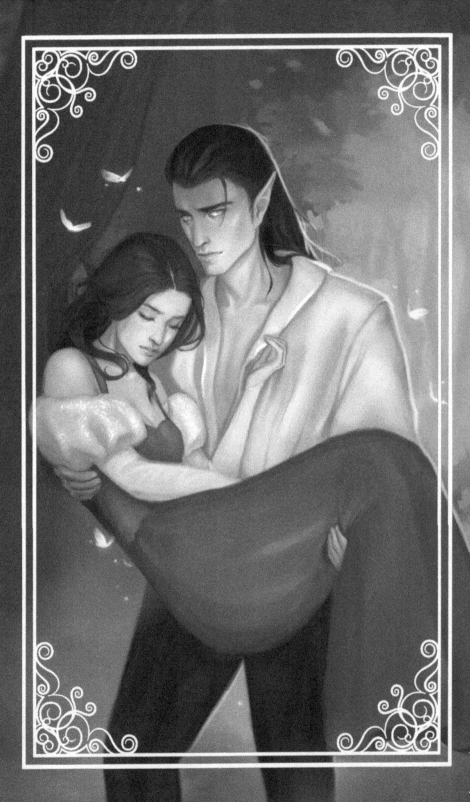

ENSORCELLED

PRINCE OF THE DOOMED CITY:

BOOK 3

© 2022 by Sylvia Mercedes

Published by FireWyrm Books

www.SylviaMercedesBooks.com

Cover illustration by Amira Naval

This one is for Andra,
for all the encouragement

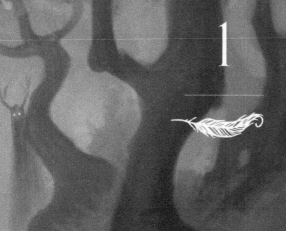

1

A LOCK OF HAIR HAS FALLEN ACROSS HIS FOREHEAD. My fingers twitch. Again. This is the fifth time I've almost leaned forward in my rocking chair, bent over the recumbent form at my feet, and tried to swipe that glossy strand back into place. It's an unconscious urge, no doubt stemming from my need for order in the current chaos of my life. It certainly can't be that I actually *want* to discover if his hair is as soft and silky as it looks . . .

There I go again! I snatch my hand back, clench it tight in my lap. My chair utters a disconcerting groan and lurches to one side on its broken runner. I quickly grip the arms to brace myself. A curse bubbles up on my lips. Biting down hard, I refuse to let it out. Instead I close my eyes and breathe a silent prayer: *Seven gods above, give me strength.*

Another breath. Another. I'm centered now. Calm.

Slowly I open my eyes. This time I'll find somewhere else to look. The sparse little room doesn't offer much, however. All the nicer furnishings were sold off long ago. Only the brightly painted porcelain shepherdess remains on the mantel. Her face was smashed; otherwise, she might have fetched a penny or two at the trinket stalls. As it is, she stands in her accustomed place, covered in a thick layer of dust. As sad and decrepit as everything else in this house that was once my home.

My gaze drifts. How can it not? By contrast to the rest of the room, the figure lying on that pile of blankets close to the hearth is altogether glorious.

I chew my lip, my brow puckering. Of course the Prince has always been beautiful. That's no great surprise. Just now, however, he's more beautiful than usual. Drained of his human blood, his fae nature fairly shines through his skin, pulsing from his very core. As I sit here studying him hour after weary hour, I cannot help wondering if he's changed in more than appearance. When he wakes, will he be the same man I've come to know over the last few months?

Do I want him to be the same?

Gods blight me, that lock of hair is going to drive me mad! All coiled and falling delicately across his wide, smooth brow and down the plane of his cheek. Maybe I should just swipe it back and have done with it? It's so unusual to see the Prince even slightly mussed. Just now, he's nothing but mussed. Pale and rumpled and nearly naked underneath that rough cloth blanket, and so, so beautiful. Heartbreakingly beautiful.

And here I sit. Ogling him. My Obliege Lord, my tormentor. The source of all my problems and woes. The man who saved my life at risk of his own. The man who goes on risking his life day after day for the sake of Vespre's people, regardless of how deeply they hate him.

I bury my face in my hands, push my palms hard into my eyes. Then, with a little huff, I spring from my chair. It rocks wildly and nearly tips over behind me as I stride to the window. I peer through grit and grime. Darkness falls; the day draws to a close. A little lamplighter scurries along at the intersection some doors down, but nobody bothers to illuminate Clamor Street. As night descends, I feel more and more cut off from the rest of the worlds.

What is happening back in Vespre? I left in such a rush with the Prince following our battle with the Noswraith. How extensive was the damage wrought by the Eyeless Woman? Did any other Noswraiths work their way free while the librarians were distracted? And what about Nelle? I close my eyes fast against a sudden flood of tears. For a moment, I see myself once more back in the library. I'm in a darkened passage, looking beyond the arch to where Nelle stands. She holds a flaming dagger in her hand, and its light illuminates her face—young, pale and beautiful, brilliant with fierce courage. She glances swiftly back at me, face shining.

The next moment, red mist envelops her. And the screaming begins.

With a gasp, I open my eyes and press a hand to my pounding heart. Nelle is dead. I'm sure of it. Killed by the Eyeless Woman. By the very Noswraith I called to life and then . . . forgot about. The Noswraith I failed to contain because I could not remember its name. Another life counted to my bloody ledger. Right along with the life of the Prince's own mother.

Sniffing loudly, I dash hot tears from my cheeks. Where is Lawrence anyway? After the Prince woke this morning feeling better, his manservant returned through the Between Gate to carry word back to Vespre. I expected his return hours ago.

I wrap my arms tightly around my stomach as I turn and face the room again. Truth be told, it's not really Lawrence I'm worrying about. It's Oscar. My little brother. He should be here. But he wasn't home when we arrived late last night, and he's not made an appearance all day. Now night is falling once more, and he's still not back from . . . from wherever he slinked away to. Some pub or, worse yet, some opium den. Perhaps he's even now carousing with the new lover about whom he's dropped broad hints. Getting high on *rothiliom*.

My hands knot into fists, pressed tight against my ribcage. If only I could go out searching for him. But I wouldn't know where to begin! Besides, I can't just walk out and leave the Prince like this, can I?

I cast my patient a baleful glance. Once more, his awful, terrible, gods-blasted beauty strikes me like a blow to the chest. Why does he have to *be* like this? *Why?* Why does he have to lie there, all vulnerable and glorious, with that muscled arm thrown back over his head, and that strand of hair fallen over his brow, his full lips gently parted, his broad chest rising and falling with the rhythm of his breaths? Why does he have to affect me like this . . . like . . . like . . .

Like I could fall in love with him if given half a chance.

Oh, gods. Won't someone—*anyone*—come home already?

As though responding to my silent wish, the front doorknob jiggles. I start, turn from the window, and take three steps forward, Oscar's name on my lips. The door opens.

Danny steps through.

I halt. A storm of confused feelings whirl in my head. Danny has always been a source of comfort and security in my life, but all that changed last night. Last night, I lied to him. Lied to him in order to manipulate him, forcing him to save the Prince. He believed that by doing so he saved my life as well. Which wasn't true at all.

The weight of my lie presses hard on my conscience. But what else could I do? Danny was determined to let the Prince die. I couldn't let that happen, not when I . . . that is, not when Vespre needs him so badly. He's the only protection the denizens of that dark city have against a veritable onslaught of doom.

I straighten my spine and compose my face into a careful mask of welcome. A little cold, perhaps. Danny removes his hat and hangs it on a peg before turning. Seeing me standing there, he starts to smile, then stops. Something about his expression looks guarded, like a wounded puppy expecting another kick. But he's here still. Come back to offer his help. Because he's Danny and he cares. He will always care. He can't help himself.

"Miss Darlington," he says, slipping into that painful formality we've erected as a barrier between our hearts over the last few years. "I can't stay long. I've a patient in critical condition down at Westbend Charity. But I wanted to check on . . . on . . ."

He can't say what he truly means, but we both know his concern isn't for the Prince. He's here to see that I'm all right, to make certain I haven't already been whisked back into a world of darkness and danger he cannot begin to imagine. Leaving him behind. Again.

"Danny," I say, then hastily correct myself, "Doctor Gale."

Before I can go on, he pushes past me into the room where the Prince still sleeps soundly on the floor. I've managed to keep a small fire burning throughout the day, but the room is still bitterly cold. To combat this, I've done my best to keep the Prince covered in blankets. In this particular moment, however, he's thrashed free of them, displaying his sculpted torso to full effect. Gods blast him! I half suspect he's done it on purpose. Is he truly as sound asleep as he seems?

Danny's face speaks volumes as he stands silently over the Prince. I don't like the look in his eye. As though he even now contemplates murder. It's such an unnatural expression, one that doesn't belong anywhere on Danny's face. He's a healer through and through.

Have I driven him to this dark place?

I bite my lip, trying to decide what I might say to alleviate this terrible silence. Before an idea springs to mind, Danny kneels, opens his bag, and pulls out a wooden stethoscope. With quick, practiced movements, he screws the three parts together, then presses the bell to the Prince's chest, listening to his heartbeat. After that, he takes his pulse, places the back of his hand across the patient's forehead, and even lifts one eyelid, then the other, peering closely into each eye. Throughout this examination, the Prince remains, to all appearances, deeply asleep.

At last, Danny sits back on his heels. "He's improved," he says grudgingly and casts me a fleeting glance. "His vitals are sound, his heartbeat stable. It will take time for his body to replenish the lost blood. Best to let him sleep as much as possible." His voice is cold, clinical.

I nod, taking care to maintain my neutral expression. "Thank you," I manage after a silence that lasts a little too long. "I . . . I just want to . . ." I stop. Whatever I try to say sounds lame. Finally I settle for simply repeating, "Thank you."

Danny unscrews the parts of his stethoscope and places them back in his bag. Closing it, he rises, then makes his way to my side. He stands a moment, looking back into the room. I listen to him draw a long breath, feeling the tension in the air between us.

"Don't move him," Danny says at last, still without looking at me. "Not yet. I'll be back again in the morning." With that, he turns away and makes for the door. Returning to the patient in critical condition, no doubt. Because that's who Daniel Gale is—a man who has devoted his life to helping other people. A good man.

A man I've hurt more deeply than I ever meant to.

I wish I could just let him go. Let him walk out of my life so I can't hurt him anymore. If it were just about me, I would. As painful as it would be to lose Danny—and, necessarily, his sister Kitty as well—it would be better than knowing I'm causing them both continuous pain.

But this isn't just about me.

"Doctor Gale," I say, hastening after him.

He stops on the doorstep and looks back at me. For a moment, my heart seems to stop. The last time we stood here like this, he kissed me. A rough, angry, possessive kiss, not at all like the first kiss we shared. I know he's remembering it too. I see it in his eye.

I drop my chin but force my next words out. "I have to ask . . . It's about Oscar."

"Oscar?" Danny frowns, glances beyond me to the figure on the floor again, then meets my eye. "Where is Oscar?"

"That's what I'm wondering. He's not here. He wasn't here when we arrived last night, and I haven't seen him all day. I'm just . . . I'm worried."

The crease between Danny's brows deepens. "He will probably turn up when he's ready."

There's something evasive about the way he says it. "You know where he is, don't you?"

His lips press into a tight line. He shuffles as though ready to make a darting escape from my stoop. I start to reach out, to catch his arm, but stop myself at the last second. He notices, however, and his gaze flashes back to hold mine. The reflection of the low firelight on the hearth dances in the depths of his pupils.

"I don't know," he says. But he's lying.

"Where is he?" I urge. "Is it the Siren Bell? That's where Dad used to lounge with his mates back in the day. Or is it worse than that?" Danny sets his jaw, turns away, and looks down the street as though he wants to run. My stomach plunges. "It's the Old Docklands warehouse district. Isn't it? That's where he's gone."

Danny whips his head back around. "You shouldn't even know a place like that exists."

That's all the confirmation I need. I step back from the door and lean against the wall, suddenly light-headed. "There's a lot of things I shouldn't know," I admit.

I close my eyes. Suddenly, I'm a girl of twelve once more. Mama holds me by one hand and clings to Oscar on her other side. We're walking fast, trying to keep up with her anxious stride as she leads us down the winding streets of the old docking district. Despair permeates the air around us as Mama searches and begs for directions and searches some more.

She finds my father at last in a derelict warehouse. I'll never forget the sight—Edgar Darlington, famed writer, one of the most celebrated minds of the age, sprawled on an infested mattress in a pile of limbs with numerous half-clad women. Every one of them lost in a stupor, unwashed and unkempt. Minds wandering in darkness.

"*Edgar!*" Mama cries, her voice choked with emotion. "*Remember your children! Remember your wife! Remember how we need you!*"

He lifts his heavy head, gazing up at us without even a trace of recognition. *"G'way, you bi—"*

Shuddering, I rub both hands down my face. I've never wanted to remember that night. Not long afterward, Mama died, and our lives were never the same. So why would Oscar return to a place that caused him only loss and pain?

"Are you sure?" I ask, finally managing to look at Danny again. "How can you possibly know where he is?"

Danny hangs his head. "I've found your brother there before. On several occasions."

A sob threatens to choke me. I fight it back with an effort. When Danny reaches for me, I push his hands away, shaking my head.

"Clara, you know it does no good to take away the poisons," he says, his voice low, reasonable. "If a man is determined to poison himself, he can always find more."

I nod. There's little point in denying a truth I know too well. With a quick shake of my head, I reach for the old cloak hung by the door. It's one of Mama's, as is the dress I'm wearing. When I left Vespre last night, I was still clad in a silver ballgown. I was lucky to find a trunkful of Mama's old things stashed away in her bedroom.

"What are you doing?" Danny says as I lift the cloak from its hook and sling it around my shoulders.

"I have to get him."

"No!"

I look up, my face hardening into severe lines. "I won't leave him there, Danny. I won't. He's my brother. He's—"

"You cannot go to Old Docklands. It's no fit place for a lady."

I raise an eyebrow. "I am no lady." Pulling the hood up over my head, I step toward the open door.

Danny blocks my way. His hand clamps down on my upper arm. "Don't be a fool," he growls. "Do you really think I'm going to let you march out at this time of night to a place like that? You'd never find him anyway. Old Docklands is huge. The last time I dug him out, it took me hours, and I was lucky I didn't get knifed in the gut and left to bleed out. At some point, you're going to have to let Oscar suffer the consequences of his own choices."

"His own choices? Do you think he chose to be this way? Do you think he woke up one morning and just decided to become enslaved to *rothiliom?* Do you think this is Oscar's fault?"

"It doesn't matter what I think. It's not *your* fault. So why should you risk your life to save a boy who doesn't want to be saved?"

I twist my arm, trying to get free. "You're hurting me!"

But he won't let go. "I'm not going to let you do this." He leans into me, pushes me against the wall. "I'm not going to let you—"

Suddenly, the pressure relents. A whirl of movement leaves me gasping, confused, struggling to make sense of what is taking place in front of me. Then Danny is slammed hard into the wall across from me, and a bare muscular arm presses into his neck, pinning him in place.

"I beg your pardon, sir," purrs a deep velvety voice, "but who are you to impose your will upon Clara Darling?"

It's the Prince. Still shirtless, of course. Shirtless and shoeless, clad in nothing but a pair of trousers slung low on his hips. Firelight plays across his bare torso, and I find myself hyper-aware of details—like the way the blue veins stand out under his unnaturally pale skin; the way little beads of sweat gather on his brow; the way that same stupid lock of hair still falls across his forehead, dangling between his eyes.

With a gasping inhale, I kick myself into motion, lunging at the Prince and grabbing his arm. "He didn't mean any harm! Please, let him go! Let him go!"

He resists for no more than a breath. Glancing sideways at me, he bares his teeth in what might almost pass for a smile. Then he sags, steps back, and releases his hold.

Danny pushes away from the wall, straightening his jacket. "What?" he demands, his voice choked and furious. "Are you so chivalrous? Defending her honor? You, who *own* her! You, who control her every word and deed, even to the point of forcing her to save your miserable life!"

With a toss of his head, the Prince finally flicks that hair back into place. "For a man who dislikes seeing the lady controlled, you have a strange way of showing it."

"Only a man who doesn't care about Clara's wellbeing would stand by and watch her do something so foolish! Not when he has the ability to prevent it."

"And you know better than she how she ought to conduct herself, is that right?"

"Sometimes, yes. I've known Clara all her life. I've been her friend; I've cared for her when no one else would."

"A funny way of caring, fitting her so tightly into your narrow little box."

"I am trying to save her!"

"No doubt. But I've watched her face down monsters far beyond anything you could possibly imagine. If you knew her at all, you'd know she's perfectly capable of saving herself."

Danny spits a vile word. I've never heard him speak like that before. I never thought he could or would. Not my Danny.

Hastily, I step between him and the Prince, taking hold of his hand. "Please," I say desperately, staring into his sparking eyes. "Just go."

Danny's gaze shifts from me to the Prince and back again. He's at war with himself. In the end, however, he allows me to guide him to the door and out onto the stoop. There he grabs the doorframe and holds on tight, as though afraid some hurricane blast will rip him away from me. "Please, Clara," he says, "promise you won't go anywhere tonight. I've got to see to my patient now, but I'll return in the morning, I swear. I'll help you find Oscar then. Just promise me you'll wait until I come back."

I open my mouth, about to speak the truth. But how can I? Battle wages in his eyes. I know how hard he will fight to get his way. I don't want to lie to him, but . . .

I squeeze his hand gently. "I'll see you in the morning, Danny."

His eyes flash, igniting with painful hope. I start to pull away, but he catches my wrist, holding me in place with a grip that's almost painful. My breath hitches. I'm far too aware of the Prince standing in the foyer behind me, watching my back.

As though reading my mind, Danny glances briefly over my shoulder. Abruptly he lets go and steps off the stoop. He holds my gaze a moment longer. Then, to my relief, he turns and strides down the dark street, making for the streetlamp at the intersection. Soon he blends into the shadows, but I listen to the sound of his footsteps retreating. He appears again just under the light, takes the turn, and is gone.

I draw back into the house and shut the door. Closing my eyes, I count slowly to ten.

Then I turn around and face the Prince.

He smiles. Just an uptilt of his lips on one side, creasing his cheek and bringing forth a devilish dimple. "Neatly done," he says in that wretched purring voice that does funny things to my blood. "You'd make an excellent fae, you know."

I draw myself together, folding my arms tight. "I don't know what you're talking about."

He tips his head. And that same blasted lock of hair slips free and falls between his brows. "That was a delightful little bit of trickery just now, deceiving your handsome beau without overtly *lying* to him."

"I . . . What do you mean?"

"Come now, don't play coy. We both know you have absolutely no intention of staying put until morning, have you?"

2

WITHOUT WAITING FOR A RESPONSE, THE PRINCE leaves the foyer, returning to the pile of blankets on the floor. He idly shuffles through them with one foot, his mouth pressed in a pensive line.

"What are you doing?" I demand, gripping the folds of my cloak.

He looks up, his expression deceptively placid. "What does it look like I'm doing? I'm searching for my shirt. I seem to have lost it in all the excitement. Happens to me rather more often than I like to admit in the presence of a lady. Have you seen it, by the way?"

"Seen what?"

"My shirt, of course."

I gape at the Prince. Then, realizing I'm gaping, I turn away quickly to hide my blush. "You have no need of a shirt." Stepping over to the pile, I crouch and begin to straighten out the blankets. "You're making a mess of it! Just lie back down, why don't you?"

"Oh, no, certainly not. Do you think I could nestle in all nice and cozy while you make your way to this . . . what was it called again? This Old Docklands. A den of ill repute in more ways than one, I take it. Don't try to shield my delicacy!" He places a hand to his heart. "I've seen more of the worlds than you and have accumulated my fair share of experiences. You needn't worry about shocking me."

"I'm not worried about shocking you." I rise and face him, crossing my arms. "I'm worried about you keeling over any second now. I've got no one here to help me get you back into bed. For all you're so skinny, you're not light, you know."

"Skinny?" He looks down at his lean, muscled frame. "Come now, that's a bit harsh, don't you think?"

I refuse to be baited. "Go on." I point to the bed firmly. "Put your head down and go back to sleep."

His violet eyes flash as he catches my gaze. "Are you *obliging* me, Darling?"

My blood runs cold. Somehow in my worry over Oscar, I'd allowed myself to forget that vital piece of information—the fact that I am, however inadvertently, the Prince's savior. According to him, that means he's Obliged to me.

But surely that can't be true, can it? It must be some trick, some manipulation. He's trying to lure me into a false sense of security so that he can . . . what? I don't know and cannot possibly guess.

I lick my lips, considering my next move carefully. "What will happen if I do oblige you?"

He tilts his head, sending that ridiculous lock of hair tumbling across his cheek. My hand positively itches to reach out and tuck it behind his ear. Gods on high, this isn't fair! Why does he have to be so distractingly beautiful? It unnecessarily complicates everything.

"This situation is unusual," he says. "Only a handful of times throughout the vast and twisted histories of Eledria has a fae become Obligated to a human. As for a *mutual* Obligation? I'm fairly certain there have been no more than two previous instances throughout the whole history of fae-human interactions."

"Mutual Obligation?" My brow puckers. "What do you mean?"

"Oh, you didn't think your own Obligation ended, did you?" The Prince chuckles, a sound that makes my toes curl and my stomach do a little flip-flop. "No, Darling. I'm afraid your Obligation stands as firm as ever. Only now we find ourselves in the unlikely situation of being Obligated *to one another.*" He rubs his chin thoughtfully. "As I recall, a mutual Obligation requires a certain back-and-forth. The same rules of the original agreement stand, including the day off once every lunar cycle. But only one may be the Obliged and one the Obliege at a time."

"So," I say slowly, my mind racing to catch up, "if I were to oblige you to lie down and sleep now, you would have to do so. But I won't be able to oblige you again until you've enacted *my* Obligation."

"Indeed." He smiles, but there's a fierce glint in his eye. "Which means, if I never choose to do so, you will effectively cease to have power over me."

I take this in, mulling it over carefully. "Is it my turn then? To oblige you?"

"Considering I've never obliged you to do anything against your will, there has been no start to the cycle yet."

"You obliged me to go with you to Vespre. To work in your library."

"There you are wrong." His eyes narrow ever so slightly. "I brought you to Vespre, yes. I taught you what you need to know. Not once, however, did I force my will upon you. You were Estrilde's Obligate before you were mine. You know the difference."

I do. I can't deny it. All too vividly I remember what it felt like when Princess Estrilde issued one of her many flippant commands. The hold of her voice, her power, clamped down around my very spirit. To resist was to suffer, and I learned quickly to jump in obedience if I wanted to avoid pain.

The Prince, by contrast, though imperious, demanding, and exacting, has never crossed that particular line. Always I've had the choice whether or not I would submit to his commands. A fine line of difference, perhaps, but a difference, nonetheless.

"So tell me, Darling," the Prince says, when my silence has lasted a little too long, "is this where we begin? Is this where you assert your will over mine? Will you insist on venturing alone into this den of depravity as you search for your missing brother, leaving me to snooze peacefully in my bed?"

I want to. I want very badly to speak the words, to see him obey me. For years now, I've railed against my own Obligation, longing to be free, to do as I wished with my own life. The satisfaction of turning that power on another is undeniably appealing. But to do so would be to become what I hate. How can I in good conscience play the role of Obliege Lady?

I bite my lip. "You're going to slow me down."

"Maybe," he answers placidly. "But if you don't take me hobbling with you, I will crawl along behind you. Either way, I'm coming."

"What happened to my facing down monsters beyond imagining and being capable of saving myself? Was that just posturing?"

His lips curve again. "I meant every word. That being said, the monsters one finds in this world are worse than anything to be met with in Vespre. While I don't doubt your capabilities, I would nonetheless rest easier knowing you won't face such monsters alone." He tips his head, looking at me from beneath his puckered brow. "And you *do* want me to rest easy, don't you?"

"Of course, but—"

"Well, there you have it. I cannot rest until I know you're safely home, therefore I must see you home safely. Yes?"

I toss up my hands, exasperated. "How could you possibly help if we run into trouble? You're so weak, you can barely stand!"

"Oh, I have many ideas, never fear." He counts them off on his fingers. "I could fall on the enemy. Land in a heap of bones to trip up pursuers. Shoot them a deeply unsettling, glassy-eyed stare." He shrugs. "The possibilities are endless."

I don't want to smile. And I don't want to feel this sudden upswelling of relief at knowing I won't have to face Old Docklands alone. But I can't help myself. I've been alone so much of my life that I've come to prefer it that way, to never let myself be dependent on anyone. But just now . . . just now, it would be good to know someone walked beside me in the dark.

"All right," I say at last, pulling my cloak tight around my shoulders. "Get a shirt on, and let's go."

I find an old, ragged, moth-eaten coat of my father's for the Prince to wear. Otherwise his finery will attract far too much attention down in Old Docklands. The sleeves are too short, and the buttons won't close across his chest, but at least it's some measure of covering.

"Here, wear this," I tell him, and plunk a much-battered hat on his head.

It sinks to his eyebrows. He pushes the brim up with one finger and looks at me. "Well, Darling? Do I look like a down-on-my-luck dockworker yet?"

He doesn't. Just now, with the human blood mostly drained from his body, his fae nature dominates, rendering him unreasonably beautiful. He could wear a bag over his head, and he'd still draw every eye on the street. But I don't tell him that.

"You'll have to do," I say and usher him out the door. Once I've locked it behind us, I start down the street, making for the lamp at the intersection.

The Prince lays an arresting hand on my arm. "Where are you marching off to with such determined purpose, may I ask?"

"Old Docklands, of course," I growl, shaking his hand off. "It's a long walk, and we haven't time to dally."

"If the walk is long, why not order a cab?"

I look up and down Clamor Street, illuminated by just enough moonlight to reveal creeping shadows in the darker corners. "Do you think any cabbies are foolish enough to try their luck around here?"

In lieu of an answer, the Prince sticks two fingers in his mouth and utters such a piercing whistle, I yelp and leap back several paces. Before my heart has a chance to settle down again, there's a clatter of hoofbeats. Whirling in place, I let out another yelp just before the Prince grabs my arm and yanks me out of the way of an oncoming hansom cab. The horse comes to a stop, tossing its head and rattling its harness, while the driver, blinking with some perplexity, turns in his seat, looking around.

"Down here, my man," the Prince says.

"Oi, 'ere!" The cabby doffs his hat, then rubs a finger along his drooping mustache. "Were it you what called for a cab, then?"

"Indeed, I did, sir."

"What are you doing?" I hiss. "We don't have any money to pay for a cab!"

"Not to worry, Darling." The Prince smiles brilliantly, his teeth flashing in the moonlight. He turns that smile from me to the poor unprepared cabby and says, "Will you barter for a ride, my man?"

The cabby's bewildered expression sinks into sullen wariness. "Sorry, sir, and meanin' no disrespect, but I've got mouths to feed. It's coin or nothin'."

The Prince's smile never falters. He pulls a single hair from his head and holds it out, pinched delicately between two fingers. "And what would you give for a year of solid good luck?"

The cabby's gaze fixes on that hair with unexpected intensity. He rubs his mustache again. "What's the catch?"

"No catch," says the Prince. "Simply weave this strand into your horse's tail, and you'll only take heavy tippers for the next twelve months. The first tip alone will more than cover the fare to our destination and back again."

I hold my breath, watching the cabby's face as he contemplates the idea. Then he snuffles loudly and holds out his hand. "Give it over then."

The Prince drops the hair into the man's grasp. Then he offers me his hand. "After you, Darling."

Part of me wants to protest. But what's the point? I allow the Prince to assist me into the dark cab interior. I've just settled my cloak and skirts when he climbs in and takes a seat on the bench beside me. He's suddenly very close. I try to sidle away only to find I'm already as far over as I can get, and he's pressed right up against me.

He smiles. "This is cozy, isn't it? But the night is cold, and this coat you've got me wearing doesn't button properly up the front. Perhaps we could share your cloak?"

"Perhaps you could try buttoning your shirt instead."

He smirks and glances down at his exposed chest. His shirt is made from some lovely shimmering fabric with a satin weave, but he seems to have grown weary of doing up its delicate flower-shaped buttons, leaving the top five undone. Typical. When I growl that he's sitting on my skirt, however, he does slide back a little, giving me room to breathe.

"Will it work?" I ask, keeping my voice low.

"Will what work?"

"The year of good luck."

"Of course, it will work." He shoots me a look. "I'm fae, remember. I cannot lie."

"You're half human. You can lie half the time. And something tells me you probably do."

He shrugs an elegant shoulder. "Since you bullied your handsome beau into bleeding the human blood out of me, I'm far less capable of human trickery at the moment. So yes, the bargain is good."

"I thought the fae were particular about not giving pieces of themselves away."

"Naturally. But that hair had a split end anyway, so I'm just as happy to be rid of it."

The cabby finishes tying the hair into his horse's tail and scrambles up into his seat. "Where'd you wish to go then?" he calls back through the little window.

"Old Dockside, please," I answer, my voice firm.

The cabby hisses a little breath through his teeth. "And what would a nice lady like you'un want to be going to a place like that for?"

"Our bargain does not extend to personal questions," the Prince says sharply and smacks the ceiling. "Quickly, man, if you want your luck to hold!"

Muttering, the cabby shuts the window and gives the reins a smart slap. "'Ere, ge'yup!" The cab lurches into motion, and we are on our way.

"I cannot believe he bartered with you," I say, settling deeper into my seat. "I didn't think folk of our world had dealings with Eledria save in rarest cases. When I was growing up, I thought all those stories of fae and bargains and magic were just that: stories."

"When two worlds exist in such close proximity, it would be strange indeed if they didn't bleed into one another rather more often than not." The Prince tries to cross his legs but finds the space too confining. He grunts and shifts uncomfortably. "So tell me again who we're on our way to rescue? Some brother of yours?"

"Yes," I answer softly.

"I remember him—a young fellow, all knees and ears. He should be about eighteen now, I think."

"Twenty."

"A bit of a troublemaker, is he?"

"You could say that."

The Prince's gaze burns into the side of my face. It's dark within the carriage, the only light coming from the flickering streetlamps flashing past the window at intervals. But I suspect he can see me clearly enough. I keep my expression perfectly pleasant, perfectly neutral. Give him nothing.

We lapse into silence. My nerves spark with heightened awareness as the cab ventures into the darker, more twisted streets of the old city. Memories of that long-ago night with Mama and Oscar down in Old Dockside have haunted me for years. I have no desire to revisit them. But how can I bear to leave Oscar there?

Of course, even if I manage to find him, manage to drag him out . . . I can't stop him from crawling right back again.

A tear escapes, spilling onto my cheek. I dash it away quickly, determined not to let the Prince see. Tomorrow is not my concern. Nor the next day, nor the day after that. I need to find Oscar tonight. I need to do what I can right now. The rest will simply have to wait until it happens.

Finally the cab comes to a stop. "Here ye are, Master and Missus," the cabby calls out. He doesn't get down to open the door for us. The Prince climbs out, then offers me a hand. I pretend not to see it as I hold my skirts out of my way and step out onto the street. The stench of Old Docklands hits me like a blow to the face. This section of the city used to boast the primary shipping docks. Enormous derelict warehouses extend along the waterfront for several blocks. Most of these have been converted into brothels and illegal gaming houses. The city constabulary are well aware of the doings down here but are too frightened to venture in save in absolute need. Thus, vices planted by the dregs of society are left to take root, flourish, and fester at will.

The most infamous of these converted warehouses is called the Den of Vipers. I recognize it at once, standing at the end of the street. It was there we found my father all those years ago. Letters over the door used to spell out the name of some shipping company, but they've been painted over with a crude scrawl and an ugly squiggle of green that might be intended as a snake.

"Wait here for us," the Prince says, casting a quick glance back at the cabby.

"Oh, now, sir, we ain't agreed 'pon—"

"If you want your luck to hold, you'll be here when we return. Understand?"

The cabby looks as though he's not sure twelve months of good luck are worth another second sitting exposed on a street like this. But he meets the Prince's eye and nods grudgingly. I doubt his courage will hold once the Prince is out of sight. We'll just have to risk it.

"Shall we, Darling?" the Prince says, offering his elbow. I take it hesitantly. In just a few paces, I realize he's not simply being gallant. He leans into me, his pace a little staggering, his breath uneasy.

"Are you all right?" I whisper. "Perhaps you should wait."

"And miss out on all the fun? I think not."

An emaciated someone stands watch at the door. Light from a low-burning lantern flickers red on features pinched with sickness and eyes sunken into deep hollows. The long skirt and ragged lace-trimmed blouse seems to imply a woman, but the nearer we come, the less I'm sure. I'm not even fully convinced it's human. It flashes a knife as we draw nearer. I catch a glimpse of catlike yellow eyes with narrow pupils, but the person blinks, and the image vanishes. The lantern swings away, and the face falls into deep shadow.

"Password," an unexpectedly deep voice slurs.

I stop short, uncertain. How did Mama get us through that door? Had she learned the password somehow? If so, I certainly don't remember. Not that it would be the same anyway, so many years later.

The Prince doesn't hesitate. He draws himself up and, though he was breathing heavily only a moment ago, speaks now in a clear, commanding voice: *"Felaadar."*

The being blinks at him several times. With each flutter of lashes, I glimpse those cat eyes again. At last, it bows and steps back. "Careful you keeps to the right," it says. "The left . . . it won't take you where you wants to go."

The Prince offers the faintest inclination of his head, then glances down at me. "Shall we?"

I swallow hard and nod. Stepping through that door again takes far more courage than I like to admit. But Oscar is in there. I'm certain of it.

I gather my skirts in both hands and duck into the shadowed interior with the Prince following close at my heels.

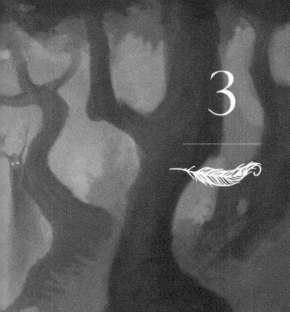

3

"WAS THE DOORKEEPER FAE?" I ASK IN A TIGHT whisper.

"Indeed." The Prince ducks his head low, speaking close to my ear. "This whole place stinks of Eledria."

A shiver prickles the back of my neck. I remember Danny telling me there are places in the city that lie closer to the fae worlds than I ever realized. I never considered the possibility that Old Docklands might be one such place.

The entrance has brought us directly into a narrow passage. A blank wall stands before me, shabby with chipped paint. With the doorkeeper's warning still ringing in my head, I can't help glancing first to the left. Nothing to see but a little globe-shaped lamp, its flickering light illuminating bare board walls and what looks like an open doorway at the far end. A sudden and indescribable curiosity overcomes me. I take a step in that direction without realizing it.

The Prince's hand closes down hard on my elbow. "Now then, Darling. You've lived in Eledria long enough to know it's best to follow the directions of mysterious personages standing at gates."

I catch my breath with a little "Oh!" Then, shaking my arm free of his hand, I turn to the right. When he tries to take my arm again, I snap, "Let me go."

"Of course," he answers at once, removing his hand. "If you don't mind my sagging to my knees and gasping out my last breath here in this darkened passage."

I glare at him. The light of the lantern behind me casts his face in strange highlights, revealing the flash of his teeth when he smiles back. But I allow him to take my elbow again, ostensibly for support. He doesn't lean on me this time, however. Is he doing this as a pretense to keep me closer? Quite probably, but in the moment, I don't care to argue.

We proceed along the righthand passage. There's no door at the end, just a ratty old curtain. The Prince sweeps it back and steps in first, drawing me after him. We emerge into an enormous square space, heavy with darkness. Light from barrel fires illuminates patches at odd intervals. I glimpse moldy mattresses and recumbent forms. The air is dense with smoke and reeks of human waste overlayed by thick, cloying perfumes. Scantily clad women lounge with their arms thrown over their heads, lying beside naked, emaciated men. Laughter erupts from one of the nearby clusters, sounds of fights and . . . and other things I don't want to study too closely.

I come to a stop three paces in. Frozen. Stunned. Memories of the last time I was here scream at the corners of my mind. Of Mama's iron-fast grip on my hand. Of Oscar whimpering, weeping. Mama crying out to our father: *"Remember your children! Remember your wife! Remember how we need you!"*

We shouldn't be here. We shouldn't be here, we shouldn't be here, oh gods, what am I doing here? I need to go, I need to escape. I need to . . .

My knees buckle. I start to sink. But the Prince's grip on my arm keeps me upright. He pulls me against his side, murmuring, "Steady now. Be strong." I close my eyes against a sudden upswell of tears. Dragging a steadying breath into my lungs, I hold it for a count of five, then let it out in a measured gust. "Better?" the Prince asks. I nod. "Excellent. Where to next?"

I open my mouth, not at all certain what I'm going to say. Before I can speak, however, a laugh rings out across the echoing rafters. High, keening. Heartbreaking. A laugh I would know anywhere.

"Oscar!" I whisper.

Suddenly galvanized, I dart ahead, heedless of the Prince's, "Darling! Wait!" Nipping between mattresses, barrels, and shadowy forms, I push through several more curtains in pursuit of that elusive siren call. "Oscar!" I try to cry. My throat closes up, choking on the stink and fear and desperation in that putrid atmosphere. I pull a handkerchief from my sleeve and press it to my nose, trying not to breathe too deeply. Stumbling, I take a few more steps.

The air inexplicably changes.

I'm still in the warehouse. I can see its listing walls, broken windows, and sagging rafters overhead. Somewhere, far off, I can still smell the funk of refuse and waste. But all of that seems to exist behind a shimmering mirror, like a reflection world that cannot quite reach reality. Here, dominating my immediate senses, are the sweet perfume of apple blossoms, the soft whisper of green leaves and silken petals, and the play of light filtered through lacing branches. Music lilts, mingling with laughter so that it's impossible to tell where song ends and voices begin. Figures dance amid silvery tree trunks, naked and wild, beautiful and free.

I blink . . . and the trees are gone. Instead I see only old posts and broken boards, propped up and nailed in place. The figures dancing among them shamble awkwardly, drunken and manic. There is no music, only their laughter, which now sounds more like weeping and wailing.

I spy Oscar at once. He's at the center of the throng and happens to pass near one of the barrel lights. The red gleam lights up his face. Eyes shining bright with *rothiliom,* he links arms with two other young fellows. They, like him, are stripped down to their trousers, barefoot despite the cold. He looks ragged, hideous. Like a phantom creature only just clinging to corporeal life.

Oscar! I try to cry for him but cannot get his name out through the thickening in my throat. With a growl of frustration, I hurtle forward, pushing into the crowd. Shadowy figures move and gyrate, and Oscar passes beyond my range of sight. I try again to call his name, elbowing my way deeper.

Someone catches me around the waist and yanks me into the dance. For a terrible moment, I hear that lovely, lilting song again, feel the softness of a spring breeze, glimpse the white-and-gold light shimmering through pale blossoms. I scream, twist, fight to get free. Laughter rings in my ear. I'm pulled against a broad, muscular chest, but when I pound my fists against that hold, I see skeletal bones, sagging flesh, oozing sores. Wet lips press against my neck. I scream again when I feel the edge of teeth scrape against my skin.

The next moment, I'm pulled free. My vision spins, but when I manage to reorient myself, I'm positioned just behind the Prince's back. He holds out one arm, shielding me even as he faces down my captor. The man is a ragged individual, bearded and broken. He sways on his feet, blinks blearily up at the prince. "I was'na gonna . . ." he starts, but his voice trails off, unable to finish the sentence.

The Prince's hand curls into a fist. "No!" I say, taking hold of his sleeve. He looks down at me, and I shake my head. "Leave him. It's not worth it."

"It might be."

"Please!"

The Prince's brow tightens. Then, with a short nod, he lets his fist relax. Tipping his head, he indicates the dancers behind me and says, "Is that young fellow the one we seek?"

I turn. To my surprise, Oscar stands but a few paces behind me. His companions have abandoned him, flitting off into the darkness, away from the barrel fire. Without their support, he sways heavily but manages to keep his feet. This close, I can see the twin circles of green light swirling around his pupils as he blinks and tries to focus his swimming gaze. "C-Clara?"

"Oscar!" I leap forward, take hold of both his hands. "Oscar, what are you doing in this place? I've come to take you home."

"Nnnaaaow." His voice sounds like the wail of a sickly tomcat. He shakes his head, and his hands twist to pull free of my grip. "Nnnnaaaaow, I'm not leaving. My friends is here. My . . . my sweet . . ." He looks around vaguely, but the throng of dancers has dispersed. Frowning, he turns to me again.

Then his gaze lifts, focuses on the figure standing just behind me. "You!" His eyes widen, burning bright with green light. He lifts a trembling finger to point wildly. "You! You! Stay away from me!" With an inhuman shriek he turns, tries to run. He trips over his own feet and falls flat on his face, hitting the floor hard.

"Oscar!" I crouch over him as he curls up into a tight ball of misery. He's weeping. Sobbing. Open-mouthed and wailing like an infant.

"I lost it!" he blubbers as wetness trails from his eyes and nose. "I lost it all! Maybe I never had it. But it's gone now, gone, gone, gone." The words devolve into incoherent sounds of agony. He doesn't resist when I draw him into my arms. I cradle his head against my shoulder, wiping strands of sweaty hair from his face. Urgently, I look up at the Prince. I have no words, not even to ask for help.

The Prince doesn't wait for me to ask. He kneels across from me and places a hand over Oscar's face. "See only she who loves you," he says.

At once all the tension seeps out of Oscar's body. When I look down at him, he blinks at me, innocent as a newborn babe. His chapped, bleeding lips part, forming a little O as though of surprise. Then he closes his eyes and simply tucks up against me.

"What did you do to him?" I demand.

"Placed a glamour over his eyes." The Prince sits back on his heels, his expression grim. "It doesn't take much—the *rothiliom* in his system has already addled his senses. He'll be calmer now. Let's see if we can get him up, shall we?"`

While I dislike the idea of my brother's perceptions being meddled with, I can't very well argue. Not here, not now. Too many eyes watch us from the shadows, and my neck still feels slimy from that disgusting, unwanted embrace.

I draw Oscar's arm over my shoulder. The Prince does likewise, and between us, we get him upright. I've the distinct impression the Prince is taking more of the weight than he should. When I glance at him, his face reveals deep strain. He shouldn't be doing this. But what choice do I have other than to accept his help?

We stumble back through the pockets of light and stretches

of darkness, past vignettes of sorrow and horror I cannot bear to look at directly. At last we make our way to the curtained doorway and step out into the narrow passage. Sidling awkwardly, we reach the door. A different doorkeeper stands watch now, a startlingly tall and painfully skinny woman wearing nothing but a shift and corset. She trails long, large-jointed fingers across the Prince's shoulders as he steps past her, crooning, "Come again soon, sweetheart." There's an odd, serpentine quality to her voice.

But we're out now, back into the night air of Old Docklands. To my unending relief, the cabby still waits for us at the end of the street. He jumps in his seat when the Prince hails him. "Gods above me!" he exclaims. "I thought yer wasn't coming back! I started to think I were going to be here till morning!"

I frown, surprised. "How long were we inside?"

"Gone on four hours now, miss, by the belltower's toll."

My gut clenches. It seemed like no more than twenty minutes. But perhaps he's exaggerating. Perhaps it only *felt* that long, waiting in the dark in this part of town.

Rather than press the issue, I push Oscar into the cab. Shivering hard, he keeps saying my name in a plaintive little-boy voice: "Clara? Clara? Clara?" I remove my cloak and wrap it around his naked shoulders. The Prince shoots me a look, but I ignore him. I'd rather freeze than watch my brother suffer.

Once the Prince climbs in and the door is firmly shut, the cabby snaps his horse into motion. We roll on through the night, leaving Old Docklands behind. I breathe a sigh, resting my head back against the threadbare seat cushion. When Oscar says my name again, I pull his cheek against my shoulder and croon for him to sleep. He obeys, closing his eyes.

I meet the Prince's gaze over the top of my brother's head. He's uncharacteristically solemn. "So," he says. "*Rothiliom.*"

I nod.

"How did he come by it?"

I shrug. "He claims to have fallen in love. I suspect his lover is fae. But I don't really know." A few silent moments hang in the air between us, full of unspoken things. I don't like it. "This isn't who he really is, you know," I say suddenly, the words falling out in a tumble. "Oscar is a lovely boy and so . . . so . . ."

I stop. I was going to say *so talented.* But something stops me. Instead I turn away, unwilling to meet the Prince's eye. He knows too much already. In fact, I suspect he knows more than he's letting on. I must be wary at all times. *Never anger the fae. Never trust the fae.* Not even this one.

The cabby drops us just outside my door on Clamor Street. Ready to see the last of us, he stops only long enough for us to drag Oscar out and to demand reassurance that his luck will last a good twelve months. "Indeed, it will," the Prince responds. "If not, the rest of my glorious hair will fall out by the handful, and we can't very well have that now, can we?"

The cabby snorts but seems satisfied. He clucks to his horse and drives off, making for the light at the end of the street with all speed. The Prince helps me get Oscar inside. Between the two of us, we manage to drag him up the stairs and into his bed. I wrap my cloak around his frail, thin body, tucking the end over his bare feet. Only then do I look up and notice the Prince has sagged heavily against the wall, one hand pressed to his forehead.

"You're not well," I say, straightening upright. "Go downstairs. Lie down and shut your eyes. I'll be in to see to you shortly."

"You know, I don't mind if I do." With an effort, he pushes off from the wall and makes for the door, calling back over his shoulder, "See what an obliging sort I am?"

I scowl at his retreating back. He knows perfectly well that, curt though my commands were, I did not implement the Obligation over him. There's no point in protesting, however, so I go back to seeing to Oscar's needs. There's little enough I can do to make him comfortable, but I try my best. When I'm done, I search his room carefully for any drink or powders or little vials of green liquid. There's nothing of the kind, not that I can find.

Finally I turn to the bed once more. Oscar's eyes are cracked open. *Rothiliom* glints behind his lashes as he looks at me. "Clara," he says, his voice hoarse. "You won't leave me again, will you?"

Gods on high! My heart feels as though it must break. Because of course, I will leave him. I can't stay here forever no matter how I wish to. I've got my Obligation to fulfill.

Rather than answer, I kiss his forehead. Tears slip down my cheeks to splash on his face. "I'm going to fetch you some water," I say softly, stroking his forehead. "I'll be right back, I promise."

He whimpers but closes his eyes, turning his face into his pillow.

I slip away, down the stairwell. In the kitchen I find water someone hauled in from the city pump three streets over. I fill a cup, telling myself I'm unaware of the Prince's lounging form on the floor by the hearth. But as I make my way back to the stair, I cannot help a swift, covert glance.

He's somehow lost his shirt again. Of course. He lies with one arm thrown across his eyes, his chest rising and falling in deep rhythmic breaths. Low firelight plays across his form, illuminating his too-pale skin. I swallow the lump in my throat and turn away, cup in hand.

Before I've slipped into the stairwell, however, the Prince's voice startles me from behind: "A moment, Darling. Before you go."

I pause. Slowly, I look back. The Prince is watching me from under his bent arm. His eyes glitter in the dim red light. "What?" I demand.

"When I'm quite recovered, and the time has come for my return to Vespre . . . will you be joining me?"

"Of course," I answer at once, without thinking.

He smiles. The next instant his eyes are closed, and his arm rests across them again. Heavy breathing fills the air, accompanied by a most unexpected snore. He's asleep. Already. Almost miraculously.

I frown, biting the inside corner of my cheek. Why would he ask me something like that? As if I have a choice. Is it something to do with this new mutual Obligation of ours? And if I have a choice, what should I do? Stay with Oscar, of course, but . . . but . . . there are the children to think of. Not to mention Lir. Mixael and Andreas.

Captain Khas. And all that vast, horrible library full of Noswraiths eager to burst free and wreak destruction on the worlds. Could I really choose to abandon my role in Vespre City?

No. No, I won't think about that. Not right now.

Ducking my head, I slip up the stairs to Oscar's room. There I shut his bedroom door fast against any questions that might try to plague me in the wee small hours before dawn.

THE PRINCE

I WAKE WITH A START, BLINKING INTO DARKNESS.

For a moment, a hazy image manifests before my sight. An awful visage—pale, sunken. Eyes sewn up shut with dangling black threads which tickle my cheek.

I gasp, try to draw back. Only I'm flat on my back and cannot move. My body is heavy, paralyzed. The vision tilts its face, brow puckering slightly. Hair falls across its features. But when it shakes that hair back, the ghoul is gone.

Instead it's Clara's face I see. That soft, gentle face, her eyes shining with concern.

She's never looked at me that way before.

My heart leaps to my throat. With everything in me, I want to reach out, to touch her cheek. To slip my hand through that long hair, round to the back of her head. Pull her face down, claim her lips with mine. To show her with my body everything that burns in my soul.

If she knew . . . if she only knew . . . surely then she must . . . we could . . .

My eyes open. Again.

This time it's real. This time I am truly awake. Not trapped in a hazy half-sleep dream but lying on a pile of old blankets beside a cold hearth in a room smelling rather pungently of humanity. Grimy dawnlight forces its way through dirt-caked windows and dust-heavy curtains, falling across the floor and driving back the shadows. The air tastes stale. And worse. Despair has worked its way into these walls, these floorboards, the very beams over my head.

Slowly I sit up. Aches and pains erupt across my body. But nothing worse. No fiery jolt in my blood followed by an icy wave of unadulterated anguish. I roll my shoulders, twist my spine. Everything feels much better than it did during last night's little escapade. In fact I'm stronger than I have been these last five turns of the cycle. My fae blood, purified for the time being, flows fast. I feel I could, with very little effort, leap rivers and soar over mountains.

Only when I reach for my human magic does something shiver inside me. Hastily I retreat from that sensation. The curse is still alive, after all. Dormant, perhaps. But I'd prefer not to wake it.

I turn in place, cast my gaze about the dingy little room. It's empty. No sign of my hostess. But I know where she is. With a groan, I press my palms into my eyes, run my fingers through my hair. Then, grabbing my discarded shirt lying nearby, I pull it on over my head and push to my feet. For a moment I stand still, waiting to make certain the room doesn't suddenly decide to upend me. When everything remains as it should, I kneel, pick up one of the blankets, and step away from the hearth.

The stairwell is narrow and dark. But that unseen, unmistakable thread of connection which always leads me back to her plucks gently that way. I used to resist it. I used to pretend it wasn't there. Now . . . what's the use? It's not as though I'm fooling anyone. Least of all myself.

The blanket draped over one arm, I climb the creaking stairs to the floor above. It's a short passage with only a few bare little rooms. I peer into the first one. And there she is. Just as I expected. Propped on a chair beside her brother's bed. Holding the boy's hand. Her head is tilted at an awkward angle. She looks cold and so exhausted.

I step into the room, moving softly so as not to disturb her. Gently I wrap the blanket around her. She stirs, but does not wake, not even when I crouch beside her, studying her pinched face. There's little light in this room, but my fae senses see her clearly enough. I study her at my leisure, those delicate features which I long ago memorized. The little bump midway down her nose.

The soft bow of her upper lip. The line of her jaw, so sharp and determined.

What a reckless creature she is. Reckless and wild and so grimly resolved to throw herself into peril without the least regard for her own safety. She would die for those she loves. Gods above know she would die for those she felt nothing more than a passing concern for! She is selfless to a fault. Selfless and courageous and . . . and . . .

And she saved my life.

What did I ever do deserve this? To become the recipient of her care and concern? I treated her with such scorn, such contempt. I tore her away from the comforts she knew and hurled her headlong into a war for which she was wholly unprepared. I lectured her and berated her and demanded far more from her than I had any right to demand.

Yet there she was by my side that night. In the depths of the Nightmare. She did not flinch from the fight. She did not retreat, even when I ordered her to. She refused to let me face the wraith alone.

But that had nothing to do with me personally. Did it? No, I shouldn't flatter myself. I know better. That's just who she is. A fighter. A unique kind of warrior. The sort of woman who takes in unwanted troll orphans and claims them as her own, braving the wrath of an entire city. Risking her life for the chance to make theirs a little better. Sacrificial, selfless, eternally committed to loving and to giving, no matter the cost.

The kind of woman who will fight tooth nail for those who don't give a damn about her.

My lip curls. I turn my gaze from her pale face and let it rest instead on her brother. He lies quiet for the moment. Not peaceful—the aftereffects of *rothiliom* play havoc on human bodies and minds. His dreams will not be pretty, and he will wake in pain. After what he put his sister through last night, I cannot summon much sympathy.

I still remember the first time I laid eyes on the boy. He was little more than a child then, gangly and terrified. But magic stirred deep in his soul. So much power. That power is still present now, but suppressed. Deeply hidden behind terrible barriers. A curse—as vicious as any curse I've ever seen. Magic of the absolute blackest variety.

I grimace. The weight of a curse like that must take its toll on both body and soul. It's not right for anyone to live under such malice. *Rothiliom* might counteract some of the effects, but the relief would be temporary.

Someone is trying to get through that curse. Someone is trying to break down those barriers. Not Clara. No, she is both innocent and ignorant in this matter. I doubt she even knows there is a curse at play. Even if she did, she wouldn't think to treat the symptoms with something as dangerous as *rothiliom*.

What about this fae lover she mentioned? Is it possible someone is supplying the boy, attempting to break through the curse? Someone who cannot fathom the potential consequences . . . or someone who simply doesn't care?

I let my gaze return to Clara. Her brow is so tense, the line of her lovely mouth so severe. She suffers too much for this boy's sake. If only I could convince her not to waste her affections. A useless wish; just as useless as trying to convince her to leave the troll children and their people to their fate.

But maybe there's something I can do. Maybe . . .

I rise. Stand a little longer, looking down at her. Temptation burns in my veins. I fight to hold myself in check. Then, in a moment of impulse, I allow one hand to reach out, one finger to brush ever so lightly down the curve of her cheek.

Her frown deepens. She shifts under the blanket, turning her head slightly.

Pivoting on heel, I hasten from the room and descend the stair on silent feet.

CLARA

4

THE LAST THING I WANT TO DO IS WAKE UP. IF I weren't so precariously propped on a spindly chair beside my brother's bed, I would most likely just roll over and continue sleeping for another ten hours straight.

As it is my foot slips, and my body jerks, and I have no choice but to slide back into the waking world once more. Groaning, I rub the heels of my hands hard into my eyes before blinking and looking around. Pale gray light filters through the grime on Oscar's window, illuminating his sparse cell of a room and the harsh contours of his drug-ravaged face. At least his expression is relaxed. Perhaps I could slip out to the market, get some supplies to make a small breakfast for him when he wakes.

This resolution in mind, I sit upright. It's bitterly cold, and my cloak is still wrapped snugly around Oscar's frail body. But there's a blanket draped over me. Strange. I look down at it, frowning. I don't remember bringing a blanket upstairs with me. I certainly wouldn't have kept it for myself, not when Oscar is in such delicate state.

With a shiver, I rise and quickly drape the blanket over my brother, on top of my cloak. Then, rubbing my arms, I slip from the room and descend the stairs, little puffs of white vapor drifting from my lips with each breath. Downstairs is somehow even colder.

I only allow myself a brief glance at the hearth and the pile of blankets lying there. The last thing I want is for the Prince to catch me staring at him, so I hasten instead to the kitchen. No sign of Lawrence anywhere. What is keeping him so long? A number of possible answers spring to mind, each darker and more desperate than the last. But no. Best not to dwell on what may or may not be happening back in Vespre without its Prince there to protect it. I have troubles enough of my own just now.

It's cold out in the city streets without a cloak. I wrap my arms around myself and trot all the way to Sloaner Square, nine streets over. There, Farmer Gavril is just setting up his stall and, after a little cajoling, agrees to sell half a dozen eggs to me on credit with the understanding that I owe him twice the usual rate. Another seller is likewise convinced to give me bread, and a third parts with a single small bottle of milk. It's not much, but it's all I can manage for now.

Laden with my purchases, I return home, freezing and utterly ravenous. I've not eaten since yesterday morning, before Lawrence set out for Vespre. My stomach growls. I wish I could tuck into the loaf of bread. I can't bear to deprive my brother, though. Once I return to Vespre, I'll have food aplenty; meanwhile, how will Oscar get by without me here to remind him that his body needs sustenance?

My head heavy with problems for which I can find no solutions, I shoulder the door open and hasten inside. My glance flashes idly toward the fireplace and away. Then, with a little kick to my heart, I turn sharply back again, blinking hard.

The Prince is gone. The pile of blankets, which I had mistaken for his sleeping form earlier, is just that—a disheveled heap of tangled fabric.

I stand a moment, staring at that cold hearth. Staring at those blankets. At that empty spot where my patient ought to be. He seems to have taken his shirt, at least. And my father's old coat. But where could he have gone? Is he searching for me? Did he venture out into the streets on his own?

I take a half step back toward the door, but some practical side of my nature stops me short. If he's gone into the city, there's no telling where he may have wandered. Best to stay here where he knows he can find me. Besides, the house is freezing. And Oscar needs food.

I force myself to enter the kitchen and unload my purchases, then go about building a meager fire in the stove. All the while, I refuse to let my brain run wild, refuse to let one awful, dangerous question intrude upon my thoughts: *Did he leave for Vespre without me?*

I stare at the little fire I've coaxed to life in the belly of the iron stove. As the flames flicker in their erratic ballet, I seem to see again the whirl of glorious golden dancers. I hear wild fae music and the rush of a million tiny wings mounting to the sky. When I close my eyes, I feel a warm hand slide around my waist, drawing me close.

"Blight and blast it!" Pushing up from my knees, I turn to face the door. Foolish or not, I'm going to find the Prince. If he went tottering out into those frozen streets on his own, who knows what might have happened to him? He's not well, and he shouldn't be overextending himself, and—

Just as I reach for the doorknob, it turns. I stagger back, surprised, as it swings open. A tall figure stands silhouetted in the opening. My heart springs to my throat, and my mouth starts to form a greeting or a chastisement, I'm not certain which. At the last instant, however, I choke back the words I was going to speak.

"Oh!" I splutter instead. "Doctor Gale. You frightened me."

Danny steps into the foyer, his brow puckered. He looks worn after his long night at the charity hospital. Was he able to get any sleep? No more than the rest of us, I imagine.

His gaze slides over my unkempt appearance. "Are you all right, Miss Darlington?" He removes his hat, hangs it on a peg. "Gods above, it's freezing in here!"

I smooth a hand over my hair and tuck a strand behind my ear. "Yes, I . . . I'm lighting a fire."

"Were you going out?" His brow puckers. "Without a cloak?"

What am I supposed to tell him? That I was about to plunge into the city streets, shouting for the Prince? He looks at me closely as though reading the truth in my face. Hastily, I avert my eyes to the covered basket he carries on his arm. "What is that?" I ask rather too briskly.

He hefts the basket and offers me a small smile. "Food. I know how little there is to eat in this house."

"Oh, you didn't need—"

"I wanted to." He tilts his head, brows lifting slightly. "May I?"

I step aside, allowing him to carry his offering to the kitchen table. I don't like the way my heart melts at this kindness. I want to stay angry, resentful, and distant. As distant as I can manage. But it's so hard to remember when Danny goes and demonstrates his thoughtful, generous nature like this.

I trail after him, chewing my lip uncertainly, and watch as he unloads fruits, vegetables, several hard-crusted loaves, and an assortment of meat pasties. It's a small feast. "Thank you." The words seem too small, almost foolish. I catch his eye and put as much sincerity as I can into my voice. "Truly, this is too much."

One of his eyebrows lifts slightly. But all he says is, "You should eat quickly. Then we'll go."

"Go?"

"To Old Docklands. Like you asked." He notes my sudden shift of expression, and his eyes brighten with hope. "Unless you've decided against it after all?"

"Oh." A cloud of shame passes over my soul. I drop my head, lowering my lashes. "Yes." I can't manage anything more.

It doesn't matter. I feel all the brightness go out from Danny in a rush. He's silent for a terrible moment, and when he finally speaks, his voice is cold: "You went there. Last night."

It's an effort of pure will to meet his gaze, to see that stricken look of betrayal in his face. "I couldn't leave Oscar—"

Spitting a curse, Danny turns away from me. His hands clench into fists as he draws deep breaths, trying not to let his feelings get the better of him. At last, he looks around, his eyes hard beneath his drawn brows. "Why would you go without me? I told you to wait! I told you to let me accompany you! Anything might have happened to you. Anything!"

My hand rubs at that place on my neck where a stranger's wet lips kissed me. I grimace but shake my head and draw back my shoulders. "I can handle myself."

"Handle yourself?" His gaze slides from my face to the pile of blankets on the floor. "You took *him* with you."

"Danny—"

He pounds the wall with his fist, leaving a crack in the old plaster. I yelp and start back another two paces. I've never seen Danny display temper in such a way. It's not like him at all.

"I'll remind you this isn't *your* business," I say angrily. "Oscar is *my* brother, and I am responsible for—"

"Not my business?" He shakes his head in disbelief. "Do all these years mean nothing to you? All the times I've stepped in to help when I didn't have to, when others urged me to let you go. All the times I've been here for you, for Oscar. All the times I've been the one to venture into various dens and brothels and gaming houses, dragging your brother home by the collar to dunk him in cold water, trying to pull him back together while you . . . you're off galivanting in other worlds! Dancing with fae folk and making eyes at handsome princes."

"That's nothing like what I've been doing!"

"Oh, isn't it? Because that's how it looks from where I'm standing."

I draw breath through my teeth. "I don't owe you anything." The words grind out, each one painful but necessary. "I'm grateful for the help you've rendered me over the years. But that doesn't mean I belong to you."

"No. You *belong* to him." Danny's arm swings around, one finger pointing at the pile of blankets as though the Prince still lies there. "You belong to him, signed, sealed, and delivered. And what kind of services do you render him exactly?"

I feel all blood draining from my cheeks. How dare he? How dare he speak to me like this? I want to slap him. I want to tell him to get out of my house, to get out of my life. In that moment I cannot remember the boy I've known so long. He's been replaced by a stranger, a cruel, angry, jealous stranger. Instead of speaking, I turn my back on him. Tears well up, frustrated and heartbroken and furious. Though I try to suppress it, one choking sob escapes.

"Clara!" Shame colors Danny's voice. His footsteps sound on the floorboards behind me. "Clara, I'm sorry. I don't know what came over me! I'm such a cad." He's there the next moment, his hands on my elbows, trying to turn me, to take me in his arms. Part of me longs to give in and fall into his embrace. He's comforted me before. Would it be so wrong to accept such comfort again? This is Danny, after all. My Danny.

I set my spine like iron. "You should go."

His hands drop away. I listen to his ragged breathing. Then he draws a deeper breath, and I brace myself for whatever he's about to say.

"Enough is enough. I'm going to break your Obligation. Once and for all."

I whirl on one heel. He's already marching across the room, striding for the door. As though he even now heads for some hidden gate into Eledria, off to present himself before Princess Estrilde in the Court of Aurelis, to subject himself to her dangerous whims. Whims he cannot hope to satisfy.

"No!" The word bursts from my lips. I leap forward, grab his arm. He looks down at me, eyes snapping with passion so hot, it burns. I nearly let go but somehow manage to maintain my grip. "No, please. You mustn't."

"How can I not?" He rests his hand on top of mine, his fingers gripping hard. "Can't you see what's happening here? How we're becoming poisoned against each other? Clara." He turns to me fully, takes hold of my upper arms. "We are meant to be together. The only thing standing in our way is this cursed Obligation of yours. I know it can be broken. I know I am the one who can break it, the only one. I should have done it years ago, should never have let you suffer so long. Gods! How could I have been such a coward? But no more. I'm going to save you. And then all will be right again. You'll see."

"Danny . . ." I hesitate. I don't want to say what I must. After all, I only just came to the realization myself a short time ago. Part of me had hoped I would never have to speak this truth out loud, because I hate, hate, *hate* to cause him pain.

But now, seeing that determination blazing in his eye, I know I must speak now or forever regret my silence. "Danny, you have to know I can never marry you."

The whole world seems to freeze. I watch the blood drain from his face. His grip on my arms tightens painfully. "You don't mean that."

I nod. Tears catch in my eyelashes. I blink them free, let them race down my cheeks. But my jaw hardens. "I do mean it. I cannot marry you. Not now. Not when the Obligation is complete. Not ever."

He shakes his head. "No. No, no, no, Clara. You're ensorcelled. That's what this is. It's that prince! I've seen the way he looks at you. He's put you under his spell." His lips roll back, baring his teeth in a terrible grimace. "I will break it. I will save you."

"Can't you just listen to me for once in your life?" I wrench my arms, freeing myself from his grasp. My voice sounds thin, shrill. "I am *not* ensorcelled. I am not glamoured or persuaded or cursed. This is *my* choice. This is *my* life. You don't have to like it or approve because I am not *yours*. I never have been, and I never will be."

"You can't stop me, Clara. You can't stop me from loving you. You can't stop me from saving you."

"Maybe not. But I get to choose where I give my love. You may have my friendship forever and a day. But not my heart. Never my heart."

He lunges, catches hold of my arms again. Before I can even cry out, he pulls me into him and presses his mouth against mine, a painful clash of lips and teeth that might have been a kiss if it weren't so terrible. I yank my head back, but he won't let go. "I'm going to save you," he growls, staring down into my eyes. "I'm going to save you if it's the last thing I do. I love you! I will never stop loving you. I will—"

Suddenly, he staggers, knocking me off my feet. His swinging arm flies just past my head, very nearly knocking me silly. As it is, when I hit the floor, my breath bursts from my lungs. I pull myself up, my spinning gaze looking wildly to the jumble of forms on the floor. Someone kneels on Danny's chest, pounding his face with both fists.

"Oscar!" I cry. Scrambling forward, I throw myself at my brother. "Oscar, stop! Stop it, please!"

"Keep your dirty paws off my sister!" Oscar roars, his voice high and strangled, almost inhuman. Danny gets his arms up, deflecting the blows raining down, but I see the *rothiliom* glowing in my brother's eyes. I know the drug can instill bursts of extraordinary power.

"Please, Oscar!" I cry again, grasping at his arm. One flailing fist strikes me in the stomach. Winded, I grunt, stagger back . . .

. . . and fall into a pair of waiting arms.

"I seem to have arrived in the nick of time," a warm voice speaks close to my ear.

I have no chance to register anything clearly before I'm set back on my feet. Leaving me to gather my balance, the Prince strides across the room, my father's old coat swirling behind him like royal robes. He plucks Oscar up by the back of his shirt and lifts him off Danny, who scrambles backward across the floor. Blood pours from his nose, spilling over his lips and chin.

"Well?" The Prince looks from one to the other. "Shall we kiss and be friends again? Or do we need a little time to cool our heads?"

Oscar yanks free of the Prince's hold. "Let go of me, you monster!" he snarls, his eyes sparking with pure terror. Then his legs seem to fold up beneath him, and he collapses in a little huddled ball, arms wrapped over his head.

The Prince raises an eyebrow. "While I admit my personality may be a trifle overwhelming, most people don't react to me with quite such vehemence."

I rush to my brother's side, kneel, and put my arms around him. "Please," I say, my gaze seeking first the Prince, then Danny. "Please, just go."

The Prince eyes Danny as he climbs to his feet. Danny wipes blood from his face with the back of his hand, his shoulders hunched to his ears. "This isn't over, Clara," he says between heavy gasps. With that, he staggers to the door and disappears out into the cold street. It's pure relief to have him gone.

"Friendly sort, your handsome doctor." The Prince turns to me, his expression placid. "Shall we get the boy up to bed?"

When he takes a step toward us, however, Oscar lets out a bone-rattling scream and buries his face in my shoulder. I shake my head, unable even to form words.

The Prince meets my gaze. His brow puckers a little. Then he nods. "I'll be just outside," he says. The next moment, he too disappears through the door. But I can feel him there, close at hand. It's more comfort than I like to admit.

"There, Oscar," I say, rocking my brother gently as I used to when we were children. "There, I have you. I have you now. I promise."

My brother sobs on and on. And there's nothing I can do but sit and hold him for what seems like a long, long time.

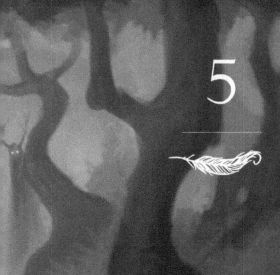

5

I N BETWEEN CALMING OSCAR THROUGH SHAKING FITS
and bouts of irrational terror, I spend the better part of the day
trying to convince him to eat. I also question him about this
new lover of his, the one I suspect of introducing him to *rothiliom*.

My brother won't open up to me. He turns to stare at the wall,
his shoulder a rigid fortification against all offers of love or care.

The sun is setting when I finally leave him and venture back
downstairs, so tired that I'm obliged to lean heavily against the
wall to keep myself upright. Warmth greets me, however, and
when I emerge from the narrow stairwell, I'm surprised to find a
cheery fire. The dancing flames are violet and blue, but the heat
they shed is real enough, and they seem to burn on mere wish
alone, no need for other fuel.

The Prince sits in my mother's old chair, rocking gently. He makes an unexpectedly amusing picture, lounging there with one ankle draped across the opposite knee, a magazine in his hands. His long fingers idly turn a page even as he looks up at me. "Ah! Darling," he says, his expression mild. "How is the boy?"

"Sleeping." I let out a breath and sag against the doorframe. "Deep sleep this time. I think . . . I hope when he wakes, the *rothiliom* influence will be past."

The Prince nods. Then he stands suddenly and steps behind the chair to hold it steady. "Please, sit. You are exhausted."

"Oh, no, I shouldn't. You're the one recovering."

"Though I don't wish to speak too soon, I believe I am, for all intents and purposes, recovered." He looks down at his own body, and shrugs. "Perhaps as my human blood regenerates I'll sicken once more. For the moment, however, I feel quite as spry as ever."

He's donned a shirt. What's more, he's taken the time to fasten almost every button. It cannot disguise the fitness of his frame, and the firelight tends to shine revealingly through the delicate fabric. But I'll take the effort for what it's worth.

Sighing, I step into the room and, without further protest, sink into the chair. Once I'm settled, he lets go, and I rock gently back. It's the first time in years my mother's chair has worked properly. Did the Prince take the time to fix the broken runner? Or is this just a fae glamor of some kind? Rather an effective one if so. I close my eyes, momentarily luxuriating in both the warmth from the violet fire and the sheer bliss of letting my limbs relax for the first time in days.

"I need to send a message," I say after a few quiet moments. "To the Gale household."

The Prince speaks from the shadows behind me. "Your doctor friend?"

I bite my lips, considering my words. "Danny has been good to Oscar and me. He and his sister were our only friends when . . ." I stop. I don't want to get into all of that. It's none of his business anyway.

The Prince is silent for a little while. Then, finally, he says in a low voice, "Good friends are hard to come by."

"Yes."

We're silent again. But there's nothing peaceful about the atmosphere. Despite the fire, despite the gentle creak of the rocker treads. There's something here, something between us I couldn't define in words if I tried. Or possibly something I *shouldn't* define.

He steps into view, just in the tail of my eye, staring down at the fire. His hands are at his sides, but I can see the one closest to me slowly clench, knuckles whitening. "Darling," he says.

"Yes?" I turn, look up at him directly. It's in that moment I notice what magazine he's got tucked under his arm. *The Starlin,* the premier literary magazine in the city. I can just see the beginning of the lead title: *Black Heart Beating.* My stomach turns over. "Where did you find that?"

"This?" The Prince purses his lips and looks at the magazine as though surprised to see it. "Oh. They're selling them all over town. I spied a familiar name on the cover and thought I'd pick up a copy. You're not the only literary one in your family it would seem."

I stand so abruptly, the chair rocks wildly backwards, almost tilting over. With a dart, I pluck the magazine from his grip and press it to my chest. "I . . . um. Yes. Oscar and I both take after our father. Writers. Storytellers."

"Your father. Yes. I remember him."

His words hit me like shards of ice. With each strike, I see an instant of memory, like glimpses of a nighttime scene caught in flashes of lightning. Kneeling on hard cobbled stones, my hands splayed in front of me. A golden figure holding a bloodstained sword. Fingers tangled in my hair, lifting my head up. A broken form on my right. Blood. So much blood. Soaking into my skirts . . .

I shake my head hard. Then I look up at the Prince, eyes flashing. "You were there. The night I was Obligated. You know what happened."

He holds my gaze. "And you? Do you remember?"

He'd told me this moment would come. He'd told me that once my Obligation became his, once he broke Estrilde's hold over me, my memories would return. They've been pressing in around the edges for a while now. Part of me longs to turn to them, to look upon them fully. To know my history and know myself.

I take a step back, fingers crumpling the cheap magazine cover. "I don't want to." The words slip out, thin as a shallow breath. "I don't want to remember."

He dips his chin and peers at me from beneath his dark brows. "And that's the whole problem. Isn't it?"

Before he can utter another word, there's sudden frisson in the air behind us. We both feel it at the same time and turn. A ripple of energy passes through the empty space on the far side of the room, forming an ever-widening circle. I know what this is: a Between Gate, opening directly into my home. But who or what will step through? Am I about to meet this mysterious lover of Oscar's? Or something worse?

The circle widens to its greatest width. A silhouetted figure becomes visible, stepping through layers of reality. The next moment, a plain freckled face with a shock of floppy fair hair manifests, shedding layers of sparkling *quinsatra* dust as his body solidifies. He blinks and shakes his head, making the comical jaw-twisting expression we all make upon arriving between worlds.

Then his gaze turns to us. "Prince!" he cries with obvious delight. "Good to see you up and well, sir!"

"*Upright,* at the very least," the Prince responds. "How are our people faring back home, Lawrence?"

The Prince's manservant shakes his head. "There's trouble aplenty. Rather more than usual, I should say. The grimoires are all in an uproar following the last outbreak, and your librarians are stretched to their limits. Masters Silveri and Cornil are keeping a tight rein, but . . ." He shakes his head heavily. "It's going to get nasty very soon if they don't have reinforcements."

The Prince turns to me. I feel his gaze but cannot meet it. My whole body seems to clench with dread. "Well, Darling?" the Prince says. "The time has come for our return."

I close my eyes, forcing back the sudden swell of tears. *Oscar.* How can I leave him? How can I let him wake from yet another agonized sleep to find himself all alone in the world once more? I know exactly what he'll do: crawl right back to Old Docklands. Lose himself in the bliss of *rothiliom,* killing himself by degrees.

What will happen if I tell the Prince I'm not coming? What will happen if I say I must remain behind to help my brother? I know how desperately he needs me back in the library, how desperately all of them need me. Will he command me to obey? Would he, for the first time, make use of the irresistible Obligation ties?

What if he doesn't?

I draw a long, careful breath. Lifting my eyelids, I face the Prince, set my face into lines of neutral submission. "Of course," I say. "I shall be ready momentarily."

I cannot find a runner to take a message to the Gales. In the end, Lawrence agrees to carry the message himself to the address on Elmythe Lane. While he's gone, I climb to Oscar's room and sit with my brother. He doesn't wake, not even when I perch on the edge of his bed and take hold of his clammy hand.

When I finally hear Lawrence return downstairs, I kiss Oscar's brow and smooth hair back from his forehead. "There's food in the kitchen," I say quietly, though I know he cannot hear me. "A few days' worth. I'll be back as soon as I can, I swear it.

I'll never truly leave you. Not for good. Just please . . . please, be here when I get back."

The Between Gate journey is as unpleasant as ever. We step through to the other side, emerging on a dark shore beneath a perpetually starry sky. A carriage drawn by monstrous morleth waits for us at the end of a long pier. The Prince and Lawrence climb inside, and though I'm prepared to take my place beside the driver—a great rock-hided troll man in a top hat—the Prince bids me join them within.

I tuck into the corner of the bench opposite the Prince and keep my gaze firmly on the window. The morleth climb into the sky, treading lightly on darkness as they carry us out across open ocean. Before long, the Prince is snoring softly. When I glance his way, I note the pallor in his cheeks, the pinched quality around his eyes. Despite his protests of perfect health, I know his recovery is ongoing. Still, considering the state he was in when we left Vespre, I would never have hoped we'd return so soon with him alive and relatively whole.

Shuddering, I turn back to the window and gaze out over the dark water. When I crane my neck, I can see Vespre City on the horizon. My heart gives a traitorous little leap of . . . of . . . What is this feeling? Certainly not joy. Who could joyfully return to a place known throughout the worlds as the *Doomed City?* Anticipation, perhaps. I do long to see my little troll children again. And I could certainly use one of Lir's affectionate embraces, not to mention her gifted hands running a brush through my snarled hair.

The ride feels endless. Eventually, however, we soar across the city proper and touch down before the great front steps of the palace. The Prince wakes with a snort as we rumble to a halt. "Seven gods spare us, are we caught in a hurricane?" he demands.

"We're home, Prince," Lawrence soothes.

The Prince leans forward to peer out the window. "Ah! So we are." He sits back and draws a great breath. When Lawrence reaches for him, however, he bats his manservant's hand away. "I can get myself in and out all right. Run on ahead, why don't you? Draw me a hot bath and lay out some clothes. Preferably something with as few buttons as possible," he adds with a glance my way.

Lawrence starts to protest, but the Prince waves an imperious hand. His Obligate relents, grudgingly. He hops from the carriage and runs up the front steps without stopping to put down the box step first. A troll footman lumbers up instead and sets the box in place. Then he stands at attention with a great boulder-shaped hand extended.

"You first," the Prince says. I nod and awkwardly unfold my limbs, stiff from the long ride. I'm grateful for the troll's assistance as I step down and move quickly aside, making room for the Prince. He's even more stiff and awkward but refuses help, gripping the edges of the carriage doorway instead.

I wait until I'm certain he's steady on his feet. Then, without a word, I turn and quickly start to climb the steps.

"Darling!"

I pause. I've managed to climb only three steps, but they're such great, tall things, meant for beings much larger than myself. Closing my eyes, I paint a meaningless smile on my face, then turn. The carriage is pulling away already. The Prince stands below, looking up at me.

He approaches. Though the steps are overlarge for him as well, he takes them more easily than I did. One step. Two. Now he stands a single tread lower than me, his eyes level with mine. He seems very close. Too close. I want to back up but can't without scrambling up the next step. So I hold my ground.

"Well, Darling," he says, his voice low and rumbling. "Would you rush off without a word?"

I open my mouth. Close it again. I drop my gaze for an instant before forcing it back to meet his. "I have nothing to say."

"You saved my life."

Can he see the telltale flush warming my cheeks? "I suppose I have."

"I feel I've not thanked you properly." He tilts his head. "The truth is, I'm very grateful to be breathing, even if it means I find myself obligated to my Obligate." He holds out his hand, palm up, fingers gently curled. "Will you shake hands with me?"

"I . . ." My lips are suddenly very dry. "I don't see the need."

"Don't you? Do you not think it right, before we enter back into whatever darkness this world has in store for us, to take a moment to honor a victory? I saved your life. You saved mine. We are perhaps building some small semblance of trust between us. Indeed, if that is not worthy of a handshake, I don't know what is."

I stare at his hand in that little space of air between us. "It's not wise to shake hands with the fae," I say softly.

"If this were a bargain, that would be true enough. But I am not bargaining. I am offering. Freely, with no compunction and no guile. Not even with any hope. Merely offering."

My lashes lift, my gaze rising to meet his again. Strange energy limns his voice, and strange fire sparks in the depths of his eyes. What is he offering exactly? Mere thanks? I don't think so.

"Very well," I say coolly and place my hand in his. A jolt of pure heat races up my arm at that contact of my skin with his. I try to withdraw, but he tightens his grip and rests his other hand on top of mine. He looks down at my fingers, his brow puckered, curious.

"It is strange," he says, and for once his voice contains none of its habitual mockery, "how swiftly changes may come over one's soul. So swiftly, one hardly recognizes what's happening until it's too late. One moment, I look at this hand and see only that instrument by which cruel death has been wrought. The next moment . . ." He rubs his thumb along my knuckles, a small gesture that sparks across my senses. "How is it that this same hand may be an instrument of such tenderness? Such healing? Such strength?"

The world turns around me, but here in the center of everything, I am still as stone. I cannot breathe, cannot move, cannot think. I should yank my hand free, turn, flee up those stairs as fast as I can. And yet all I do is stand. Mutely. Stupidly.

He lifts his gaze suddenly. "Darling," he says, "I want to—"

Before he can utter another word, the air behind me erupts

in high-pitched squealing. I gasp and whirl about. The Prince releases my hand, and I only just have time for a fleeting sensation of coldness where his warm fingers had been before I'm swarmed by small, hard, leaping, screeching bodies. I gasp as arms wrap around my legs and very nearly send me toppling down the steps. One of them springs straight for my face, and I'm only just quick enough to catch the living missile in midair.

"Mar!" Sis screams, wrapping her arms around my neck. *"Mar! Mar! Mar!"*

Laughing and quite certain I'll discover any number of bruises when I change my gown later, I kneel and hug as many of my children as I can manage at once. Three ugly little faces and one more perfectly beautiful than a new spring moon upraise to mine, seeking kisses. "Yes, my dears, I'm home!" I laugh through prickling tears. "I'm home!"

Guilt strikes me like a wave. Because the truth is, this does feel like a homecoming. But that can't be right, can it? Home is where the heart is, and my heart must be with Oscar. These little beings, so dear to me, could not have replaced him in prominence. I'm fond of them, surely, but . . . but . . .

Lir is suddenly there as well, crying out, "Mistress! They said you were home, but I didn't believe them!" She joins the children, dropping to her knees and throwing her arms around me, ignoring the boys and Sis as they kick and growl, "Mine! Off! Mine!"

"Oh, Mistress," she says, drawing back enough to look me in the eyes. "I have all sorts of news to share! There's been another outbreak of a Greater Noswraith, the one they call Boney Long Fingers. Mixael and Andreas managed to get it in order, but not before it escaped the library and broke Captain Khas's arm! Oh, it was awful! Andreas was so brave. They both were, I'm sure. But I'm so glad you and the Prince are home now, for I don't know how they can go on by themselves."

The Prince.

I struggle to my feet, impeded by grasping, affectionate trollings, and look around surreptitiously. But the Prince is long gone.

6

A LIBRARIAN'S FUNERAL IS A STRANGE THING.

Peronelle Silveri was an old woman by the time she met her end. She'd served in the Vespre Library for three hundred years, battling nightmarish horrors with a tenacity of spirit unmatched save by her own brave husband. These battles—not to mention the loss of her husband—had aged her, leaving her wrinkled and withered despite the rejuvenating power of Eledria's air in her lungs. Had she wished to remain young and beautiful, she could have chosen to do so, but the will for youth had gone out of her.

Now, however, laid out in funeral state, the shadow of what she once was lingers about her face. It's as though she cannot be fully contained by any one age. Hers is a beauty of all ages: the delicate lines and age spots of an old woman, the radiant glow of a maiden, the full soft lips of a child, the warm, welcoming roundness of a mother. All simultaneous, the many facets of this single fascinating person.

They arranged her body on one of the library lifts. It's not unlike a funeral barge, I think, as once were used for warrior kings. She's surrounded by books—none of the active grimoires containing Noswraiths, of course, but rather the volumes of poetry and works of fiction she once loved and enjoyed during her few spare moments. She wears a gown of deep green velvet cut in an old-fashioned style that perfectly suits her vibrant red hair.

How much of her current appearance is glamour? I know all too well the painful death Nelle suffered, for I nearly shared the same fate. The pummeling. The breaking of bones. The crushing of lungs and skull. The fear.

I choke back a sob, pressing a hand to my mouth. This is my fault. I am responsible for this woman's death, for the emptiness left behind in the worlds at her passing. It was my Noswraith that did this. My Noswraith, which I called to life from some dark center in my being and then failed to properly bind. If not for me, Nelle would still be alive.

A small stony hand slips into mine. Startled, I look down into Calx's ugly little face gazing soulfully up at me. He shows me his diamond teeth in a smile. I cannot help tilting my lips in response. Then, holding my chin higher, I blink back my tears and focus on the ceremony taking place.

The Prince stands to the right of the lift. He's clad in somber robes as black as his raven hair and trimmed in gold. For once, the buttons are done up all the way to his throat, and the overall effect is impressively magisterial. "Peronelle Silveri was the bravest soul ever to serve in Vespre Library," he declares solemnly to the gathering. "I owe her my life many times over. In fact, the first time I met her, she saved my life when I was at my most vulnerable. Years later, when I found her and her husband again and brought them with me to Vespre, they transformed what should have been an impossible task into . . . well, into something a little less impossible than it was before. I will be forever grateful for her courage, her wisdom, her hard-honed skill, and—if I dare say it— her friendship." He sweeps one arm, indicating Mixael, standing across from him. "Thank the gods she leaves behind a worthy successor to her role of senior librarian."

Mixael's eyes are wet with tears. He looks younger than he did just a few days ago, but his eyes have aged tremendously. They are the eyes of a very old man.

I glance around at the others present. At Andreas, whose glasses are broken and pieced back together with a bit of sticky plaster. At Captain Khas, her arm in a sling following her most recent brawl with a Noswraith. At the other children, and Lir, and various members of the Prince's household.

I try not to let my gaze wander to the golden figure standing just beyond the Prince. Every now and then my eyes are drawn her way, against my will. Ilusine. Princess of Solira. Somehow, I'd hoped she would depart with her people long before our return to

Vespre. But of course, she remained behind to make certain the Prince came home all in one piece. Her exquisite face is solemn, though there's a hint of perplexity about her brow. As though she cannot quite fathom the reason for all this to-do over a mere human. Sensing that this human was important to the Prince, however, she maintains her dignity, for his sake.

Something burns in my heart at the sight of that woman. I swallow it back and concentrate my attention upon Nelle. The old librarian deserves better than my impotent jealousy at her funeral.

When the Prince has finished his short speech, Mixael clears his throat. "Every one of—" he begins, then stops. We wait, watching him gather himself for the next attempt. Finally, he starts again, this time in a lower voice. "Every one of us knows what our fates will be. No one gets out of this job alive. We don't expect to, don't even try to. It is our honor to protect the worlds from what we imprison here within these walls, within these bindings." He draws a long, shuddering breath. "My parents lived and died for the work here in Vespre. Now, we must carry on their legacy. Together."

With those words, he turns to the lift levers and grips them with both hands. He stops. A little shudder runs down his spine.

"In your own time, Silveri," the Prince says.

Mixael nods. Then, gathering himself, he begins to work the levers. Chains creak and move. The book lift begins its descent down the many hundreds of floors of the library citadel.

Before it's gone more than a few feet, however, a little squawk draws everyone's head whipping to one side. An awkward creature emerges from Nelle's cubicle, scrambling out from under her desk. It stands upright on its two hind feet and waddles toward us, arm-wings held up and out behind it, tail dragging along the ground for support. The wyvern makes its way through the gathering and marches up to the lift. There it scrambles down and settles itself on Nelle's stomach. It curls into a little ball, wrapping its wings tight and draping its tail over its nose. It closes its eyes, and . . .

I blink. There's no wyvern anymore. Nothing but a piece of folded parchment. I can't see the shape of the draconian creature at all. Just old faded paper covered in close, neat handwriting.

Mixael kneels. Tears fall from his face and splotch the page as he lifts his mother's hand and rests it atop the parchment. "Sleep now," he says. "Carry my love to Father."

Rising, he returns to the levers. Slowly, steadily, he works the mechanism, and the lift descends. The rest of us gather at the rail and watch as Nelle's body is carried down and down, past the upper ten floors and into the shadows below. Is there a bottom story where the lift will eventually come to rest? Are the remains of other librarians down there somewhere, their bones slowly turning to dust?

At last, Mixael stops. The Prince steps forward and, using a sharp tool, cuts the last few chain links. The whole long chain goes slithering and skittering over the edge and down, following the lift. I never hear it land.

The ceremony seems to be complete now. The Prince gives Nelle's final quill pen to Andreas and bids him take it down to the fifth floor, there to be placed with honor in a display beside her husband's. While Andreas hastens about this task, Captain Khas speaks to those of her guards who came to pay their respects, and they disperse back to their posts. The beautiful captain remains behind a little longer, stepping to Mixael's side and lowering her head to speak softly in his ear. I think she may even have taken his hand, but Lir draws my attention away before I can be certain.

"The children are tired and hungry," she says. "I'm taking them back to their room now. Will you be joining us?"

Their room. I note the words with a smile. It may not seem like much, but it means a world of difference to me—knowing my little ones have a room of their own in which to sleep and won't need to pile up all together in my bed every night. "I'll come as soon as I can," I assure Lir. "There's work yet to be done, I'm afraid."

Lir nods her understanding. "Take your time, Mistress," she says, and raises her eyebrows significantly, her gaze shifting to look at something behind me. I turn, curious.

The Prince stands by the rail. Looking at me.

Heat rushes to my cheeks. I turn away, trying to catch Lir's attention, but my maid has already made good her escape, abandoning me to my fate as she hastens to chase down the troll siblings. I'm left to gather my senses, taking a few deep breaths. I've not spoken to the Prince since that moment yesterday on the front steps. What did he almost say to me then? Does he intend to pursue that conversation now? Perhaps it would be best to leave well enough alone. After all, I most likely misinterpreted his demeanor, read more into the encounter than I should.

This thought firmly in mind, I lift my chin and turn again to face the Prince. He's still there by the rail, his arms crossed over his buttoned-up front, his lips ever so slightly quirked to one side.

Before I can take more than a single step toward him, however, a statuesque figure all in gold glides between us.

My heart gives a painful beat. Rather than a second step, I perform a swift sideways shuffle, slipping into the nearest desk cubicle, out of sight. The moment I've done so, I curse my stupidity. Now what am I going to do? Crouch here like a trembling mouse and hope not to overhear something I oughtn't? I should reemerge at once and hope the Prince doesn't notice me as I slink ignobly away to my own desk and the pile of work awaiting me there.

But I don't. I stay where I am.

And I hear every word of what transpires.

"You're looking well, Castien," Ilusine begins, her voice as rich as wild honey and equally sweet. "Better than ever, I should say. It suits you to be more fae and less human."

"I suppose I'll take that as a compliment," the Prince answers dryly. "Would you still think so, however, if you knew how sadly reduced my magic is without the human blood?"

She sniffs. "With that curse you were carrying, whatever power your human blood granted you was too badly compromised to be of much use. No, I definitely like you better this way."

"Perhaps I should make a point of having myself bled close to death regularly for your sake, dear Ilusine."

"Perhaps you should." She matches his sarcasm with total seriousness. Then her voice drops an octave, transforming from sweet to something much warmer, more urgent. "You would never need worry about power again if you aligned yourself with Solira. You know my mother would back you."

"Your mother would give just about anything to see her favorite daughter seated on the throne of Aurelis. Even see her wed to a hybrid."

"Why do you sound so bitter? If it's true, it's a truth that can greatly benefit both of us."

"Ilusine," the Prince says suddenly, "why do you pretend with me?"

The air beyond my cubicle seems to drop in temperature by several degrees. I remain hidden, my back against the wall, my hand pressed to my beating heart.

"Whatever do you mean?" Ilusine asks, her tone guarded.

"Only that I know you find my human nature repellent. Why play these games, acting as though you want to marry me? Are we not better friends than that?"

I shouldn't be here. Does the Prince realize how close I am? I cannot imagine he wants me overhearing this conversation. By rights, I ought to cover my ears, hum a little tune, anything to give them privacy. Instead I crane my neck.

"Really, Castien, you can be so boorish sometimes."

"Is it boorish to speak the truth?"

"This is what you truly think of me?" Her words come sharply. "Have I not been more than clear about my feelings all these turns of the cycle?"

"That's just the problem, my sweet. You have. Perhaps my human blood allowed me to delude myself for a time into thinking otherwise. But at the moment, due to the not-so-gentle ministrations of my physician, I am rather less human than usual. In this state, I am better equipped to hear the fae falseness behind your pretty words. You have never lied to me, of course. But neither have you been wholly truthful."

The silence is acute. I don't have to see them to feel the tension in the air surrounding them.

At last, Ilusine says in a voice as low as a tiger's growl: "I'm willing to give you everything."

"Maybe I need more than *willing*. Maybe I need *wanting* too."

"This is what I want."

"Perhaps. But am *I* what you want? Or am I merely the clearest, simplest means to an end?"

"What does it matter if I am your means in return? So long as the means isn't entirely loathsome, I don't see how we cannot both benefit in the long run."

I can't see what's happening. But I'm convinced she's edged closer to him. I'm convinced she's even now twining her long slender arms around his neck, drawing him toward her. And she's so beautiful, so achingly beautiful. He cannot be immune to all that she is and all she has to offer.

"Be honest, Castien." Her voice is lower than ever, so seductive it makes the small hairs on my skin prickle. "I am more than a *means* to you, aren't I?"

What is in that lingering silence? Is he considering her words? Or are they even now locked in a passionate kiss? Everything in me wants to peer out of my hiding place, to see, to know. But I can't. I hold tight to my resolve, squeezing my eyes shut. Even so I cannot shake the memory of the first time I saw Ilusine. Of the moment she descended, walked straight up to the Prince, and kissed him soundly. One certainly doesn't kiss a mere *friend* like that.

The Prince speaks at last, his voice rougher than before. "You will be a great queen one day, Ilusine. You will reshape kingdoms according to your will. As for me? I am not willing to be reshaped by you. You have my friendship. You may not have my heart."

Another painful silence. Blood thunders in my ears. I'm dizzy, almost sick.

Suddenly I hear footsteps. To my great horror, Ilusine appears in my line of sight, marching away from the Prince with long strides. Her golden gown swishes in her wake. Just as she draws level with my hiding place, she stops. Her shoulders are set and straight, her head high, her gaze clear and fixed upon some point ahead of her.

"I wish I could lie." She speaks clearly, without looking back. "I wish I could tell you I hate you."

"I will accept the desire in place of the hatred itself," the Prince replies.

"I'm going now. And when I go, I'm not coming back. You may find you have lost a powerful ally."

"I may indeed. Or I may find there was more to our friendship than either of us credited. Time alone will tell."

I watch the effect of his words. She controls her features expertly, not even the faintest trace of tightness in either brow or jaw. She merely blinks. Once. Then she's in motion again. Her gaze never slides my way as she crosses to the library exit.

In another moment she's gone, vanishing like the sun behind the far horizon, leaving only darkness in her wake.

My knees are weak. Back pressed against the cubicle wall, I sink slowly to the floor, unable to draw breath. I shouldn't have been here for this. Not that Ilusine would care if she knew; she views me as little better than a semi-intelligent pet. But the Prince? What would he—

"You can come out now, Darling. The danger is past."

Gods on high! He knew all along. I close my eyes and clench my jaw, trying not to bite out a curse. Should I pretend I'm not here? Is there any point in trying?

Before I can decide, the Prince arrives. He leans one elbow against the cubicle wall, gazing down at me where I sit on the floor, and lifts a wry eyebrow. "What do you think? Have I well and truly fulfilled my princely role?"

I swallow painfully but manage to gather some dignity and answer, "What role do you mean?"

"Why, toying with and subsequently destroying the lady's heart, of course."

"I . . . I don't think it fair of any gentleman to lead on a lady's feelings. Prince or otherwise."

"Quite right. And I truly regret if I have done so. But tell me," he leans in a little closer, looking almost conspiratorial, "do you think I've led on the lovely Ilusine?"

I open my mouth to answer but stop. The truth is, I'm not altogether certain. I can recall many instances of Ilusine presuming upon familiarity. Touching the Prince, kissing the Prince, caressing the Prince. Speaking to him in a proprietary manner that made my stomach twist and churn with emotions I do not wish to name.

Try as I might, however, I cannot recall the Prince answering in kind. In fact, what I do seem to remember are numerous instances of him distancing himself. Putting her off. Sometimes he would respond to her overtures with light flirtation, but nothing more. If I'm honest, he seemed more determined to repulse her advances than anything.

"I'm not sure it matters what I think," I say at last. "It is not my heart at risk."

His eyes sharpen. "Indeed?" Then he draws a breath, his nostrils flaring, and stands back. No longer leaning over me, he crosses his arms and tilts his head a little to one side. "And you truly believe Ilusine is heartbroken?"

I consider the glimpse I had of the lady's face. She had not looked heartbroken, but . . . "I couldn't very well offer judgment. After all, I do not know the particulars of the relationship. I have only my impressions to go by."

"And what were your impressions?"

"That you intended to marry her. That in marrying her, you

would further your cause with Aurelis."

"What cause with Aurelis?"

"Your play for the throne."

"And who ever gave you the impression I intended to make a play for the throne?"

"You did," I answer hotly. I'm painfully aware that I'm still seated on the floor, a most undignified position. To scramble to my feet now would only make matters worse, so I merely lift my chin. "You've all but admitted it gives you pain to see Lord Ivor favored by Lodírhal. Why should you not contrive to take the throne which by rights is yours?"

He smirks then. His face is so bitter and so beautiful, it pricks my heart. "While I may pity any kingdom handed over to Ivor, and while I may doubt my father's good judgment in handing it thusly, it doesn't follow that I should want the same favor bestowed upon myself." He sweeps an arm then, indicating the vastness of the library in a grand gesture. "Have I not already been the recipient of Lodírhal's generosity? Gifted with power and responsibility far beyond what your average disappointing son might expect to receive?"

"You will not leave Vespre then?" I hate how hopeful my voice sounds, how it quavers and nearly breaks. "You'll not abandon the library?"

He meets my gaze. For a long moment he doesn't answer. Finally, he says only, "I do not know." He draws back then and gives his head a quick shake. "None of it matters now. Set aside your fearful musings and fetch your book and quill. We have work to do that cannot wait."

With that, he turns on his heel and marches for the nearest of the spiral stairways leading down to the lower levels. "Quick, Darling!" he calls back over his shoulder.

What choice do I have but to follow?

7

THE PRINCE CALLS FOR MIXAEL AND ANDREAS AS WE descend. The four of us converge on the eighth floor and from there step onto one of the book lifts. Were Nelle still alive, she would never stand for us to use the lifts in this fashion. She was always adamant they were for books, not librarians.

I know I'm not the only one thinking of her now as the Prince works the mechanism. Mixael is very pale, holding onto one of the four main posts, not meeting anyone's eye. Andreas leans against the side rail, arms crossed, chin tucked, expression thoughtful behind his glasses. The Prince is turned mostly away from me. What little I can see of his face is an enigma. As usual.

Chains creak as they lower us into the darkness below the tenth floor. I tip my head back, gazing up to the crystal dome high overhead, at the twilit sky beyond. I feel like a drowning soul gazing up at my last view of the world before the deeps drag me down. Shuddering, I drop my gaze, close my eyes, and cling to the rail. I knew this hour would come sooner or later; the hour in which I would return to the lower vaults of the library. To the thirteenth floor.

To the cell of the Eyeless Woman.

The lift creaks to a stop, settling against the thirteenth-floor landing. Swinging open the little gate, the Prince steps out, leading the way. Mixael and Andreas follow, but I remain where I am. Gripping the rail. Immobile. Alone.

The Prince lifts a moonfire lantern from its hook on the wall, turns, looks from Mixael to Andreas, then notices the empty space where I should be. Frowning, he raises the lantern higher. I flinch from the glare, lifting one hand to shield my eyes. The next moment, the lift floor shifts as the Prince steps back onto it. I turn away from him, facing out into the open emptiness of the central citadel. My entire body shivers uncontrollably.

"Darling." His voice at my back makes my nerves jump. "Come. You must be brave."

A pathetic whimper vibrates in my throat.

"Look at me."

I shake my head.

"Look at me, Darling."

I search for some sense of forced Obligation. It isn't there. I must act on my own will. I must find the strength either to resist or to obey. In that moment, I'm not sure which I find more terrible.

Swallowing a sob, I turn slowly, peering over my shoulder. Moonfire glow illuminates the Prince's face as he stands with his hand outstretched to me. "You are in command here," he says, his voice low, urgent. "Do you understand? That which waits in the darkness is subject to you. You are her creator. You have the power to bind her. You are strong enough. But you must believe it. Can you do that for me?"

I shake my head. "I can't."

"You can."

"No." I've never been strong enough. Not when it counted. I couldn't protect Oscar. I couldn't protect Mama. I couldn't even protect myself. My very existence is futile, pointless . . . The shivering intensifies, wracking my whole body. I'm coming apart at the seams, panic thrilling through every nerve, every vein.

Suddenly, the Prince's hand wraps over mine as I grip the rail. That touch—that contact of his skin against mine—shocks me. I catch my breath, my gaze flicking to meet his. "It's all right," he says. "You don't have to believe it. Not yet, not if you're not ready." He steps closer, leans his forehead close to mine. The space between us is scarcely more than an inch or two. His eyes are deep and dark but with an inner light of soul that is undeniable.

"I'll believe for you," he says.

I see the truth there in his eyes, clear as day. He's believed in my power from the very first moment he saw me, from even before I remember. And he's feared that power all this time. Fear is still present in his gaze, underscoring his confidence with a deep harsh line.

I draw a breath. Then I pull my hunched spine straight, draw my shoulders back. "All right," I say in a small tight voice. "All right, I'm ready."

I'm not ready. Not even a little bit. But there's no point in delaying. The Eyeless Woman is waiting, and she must be bound.

The door to her vault is shut fast, but as we approach along the curved corridor, I feel the force of her malice swelling on the other side, seeking some means of escape. Without a trace of hesitation, the Prince marches up to the door and turns the great lock. When he pulls it open, a blast of foul-smelling air billows forth. Mixael and Andreas draw back a step, pulling close together behind me. I hold my ground. But only just.

The Prince stands a moment in the entrance. His face, illuminated by his lantern, reveals little of his thoughts. The last time he was here, he nearly met his end. He has no doubt faced death many times over the course of his long existence, but I'm not sure that makes the experience any easier. He draws a long breath, then steps inside, approaching the pedestal in the center of the room where lies a single large grimoire: the most recent vessel of the Eyeless Woman's spell.

Even from the doorway I can see that the binding is weakening, rotting from the inside out.

The Prince picks up the book, turns it over, and grunts thoughtfully. Carefully he opens it across his arm and turns the first few pages. Then, shaking his head, he sets it down and rests a hand atop it. His shoulders bow as though bearing a great weight.

Finally, he turns to the three of us clustered in the doorway. "The binding must be reaffirmed. Which means the spell must be read through, beginning to end, and made secure. Without the Eyeless Woman's true name, we will have to keep reaffirming the spell every few days to keep her contained. A fresh version of the spell will need to be written sooner rather than later. Now that she's had a taste of fresh blood, she's hungry for more."

As though proving his point, the pages of the broken books littering the floor of the vault all seem to rustle and hiss together, a soft but undeniably bloodthirsty sound. Strange, for the Noswraith herself hadn't seemed violent when I encountered her a few nights ago. She had been . . . sad. So sad, so pathetic.

Of course, she had killed just as savagely as any other wraith I've met.

The Prince turns to the grimoire again. I cannot see his face from this angle, but his shoulders look undeniably tense. After a moment, he lets out a gust of air and a short curse. "I cannot do it myself," he says. "My human powers are still too weakened. None of the words make sense to me."

Mixael steps forward. "I'll do it."

But the Prince shakes his head. And his gaze fixes on me.

I don't want to do this. I don't want to be the one to read this spell, to reassert the binding. I don't want to be here.

My feet move. Slowly, almost painfully, they carry me through the doorway and into the vault. The books on the floor whisper and shush in quiet impotence. Holding the Prince's gaze, I ignore them. He steps down from the stool, making a place for me at the pedestal. Though every instinct screams for me to turn and run, I climb the little steps and stand there, facing the grimoire.

It's a simple, unadorned binding. Different from the last grimoire I'd seen containing this spell. That one had been black with silver buckles shaped like demon's heads. This is just a leather-bound journal with simple straps wrapping it shut. It takes no more than a glance to see how badly broken down it is as the spell inside struggles to get loose. Foul magic fairly oozes between the pages.

"H-how do I do it?" I ask softly. My training is not yet complete. While I've worked a few small bindings, I've never attempted anything quite like this.

"Read the spell," the Prince answers. He stands at my elbow. "Let the words travel through your mind, filter through your soul. Then send them forth again from your lips. Once you begin, you must not stop. Read straight through to the end. Don't let yourself be drawn too deep. You must remember who you are and why you are there. And when you reach the end, you must leave as swiftly as possible. And Darling!" The sharpness of his voice draws my gaze to meet his. "You must remember her name. Without it, everything you're about to endure will be for nothing."

My lips quiver. I press them into a tight line, nod once, then turn back to the grimoire. I grip the edge of the pedestal with one hand even as I reach out with the other. The cover feels as frail as an old autumn leaf when I lift and turn it, exposing the first page. The lines of text written there are rather jumbled, but when I lean forward, I can just discern words by the light of the moonfire lantern.

"*They were brother and sister,*" I read softly. The opening lines of the spell. My spell. The one I created long ago, though I have no memory of doing so. "*But people observing them might almost mistake them for mother and son. Not for any great difference in their age—they were only two years apart—but by the way she cared for him. As though he were the only thing in the world that truly mattered to her . . .*"

"Sister?"

I look up from my book, turn around sharply. My brother stands in the doorway, wearing his nightshirt, his little feet bare. I close my book with a snap. "What are you doing out of bed? I thought you were asleep."

"Can't sleep. Not sleepy," he says, though the way he rubs the heel of his hand into his eye tells a different story. "I'm scared, sister."

"Scared of what, silly?" I say, though I already know the answer. We've had this conversation before, more times than I like to count.

"The monster in the cellar," he answers. "I'm scared it's going to get me. It's hungry tonight."

Though my lips twitch, I force back a smile. My brother's vivid imagination makes him popular among his school friends, for he can come up with the most outrageous and rambunctious games. But at night such a gift can be more bane than blessing. "Come on," I say, taking his hand. "I'll tuck you in. And I'll have a word with the cellar monster too, tell him little boy is not on the menu tonight."

He reluctantly lets me lead him across the hall to his own room. I tuck him into bed, snugging the quilt under his chin. "Good night," I say with a brisk kiss to his forehead. "I'm off to speak to the cellar monster now."

"Don't let it eat you, sister," he says, his eyes very wide above the white edge of his blanket.

"Silly. Cellar monsters don't eat girls, remember? We're much too spicy for monster mouths."

He tries to smile, but I can tell he's still too frightened. So I leave the door a little bit open behind me when I venture downstairs to the kitchen.

Mama is still up, working on a bit of mending beside the hearth, her bright thimble and silver needle glinting in the firelight with each careful stitch. She wears a green headscarf, but a strand of hair has escaped and fallen in her eyes. Looking up at my approach, she brushes the hair away with the back of her hand. "And what are you doing up at this hour?" she demands.

"Oh, someone's having trouble sleeping again." I snatch a biscuit from the tin in the corner cabinet, hiding it in a fold of my nightgown. "I promised I'd have a word with the cellar monster."

Mama gives me a look. "You encourage the boy too much in his fancies. Really, my love, you must leave him be. Let him discover his own strength."

She's probably right. I've always been there for my brother, always done my best to shelter and shield him. I'd hardly know myself if I stopped. So I say only, "Yes, Mama." We both know I don't mean it.

She rolls her eyes as I plant a quick kiss on her cheek, then shoos me back up the stairs to bed. Moonlight illuminates the passage, falling from the little round window at the far end of the hall. The whole upstairs feels strangely disconnected from the light and warmth down in the kitchen, and my feet are cold on the bare boards.

I creep to my brother's door, whispering softly as I go, "Are you still awake? I've brought you a biscuit if you're . . ." My voice trails away. Little brother isn't in his bed where he belongs. He's standing at the open window, silhouetted by moonlight.

"Brother?" I say, pushing his door wider. "What are you doing?"

He turns slowly. I cannot see his face, for the light is behind him. "I'm saying goodbye to the nice lady," he says.

"What nice lady?" I cross the room to the window. No one is out there, of course. We're on the second story, overlooking the street. I peer down at him, my brow stern. "Were you sleep-walking again?"

He shakes his head. With the moonlight on his face, I can

see that he is fully awake. "She's very nice," he says. "She made me feel better."

"Feel better about what?"

"About the monster in the cellar."

"I thought I was the one who made you feel better about the monster in the cellar!"

"You try," he acknowledges with a shrug. "But all you do is tell the monster to stop. And it never stops. It's always there and always hungry."

"Yes? Well, what does your lady do that's any different?"

"She says it isn't a monster at all."

"What?"

"She says it isn't a monster. She says it cannot help being scary. But it's not actually hungry. In fact, it's really quite nice."

I frown. This is certainly a new twist. I'm not certain I like it. After all, I'm supposed to be the hero here. "Monsters aren't nice," I say. "Monsters are monsters. It's just their nature."

"There, see?" My brother pouts, his brow darkening. "The lady is kinder to me. She tells me nice things."

"Well, what's the point of *nice* things? I tell you *true* things." Remembering what Mama said, I set my jaw and glare at him. "The truth is, you need to be strong. You need to be brave. Otherwise, you can never be a man."

He shudders, his eyes flashing in the moonlight. "There, see? You don't care for me. Not like the nice lady does."

"I've had enough of this nice lady!" I grip my brother by his shoulders and turn him away from the window. "Get back into bed."

In short order, I get him tucked in again and press the purloined biscuit into his little hands. When I bend to kiss him, however, he turns his face away from me. Scowling, I tell him to go to sleep, march from the room, and shut the door firmly behind me. Crawling into my own bed, I pick up my book. But when I try to read, the words won't come into focus.

I can't stop thinking about what my brother said. About the nice lady . . .

"Steady, Darling."

The Prince's voice plucks at the edge of my awareness. I lean into it, grounding myself in reality. In this dark chamber vault, surrounded by dead and broken books. Standing on that stool, gripping the pedestal for support. Pages turning beneath my hand as the story—the spell—flows into my mind and out again through my lips.

The magic is intense. Stronger than I'm used to dealing with. It's all too easy to let myself be drawn in by the written words, to cease reading and begin living. But I'm still in command here.

I nod to let the Prince know I've heard him. And I continue reading the spell: "*Her jealousy sparked, the elder sister spent all the next day thinking about what her brother had said, particularly about the nice lady and her words. Part of her thought she should be glad. After all, if this mysterious personage could bring her brother comfort and help him sleep, wasn't that for the best? But she couldn't shake the feeling something was wrong.*

"And so that night, she decided to discover the truth . . ."

I lie in the dark, staring up at the ceiling. Mama has long since gone to her room at the end of the hall, shutting the door behind her. The house is still.

My brother hasn't come to see me. Usually, he comes at least once if not several times each night. I'm the one who comforts him. I'm the one who holds him and soothes him and tells him everything will be all right. But he doesn't come.

Finally, I hear the tower bell strike twelve. It's the hour I've been waiting for.

I push back my covers and climb out of bed. I have a candle stub and a single match I'd managed to sneak, which flares brightly when I strike it. My candle lit, I tie my robe and slip to my door. It creaks softly as I peer out into the silent moonlit hall.

My brother's door is shut. Which is strange. He always begs to leave it a little bit open. Claims he doesn't feel so lonely that way. I step across the moonlight and press my ear against the door panels. Is that a murmur of voices I hear inside? My brother's voice and . . . and who does that other voice belong to? Is it Mama? I turn the knob ever so gently. It doesn't make a sound. It's as though a magic charm has been worked on the hinges, for the door is silent as I crack it open and peer into the room.

My brother sits upon his bed, bathed in moonlight. Someone is with him. A lady. Mama? I can't tell from this angle. She's dressed in a white nightgown, and her hair is dark, long, and loose down her back. She holds him in her arms, pressed up against her chest, and rocks him gently back and forth.

"He's really most kind," she says in a soft sing-song voice. "You don't even know how kind he can be."

My brother looks up at her. I can see his little face illuminated by moonglow. His eyes shine with trust, with adoration. But I cannot see the woman's face, for her dark hair falls across it, covering her like a veil.

"Give him another chance," the woman says. "He really loves you, you know. Why don't you come and see?"

I've had enough. I push the door wide and step into the room, raising my candle high. "Who are you?" I demand in a ringing voice.

My brother screams and pulls back from the lady, whirling to stare at me. The lady is slower to react. She remains a moment, seated in exactly the same position, her hair falling in a curtain across her face. Then she turns, slowly. And I see her. Empty, sunken hollows where eyes should be. Black stitches sealing them shut. Dangling threads hanging down her cheeks like streaming tears.

A scream tears from my throat. Acting on instinct rather than rational thought, I hurl my candle straight at that face. For an instant, the flashing red glow lights her up like some demonic apparition. She opens her mouth wide in a silent scream, and it looks as though she will swallow the candle and light whole.

Instead she vanishes.

My candle hits the far wall.

8

WE SHOULD PULL HER OUT."

Mixael's voice is close at hand. I blink, shifting my gaze from the text just enough to glimpse him standing to my right. He stares up at me, but it's the Prince to whom he speaks. "She's in too deep. It knows she's vulnerable."

"It's afraid of her," the Prince answers at once. "It knows she can bind it if she remembers. It won't want her to get too close. She's safe enough. Safer than you or I would be under the circumstances."

"I hope you know what you're doing."

"Me too, my friend. Me too."

I continue reading, my voice clear and steady: *"She tried to take her sobbing brother in her arms, to comfort him with soothing words, to hold him as she once had. But he struck out at her, demanding why she would do such a thing, why she would banish his friend? She told him that awful being was no friend at all but rather a vengeful ghost, a spirit intent upon malice. 'Hear me, brother!' she cried in desperation. 'That fiend seeks to bewitch you. She intends for you to venture into the cellar all unsuspecting. But you mustn't! You mustn't listen to her!'*

"Her brother however, claimed she sought only to make him *more afraid. He hated her for it, declaring that he did not wish to be afraid anymore. His voice rose with the heat of his passions until finally their mother came and sent the elder sister from the room. 'Can you not see how you disturb him? Away with you, child, and give him peace!'*

"But once alone in her bed, the girl could not stop thinking about *what she had seen. And she resolved by all the saints and angels to help her brother, somehow . . ."*

"What are you doing, child?"

I look up from my place on the floor just outside my brother's room. I sit with my knees drawn up under my nightgown, a candle beside me, an iron poker gripped in both hands. My attention has been so entirely fixed on even the slightest sounds from within the room that I did not hear Mama's approaching footsteps.

She stands over me, arms crossed. Straggling hairs escaping from under her green headscarf frame a face lined with the worries of the day.

"I've got to find out what's happening, Mama," I say in an urgent whisper. "I've got to help him."

"All the saints preserve us!" Mama sighs, making a holy sign with one hand. Then she fixes me with a stern stare. "I've had about enough of your nonsense, young lady. It's you who've filled his head with these foolish notions! Get up off the floor, and back to bed with you. Get up, I say!"

I rise but continue to grip my poker defiantly. "Please, Mama! I can't just pretend nothing is happening! He needs my help. If I can only—"

Before I get another word out, Mama takes hold of my ear and drags me forcibly across the hall to my room. Wrenching the poker from my grip, she pushes me inside and slams the door shut. With a little shriek of rage, I hurl myself at the latch, scrabbling to get it open. I'm not quite fast enough, however. Mama drops the lock.

"No more of this unladylike display!" she declares, her voice muffled through the panels. "You'd think a girl of your age would have acquired some decorum. Go to bed at once and forget all these silly fancies!"

Howling, I pound at the door, twist the latch, and slam my shoulder again and again against the panels. All to no avail. Mama leaves me to my impotent wailing, shutting her own door firmly against my pleas.

As for my brother? Not one sound does he make across the hall. It's as though he cannot hear me, as though he's vanished into another world entirely.

Tears stream down my cheeks. One splashes on the page, marring the scrawled handwritten words.

I remember. Not everything . . . at least, not yet. But enough. I remember the darkness from which this story was born. I remember pouring my heart onto the page, ink trickling from my quill nib like drops of blood. I remember the desperation that drove me to find words to express the pain in my heart.

No wonder I'd been so eager to forget.

But I cannot hide in ignorance anymore. This monster I've created has killed and killed again. It will go on killing if it is not stopped. And I am the only one who can stop it. So I must keep reading. Even as my heart quivers with pain.

"Darling?" The Prince's presence on my left comforts me. I know there's nothing he can do, but I'm glad he's there even so. "Can you keep going?"

I nod. I can. And I will.

"*She could not get the door open,*" I read on, my voice steady despite the fall of tears. "*She fought and struggled, but to no avail. The night deepened, and moonlight once more poured through the round hall window and fell on the floor. When she peered through the keyhole, she could just see the silvery gleam falling on her brother's door . . .*"

I hear his door open.

My senses quicken. Every hair on my body stands on end. I press my ear against the door, struggling to detect even a hint of what takes place on the other side. That telltale floorboard just outside his door squeaks. Then it squeaks again.

"Brother?" I call. But my voice sounds oddly muffled in my own ears, as though I'm shouting directly into a pillow. Frustrated, I put my eye to the keyhole again. His door is open. Biting back a small cry, I drop to the floor, struggling to peer through the crack underneath.

A single foot appears in my line of vision. Bare, boney. A woman's foot with nails overlong, blackened, and curled. The toes touch first, then the heel. Deliberately placed, like a dancer's tread.

It lifts and proceeds. In its place another foot appears, ghostly in the moonlight. Small, clad in a stripey red-and-white sock. "Brother!" I call again uselessly.

I hear another voice speaking. Calm, gentle. Lulling and soft. "He's in pain. But he'll be so much better once he sees you. He really loves you, you know."

Warnings explode in my head, loud as alarm bells. "Brother! Don't!" I cry, rising to my knees. "Don't go with her! Don't go to the cellar!" I pound the door with both fists, breaking my skin until blood pours down my arms. It doesn't matter. He cannot hear me.

Desperate, I rise and stagger back several paces. The door is fastened, but what of the window? Racing to it, I push it open, gaze down to the street below. It seems so high, but my courage is higher. I strip the sheet off my bed and secure it to the windowsill. Best not to think too closely about what I'm doing. Now is the time for action, not thought. I swing one leg over the sill, grip the sheet, and try my weight against it. It holds.

Hand-under-hand, I scramble down until my feet touch cobblestones. Some distant part of my brain knows this should not have worked, that the only thing supporting me is the power of the narrative I myself wrote. But that's enough in this world. More than enough, in fact.

"I'm coming, brother," I hiss, racing around the side of the stone house to the alley on the far side. It leads to the tiny backyard surrounded by a small iron gate, which I scale in a trice. Then I fling myself at the kitchen door. To my utmost relief, the knob turns in my grasp. I push the door open, stagger through into the kitchen.

And stop.

Mama's there. She'd not gone to bed after all.

She wears her faded dress and pinafore, her hair pulled up under that green headscarf. Little strands escape down the nape of her neck, resting on her shoulders. I can see the thimble on her forefinger, the needle and thread held in the opposite hand, all so homey and familiar.

She stands at the door to the cellar. Red mist pours up the stair like vomit rising from a gullet, spilling across the kitchen floor. It surrounds her, thick and impenetrable, but she does not seem to care. She stares down the steps into the darkness below.

Someone down there is screaming.

"Mama?" I call out. "Mama, where is he?"

She turns. Slowly. Inexorably. Her face is lined and heavy, her lips tilted in a sad little smile. Dark threads hang down her cheeks, dangling from the tight stitching that seals her eyelids shut. She tilts her head toward me and heaves a little sigh.

"He really loves you, you know."

That's it. There is no more. I've come to the end of the spell.

The story is told and done.

Yet I stand here in that kitchen doorway, listening to screams erupting from the cellar even as red mist pours out and around the spectral figure of Mama.

Mama.

She tilts her head. The green scarf melts away, and her hair tumbles over her shoulders. She takes a step, and now her wool gown is gone, replaced by the white shift that makes her so phantomlike, so ominous.

"Welcome, sweetheart," she says in a voice both low and sibilant.

Somewhere far off, I hear the Prince calling, *"Darling? Darling, do you hear me?"* I cannot answer him. He's too many realities away. He cannot help me.

The Eyeless Woman draws near, one step after another. She holds out one hand. The thimble drops away, clatters to the ground. In its place is a long black curved nail. Her lips tip in a gentle smile. "Come, join your brother. He is waiting for you. Just downstairs."

I turn to flee. But when I dart out through the door, it's not the open street that awaits me. Instead I'm back in the upstairs hall, bathed in moonlight pouring through a round window. I stagger to a halt, heart hammering, every sense singing with terror. The door on my left stands open, and I peer into the small bedchamber.

She's there. Seated upon little brother's bed.

"Don't be afraid." She rises slowly. Red mist pours out from under the bed, streaming between her feet and rushing out into the hall. "He's in pain. But he loves you so much."

I back away, stumble to the doorway of the opposite room, the room that belongs to the sister character of this tale. It feels like safety, like a haven. I step into the doorway, but a yawning openness at my back makes me stop, grip the frame, and turn to look over my shoulder. There is no room. The cellar stair drops away below me, down into darkness. Red mist rises fast and roiling. Choking on a scream, I face forward.

The Eyeless Woman is there. Right in front of me. She smiles even as her head tilts. "You'll learn to see as I do," she says.

Then she plucks my right eye from my head.

With a scream, I fall backwards. Rather than hit the floor, however, I land in a pair of strong arms that grip me fast. I writhe, lashing out, struggling in blind panic. One of my hands reaches for my eye, expecting to find an empty socket and pouring blood. My head explodes with pain so real, it takes me a full minute at least to realize my eye is still intact.

"Stand to it, Silveri!" the Prince barks, his voice close to my ear.

Mixael has already leapt to the pedestal. He brandishes a quill and begins writing furiously. Red mist roils in the corners of the room. All the dead books are stirring, whispering, as the power of the Noswraith grows, threatens to break loose. "I can't hold her!" Mixael shouts, desperately. The room shakes, and he nearly tumbles, obliged to stop writing and catch the pedestal with both hands. "I can't hold her without her name!"

I gasp. My throat is ragged, raw with screaming. But I breathe out a single word: *"Emma."*

"What's that?" The Prince whips his head down, staring earnestly into my eyes. "Darling, what did you say?"

"Emma." I choke on a sob but manage to get the word out somehow. "The Noswraith. Her name is Emma."

"Did you hear that, Silveri?"

"Aye!" The senior librarian bows over the book, quill in hand. Magical energy churns around him, dragged straight from the *quinsatra* and channeled through his mind, his body, his spirit, into the words he writes. All around us, books roar and rage while red mist hems us in. The Prince sweeps me up in his arms, plucking me out of reach of tendril-like fingers that brush against my skirts.

Then, with a sound like a great iron door rattling in its hinges, Mixael slams the book shut. "It's done!" he cries.

9

SHOULDERS SLUMPING, MIXAEL SINKS ONTO THE STEP
stool below the pedestal, leaning his head back against the
post. His face is pale, drawn, and deeply shadowed. His
breath comes in ragged gasps.

But the red mist dissipates swiftly. And the old paperback
books lie still.

I turn into the Prince's shoulder. Tears stream down my
cheeks, soaking into the rich fabric of his black robe, but I
cannot stop them. My face hurts—a stabbing, agonizing pain
where the Noswraith ripped the eyeball from my socket. I know
it was just a nightmare. I know it isn't real. But it's all too easy
to believe the dampness on my face is thick warm blood, and I
cannot stop shuddering.

"Is she all right?" Mixael sounds exhausted. I'm surprised he even has the energy to be concerned for me.

"She's strong," the Prince replies. "And she's only going to get stronger."

"I hope you're right." Our senior librarian lets out a heavy sigh. "That binding should hold for a while now. But the whole library will be testing our limits. The other wraiths must sense how close she came to breaking free again. How will we get them back in line with our ranks so badly reduced?"

"Is it possible for Vervain to be reinstated?" This time it's Andreas's soft voice speaking.

My stomach tightens painfully. The last time I saw Vervain, she was locked in a tower on the opposite end of the palace, as far from the library as she could be housed. Her mind was broken from an encounter with her own Noswraith . . . a fate far too many of the Vespre Librarians have shared over the years. A fate that suddenly seems much too close for comfort.

"Vervain will not be rejoining us anytime soon." The Prince's voice is close to my ear, and when he speaks, his arms tighten ever so slightly.

"Then what are we to do?" Mixael demands. I've never heard him speak with such dangerous desperation. He's lived his whole life in Vespre, born the son of librarians, raised in the shadow of the imprisoned Noswraiths. There isn't much he hasn't seen or endured, yet he's always maintained extraordinary optimism of spirit.

That was back before my Noswraith battered his mother to

death, however.

"There're only three of us," he says heavily. "And you, of course, sir. But at the moment you can't even read, as your fae blood is too dominant. How long will it take before your human blood replenishes?"

"I couldn't say. I've never been bled half dry before. Besides, once my blood *does* restore, I must assume the curse will renew as well. And it might be worse than before."

"So it really is hopeless. Vespre is doomed."

"Did you ever doubt it?"

Mixael laughs bitterly. "When you grow up in a doomed world, it's rather too easy to forget just how doomed it is."

"What will we do?" That's Andreas again, mild as ever. "Is it . . . Should we try to convince the denizens of the city to evacuate?"

"Our situation is not yet so dire," the Prince answers quickly. "Not that I believe the trolls will actually go in any case. They cling to their city with tremendous tenacity, no matter how many horrors we bring into its heart."

"Then what *is* the plan?" Mixael demands.

The Prince shifts his grip around me. For a moment I fear he's about to push me away, set me on my feet, tell me it's high time I pull myself together. The truth is, I'm not ready. I'm not sure I ever will be. The stabbing pain in my head is matched only by the throbbing pain in my heart. While I know neither is a true physical pain, I cannot help clinging to the Prince, holding myself together through sheer willpower.

As though he senses my sudden flare of fear, the Prince's arms only press me closer. His voice is firm and even as he speaks: "First, I will be expediting Darling's training. She's done well over these last few weeks. Following the events of tonight, she should soon find access to her deeper powers. Beyond that, we shall have to wait and see."

Another shudder ripples down my spine. What he says should be encouraging, but . . . the truth is, I don't want access to any deeper powers. I want to shut them down fast and tight and never speak of them again.

At length, the Prince rises, still cradling me in his arms. He does so easily, as though I weigh no more than a feather. His strength and grace are positively inhuman. A word of command from him, and the other two librarians slip from the vault. He leaves last of all, carrying me with him.

As we pass through the door, I feel a chilling sensation like cold fingers brushing against my cheek. Longing. Sad. Desperate. Then we're through. Mixael slams the door behind us and shifts the heavy lock into place.

The Prince declares that he and I will take the night shift, giving Mixael and Andreas a much-needed reprieve.

By this time I'm able to sit upright on my own at my desk. I try not to let myself feel the lack of the Prince's warm, steadying embrace. I try not to let myself long to go to him, to rest my head on his shoulder, press my body against his chest, and feel his arms envelop me.

Instead I sit straight and tall, my face a careful mask of blankness. Mixael and Andreas both shoot me uncertain looks as they take their leave. I can see protest in their eyes, but just now their exhaustion is much too great. In the end they slip away to their beds, and I can only pray their sleep will be deep and undisturbed by nightmares.

Long hours stretch before me. The Prince leaves me at my desk and vanishes down the stairs about some business I cannot guess. I know perfectly well that he can't do any of the work required of a librarian just now. Whatever transpires tonight, it will be my responsibility to keep the Noswraiths contained and quiet.

I lift a hand to my face, pressing my palm against my right eye. Funny. Even now I could almost swear I feel a gaping wound and warm, flowing blood. But when I lower my hand and stare at it, there's no brilliant red smear. The phantom pain has mostly faded as well, leaving nothing but a dull memory.

You'll learn to see as I do.

I shudder at the whispered hiss in the back of my head. Closing my eyes tight, I tuck my chin and breathe a prayer.

When I look up again, the Prince is approaching, a stack of books in his arms. He scarcely glances at me but sets his stack on my desk with a loud thump. "These were on your fellow librarians' desks," he says. "Small bindings, but good opportunities to improve your skills. Shall we get started?"

I stare at the pile of ragged volumes, each one on the verge of collapse, the power contained within ready to escape. None of these are great wraiths. I doubt they could harm any but the very weakest mind should they manage to escape. They pose no challenge even for my fledgling skills.

I feel the Prince's eyes on the side of my face. If I meet his gaze, what will he do? What will he say? Will he ask how I knew the name of the Eyeless Woman? The name I have for so long suppressed? Will he ask what drove me to write such a monster into existence?

Without a word, I reach for the topmost book. My actions crisp and efficient, I select an empty volume from a stash in my desk drawer, trim my quill, dip it in ink, and begin the labor of writing the damaged spell afresh. The Prince leaves me to the task, returning only now and then to check on my progress. It's a simple enough spell, almost laughably easy. I complete it in record time, seal the binding with a flourish of my quill, and slam the book shut.

Then I rise and, taking the volume with me, leave my desk.

I find the Prince several floors below. He's running his fingers over book spines, feeling for weaknesses in the spells contained therein. The whole library gives off an uneasy sense of instability. Even I can sense it, inexperienced as I am. But, for the moment at least, peace holds sway among the stacks.

The Prince turns at my approach. One eyebrow rises slowly up his forehead. "What is it, Darling? Have you encountered difficulty?"

I keep coming until I stand just before him, the new binding still held tightly in my arms. I meet his gaze and hold it hard. His eyes travel across my face. That risen eyebrow falls as his forehead puckers into a slight line.

"I remember that night," I say at last.

He blinks. Once. Slowly.

"You were there," I continue. My voice is measured, calm. It does not match the galloping pace of my heart. "You were there when they brought us before King Lodírhal. You had me by the arm, and Estrilde held my father. The two of you forced us to our knees in front of him."

I cannot read his expression. He offers neither confirmation nor denial. But it doesn't matter. The memories are there now. As clear in my head as though I've just lived them.

"It was the first time in years Father had written a success." The words rise to my tongue and spill over, a relentless flood. "We'd been struggling. Starving. He'd given up for a time, declaring he would never write again after the last story failed. We lost everything. Our home, our standing in society. Our dignity. And Mama. She died, leaving us behind. Father nearly went mad with grief."

I close my eyes, remembering it all. All those memories Estrilde suppressed over these last five years, now unlocked. Part of me wishes I could return to my former mistress and beg her to reestablish her curses. But there's no going back.

"He found a story I had written. I tried to keep it secret from him, but there wasn't any use. He found it, read it. Liked it. He submitted it to *The Starlin*, and they published it as one of his. *The great return of Edgar Darlington.* That's what the reviews all said. It was so popular, his publisher reprinted it in a special edition, and it sold even more."

I see it again—all those cheap paperback volumes printed on low-quality paper for ease of production and swift distribution. Now they lie in ignoble piles of ruin and decay down in the thirteenth vault on the thirteenth floor below, but at the time they were everywhere. Sold at every magazine stand, in every shop. Found in the front pockets of every gentleman's overcoat and tucked into every lady's reticule. Gentry and lowlifes alike snapped up copies for pennies and read with great relish the ghoulish tale. A tale reminiscent of Edgar Darlington's early work, back when he first made his name. Only this tale outsold all his previous efforts, catapulting him to a level of acclaim such as he'd never before known.

And the combined imaginations of all those readers—so full of vitality and power and magic beyond even fae understanding— gave life to the creation captured in those words. To my creation. My Noswraith.

The Eyeless Woman manifested. Not in the mortal world, for the air there could not support her substance. No, she came into being here. In Eledria. In Fairyland, where the very atmosphere teems with magic. Only here may Nightmares take solid form. So she manifested, and so she walked the halls of Aurelis, dragging her red mist in her wake. Slaughtering all who met her. Including Dasyra. The Prince's mother.

Tears escape through my lashes, roll down my cheeks. "When Lodírhal asked who was responsible, Father admitted the story wasn't his. He admitted he had only found it, secreted within the pages of my diary. It was mine. My work. My words. My sin." I sniff and look up at the Prince again. "Lodírhal killed him anyway."

He took out his sword and cut my father's head from his shoulders in a single swift stroke. I can still feel the spatter of blood hitting my cheek, the warmth soaking into the hem of my skirt where I knelt beside the broken, headless body. And I wept. Not for fear, but for heartbreak. For devastation over the death of the man I'd hated my whole life. I wept and could not be comforted.

I draw a ragged breath now. "It was my fault as much as his. The story was mine." I look up and catch the Prince's eye. "You knew as much. That's why you hate me."

Now that the memory has returned, I know I will never forget it. Never forget the feel of the Prince's fingers twined in my hair, holding me upright where I knelt. He stood over me, bloodstained and bruised, having just narrowly survived his own battle with the Eyeless Woman. The hatred rolled out from him, mingled with his sorrow.

Yet he had not demanded my death. He had urged Lodírhal to be satisfied with Edgar's head, to send me back to my world. It was Estrilde who insisted on taking me under Obligation. And when at length the bereft king agreed, she had taken me and bound me, suppressing these memories and most of my power. Thus had my fifteen years of servitude begun.

It could have been worse. It should have been worse.

"Why did you stop him?" I demand. "Why did you not want me dead?"

"I did want you dead," he admits, his honesty as brutal as a blow. "For a long, long time, I wanted nothing more."

"But you defended me."

"Yes."

"Why? I should have died with my father that night! Why did you spare me?"

The Prince holds my gaze. "I will not tell you."

His words are simple. But they strike me straight to the heart. I stare at him, unable to breathe. Finally, I ask: "Will you tell me one day?"

"Yes."

"Will I understand when you do?"

"I hope so."

A sob swells in my throat, threatening to choke me. I gasp and turn away. With one groping hand, I find the rail ringing the center opening of the library citadel and lean heavily against it. I feel the great yawning depths of the darkness below, the very darkness into which Nelle's body disappeared not many hours ago. The darkness which will, eventually, claim us all.

"How can you bear to have me here?" I whisper. "How can you

bear even to look at me? Knowing what I am. Knowing what I am capable of. That monster . . . she killed your mother. And Nelle. And who knows how many others. I am as guilty as any murderer."

"Perhaps." The Prince draws near, standing but a pace or two behind me. "But from the very first moment I saw you, I knew you were innocent as well."

"How can I be both?" I choke on something that would almost be a laugh were it not so bitter. "I must be one or the other."

My words seem to echo in that dark space below me, hollow and terrible. Behind me, the Prince is silent and still, so very still, I would almost think he had turned and slipped away, leaving me alone in this place.

At last, however, he answers softly: "What a very human perspective."

10

I WORK BY WHITE MOONFIRE GLOW THROUGH THE LONG hours of my watch. When my eyes grow bleary, I set aside the bindings to walk the stacks, checking for signs of bookwyrms or spellrot or Noswraiths testing the boundaries of their ink-and-page prisons. These strolls are good for resting my gaze and giving my tired hands and arms a rest from writing.

But it's too easy to let my mind wander back to the memories I've only just recovered. To dwell in those places of horror and sorrow. Soon I find myself scurrying back to my desk, eager for the binding spells to wholly absorb my attention.

I see little of the Prince. Following our conversation, he has kept himself to further reaches of the library. Always within earshot, I suspect, but just beyond sight.

At long last the hours of the night watch give way to morning.

Dawn looks much like night in the Umbrian Islands, caught in perpetual twilight. The pattern of the stars dancing above the crystal dome changes, but the purpling gloom remains ever constant. I tell the time by the tolling of distant bells. When I hear the bells ring out six, I breathe a sigh of relief, drop my quill, and lean back in my chair, rubbing both hands down my face. I've survived my first night on watch in Vespre Library. Soon my replacements will come, and I will be afforded a few hours of sleep.

Sure enough, Andreas and Mixael arrive, one after the other. Andreas heads straight for his station, but Mixael stops by my desk to check my work. Now that he's slept, he manages to summon one of his familiar smiles. "Well now, Miss Darlington!" he says, looking over the stack of bindings I've completed during my shift. "You've been hard at work, haven't you? Turning into a proper librarian, I should say."

"And so you should say."

Startled, I turn in my chair to see the Prince approach, looking as fresh as though he's just come from a long sleep and a bath. The only difference between his appearance now and last night is that he's unbuttoned the collar of his black robe, letting it hang open to reveal the loose, unfastened shirt beneath. And rather a lot of exposed chest. Naturally.

He leans against the wall of my desk cubicle and smiles easily. "Darling, here, has proven herself to be most capable. My mind shall be quite at ease when I go."

"Go?" Mixael's voice is sharp, an echo of the sudden tumultuous lurch in my own heart. "You're leaving Vespre? Again?"

"I am," the Prince replies. He looks at his nails, buffs them on one sleeve. "I hope not to be away for long. A few days, no more."

"But where are you going?" Mixael persists. "You've only just returned. Regardless of Miss Darlington's abilities, we are hardly stable as of yet."

"Precisely why I must go. We are in desperate need of new blood. I have a lead on a possible recruit, and I want to follow it."

His voice seems to echo in my head like the beat of hollow drums. What lead does he mean? Surely, he couldn't . . . he wouldn't . . . ?

Before I can form a coherent question, the Prince stands upright and steps away from my desk. "The library is in good hands among the three of you. See that she's still standing strong when I return, will you, Silveri? I shan't be long."

Mixael offers grudging compliance. Then the Prince is striding away, making for the exit. I stare after him, vaguely aware that Mixael is speaking to me but utterly incapable of comprehending his words. "Miss Darlington?" he says, snapping my attention round to him. "Are you listening? I was saying you really must get some sleep. You look quite done in."

I gape at him. Then with a little gasp, I spring to my feet. "Yes, Mister Silveri! Of course!"

Grabbing my skirts, I dart to the doors. They've already shut heavily behind the Prince, but I yank one open and slip out onto the landing above the stair. "Prince!" I call out.

He's there. No more than ten or twelve steps down. His hand

rests on the banister, and I see his fingers tense as he turns to look back at me. A nearby lantern bathes me in light but leaves him partially obscured in shadow.

My mouth hangs open. Though I try, I cannot seem to make further words come. I just stand there. Stupidly. Looking at him.

His brows pucker slightly. Slowly he climbs back up until he's merely a step or two below me, his face level with mine. "I must say, Darling," he speaks in a lazy drawl, "I find it rather strange, hearing my title shouted after me like that."

My face heats. "Forgive me," I say quickly, ducking my head. "I don't mean to be rude. You asked me to call you that, so . . . so . . ."

"I did?" The Prince tips his head ever so slightly. "Well, I don't much care for the sound of it coming from your lips. Why not give my proper name a try for a change?"

A shock shoots through my heart. I stare at him, aghast. Then, realizing I must say something: "Oh, I couldn't."

"And why not? It's very easy." He joins me on the landing and gazes down into my eyes. "It's not as though it's my *true* name. That is a secret I must keep a while longer, I fear. But I see no reason you shouldn't call me the name by which I am known throughout the worlds." He bows his head. "Well, Darling?" he says, his voice low and somehow dangerous.

I shake my head. I'm dizzy, not thinking straight. The events of last night threaten to overwhelm me, pushing me toward the edge of a cliff. I cannot safely balance. If I do not retreat soon, I will fall.

His hand reaches out, drawing near to mine. His fingers move, wafting in that little space of air, so near that my skin prickles in response. It would take no more than a twitch of my wrist to bring my hand in contact with his.

"Go on," he breathes. "You came after me for a reason. Is there something you want to ask me? Before I leave?"

"Y-yes."

"What is it?"

"I . . . I . . ."

His eyes are so deep. So vivid in color, so expressive, and so dangerous. I feel the wild fae-ness of him, the otherworldly beauty and brilliance that both draws and repels me by turns. I long to close the space between us, between our hands, between our bodies. I long to feel the sensation of his arms around me as they were last night when he held me trembling against him. I want . . . I wish . . . so many terrible things. Things I have no business wanting or wishing. Not now.

I must remember who I am. I must remember why I am here. And I must be strong.

"Are you going to see my brother?"

The words fall from my lips like iron blocks: heavy, ringing. They land between the Prince and me, driving him back. His foot lands on a lower step, bringing his line of sight level with mine. "What if I am?" he asks.

"Oscar does not deserve to be Obligated." I pull my shoulders back, my hands clenching tight. "He's done nothing wrong."

"Your brother has incredible magic potential."

I know it. I've always known it. He is, of the two of us, by far the more gifted. The true son of Edgar Darlington, with the potential to surpass even his father's reputation in the literary world. But the darkness in his heart, all the demons haunting him every hour of every day and every night . . . they make him dangerous.

And the Prince has now read one of my brother's stories.

"It doesn't matter what he *could* be," I say. "He has not yet done anything to deserve Obligation. You cannot take him against his will."

"And you . . . what? Expect I would lay hands on your brother and drag him across the worlds, kicking and screaming?" The Prince narrows his eyes. "Is this your opinion of me?"

"I . . . I just don't . . ." I lick my lips, staring down at my feet. "I want what's best for Oscar."

"And what about you? What is in your best interests where that brother of yours is concerned?"

I shake my head sharply, my jaw firming. "I don't know what you mean. I only want him safe and well. I only want—"

"Mistress!"

The bright voice ringing against the stone walls startles me. With a little cry, I leap back from the Prince. Then, recovering myself, I look over the railing, all the way to the floor down below. There stands Lir, her pale hair snarled around her face, her eyes wide and a little frantic.

"Mistress, I thought I heard you!" she cries, her hands cupped around her mouth. "You are needed at once! These children of yours have refused to sleep and are running positively wild about the halls. Captain Khas declares she will throw them out on their ears unless something is done right away. You're the only one who can keep them even tolerably in line. I beg you, let the Noswraiths have the whole blighted city, but *please* come put these children to bed!"

"Oh, Lir!" I laugh nervously and wave a reassuring hand. "I'm coming, I promise! Wait a moment." Turning from her, I look for the Prince again, several final words quick upon my tongue. They fade away and die before they are spoken, however.

The Prince is already gone.

The children put up some resistance to being tucked into their beds. For one thing, they are not used to being separated from each other, preferring to sleep in one great mound of rocky limbs rather than rest comfortably on individual pallets with pillows and blankets. For another, they've spent the last several weeks with me in my bed when I thought I was hiding them from the Prince's notice.

That pretense is over now. The Prince has given the children a room across the hall from mine, complete with four little beds piled with cushions and satin-weave blankets. There's a bathroom as well, though how often I'll be able to bully any of them into the big stone bathtub remains to be seen. One step at a time.

"I sleep with *mar*," Sis says petulantly when I turn from tucking in the last of her three brothers. She stands on the footboard of her bed, precariously poised without a care in the world. To my surprise, she's actually wearing a scrap of clothing—a little slip of silk that scarcely comes down to her knees and tends to fall off one shoulder. Considering she's insisted on running around stark naked for as long as I've known her, it's a great improvement.

"Not tonight, sweetness," I tell her sternly and point to the pillow. "Sometimes, yes. But now, you need to be a big girl and sleep in your own bed."

She gives me such a look, my spine tenses, preparing for battle. Perhaps it would be easier to give in this time, to let her snuggle up in a little lump beside me while I sleep.

No. I will begin as I mean to continue. Besides, I'm painfully exhausted after my night in the library, and I desperately need a proper rest without little legs kicking me in the small of my back.

I hold up one hand. "I'm going to count to three. Then your head needs to be on that pillow."

Sis's eyes narrow. "What if don't do?"

I match her stare with one equally fierce. "*Consequences.*"

I doubt she has any idea what the word means. But my tone is unmistakable. Her perfect little mouth set in a pout, Sis climbs down from the footboard and flounces to her pillow. When I smile sweetly and drop a kiss on her forehead, she deigns to pucker her lips and press them briefly to my cheek. So we're still friends, at least.

The three boys watch wide-eyed, peering out from under blankets held up to their broad, flat noses. I blow each of them a kiss as I cross the room, obliged to duck and dodge as I go. Sis has been hard at work these last few days constructing another . . . what did Lir call it again? A *tangle*. A mad weaving of string and random bric-a-brac collected from all over the palace. One elaborately embroidered slipper dangles in front of my face as I push through to the door. I'm almost certain it belongs to the Prince.

Swatting it aside with a sigh, I silently vow I'll make her clean it all up. But later. Now, we could all use a rest.

Lir is waiting for me across the hall when I step into my own room. She looks up from her work with an expression of utmost relief. "Are they asleep?"

"Not yet. Judging by the number of yawns, though, I should say very soon."

"Deeper Dark be praised!" she answers with sincerity. She's laying out a nightgown for me and performing other small tasks to make the room ready for repose. "And how was your night in the library, Mistress?" Her tone is deceptively disinterested. As though we're not both perfectly aware how eager she is to know how everything went between the Prince and me during those long, dark hours.

I sink into the chair before my vanity mirror, breathing out a long sigh. How can I possibly begin to answer such a simple question? Last night was horrible. Incredible. Terrifying. And . . . and just a little bit . . . *wonderful.*

"It was fine," I answer flatly.

Lir's look is too knowing for comfort. She bites her tongue, however, and serves me a hot meal, before helping me into my nightgown. Then she gently prods me to bed. I'm fairly certain I'm asleep before my head even hits the pillow. Some vague part of my awareness hears Lir's whispered, "Sleep well, Mistress," just before the door clicks shut. I may have even grunted some sort of response. Beyond that, nothing.

I sleep long and hard. No dreams, thank the gods. Perhaps even the Noswraiths took pity on me. Or perhaps they simply did not consider me interesting enough prey in my pathetic, weakened state. Whatever the reason, I sleep the sleep of the dead.

It's not until hours later that a pressure on my arm stirs my slumber. At first, I ignore it. The pressure comes again, a persistent prodding. I try to roll over, to get away from the sensation. But I've entered that strange state of sleep in which I'm aware of the physical, waking world around me, but my body remains inert. A disconcerting feeling, especially in a world so rife with living Nightmares.

That pressure on my arm again. A bit heavier than before. Is it one of the children, poking me with a rock-hard finger? But no, a second pressure follows, then a third, and a fourth, all at the same time. It reminds me of the old tabby cat I had when I was little. He used to wake me in the morning by walking across my body like this. "Get off, Maulkin," I try to grumble. It comes out in a series of rough grunts, not quite words.

Now the thing—whatever it is—stands on my shoulders.

"*Heheheh.*"

The hairs prickle on the back of my neck. Was that a laugh I just heard? Low, soft. Almost a whisper. Perturbed, I try to force my eyelashes apart. Just a little. Just enough that I can see a blurry impression of my bedroom.

The weight on my back shifts. A scramble of dark limbs passes before my eyes, followed by a thick-sounding *thump*. The next moment, something scuttles across my narrow field of vision, crosses the room, and dives into my open wardrobe. I try to blink. But I can't. I can only lie there, one eye partially open, staring as hard as I can into that shadowy space beyond the sagging wardrobe door. Why is it open? Lir is always so meticulous. Surely, she would have closed it properly.

I'm still puzzling over this question when new movement makes my heart leap. A long black hairy limb extends from the wardrobe interior, plants on the floor. Three curved claws, like raptor talons, tap the stone floor. But the leg joints are weirdly angled, like a spider's.

Another limb emerges. Then another, and another. Then a big bulbous body sinks nearly to the floor. It crouches there for some moments before a stalk-like neck stretches up and up, unfolding in sections, like a telescope. Two yellow eyes blink owlishly.

Quick as a flash, the neck retracts. The shadowy head sinks back into the dark fur of the body. Before I can begin to process what I'm feeling—fear, disgust, amusement, or sheer horror—the thing scuttles across the room. I can't see it anymore. Not from this angle.

My lungs are tight. I can't draw breath. Ice-cold dread pulses through my veins. More scuttling, claws clicking with each step. It's beside my bed now. I know it. I try again to move, to make my limbs obey me. But that terrible, heavy paralysis holds me captive.

Slowly, tentatively, a round black head rises. Comes into view over the edge of my bed. Yellow eyes blink at me, one after the other, just slightly out of synchronization. Then, the black hairiness breaks in an enormous, toothy, crescent-moon smile.

"Boo," it says.

11

THE ACCUMULATION OF AIR IN MY LUNGS BURSTS
from me in a glass-shattering scream, jolting my mind and
body back into consciousness. Flailing, still screaming,
I toss blankets and pillows aside and spring upright. My hand
latches hold of one pillow. I swipe it like a sword, striking the
creature in the head, a sound hit.

It vanishes. Nothing but a puff of cloud and a putrid stink remains.

The next instant, the tail of my eye catches movement scurrying
across the floor, making for the door. I turn just in time to see
the leggy, bulbous form duck and slip right through the half-inch
crack between door and floor.

I sit there, my own screams still ringing in my head, staring.
Noswraith. It's a Noswraith. A gods-blighted Noswraith, escaped
from the library. The Prince and I must have missed one last night,

and Mixael and Andreas didn't realize, and . . . and . . .

The children!

I fall out of bed, right myself, and grab a book and quill from the satchel slung over the back of my vanity chair. Racing to the door, I wrench it open to see that twisted monstrosity of black hair and claws and disproportionate limbs standing just across the hall. Its accordion neck pops up, its round head turning to look at me. That awful, toothy mouth forms a startled O. *"Oopsie!"* it says.

Then it darts under the door. Into the children's room.

Roaring like a warrior, I hurtle across the passage and wrench the door open. Two steps in, and I run straight into a snarl of strings and stones and bits of random debris. Swiping with one arm, I push myself through.

A dark little voice cries out, *"Ooooh, no, no, nonono!"*

I peer through the vibrating web of threads. Right in the center of the room is the Noswraith, its awkward limbs tangled up in threads. It writhes, struggles, looking more like a spider than ever with its head tucked in close. But it seems to be wrapping itself up. *"Oopsie!"* it shrieks. *"Oh, no! Oopsie! No!"* With each horrible cry, its voice becomes more muffled as threads wrap tighter, faster, and then . . . I blink. Where the Noswraith was a moment before there is nothing but a big, complicated knot.

What in the worlds have I just seen?

"Mar?"

I start and look past the snarl to the four little beds lining the far wall. Sis and her brothers are all sitting up, blankets pulled to their chins, staring at me. "Are you all right?" I gasp. I want to push through the threads and get to them but remain rooted in place.

"Arpigig gubdagog!" Sis sits up a little straighter in her bed, her pretty face darkening into a scowl. She points at me. "You broked it!" With that, she scrambles out of bed and, weaving her way through the various threads and knots and suspended bits of detritus, begins to reassemble the parts I've run through. She unwinds broken threads from my limbs and nightgown, ties them with nimble little fingers, then sets about restringing them from different points on the wall, floor, ceiling, and articles of furniture. As for me? I stand there, watching her. Trying to make sense of what I'm seeing.

"Mistress? What are you doing out of bed?"

I turn to see Lir standing in the doorway of the room. She frowns around at the threads strung all over the chamber. "Lir!" I cry, and hasten to her, stepping out of the tangle as I go. "Lir, what was it you called this again?" I swing an arm to indicate Sis's mad creation.

Lir makes a face. "It's a *gubdagog*. I'm sorry, Mistress, but I can't seem to stop her from making them. This is the third one this week!"

"But what *is* it?" I demand. "Why does she make them?"

Lir looks puzzled. "It's just a *gubdagog*, Mistress. It's something troll children do. I don't know why."

Leaving Lir where she stands, I make my way back into the room, this time taking care not to disturb any of Sis's work. I approach the knot in the center of the room. It's big, intricate, woven with so many parts I cannot begin to understand it. But it's nowhere near as big as the Noswraith I'd watched struggling in that snarl. I lean in, look closer. Am I mistaken, or is that subtle vibration in the air . . . magic? Putting out one tentative finger, I poke the knot.

It shivers. Very faintly, just on the edge of awareness, a voice whispers: *Boo!*

I draw back, breath catching.

"Murb atub." I look down at little Sis, who stands beside me, arms crossed, a stern scowl creasing her face. *"Bic gubdagog!"* she says.

"Yes," I answer thoughtfully and nod. "Yes, you're right. I should be more careful with your things." Very gently, I poke the knot one more time, feel the vibration of energy in the air around it. "You know what? I think it's high time we went to speak to the Priestesses of the Deeper Dark about you and your brothers. What do you say?"

I can't very well leave a Noswraith wrapped in a tangle of threads in the middle of the children's room. So I use my book and quill and write the awful thing into the pages. There's a strange shift in the air as it moves from one to the other, and I cannot honestly say my written spell feels as strong as the knot had been.

I take the book with me back to the library and hand it over to Mixael. "One got out," I say, placing the book on his desk.

He looks up at me, his expression shocked. "A bad one?"

"Quite small. Only, I don't know the name, so I cannot bind it properly."

"I'll see to it." Our new senior librarian pinches the bridge of his nose and leans back in his chair. "I won't lie, Miss Darlington—I don't see how we can carry on much longer. There used to be enough of us, and little breakouts like this were entirely unheard of!"

I feel for him. For all of us. The daunting task of containing this many Noswraiths has only become more daunting with time, as more nightmares are collected. But perhaps there's hope. Perhaps there might be a way . . .

"I need to run an errand. Down in the city."

Mixael shoots me a look. "An errand?"

"Yes. I'm going to speak to the Priestesses of the Deeper Dark about adopting the troll orphans."

He sighs heavily and shakes his head. "Are you sure that's such a good idea, Miss Darlington? Trollfolk are awfully particular, as I'm sure you're coming to realize. They have their ways, and while we may not always like or understand them, we must respect them."

"I know. Which is why I wish to speak to the priestesses."

"They're not going to give you permission to take the children. Troll orphans belong to *Morar tor Grakanak*. It's as simple as that." He sits forward in his chair. "You'd be better off concentrating on your duties here in the library, not trying to upset thousands of years' worth of troll tradition."

"So you won't let me go?"

For a moment he looks stubborn. I truly do fear he's going to refuse permission. Then I will have a choice to make—honor the commands of the senior librarian or flagrantly defy his authority. Exactly how much leniency does my Obligation afford me if the Prince isn't here to enforce his will?

To my great relief, Mixael finally lets out another long-suffering sigh. "You won't go alone, I trust."

"I'm taking Lir with me," I hasten to assure him.

"Take Khas as well."

"I wouldn't want to pull the captain from her duties."

He smiles. "Khas's primary duty is keeping the Vespre librarians alive. These days, that means the majority of her focus is on our newest and most vulnerable librarian."

While I don't particularly like thinking of myself as vulnerable, I can't argue with Mixael. Captain Khas, however, is less open to the prospect of a jaunt into the lower city than I might have hoped.

"You shouldn't go," she says when I broach the topic.

I sigh. This is exactly why I didn't want to involve anyone else. "And why not?" I ask. "Do you also think the children should *belong* to the God of the Deeper Dark?"

Her lip curls ever so slightly. "It doesn't matter what I think. It's the *Hrorark* trolls who should worry you."

A shiver races down my spine. "Yes, well, that's why I want you to come along. Please, Captain. It's for the children. I don't want them falling out of *Vagungad* and being forever separate from their people. If I can work out some sort of arrangement with the priestesses, perhaps this will be enough to satisfy the . . . the . . ." I take a stab at the difficult word, "the *hrorark.*"

Khas exchanges glances with Lir, who stands beside me. The two of them are alike in many ways. Both are pure white from head to toe and boast soft skin rather than the stone hides of other trolls. It is not her physical differences, however, that make Lir an outcast, but the fact that she was raised by humans here in Vespre Library. Is Khas's story similar? There must be some reason why she's devoted her life to serving the Prince and his cause. I've seen her in action multiple times, a valiant warrior quick to defend those in her charge. Though her brute strength has no effect against Noswraiths, she doesn't hesitate to throw herself into battle against them when necessary. If nothing else, she can serve as a distraction while one of the librarians works a binding spell. Her broken arm hangs in a sling even now after one such battle.

I wait, watching the solemn captain's face, trying to gauge her thoughts. Though her skin is soft, her expression is hard as stone. Finally, she says, "Very well. I will go with you to the lower city."

"Thank you!" I breathe. My heart lightens. Perhaps this will be a successful venture after all.

It takes some convincing, but in the end, I get Lawrence to watch over the children while Lir and I are away. When the Prince is gone, it isn't as though his manservant has much to occupy his time in any case.

The last sight I have of him, poor Lawrence stands before the four of them, surveying their mostly naked, disorderly state. "Well!" he says. "Someone must take on the burden of introducing you to the sartorial arts. It would seem the gods have chosen me for such a task." I close the door and say a quick prayer that my little ones won't eat the poor man alive.

Khas leads the way into the lower city while Lir walks close beside me. I've now ventured from the palace on enough excursions that some of these upper streets are familiar to me. It'll take me a while to fully understand the logic of troll-city layouts, but familiarity certainly helps.

"I must remind you, Mistress," Lir says as we go, her arm linked in mine, "that I may not be welcome at the temple." Fear underscores her voice. This is difficult for her, outcast as she is. I know she would prefer to remain behind.

"I understand," I say, offering her a quick smile. "You don't need to come in with me. I have Captain Khas, remember."

"I will not be entering the temple." The captain's voice is sharp. I hadn't realized she was listening. I frown, studying the firm set of her shoulders in front of me. She offers nothing more, but I can tell there's no point in arguing. Well, fine then. I'll enter the temple by myself. It can't possibly be worse than entering the Den of Vipers in Old Docklands, now can it?

The deeper we go into the city, the more I become aware of watchful eyes and hidden faces peering at us through shadowy windows as we pass. Rumor will, no doubt, spread through the city that one of the librarians has ventured down from the palace. Will the *hrorark* hear? Will word reach their leader's ear? I must hope I can make this visit as brief as possible. I don't want either Lir's or Khas's safety compromised for my sake.

We pass into streets so deep, I can no longer see the sky overhead. Instead the narrow roads are lit by luminous crystals propped on tall stakes, rather like lampposts. We hasten from one such crystal to the next, clinging to the light, wary of the deeper shadows in side streets and alleys.

"We're here," Khas says at last as we reach the end of the road. I peer ahead, searching in the dim crystal glow. I see no tower or structure of any kind. Nothing that I would have associated with a temple. A yawning cave mouth opens before me, ragged and totally natural, unshaped by artisan hands. It looks like a gate to the Underworld. Perhaps it is.

I draw back a step, clinging a little harder to Lir. Slowly, my eyes adjust enough to see two great boulders set on either side of the cave mouth. When Khas calls out a rough-sounding greeting, these boulders shift, stir, then stand up straight into the forms of tall, stone-hided guards.

"*Grakol-dura,*" one of them says. He grips a huge club in one hand and slowly bounces it off the opposite palm. "*Grazut orumum?*"

Khas responds in kind, her voice a series of roars and grunts.

165

She draws herself up to her fullest height, and though she is a good head shorter than either of the guards, I see one of them take a half step back. The other one, however, points beyond Khas to where Lir and I stand together. He growls something harsh.

"What's going on?" I ask, leaning into Lir. "What's he saying?"

"Oh, Mistress!" Lir's grip on my arm tightens painfully. "I knew it would be this way. They recognize me from the palace. They know I am *va-lak*. I am fallen from the Holy Cycle."

Her fear is so potent, I almost give in right then and there. But no! All this suffering Lir has endured, just because her parents chose to love her, chose not to abandon her to the dark troll god . . . it's wrong. And I won't have it, not for my little ones.

Letting go of Lir's arm, I step forward until I'm level with Khas. The captain turns sharply, her eyes snapping. "Get back!" she growls.

Ignoring her, I face the two guards, both of whom leer at me, their lips curled back to reveal diamond-sharp teeth. I try not to let myself consider how easily such teeth could shatter my bones. "I have come," I say, in a clear, firm voice, "to speak to the Priestesses of the Deeper Dark."

One of the guards takes a rumbling step forward. Khas hastily steps between him and me, her one good arm held out protectively. "Get ready to run," she says, her head low, her eyes intent upon the guards.

I stand my ground. "I seek the priestesses' council," I continue, meeting the eyes of the nearest guard, "to learn more of the ways of *Vagungad*."

He studies me. There was a time when I thought all trolls brutish lumps, scarcely sentient enough to be considered intelligent. Now, after many weeks spent in their world, interacting with their kind, I've come to recognize the deep wellsprings of thought that hide behind those stony facades. The way this troll looks at me now, I cannot help feeling I'm being weighed in the balance. Will I be found wanting?

Suddenly, he blinks and turns away. I catch a breath. "What's going on?" I whisper to Khas even as the guard vanishes into the mouth of the cave.

"I'm not sure," she responds. Her hand is still clenched in a fist. "I think your request is being carried to Umog Grush."

"Umog Grush?"

"The low priestess of Vespre." She speaks the words with reverence.

I swallow, my throat dry. "And how likely is this Umog Grush to agree to see me?"

"About as likely as daybreak," Khas replies. Which, in these parts, is as good as saying, *Not very likely at all.*

I face the cavern entrance, my heart beating fast. Every minute we stand here is another minute that word might carry to the *hrorark* of our presence in the lower city. The last thing I want is to cause trouble. But I can't simply abandon Sis, Calx, Har, and Dig. Who do they have in this world to care for them besides me? No doubt Lir's parents felt the same way once upon a time. Is Lir ultimately grateful? Or does she sometimes wish those two foolish humans had left well enough alone, allowing her to remain in the

Holy Cycle of her people and her god?

A rumbling from the cave mouth draws my attention. The guard emerges, his teeth flashing in the light of the nearest crystal. He looks at me and speaks a stream of rough troldish. The only words I recognize are *Umog Grush*.

"What is he saying?" I ask Khas.

She lets out a breath. "The low priestesshas agreed to see you." She looks down at me, her eyes wide. "You must enter alone. No companions. And no light."

My blood goes cold. But I nod. "All right. If that's how it must be."

Lir whimpers beside me. "You should go with her, Khas!"

But the captain shakes her head. "I cannot. This is the only way."

"Mistress." Lir grips my hand, her fingers squeezing almost hard enough to break bones. "Mistress, please."

With some effort, I manage to free myself from her grasp. "It's all right, Lir." I smile with more confidence than I feel. "It's all right. I'll be back before you know it."

"And if you're not?" Khas growls. "What will I tell the Prince if he returns to find something has happened to you?"

"Tell him it was my own fool fault, and you're not a bit to blame. He won't have any trouble believing that."

"But, Mistress, please consider—"

I hold up a hand, silencing both of their protests. "The children are mine now," I say. "I owe them this much."

The two women exchange glances, their pale faces etched

with concern. Lir shrugs and says something soft in troldish. The captain growls. Then, though her manner communicates extreme reluctance, she sweeps her hand to indicate the cavern entrance.

I step out from between them, immediately feeling the lack of their tall, strong forms. But I cannot ask more of them than they've already given. Whatever waits for me in the dark, I must face it. Alone.

The two troll guards stand so straight and still, I could easily mistake them for rough-hewn boulders in that eerie lighting. As I draw near, one of them speaks, his voice growling with troldish accent: "Walk straight in the dark. Veer neither to the right nor the left. Do not hesitate but trust the God of the Deeper Dark to guide your steps. So may all walk safely."

I acknowledge him with a short nod. Somehow, I feel much less confident than I did a moment ago. Nothing for it now, however. I step between the guards and into the waiting darkness.

WITHIN A FEW PACES, I'M BEYOND THE RANGE of light. The darkness is so absolute, I stop in my tracks. It requires every bit of willpower I can summon just to take another step. Then another.

"Veer neither to the right nor the left," I whisper through gritted teeth. "Do not hesitate." The guard's words were so specific, and he took care to speak them in my own language so that I would be sure to understand. What will happen to me if I do not follow through? The small hairs on the back of my neck and arms prickle.

But I keep going, my pace steady, my face forward. The passage feels terribly narrow, and I can't help the wretched sensation that the walls are closing in, that they will soon crush me between them. I want to reach out, press my palms against the stone. Instead I keep my hands knotted in the folds of my gown and continue walking. One step after another after another.

Something brushes across my cheek.

I stop. My body shudders with the need to reach up and push away whatever is causing that fluttering sensation. Mama always said my imagination would be the death of me. Just now, it conjures unseen horrors enough to bring another Noswraith into existence, with or without a written spell.

I close my eyes. It's better this way, actually. When my eyes are open, I can't help straining them, trying to make sense of the darkness. Blindness makes better sense, and the rest of my body begins to compensate. Soon I'm back in motion, moving with more confidence than before. The children's names roll around in my head, over and over, like a mantra. I'm doing this for them. For the children. My children. They have no one but me. So I must be brave. For them.

Suddenly, the walls are gone. I've come to a great, open space. The emptiness in the air before me hits like a shock. If I take another step, will I fall? Tumble through that open nothingness, down and down into the waiting dark? My knees quake. I want to sink to the ground, to weep. Better yet, I want to turn and run back the way I've just come. Forget everything. This was only a fool's errand anyway, wasn't it?

I squeeze my eyes a little tighter. Then, setting my chin, I lift my foot. Extend it out into the empty air in front of me. "Gods!" I breathe, and step down, firmly.

My foot lands on something. It's solid enough, but it sways. My stomach pitches as the sensation of a terrible drop rushes over me. Though I try to stop myself, my eyes flare open, staring out into the dark. But there's nothing to see. Nothing at all. Biting back both curses and prayers, I lift my other foot, take a second stride out onto that swaying platform. Is it a bridge? I think so. Some sort of rope bridge, suspended over the void.

I take another step. "Do not hesitate," I whisper again in echo of the guard. "Do not hesitate." The swaying makes my stomach churn, but I keep going. Five paces. Ten paces, twenty. Somewhere not far off I hear the echo of running water. Nearby, however, the air is painfully still, quiet, and cold. Another little brush of something against my cheek makes my skin crawl. It's so delicate, so fine, like spider silk.

I shake my head and hurry on. My foot comes down on firm, unmoving stone. It jars my bones. With a little gasp, I scramble off the swaying bridge. I seem to have arrived at a giant rock, uncarved and jagged. The soft soles of my slippers do little to protect my feet, and I'm obliged to reach out with my hands to catch my balance. My fingers touch sheer stone wall. Is this it? The far wall of the cavern? I still sense looming, empty space all around me. Should I try to find a way around?

I let out a careful breath in an effort to steady my racing heart. "Hullo?" I call softly. Then, raising my voice, I try again, "Is anyone there?"

"Grakol!"

I bite down on a scream and only just stop myself from jumping back. Light flares over my head. I blink, shielding my eyes against the clear blue glow of a rough-cut crystal. It's set in the end of a staff, which seems to be made of a sapling tree pulled up by the roots. As my vision adjusts, I can see a great block of a hand gripping that staff. I follow the line from fist to wrist to arm, and on to a huge naked body. A woman's body, massive and powerful, seated above me on a stone chair.

With a gasp, I struggle to find my voice. "Umog Grush?" I manage.

"Librarian Clara Darlington," the troll woman responds. Her voice is perfectly clear and crisp, without so much as a trace of troldish accent. It's not at all the kind of voice I would expect to emerge from a mouth like that.

Umog Grush notes the surprise in my face. She laughs outright, a rolling avalanche of sound. "Yes, little one. Even here, even down in the dark, I see all that goes on within the bounds of my city. I knew when the morleth arrived, bearing with them yet another trembling human. Soon after, I learned of that human's Obligation and the reason she bears it. I know she is responsible for the creation of one of the horrors which even now threatens the very existence of all Valthurg."

"What . . . ?" I hesitate. But I've come too far to shrink in fear now. "What is Valthurg?"

The old priestess extends the arm holding the staff, casting its light in a sweeping arc around us. "This! This realm in which we now stand. This city we are both bound to protect. Valthurg. Vespre. The Doomed City. It is all one and the same. Only the fae like to forget that it was our Valthurg long before it became their Vespre. Trollkind ruled here, from this very seat, long before elfkin princes came to prance about the halls of the upper palace."

As she speaks, the light from her crystal continues to grow, revealing her face. She is incredibly ugly, almost beyond description. Her brow protrudes like a ledge over her small fire-bright eyes, and her jaw extends almost as far, so that they nearly meet in the middle at the point of her huge craggy nose. She's so extreme, she would be almost laughable in any other context. Here, however, in this setting, lit by that luminous stone, she is strangely dignified.

Now that my eyes have adjusted, I can discern more of our setting as well. My gaze flicks from side to side, taking in the enormity of the cavern, the great walls, the jagged stalactites of the ceiling. Other crystals seem to catch the glow of the crystal in the staff, reflecting back its light in little winking glints, like stars. Behind me is a bridge, both longer and more decrepit than I realized, with terrible spaces between the rotten slats. It extends over a chasm so deep, so dark, I cannot bear to look any closer.

But soon I cannot be bothered with the bridge or the crystals or anything else in that great space. For as the light continues to grow, something else captures my attention: *gubdagogs.* Dozens upon dozens of *gubdagogs.* Suspended in the air around me, strung from stalactites, attached to the far walls. Massive, snarled, inexplicable, and intricate, made of knots and woven patterns I cannot begin to comprehend, strung with random pieces of debris.

One of them hangs not far from me. I bend toward it, curious. The threads hum with tension. No, with *magic*. Pure, powerful magic. I cannot help taking a step nearer.

And that's when the Noswraith lunges straight at me.

My vision explodes with gnashing fangs, slavering and snapping mere inches from my nose. A dreadfully savage face, weirdly humanoid save for the exaggerated jaw, pushes against threads and knots, struggling to reach me. I scream. My feet scrabble as I back away and very nearly pitch over the edge of the rock and fall into the chasm below. I catch handfuls of stone and cling with all my might, heart pounding, staring.

The Noswraith is gone. In its place is nothing more than a large, complicated knot. But I can still feel the power simmering in the air around it.

A low chuckle rumbles above me. "Well, now! I should have expected the oh-so-mighty Vespre librarians to be better prepared to encounter one of their little horrors."

I pull myself into a more secure position, my gaze flicking from the knot to the old priestess on her throne and back again. "What is it doing here?" I gasp.

"What most of their kind do, I expect," Umog Grush says. "Kill, maim, destroy, obliterate. That seems to be their way."

"But why? How?" My brain races, struggling to make sense of what I'm seeing.

The low priestess gives me a long look. "You're a bright little thing," she says at last. "See if you can figure it out for yourself."

I study the tangled snarl of thread, bits of bone, stone, cloth, and other random debris. All suspended in the air, turning gently as the heavier points slowly shift the balance. And in the center of it—that Noswraith. Caught in a snarl, mostly invisible to the naked eye, yet very, very present.

"I don't understand." My voice echoes hollowly in that big space. "Noswraiths are born of human magic, of written words given flesh. As such, they can only be contained by human magic. By more written words."

"So you say." The priestess sits back heavily in her throne, her stone body creaking ominously. "Despite evidence to the contrary."

Blood pounds in my temples. There must be something here. Something I'm not understanding, something . . .

"It's a *story*."

I crane my neck, taking in the *gubdagog* with all its knots and the seemingly random assortment of scraps and litter. More of them, dozens of them, are strung all over this huge space. Some are quite big, twenty feet across and more. Others are tiny, no bigger than my hand. But they're all far more sophisticated than I realized at first glance. What struck me first as random snarls I now realize are patterns. Delicate. Intricate. All but incomprehensible.

There's power here. So much accumulated magic humming in the atmosphere. Now that I've recognized it, I become more aware. It reminds me of nothing so much as the most powerful, most dangerous grimoires in the library.

"Well done, little human," the priestess says and taps the end of her staff sharply against the stone. "You may indeed be the first of your kind to see our *gubdagogs* for what they are."

"But this is fascinating!" I take a step closer to the nearest tangle, no longer concerned about the Noswraith. It manifests, snapping at me again, but this time I scarcely jump. I can see perfectly well that the knot contains it, offering it no leeway. What I cannot see is *how*.

I turn to the priestess, tilting my gaze up to meet hers. "My little girl, my . . . my Sis. She made one like this. A *gubdagog*."

The priestess raises a stony brow. "Many children try to make *gubdagogs*, just as, I would imagine, many human children like to take up pen and paper and put down what they believe will be brilliant works of written word. *Books. Stories.* They may call it what they like. It doesn't make it true."

"Of course," I acknowledge. After all, I remember only too well my initial scribbling attempts at story crafting when I was a child. "But Sis caught a Noswraith with hers. Is that normal?"

A sound like two rocks smashing together bursts from the priestess. "Indeed?"

"Not a large wraith," I admit. "Certainly not like *this* fellow. But a real Noswraith, yes."

I go on to describe how I pursued the little nightmare from my room and found it tangled up in the threads of Sis's *gubdagog*. The Low Priestess, intrigued, leans forward in her chair, studying me from beneath that massive brow of hers. When I reach the end of my story, she grunts. "It sounds to me as though this child has a natural talent. A pity she is *grakanak-balja*."

I recognize the word. Lir has used it before to describe my little ones.

Knowing I'm about to step into dangerous territory, I face the priestess again, my gaze steady and firm. "Sis is not an orphan. She may have lost her parents, but she is not alone. She is mine. As are her brothers."

Umog Grush's heavy brow lowers once more. "You speak with great conviction for a human. Tell me,"—she tilts her head to one side—"how can you possibly be mother to a creature of which you know so little?"

"Because I love her," I answer at once. "I can give her a home, a place to rest her head. I can give her arms to hold her, words to comfort her, and always, always, my support. I can do the same for her brothers. But you're right." Though the words are heavy, I continue, undaunted. "I cannot give them everything they need. I am not equipped to raise them as trolls. Which is why I have sought your help."

"People do not approach me with demands." The low priestessdraws herself up very straight, slowly twisting the staff in her hand so that the crystal light flashes and flickers. "They genuflect. They ask my prayers of intercession to the God of the Deeper Dark." She tips her chin. "They beg."

Immediately, I drop to my knees. "If begging is what is required, I will beg. I will abase myself and gladly if that is what it takes to be heard. Because my children are worth it. They're worth whatever it takes."

Umog Grush eyes me, her stone face impossible to read. At long last, her hard mouth moves once more. "Such grand gestures of humility. Yet even now, the creature reveals her pride. Pride in thinking she can do what no other has done—raise troll children when she herself is not troll. Have I not seen it? Have I not lived the cycles of this world long enough to know of what I speak? Have I not watched children of the Dark fallen outside of their *va?* Children like Lir—that poor lost soul, spirited away to the upper palace. Forced into a new, unnatural shape and made all the lesser for it."

"You're wrong."

The crystal flashes as the priestess twists her staff around sharply. "What did you just say to me?"

"Lir is not lesser. She is different, perhaps, but she is not less. In fact, she is more." I climb up off my knees and brace myself before that throne. My heart rams in my throat with terror at what I'm doing. I'm all too aware how easily this giant of a woman could squash me between her finger and thumb. But I won't back down. "Lir is everything she was naturally born to be. Everything good and true and troll. But added to that, she has the love of two other parents, who brought their otherness to her. She is the embodiment of that love, that otherness, inextricably entwined with all that her god gifted her with at birth. She is a greater being than you know. And she is perfectly capable of living within her *va* while simultaneously living beyond it."

The low priestess growls ominously. "And this is what you intend for your children? To make them into more of these blended beings? Not troll. Not human. Not elf. Just . . . *other.*"

"Are we not all *other* in the end? Are we not all more than mere eyes may perceive?" I shake my head and take a small step forward, up to the very foot of that tall throne. "Whatever happens between us now—between you and me in this moment of time—I have absolute confidence in my children. They will grow into beings as unique from each other and from me as the snowflakes that fall on a winter's night. And I will be proud of them, and I will love them. *But,*" I emphasize the word, infusing it with all my hope and longing, "what I want for them is to be as *troll* as possible. I want them to learn of their people and their ways, even as they grow to be more."

I turn slightly, indicating the *gubdagog* with one hand. "Think of my girl, great *umog*. Think of what she could do! She is already a talent, already able to catch Noswraiths with the knots she weaves. She has learned this on her own, with no instruction. What might she accomplish if she were taken in hand, trained in the art of . . . of *gubdagoging?*"

To my great surprise, the priestess laughs outright. It's a great, rolling, terrible sound that sends a quake of terror straight to my core. It takes a few moments before I realize what it is I'm hearing. "You humans!" she cries. "You speak with such passion. This is not the troll way, especially not when they are deep in *grak-va*. But I find your passionate words amusing. More than that, I find the spirit with which you speak them intriguing."

She sits back in her seat again, rubbing a massive finger across her ledge-like upper lip. The sound scrapes like chalk on a board. It's all I can do not to flinch and cover my ears. At last, however, she says, "The art of the *gubdagog* is rare. To do it well requires innate talent as well as training. So I will grant you this, Clara Darlington, librarian of Vespre: bring the child to me. I will meet her. I will speak with her. Only then will I make my decision."

"And the rest of them? Har, Dig, and Calx? Will you see they are not cast from the *Vagungad?*"

"*We. Shall. See.*" Her words are final. Like the fall of a curtain across the stage. They ring out against the stones, and all the *gubdagogs* hiss and shush and shiver.

Then, the light goes out.

13

WHEN FIVE BELLS RING, SIGNALING THE START OF a new day, Lir is obliged to drag me from my bed. Dear gods above and below, I don't remember the last time I was this tired! The overnight shift in the library followed by too few hours of sleep and an expedition into the city . . . it's all just too much. I want to crawl under my pillows and sleep for three days straight.

But Andreas and Mixael need me. No one else can relieve them at their posts.

So I slug out of bed, grateful for Lir's assistance with dressing and arranging my hair. She presses a small but hearty breakfast upon me and bullies me into taking weary bites. "Will you take little Sis to visit the temple today?" she asks once I've eaten.

I grunt and rub my eyes. "I can't. There's far too much to be done in the library, especially with the Prince gone. I must return to my regular duties for now and await a more opportune moment."

Lir sighs, obviously disappointed. After all, the children's fate may very well influence her future. "I suppose that means I must watch the littles today," she says, her face long-suffering.

Guilt stabs my conscience. It's one thing for me to decide to take in orphans, but another thing entirely when I cannot personally see to their day-to-day care. Lir was assigned to my service as maid and companion, not nanny. "Do you mind?" I ask. "Truly, Lir?"

She rolls her eyes. "I suppose I'm getting rather attached to the little biters. But don't think I want to spend the rest of my days running after them, mind you!"

I assure her I will see to more permanent arrangements for their care as soon as I have a moment to breathe. Though we both know how unlikely that is to happen anytime soon.

I peek in at the children before heading to the library. Sis has torn down much of her *gubdagog* and is hard at work repurposing her materials to make a new one. The three boys wrestle wildly all around her but somehow manage never to interrupt her work. Upon spying me, all four of them stop what they're doing and swarm in for hugs and kisses. I caution them to behave well for Lir, and they sing out a chorus of good intentions.

It's hard to leave them behind. My mind is very full as I make my way through the stone corridors of the palace. Schemes for the children's care and hopes for their future play out in my head. Is it possible the formidable Umog Grush will take Sis under her wing and train her to make *gubdagogs* like those I glimpsed within the temple cavern? I shudder, remembering the savage, slavering visage trying to tear at me through the tangles. Which Noswraith was that? No small nightmare, that's for certain. How long do *gubdagogs* hold up compared to our flimsy bindings of paper and ink? Though they had seemed frail and delicate, the magic they generated was extremely powerful, unlike anything I've ever before encountered. Could it be . . . ?

I never finish that last thought. In that moment I turn a corner. And almost walk straight into Princess Estrilde.

She's seated at the base of the great stair leading up to the library door. Someone has brought a stool, which she reclines upon with perfect grace and ease, her rose-petal gown spread out before her, her shimmering golden hair spilling over her pure white shoulders. Delicate horns coil from her forehead, burnished gold and twined with living vines.

She's not alone. Members of her entourage surround her, the usual folk I've seen any number of times gracing her salons, all exquisitely beautiful but with a careful sort of beauty. They are like the soft greenery of ferns against which the blooming rose is set, augmenting her grandeur and grace by their presence, but never competing. One of them plays a lute, picking out a delicate melody that makes the air shimmer with pale dawn light, strangely bright here in the gloom of Vespre. Estrilde holds a little mirror up to her face and seems to be working delicate glamours, perfecting her already perfect features with the tiniest, most precise of adjustments. It's painstaking work, and she is wholly absorbed in it.

Immediately I retreat back into the passage to crouch in the shadows. My heart beats wildly with shock and mounting horror. What is she doing here? Has my former mistress thought better of the bargain she made with the Prince? Has she come to reclaim my Obligation? She can't do that, surely. Not without the Prince's agreement. But the Prince isn't here. Could some of Estrilde's power over me remain? Enough that she might compel me to return to Aurelis with her in the Prince's absence?

Six bells sound. I'm due at the library. Mixael and Andreas have been working hard and will be eager for relief. Yet I continue to stand here, frozen as stone, afraid to move. I cannot make it up that stair without walking directly past Estrilde and her entourage. In that moment, I'd rather face the Eyeless Woman again!

Finally, however, I grip my skirts with both hands and step out of the passage into full view. My heart stops beating, lodged in my throat. Neither Estrilde nor any of her party so much as glance my way. I cross the little space to the stairway, trying very hard not to look at the lounging Lords and Ladies as I go. Only one of them so much as lifts an eyelid and casts me a lazy glance, a strange fellow wearing a woman's gown, his hair long and silvery, his skin a deep blue. He watches me with the same idle interest he might bestow upon an insect crawling rather too near his foot. He even pulls one leg out of my way when I pass, his lip curled in a sneer.

I reach the stairs and fairly race to the top, following the curving banister out of sight of the fae. Upon reaching the landing, I stop to catch my breath. Part of me still can't believe I made it past

Estrilde. Did she truly not see me? Or did she simply not care? Peering over the rail, I study the tops of all those fae heads. The lute player continues to pluck at his instrument. Estrilde continues to peer into her mirror.

Shivering, I draw back. She would not come all this way for no reason. I know Estrilde bears no affection for her cousin, the Prince. But perhaps she views him as an ally, especially now that King Lodírhal's life nears its end. I pinch my lips tight. The machinations of the fae courts are none of my business. Best tend to my own work and keep my head down.

Mixael is at his desk when I enter. He looks up at my approach, his eyes bleary with fatigue, and greets me with a vague, "Oh, is it six bells already? I lost track of the time." Then he sits back, drops his quill, and yawns hugely. "Seven gods spare us, I'm quite done in, Miss Darlington. I trust you are rested?"

"Rested enough," I lie, and hastily ask after the night shift. It's a relief to learn there were no major breakouts. The library has settled down following the Eyeless Woman's escape and rebinding. Mixael asks me to venture down to the eighth floor and inspect a certain series of volumes that are beginning to show signs of wear.

"If they look bad, bring them up," he says, and indicates the short stack of mismatched volumes at his elbow. "I'll finish reaffirming these spells before I turn in. Andreas is on the fourth floor, deep in the *Epic of Archithus* again. At some point, you should find him and remind him that we mere mortals must sleep eventually."

I smile. It's good to know the library is calm enough that

Andreas might return to pursuing his passion for ancient poetry. Mixael also looks better than he did. Shadows of mourning still underscore his eyes, but his color is back, and a hint of his former levity brightens his voice. I doubt he'll ever again be the same happy-go-lucky fellow I first met, not now that he wears the mantle of senior librarian. I just hope the pressures of managing the Doomed City Library won't ultimately break him.

I start for the nearest stair, prepared to begin my tasks. Before I've gone ten paces, however, I stop and turn back. "Mister Silveri, are there any Noswraiths who have escaped the lower vaults and never been rebound?"

Mixael swivels in his chair. "Why do you want to know?"

I briefly consider mentioning the *gubdagogs* but decide to hold my tongue. Best to wait until I've gathered a bit more knowledge about the trolls' strange method of story-weaving. "I'm simply curious," I say instead. "There are so many grimoires, and they're always breaking down. And with so few librarians . . ." I shrug, not finishing the thought.

Mixael looks uneasy. "It's true, some smaller wraiths have slipped through our fingers in the past. None of the Greater Noswraiths, though."

The one I'd seen in the troll temple was no minor wraith. I raise an eyebrow. "And which is the largest we've . . . misplaced?"

He rubs a hand up the back of his head, making his red hair stand all on end, his gaze edging away from mine. At last, with a little puff of air, he admits, "There was the Striker. Big fellow.

Not quite big enough to belong in the vaults. But growing, always growing. It got out not long after my father died, and no one was able to find it, not even the Prince. It killed a number of people down in the city, and then . . ." He snaps his fingers. "The trail went cold. That was more than a year ago. The Prince keeps an ear out for any word that it got off the island. It may very well be hiding somewhere in Noxaur or even have slipped to one of the other realms. Surviving on small prey, keeping a low profile. It won't want to get scooped up and imprisoned in the library again."

I consider the furious toothy face trying to rip at me through the binding threads. Something tells me that particular Noswraith might be missing its comfortable ink-and-page prison after a year tangled in a troll's *gubdagog*. "Where was the Striker shelved?"

"Level ten," Mixael answers. "But the volumes are empty. Harmless."

I know what he's saying: I don't have time to go browsing through dead books with so many living tomes in need of attention. With a hasty nod and a word of thanks, I hurry off to my tasks for the day.

The series Mixael asked me to see to down on the eighth floor isn't in bad shape. I check the final volume carefully and conclude it's strong enough to hold its spell for a few more days at least. When I continue around the curving wall of shelves, however, I find another small book—so small that it was shoved too far back on the shelf by mistake, hidden by larger volumes, and left to fester on its own. It's dangerously disintegrated, the power inside on the verge of breaking out. When I draw it from the shelf, it nearly bites my fingers. Hastily, I drop it into my trolley and set a larger, more stable grimoire on top to hold it in place. It needs to be seen to promptly.

I load my find on the nearest lift and send it up to the first floor. Before venturing after it, however, I pause to look over the central rail, down two floors below me. Down to where the tenth floor waits. Chewing the corner of my cheek, I consider.

Then, before I can talk myself out of it, I make for the nearest stair and hastily descend. I hurry among the shelves, searching out the section Mixael described, the home of the Striker. The books are exactly where he said they would be, a series of thirty-odd empty volumes, so heavy they bow the shelf on which they sit. I tug the final volume from its place and catch my breath. There's a hole in the cover. A black hole, as though something burst out from inside it. What's left of the inner pages are battered, lifeless. Even the writing is so jumbled, I struggle to make any sense of it. But there's one passage that offers a brief description: *Humanoid face. Massive fangs. Slavering.*

Granted, any number of Noswraiths in Vespre Library could boast the same. Nonetheless, it does sound very like the wraith I glimpsed in the troll temple.

"Striker," I whisper, closing the volume and slipping it back on the buckling shelf. How many times had the brave librarians been forced to rebind this one terrible Nightmare? And each time it grew stronger, each time it wore its binding out a little faster. And this is only one. Vespre Library contains thousands of these horrors, with only three librarians left to deal with them.

We need help. We need a new method. And maybe . . . maybe . . .

A sudden clamor of bells erupts in the air. I leap back from the shelf, a scream caught in my throat. I know that sound—the alarm. It's not been long since the last time it was rung. Oh, gods on high! I am not ready to face another major outbreak! My blood freezes in my veins. More than anything, I want to curl up in a ball, wrap my arms over my head, and hide.

Somehow, I manage to wrench my body around. Gripping my satchel strap with both hands, I race for the stairway.

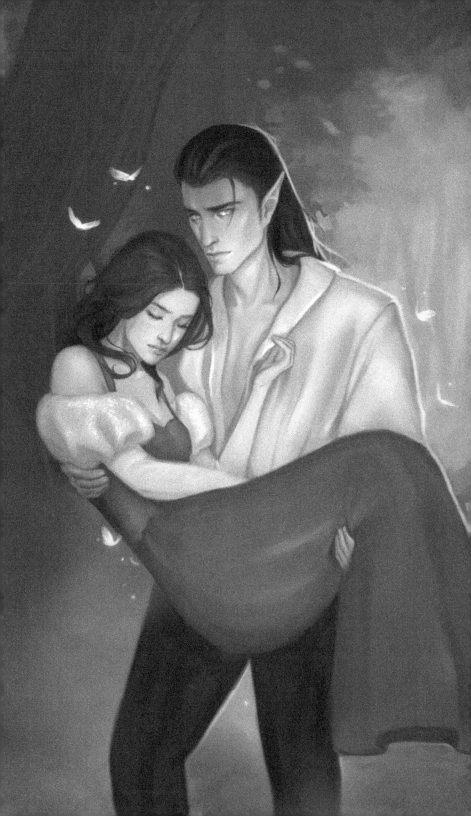

14

I FIND MIXAEL ON THE SEVENTH FLOOR BENEATH A LARGE
globe lantern which serves as a meeting point. "Did you sound
the alarm?" he demands, his voice barely audible above the bells.

I shake my head. I can hardly think straight in that clamor. My
mind is filled with images of the Eyeless Woman and the last time
I walked the floors of the library during an outbreak. I cannot bear
to face her again. Not her, nor any of the Greater Noswraiths. And
without the Prince or Nelle . . . My heart sinks with hopeless dread.

"Where's Andreas?" Mixael says.

"Here, sir!"

Our third librarian emerges from the book lift he's just ridden
up to us. Apparently, he wasn't ensconced in his epic poems on the
fourth floor all this time after all. He looks winded, his spectacles
hanging from a chain around his neck, his normally tidy hair and

neckcloth both in disarray.

"What's wrong?" Mixael rounds on his fellow librarian. "Who got out?"

"No one got out," Andreas replies. The bells are still so loud, I'm almost certain I've misheard him. Surely the alarm wouldn't go off for anything less than an outbreak, would it? But Andreas bends toward us, repeating loud enough that we can both hear him clearly. "No one got *out*. Someone got *in*."

"What?"

Andreas nods, his dark eyes darting to meet mine. "There's a stranger down on the eleventh floor, vault seven."

"Vault seven?" Mixael's face drains of color. "That's the Eight-Crowned Queen."

"Yes, sir. He's opened her grimoire. And now he's trapped inside."

The world seems to turn upside down. "But how can that be?" My voice sounds thin and small, almost inaudible beneath the still-pounding alarm. "How could anyone get down to the vaults like that?"

"All too easily these days, what with our ranks diminished," Mixael admits heavily. "Under ordinary circumstances, Captain Khas keeps the palace secure, but if someone manages to get past her, it's simple enough to infiltrate the library itself. There were only two of us on duty while you were away, and we took turns sleeping during the quietest hours. Anyone could have slipped through."

"What do we do then?"

Mixael and Andreas exchange glances. "We'll have to see who it is. Probably some mage come to siphon power from the grimoires. If we're lucky, the Eight-Crowned Queen has finished him off already. But we'll need to work together and quickly re-bind her. She's a nasty old wraith, and if she gets loose, she'll bring others with her."

Gripping our books and quills, the three of us descend in one of the book lifts. I can't help thinking how perturbed Nelle would be were she still alive to see the library rules flouted so brazenly. With Mixael as senior librarian, the three of us have been using the lifts with abandon. Probably not the safest policy, but in a place like Doomed City Library, that seems rather a minor quibble.

We reach the eleventh floor and shuffle out of the lift. Mixael claims a moonfire lantern, and Andreas goes to stop the alarm. The relief of silence is so great, I almost drop to my knees. After a few moments, however, I find the quiet all the more ominous. My own breath sounds thunderously loud in my ears.

Mixael leads the way, his lantern flashing as it swings from the end of his arm. We shuffle after him, Andreas at the rear, me between them. Part of me is proud that these two far more experienced librarians didn't make me wait in the upper floors. They see my worth, know my value, and are willing for me to join them in a crisis. Granted, this might be more to do with desperate necessity than respect for my abilities. But I'll take it.

The seventh vault awaits us. The door stands wide—whoever broke in didn't bother drawing it shut behind him. Who would be so foolish? Any mage arrogant enough to think he can steal power from a Noswraith grimoire, I suppose. A pale glow spills out through the opening, no doubt from the lantern our invader brought with him to light his way.

Mixael creeps ahead of us to the open door and peers into the vault. A look of surprise flashes across his face. "Well!" he says, his voice much too loud in the stillness. "Not what I expected, I must say."

Curious, Andreas and I hasten to his side, peering around him into the space. My gaze lands upon the tall figure standing before the pedestal on which the Eight-Crowned Queen's grimoire lies. My blood runs cold.

"Danny!"

He stands with his back to us. Though I cannot see his face, I would recognize him anywhere. Light from his lantern spills on the pages of the grimoire open before him. His hands are white-knuckled as he holds the edges of the platform, as though he's bracing himself in place. He doesn't move, not even the barest flinch at the sound of his name.

"Miss Darlington, wait!" Mixael cries too late. I've already rushed past him into the vault. I circle the pedestal so that I can stare up into Danny's face, frantically trying to catch his eye. He won't look at me. He doesn't seem to be aware I'm there. He stares down at the text before him, and I watch his eyes run along the lines, back and forth, back and forth. His lips are parted. I can just sense his faint breath. Otherwise, he's perfectly rigid, immobile.

"What's wrong with him?" I ask, turning to Mixael.

The other two librarians enter the room more cautiously, eyes wide, quills and books at the ready. Mixael approaches the grimoire, takes a look at Danny's face, then shakes his head. "It's as I suspected. He's been drawn into the Nightmare."

"What do you mean?"

Mixael sighs. "I'm sorry, Miss Darlington. There's not much to be done. The Eight-Crowned Queen is still bound, but he's gone to her world now. She presumably hasn't found him yet, as he is still alive. But it's only a matter of time."

"We should go," Andreas says softly. "Bar the door."

"Wait, what?" I stare from Mixael to Andreas and back again. "You're just . . . you're going to leave him here?"

"It's the safest precaution," Mixael answers. "The only other way to get him back is to enter the Nightmare, find him, and bring him back to his body. But who's going to risk it? Not even my father would do as much for a thief and an intruder, and he was the greatest mage I ever knew. No. This sorry fool has chosen his lot. Let him face the consequences."

The callousness of his words hits me like a slap. I shake my head, my teeth clenching. "He's my friend."

"*What?*" Mixael and Andreas speak in unison, their faces mirror images of shock.

"This isn't some power-hungry mage," I persist. "This is my friend. Danny Gale. I've known him since I was a child. He has no magic, no power. He's totally helpless."

Mixael's gaze shoots from me to him and back again. "Then what in the seven gods' names is he doing *here*?"

"I think . . ." I press my hand against my lips, forcing back a sob.

"I don't know, but I think he's trying to break my Obligation."

They gape at me. Then they gape at him. It's Andreas who finally speaks with uncharacteristic force: "Who in the nine hells would try to break an Obligation by entering a Noswraith's world?"

My stomach pitches. The answer is there, or at least, part of the answer: *Someone who was sent by Princess Estrilde.* Of course. Estrilde retained Breaker's Rights when she sold my Obligation to the Prince. That's why she's here now. Sitting at the base of the library stair, entertaining herself with small glamours. Waiting. Waiting for the poor foolish little mortal to attempt to fulfill whatever impossible task she's set him. And when he inevitably fails—if he's still alive—she'll take him. Claim his Obligation. A new toy for her collection, and quite a handsome one too. All acquired with extraordinary little inconvenience.

But why, why, *why* would Estrilde send him after a Noswraith? Of all things? It doesn't make any sense. Why would she set him a task she must have known would result in his death?

To hurt you.

I press my hands to my mouth again, forcing back another sob. Estrilde must have guessed what Danny means to me. After all, any young man willing to risk his life for the sake of an Obligate must be someone special. She wants him to fail. She wants him to die. To punish me for . . . for . . .

A golden, glorious face flashes across my mind's eye. A pair of intent, beautiful eyes. A low voice speaking in a rumble that makes my blood heat: *"I'll never give up. Not until I can bring you safely home. To me."*

Those were the last words Lord Ivor Illithor spoke to me. If Estrilde—who has always loved him, who has always longed to make him hers—if she had any idea, she would stop at nothing to make me pay.

I look up at Danny. Perspiration beads his forehead, and his lips move ever so faintly, as though he's sounding out the words he reads. He has no magic. No training. No possible hope of survival. "We can't just leave him. There has to be some way to help."

"It's no use, Miss Darlington." Mixael comes to stand by me, rests a hand on my shoulder. "He's deep in their world now. Finding him would be dangerous. Bringing him back out again? Impossible."

"You have to understand," Andreas adds, "you wouldn't face the Eight-Crowned Queen alone in the Nightmare."

"It's true," says Mixael. "She's unique in that she likes to draw other Noswraiths to her, blending their worlds into hers, layer upon layer upon layer. She's like a siren, a seductress. She poisons them, manipulates them, captivates them to her will. By herself, she's terrible. But you would encounter any number of enthralled lesser wraiths long before you reached her."

"Not even the Prince would willingly venture into her world," Andreas adds with feeling.

Their words wash over me, dark waves of understanding, threatening to pull me under and drown me. *Danny. Danny, Danny, my dear, beloved Danny. How could you have come to such an end? How could you have been so stubborn, so foolish?*

"Fine," I say, my voice cold as ice. "I won't ask either of you to risk yourselves. But I must go in after him. I must."

"I'm sorry, Miss Darlington." Mixael squeezes my shoulder gently. "I can see this fellow meant something to you, perhaps . . . perhaps rather a lot. But I cannot in good conscience let you throw your life away." He takes my hand, pressing my fingers. "Vespre needs you. Alive. If something happened to you, that would leave only me and Andreas behind to battle this whole library horde until the Prince returns. Can't you see? The lives of all the people of Vespre are worth more than that of one man, however much he means to you."

I hear him. I hear the wisdom, the sorrow, the truth he speaks. I cannot help but hear him.

I draw a long, slow breath. Then I nod. Mixael smiles sadly, releases my hand. "We must leave him here. Bolt the door. Let whatever is going to happen, happen. Once it's over, we can resecure the binding on the Eight-Crowned Queen. She'll be distracted following her kill, and Andreas and I can manage her between us. You needn't stay, Miss Darlington. In fact, let me urge you to take the rest of the day off. Go to your rooms until it's over. Rest. Sleep if you can." He looks into my eyes. "Truly, I am sorry."

"I know," I say. And when he and Andreas start for the door, I trail behind them. My feet drag. I look back over my shoulder to Danny, standing there before the pedestal.

Danny.

Danny.

This is my fault. I led him on all these years. I let him believe we had a chance together, long after I knew it could never be. Now Kitty and Oscar will be alone in that great, terrible, cold world. All because I was too selfish, too cowardly to speak the truth.

I draw another breath, hold it until my lungs start to burn.

"Miss Darlington?" Mixael calls sharply.

"Coming!" I answer in a burst and face the door again. I take a few quick steps.

Then, with a sudden rush, I grab the door and drag it shut. Surprised, Mixael and Andreas both throw themselves forward, crashing into each other in their efforts to reach the latch. In that spare instant of scuffling, I take the opportunity to grab the nearest bookshelf, heavy with old volumes that once contained the Eight-Crowned Queen's spell, and heave it over. It tumbles across the doorway, propped against the shelf on the opposite side, effectively blocking the opening. Old dead books fall in a pile to the ground.

"I'm sorry, Mixael!" I cry, staring at them over the fallen shelf and through the barred window set in the door. "I'm sorry, Andreas! Please, tell the Prince . . ." I can't finish that sentence. I have no idea what I could possibly ask them to say.

Instead I leap up to the pedestal. Reaching awkwardly around Danny, I flip the grimoire pages back to the beginning and start to read. Immediately the power of the spell swarms through my awareness. This spell is far greater than anything I've encountered before. I've read grimoires, written and reaffirmed bindings. My own Noswraith is a terrible creation, a force of great malice and destruction. But it pales by comparison to this magic.

The spell reaches out from the pages, wraps around me. Tendrils like vines creep through my eyelashes, reach down into my eye sockets, worm into the dark space behind my eyeballs. Suddenly, everything goes dark.

I stand in place. Count three breaths.

When I open my eyes again, I'm still in the vault. Surrounded by bookshelves, including the fallen shelf blocking the door behind me. But now all is murky and dark. A churning, living energy overlays the world.

I've entered the Nightmare.

Danny is no longer beside me. I stand alone on the stool before the pedestal. Mixael and Andreas pound on the door at my back, struggling to get it open. But their voices seem far away, through many layers of reality.

I lift my gaze from the book to the wall across from me, lined with more bookshelves. One of the shelves is partially swung out from the wall. It's a door. An open door. Is that where Danny went? I climb down from the stool, hastily approach the opening, and peer out, anxious, eager, and frightened all at once.

The landscape of the Nightmare spreads before my view.

Miss Darlington! Miss Darlington, no! Mixael's voice plucks at the edge of my awareness.

I draw a deep breath down into my gut. Then, gathering my courage with both hands, I step through the doorway, leaving the vault behind.

15

I STAND ATOP A HILL ABOVE A ROLLING LANDSCAPE.
Before me lie little valleys and fissures, distant crags and
forests. Lovely stone houses stand at intervals—great houses
with detached stables and sprawling gardens, all connected to
one another by little gravel roads. Mountains loom on the far
horizon while thunderclouds roll in from a distant sea, as dark
and threatening as the doom of ages.

Why is this place so familiar? Familiar enough to send a jolt of
pain straight to my gut. At first, I cannot think, but then . . . Ah, yes!
It comes back to me. This is very like the country resort my family
used to visit every summer, long ago, when Father's successes kept
us in high style. We lived like the gentry, fashionable and easy,
enjoying the cool ocean breezes at the height of summer. Oscar
and I would play with other children, laughing and romping in

our white linen summer apparel, while our nursemaid scolded us against grass stains.

Now, churning shadows shroud everything in sight, never obscuring, but clinging like mist. I seem to be standing on a little path, which winds down into the valley below me. I take a step, then look back over my shoulder. The vault is still there, the pedestal, the book, the bookshelf fallen across the doorway. No sign of Mixael or Andreas, of course. They would not enter this layer of reality. Not even to come after me.

I am alone.

Facing forward, I stare out across that dark landscape. Danny is out there. Somewhere. And if I am alone, how much worse off is he? For he does not understand this world or the beings that dwell herein. I am his only chance. I will not fail him.

That first step is the worst. Once it's made, however, the second comes more easily. Before I take a third, the sky ignites with a sudden burst of lightning. Through the clouds, I see a momentary glimpse of a massive silhouette—a great tentacled thing stretched out across the sky. It vanishes the next instant, hidden by thick cloud cover. And I'm left standing there, staring upwards, trying to decide if my eyes deceived me, trying to decide if now would be a good time to go stark, raving mad.

In the end, it's probably best to keep my wits about me.

I continue following the path, one step after another. I wish I had a weapon. A pike or a dagger. Something, anything, just to hold onto, even if I don't know how to use it. But of course, I didn't bring anything with me. If I'd been able to write myself into this world, things would be different. But I could only enter what was already here, what was already contained within the spell.

My feet are bare. In fact, now that I look down at myself, I seem to be wearing nothing but my shift. It's very cold, and a spitting rain has begun to fall. Small stones dig into the soles of my feet, and mud oozes between my toes. I'll be soaked through before I get anywhere.

The road branches before me. I stop. There are too many branches, far too many. Ten, twenty, a hundred even. Surely this isn't natural! My eyes are being tricked, made to see layers of reality pressed in on top of each other, creating this split effect. How many different worlds are gathered here? How many different Noswraiths, brought together under the Eight-Crowned Queen's thrall?

And how can I possibly figure out which way Danny went?

I close my eyes. Listen. Listen to the sound of rain splatting, of wind sighing. The distant roar of something huge and terrible hiding in the sky. Or is that merely the grumble of thunder? A soft, gentle wailing, so faint I'm almost sure I imagine it. And . . . and . . .

A scream.

I know that voice. I'm sure of it.

Gathering my shift up to my knees, I break into a run, choosing a path without looking at it, letting my heart guide me. Only after I've run several paces do I open my eyes and look where I'm headed. A stone house stands at the end of the road, through an avenue of arching elms, up a little hill, and beyond an iron gate. It's old, a gothic style with many gables, its roof set at strange angles and peaks. Once more I'm struck by a strange sense of familiarity, but it's a familiarity taken and twisted into something unsettling. Something wrong. It's as if the Nightmare realm is drawing ideas from my mind and twisting them to create a landscape specifically horrible for me.

I dart up the avenue, draw near to the gate. A wall of tall green shrubs stands on my left, and sudden movement among the leaves startles me. Heart jumping, I turn in time to see a strange creature emerge from the greenery. At first glance, it looks much like a rooster. But no, that is no rooster. Rather than tail feathers, long serpentine coils trail behind it as it flaps onto the path. Its bobbing head is skeletal, the beak overlarge and tipped with a great, poison-dripping fang. Barbed spines flare in a crest from the top of its head. Its leathery wings flap, and I see bony little arms reaching out from underneath, clawed fingers twitching. Red, roiling eyes set in a fixed stare dart hungrily this way and that.

Somehow, I know—without knowing how I know—that if those eyes meet mine, I will turn to stone.

I don't have time to think. Turning on one heel, I dart between two tall elms and into the open lawn on the far side. I don't even know if the thing—the Noswraith, for what else could it possibly be?—saw me. I only know I must get away fast.

A small shed appears through the mist. I seem to remember it from the real-world version of this place. Oscar and I used to hide there from our nanny, giggling behind our hands as we listened to her shout our names. I duck inside it now, pulling the sagging door mostly shut behind me. The hinge lets out a ragged screech. Gods blight! Any Noswraith within a ten-mile radius must have heard that!

I peer through the narrow crack out into the overcast yard. Sure enough, that creature struts into the lawn. It bobs its head, flares its wings, tiny arms stretching and flexing their long fingers. It turns its poison-dripping beak sharply toward the shed.

I pull back inside. It's coming. I'm sure of it. And I'm caught in here like a mouse in a trap. There must be something I can do, though. I didn't risk everything just to be taken down by the first pathetic little wraith I meet.

I cast about the dark space within the shed. Something tells me not to look up, not to study what lurks in the rafters. Something is up there, something horrible, and if I see it . . . no. No use in thinking that way.

A spade and hoe stand close by. And a bucket. Interesting. I could use that. Dragging it closer, I peer inside. At first it seems to be full of old nails, but when I look closer, I realize they aren't nails at all. They're fingerbones. Hundreds of pale, yellowed fingerbones, complete with nails, some long and polished, some blunt and broken.

My stomach turns. But I pick up the bucket, step as close to the cracked door as I can. And wait.

Slide, drag, slither. The Noswraith approaches, lugging its heavy, lizard tail behind it. It burbles and chuckles like a chicken, its bobbing shadow lengthening across the square of light on the ground before me. I close my eyes, count my breaths.

Then, with a cry, I burst from the shed and upend the bucket right over the creature's head. Fingerbones fly everywhere, but the bucket lands squarely in place, covering that awful crest and those deadly red eyes. The wraith lets out a hideous squawk.

I don't hesitate. Not for a second. I've already reached back into the shed and grabbed the spade. Summoning all the force in my body, I hit the monster in the spine with the edge, then smash it as hard as I can with the flat. Again and again, I strike, my ears deafened by the sound of its screeches. I don't stop smashing until it lies at my feet, bent, twisted, broken.

It should be dead, of course. But it isn't. It's a Noswraith. It can't die.

Still, it's subdued. For the time being.

I keep the spade, glad of something to hold onto. I must be cautious. That bucket of fingerbones could mean one of the Greater Noswraiths like Boney Long Fingers is somewhere close by. I don't remember much about him, only that he's big and definitely not one I can simply hit with a spade a few times. Still, there doesn't seem to be anyone close just now.

Leaving the mangled rooster-thing behind, I once more make for the house. How long has it been since I heard that scream? Too long, I fear. And how can I know for sure it was Danny's voice? How many lost souls wander trapped within this Nightmare, desperately trying to elude its monster denizens?

No point in dwelling on such thoughts. I can do nothing but forge on, trusting my instincts. And my instincts are telling me Danny has taken this path, made for this same house. I skirt the elm avenue and approach the wall and gate from a different angle, meeting no Noswraiths as I go. The gate stands open as though someone has recently passed through. I pause a moment, peering up at the stone gatehouse with its blank, dark windows.

A face appears in the uppermost window. A pale, strangely elongated face with sagging black hollows where eyes should be.

I pull away quickly. Was I spotted? Impossible to know for certain. But I can't stay here dithering and wait for that gatekeeper, whoever it is, to come find me. Feeling much like a rabbit hopping blithely into the snare, I slip through the gate and into the curved driveway leading to the front door of the manor house. I grip my spade tight in both hands, ready to swing at the first creeping shadow. Nothing leaps out at me, however, and I make it nearly to the porch steps before my pace slows.

Statues stand at the base of the porch. Two great stone angels in attitudes of graceful supplication to the heavens, their arms upraised, their eyes gently rolled skyward. Their faces are serene, carved in marble and polished smooth.

However, when I take another step, those stone eyes roll. Very softly, very gently. Just enough that I suddenly feel unnatural gazes fixed upon me.

I stop. The front door stands before me, open wide. It's deceptively welcoming, framed by potted flowers and covered in draping green ivy. My glance slides back to the two angels. Their gentle faces have shifted again. Just a little. Just enough that behind their full lips I can glimpse the edge of sharp teeth.

No chance in heaven I'm passing between those two.

Rain falls in good earnest as I dart around the side of the house, searching for another way in. I find a broken window and, with some unladylike scrambling, manage to get myself up and over the sill, pushing my spade in ahead of me. I land in a pile of ungainly limbs, hastily pull myself together, and look around to see where I've arrived. It seems to be a sort of office space, complete with built-in bookshelves lining the walls. A huge desk of solid oak dominates the center space.

Gripping my spade, I peer around the room. No Noswraiths, at least none readily apparent. No Danny either. But he's somewhere in this house, I'm sure of it. I just have to trust that he's still alive, that he's hanging on until I can find him.

I take a step toward the door.

The ceiling overhead ripples.

I stop dead in my tracks, uncertain what I've just seen. Did I imagine it? Intricate plasterwork decorates that ceiling, elegant and fashionable as one might expect to find in a house like this. No movement, not even a shifting shadow. I draw a breath and then take another step.

The ceiling moves again. An opaque sheen I'd been unable to discern before now becomes visible. Something is there, something big. Something invisible save for the way it distorts everything seen through its viscous flesh. It hides itself, flattened against the ceiling, with multiple long tentacle arms braced into every corner of the room. I cannot see an eye, but I know it's aware of me.

My fingers tighten around my spade.

Then, with a little squeak of terror, I launch myself for the door, darting around the desk and leaping over an ottoman, nimble as a deer in flight. The ceiling shifts, moves, and a huge tentacle— almost but not quite see-through—drops in front of me, landing on the floor with a *squish*. I don't stop to think. I draw back my spade and swing as hard as I can, using the edge. I feel the moment of connection, the resistance, the give.

Then the tentacle falls in half, spraying goo everywhere. I dodge, dancing away, careful not to let it touch my exposed skin, my bare feet. Another tentacle drops close by. I don't think the Noswraith can see me. I hack at this tentacle too, chopping a great gouge into its flesh. My shovel sticks. I yank hard, just manage to pull it free. Another tentacle lashes out, much too close to my head. I duck, dodge, and fling myself at the door. I can see translucent movement, something crawling down from the ceiling, ready to cover the open doorway. I plow straight ahead, determined to get free. Brandishing the spade out in front of me, I feel it strike something.

Then I'm through. Staggering into the outer passage.

I whirl just in time to catch hold of the door and slam it shut, trapping whatever that thing was on the other side. The slam echoes up and down the hall, ringing in my ears. I stand a moment, panting, leaning hard on my spade. Which Noswraith was that? I have no idea. One of a thousand-odd horrors housed within the library grimoires. Not a powerful creation, at least.

Something moves at the tail of my eye. I turn sharply in place. Nothing is there. Of course. Because certain horrors stay just out of sight until the last possible moment.

A dark hall stretches before me. The shadows are deep. Scarcely any light makes it through the heavily curtained windows. I can just discern a faint impression of green wallpaper decorated with lavender flowers, a perfect picture of the wallpaper in my memory. Only these flowers aren't delicate lilies but poisonous blossoms of some variety I do not recognize. I don't look too closely. Oh, great gods above me! Why have I come here? Why couldn't I have listened to Mixael and Andreas, left well enough alone?

I shake my head, brandishing my spade. Danny is here. I'm sure of it. And I can get him out. I've survived this far, haven't I? I will find him.

The hallway I'm standing in leads to a dead end on my right, but there seems to be a further passage branching off down the lefthand way. I turn that way and take three firm steps. A flash of lightning illuminates the darkness for an instant. In that momentary brightness, I glimpse the silhouette of a hanging body at the far end of the passage.

I stop. Swallow.

Then I turn the opposite direction. There's a door at the very end of the passage. After my encounter in the study, I can't say I'm terribly eager to discover what waits on the other side. But Danny could be anywhere. Hand trembling, I touch the latch, turn it, push the door open.

"Ah! I see our other guest has arrived. Welcome."

I freeze, my hand still on the latch, and stare into the room.

It's a lovely space despite the overcast gray light. White lace curtains grace the windows, and a low fire burns on the hearth. A table is set for tea, complete with a vase of red roses and an array of pink-and-white cups and saucers.

Danny is here. I catch my breath, my gaze fixing upon him. He sits at the table, his back very straight, his face a grim mask. His torso is bare, the pale hair on his chest displayed, his skin prickled with cold. He looks almost luminous in the strange light of the Nightmare. I try to call out to him, but my throat has closed up. I take another step into the room.

Then a woman moves into my line of view. She's beautiful. Young. Her skin is creamy, and her black hair is pulled up in an elegant chignon that accentuates her lovely features. She wears a lace gown with a round neckline and neatly trim waist. A big red rose tucked just above her ear draws my eye. Vibrant, crimson. Crawling with beetles.

She smiles widely, showing too many strong white teeth. "And what is your name, my dear?"

16

'M NOT ABOUT TO FALL FOR A QUESTION LIKE THAT.
Seriously, who lives in Eledria for any length of time and just
gives their name away?

Turning sharply away from the apparition, I fix my attention on
Danny instead. His eyelids slowly rise, his frightened gaze locking
with mine. "Let's go," I say.

He stares at me. His mouth opens and closes.

"Oh, no, no, you just got here." The apparition steps between us.
Her lovely smile fills my vision again, her lips very red against the
whiteness of her teeth. She sweeps a hand, indicating the table.
"You really must stay for tea."

I shake my head, my mouth opening to refuse. Instead,
however, I blink . . .

And find myself seated opposite Danny at the table. With no

memory of how I came to be there. I catch my breath, look around. Rain patters against the window frames. A low fire burns on the hearth, but its light is faintly green and does nothing to warm the gray atmosphere. The apparition moves to my side of the table and sets a plate of food down in front of me. Delicate lace drapes across her fragile wrist.

Something crawls across the top of her hand.

I pull back in my chair. Was I mistaken or had that crawling been . . . *underneath* the skin? My neck retracts into my shoulders. I tip my gaze up to the woman's face, and she smiles down at me. The beetles writhe among the petals of her rose. Several of them fall from her hair and land on the tablecloth.

Who is she? I cannot recall any wraith matching this description. Certainly not the Eight-Crowned Queen, of that I'm certain. But is she one of the Greater Noswraiths? Or just another small nightmare drawn into this multi-layered reality?

She wafts to her place at the head of the table and takes a seat. "Tea?" she says sweetly and lifts a teapot. Danny raises the teacup in front of him. His hand trembles so hard, the cup rattles in its saucer, but he holds it out so the lady may pour. Dark liquid glops from the spout, and an ugly stink fills the air. Danny sets the cup down, his face lined with dread.

"Drink up, please," the lady says.

He catches my eye. I shake my head, but he reaches out, takes the cup. His hand shakes so hard, dark dollops spill over the lip, over his fingers. He raises it to his lips.

With a desperate cry, I launch from my seat, lunge across the table, and whack the teacup from his hand. It crashes, rolls across the floor. Black slugs ooze out from it, trailing slime in their wake. Though I try to remain standing, some invisible force grips me by the shoulders and yanks me back into my chair. I crash into it so hard, it very nearly tips over. Gripping the arms with both hands, I sit there, heart pounding in my throat, staring across at Danny.

The Noswraith tips her chin and looks at me from beneath her dark lashes. "That wasn't very thoughtful, was it?"

Rippling movement, like many crawling legs, undulates beneath the skin of her cheek. Another similar movement crawls down her neck, and a third across her collarbone.

Gods on high, we need to get out of here!

The lady takes the little dessert plate from Danny's place and carries it to the buffet standing along the wall. Selecting dainty little treats with silver tongs, she arranges them neatly, then returns to set the plate before Danny. She does the same for me. And when we are both served, she takes her place at the head of the table and closes her eyes for a moment. Another crawling, scurrying thing flicks across her eyelid and up her forehead, disappearing into her hairline.

She opens her eyes again. "Please, eat."

My hands move against my will, selecting a delicate silver knife and fork. Though I don't want to look, though I don't wish to know, I stare down at the plate to see a little pastry shell full of wriggling maggots, a skewer pierced through the carapaces of three still-struggling beetles, and a cake crawling with spiders.

Avoiding these, I cut open what looks like a flaky puff pastry. Rather than cream, a fat white grub falls out onto my plate. I look across at Danny. His face has gone red, and a vein stands out across his forehead as though he fights with everything in him to resist compulsion. His fork and knife move, cutting a small, precise bite of spider cake.

I stab the wriggling grub on the end of my three-pronged fork. Hold it up to eyelevel. It twists and turns, fighting for life even as it suffers and dies.

The Noswraith leans forward in her seat. "Go on," she says. "Taste it. Taste it."

My lips part. My teeth unclench. My jaw opens. Slowly, slowly, I draw the fork toward my mouth.

No!

Choking on a scream, I stab my fork, grub and all, straight into the lady's chest. Once more I'm flung back into my chair, this time so hard it scoots several inches across the floor. But my fork remains where I planted it, vibrating just above her heart.

The lady looks down. Her smile melts into a little frown.

"Oh dear," she says.

The skin around the fork begins to undulate. All the little moving bits are rushing straight for that fork, where the three prongs entered her flesh. More and more, gathering, swarming.

The apparition opens her mouth. Screams.

Flying wings burst from her chest and explode into the air in a cloud of buzzing and wings and legs. More and more and more, until the lady withers up like a deflated balloon and collapses in her chair. Her rose explodes in a burst of chewed petals.

Suddenly, I can move again.

I lunge over the table and smack Danny's fork from his hand just before he can put it in his mouth. The swarm surrounds us, the air so full of vibrating wings, I cannot think straight. I can only grab his hand, yank him up from the table, and run for the door. I grip the handle, pull it open.

A pair of hanging legs, limp arms, and a body suspended from a noose. Just outside the doorway.

I slam the door shut again. "Not that way!" I shout and drag Danny across the room, through the insect swarm and to the window. It opens easily, and thank the seven gods, we're still on the first floor. It's a bit of a jump to the gravel below, but doable. "Get out, now!" I cry.

Danny doesn't hesitate. He swings his legs over the sill and drops to the ground. I scramble after him in a trice, forgoing all thoughts of modesty. The swarm escapes through the window along with us, but once we're out in open air, they seem to lose interest in buzzing around our heads and disperse into the gardens. The relief is so great, I want to sink to my knees and weep.

Instead I grasp Danny's hand again and race away from the house as fast as I can go. Instinct drives me toward the gate, but before we reach it, a tall, phantom-like figure wafts into the opening and stands there. When it turns, I see that same gaping-eyed figure I'd glimpsed in the gatehouse window. "Blight it all!" I snarl and change course. Now we race into the gardens. Not at all the direction I want to go, but I'm in no mood to face the gatehouse Noswraith just now. A gazebo offers shelter from the rain, and I haul Danny after me up the three steps and under its sloping roof.

"Clara!" He's shaking so hard his voice rattles. At least he's able to talk again. "What are you doing here?"

"What am *I* doing here?" I mop rain from my face with one arm, glaring up at the man. "What are *you* doing here is the better question!"

He leans against one of the support posts, breathing hard. Once more I'm aware of his half-naked state. Just as I have entered the Nightmare Realm wearing only my shift, he is clad in nothing but a pair of loose trousers. Even his feet are bare. I've never seen Danny in such a state of undress, not even when we were young. I hardly know where to look. He rubs a hand down his fear-stricken face. "I told you I would break your Obligation."

"Oh, is that what you think you're doing? Because it looked to me like you'd fallen into a Noswraith's snare!" I don't even want to imagine what that apparition intended to do with her tea party guests. Nothing good, that's for sure.

"What's a Noswraith?" Danny asks.

I fling up my hands. "Nothing you need concern yourself with. We're getting you out of here."

"No!" He shoots me a sharp look. "I'm going to do this. The princess said if I wished to break your Obligation, I must bring her the bloodstone of the Eight-Crowned Queen. She told me to find a certain book in Vespre Library and it would lead me to her. I found the book, but when I started reading it, I . . . I don't quite know what happened. A door in the wall opened, and I—"

"You *idiot!*" Part of me is shocked. I've never even imagined talking to Danny like this. But in the moment I can't stop myself. "Did you think you could just waltz into Eledria, make a bargain with someone like Estrilde, and escape unscathed? Look around you!" I wave my arm at the rain-soaked, lightning-streaked, shadow-churning nightmare landscape. From this vantage, I need only turn my head a little to the right or left to spy three different minor wraiths lurking in various corners of the garden, between us and the house. And those are just the few not bothering to hide.

Danny blinks, his jaw working, and I fear he's going to protest. At last, however, he slumps onto one of the benches and drops his head into his hands. "I'll admit," he says, "it's not what I anticipated." Then he rolls his face around, peering up at me. His eyes are so sad. In that moment he looks much like the boy I once knew. My anger cools, and I even feel an unreasonable impulse to reach out and take him in my arms. "Is this what you live every day?" he asks. "All this horror? All this danger?"

I shrug one shoulder. "It's not usually quite this bad."

He shakes his head. "How can you endure such a world?"

"Well, for starters, *this* is not the world I live in. This is a pocket reality, the realm of Nightmares. It's no place for humans. No place for anyone, really, other than Noswraiths. Which means we need to get out of here. Fast."

"I won't go." He sits up straighter, drops his hands from his face. "I need to find this Eight-Crowned Queen."

"No." I clench my hands into fists to stop myself from grabbing and shaking him until his teeth break. "No, no, no! You want to live, don't you? If so, plunging blindly into a Nightmare positively seething with Noswraiths is definitely counterproductive! You don't even know what the Eight-Crowned Queen looks like, much less how to find her."

His expression is mulish. He stands, and I'm impressed all over again by the unseemly nakedness of him. He's far more muscular than I ever suspected, given he spends his days hunched over patients, mixing up tinctures, and soothing fevered brows. But then, I know as little about his day-to-day life as he knows of mine. Perhaps it is more physically strenuous than I've imagined.

Either way, I fix my gaze firmly on his face, refusing to let it drop even for a moment. Nonetheless, he flushes, looks down at himself, and moves his hands awkwardly, as though he wants to hide. Then he firms his stance. "I am going on with my quest. I intend to save you, Clara, and if that means—"

The ground shakes. The whole gazebo shudders and groans. Something huge—absolutely, beyond-reason *huge*—passes overhead, blocking out what little light there is. Sort of an enormous spider with great stalks for legs, but what its body is like, I can't see above the gazebo roof. It walks directly over us and away across the garden, soon obscured by mist and cloud. The ground continues to shake for some while after.

I come to my senses to find I'm encircled in Danny's arms. Somehow, in our mutual fear, we'd rushed to one another. He clings to me now, not in protection but out of pure desperation. There's an awful lot of bare skin under my palms.

Hastily I step back, straightening my damp shift. Gods, but I hope it doesn't cling to my curves as badly as I think it does! "Look," I say, keeping my voice short. "Maybe there's still some way to accomplish this task of yours. But we've got to have a proper plan."

"We?" He looks down at me, his eyes shining. "You'll help me?"

My heart breaks a little. By lying to him once, I've only made it easier to keep on lying. I wish I could stop myself, but just now I can see no other way. "Yes. Whatever you need. But first we've got to get out of this world alive, all right?"

He studies my face, searching for some sign of duplicity. I take care to assume an expression so open and forthright that he could never doubt it. I hate myself for manipulating him so easily, knowing how badly he wants to believe me.

"Fine," he agrees at last. "We'll get out of here. Then we'll regroup and try again."

I release a tightly held breath and take his hand. "Come on then. Stay close."

It's strange, taking charge like this. Danny has always been the protector in our relationship. But he submits to my experience and falls into step behind me as we leave the shelter of the gazebo and step into the rain, which has eased up slightly, to my relief. The ground squelches under our feet, and the gravel still digs painfully into our soles. I spy a small side gate in the garden wall and make for it. A wafting figure in billowing, transparent rags drifts by on the far side, but it doesn't seem to be aware of our approach. I duck behind a shrub, signal for Danny to keep quiet, and wait until the floating thing has progressed some way on up the road.

"Quick now!" I pull him after me to the gate. It's locked. I rattle it on its hinges, biting back a string of curses. Then, gritting my teeth, I climb up, scrabbling with bare feet and legs. It's not tall, and I manage to get over without impaling myself on a finial. Danny comes after me, and I make a point not to stare at him, not to notice the flexing of his biceps or the muscles in his chest and back. Instead I search up the road for some sign of the floating phantom.

Danny lands on the ground beside me, breathing hard. "Where to next?" he asks.

I turn with the words "This way" on my lips, but they fade and die as I look out on the landscape before me. It's no longer the rolling countryside of before—no little hills and valleys, no distant stone houses. Before us lies nothing but sunken desolation. Deeply mired, reeking of despair.

"Oh no," I whisper.

It's Dulmier Fen. I recognize it in a heartbeat. The very first Noswraith spell the Prince assigned me to rebind upon my arrival in Vespre Library. Somehow it's been dragged into this space of layered realities, and now it stands between us and escape.

"This isn't good."

Danny steps to my side, his brow puckered as he peers out across the marsh, the dark pools, the clinging mist, the drooping brown grasses. "It looks calm enough."

"Don't bet on it." I turn back to the gate, of half a mind to climb back into the garden and find some other way out. My heart nearly stops. The floating phantom *thing* is there, watching us through the iron bars. Its face is covered in shroud cloth, but I feel the intensity of its gaze.

We're definitely not going back that way.

Shuddering, I take hold of Danny's hand. "Come on," I say and lead him after me, keeping close to the wall and taking care not to let my foot accidentally step in the marsh. Perhaps we can skirt around it, find our way back to the road. Danny keeps drifting, pulling on my arm as the silent lure of the fen calls to him. I tug him back to my side. "Stay close!" I hiss. "You don't want to go that way."

"Are you sure?" He gazes out to the marsh, a thoughtful expression on his face. "I don't know why, but I think . . . I think if we can just get across, there's help on the other side. It can't be that far—"

"Don't be an idiot," I snap. "Once you step foot in that swamp, you never leave it. Trust me." I pull him after me another few paces.

And that's when the howling begins.

Danny presses up behind me, his bare chest against my back. I

SYLVIA MERCEDES

cannot help leaning into him, wishing I could take comfort in his masculine strength. But I know better. He's utterly helpless in a world like this. If I can't save us, no one will.

"What's that?" he asks as another vicious howl answers the first. Before I can offer a guess, long, low, lean figures appear in the mist before us. Green eyes flash with their own inner light. "Clara!" Danny gasps.

"Back up, back up!" I hiss and start to push against him.

"No, Clara! Look!" He points back the way we came, where more of the creatures, whatever they are, wait. They, like us, keep close to the wall, avoiding the fen. But they're coming straight toward us, cutting us off.

I look up the stone wall, half wondering if we can climb it. But the creatures would be upon us before we got halfway. "Nothing for it then," I whisper and tuck Danny's hand close. "Don't let go of me!"

With that, I race into the fen. Danny hastens at my heels, and our feet splash in shallow water. We find little hillocks and clumps of firmer footing as we flee. Snarls of frustration and bloodthirsty savagery erupt behind us. I don't look back. I don't need to see those green-eyed things darting back and forth along the edge of the fen but unwilling to enter it. We've made our choice. We'll endure the consequences.

The monsters' echoing cries have scarcely faded before we're both foundering in dark water up to our knees. It's cold, clammy. My shift clings to my body, soaked through. Mist closes around us, parting only enough to reveal the next few steps ahead. The rest of the world—the rest of existence—fades from view.

"Don't worry, Danny," I say, staggering up onto what looks like solid ground. It breaks away beneath my toes, and I fall into the mud. Spitting stagnant water and dead grass from my teeth, I right myself and shake wet hair back from my face. "Don't worry. We're going to get through this."

He doesn't answer. When I glance back, his head is bowed, his shoulders bent. He's covered in mud, shivering with cold. How long have we been here? It doesn't seem that long, a few minutes at most. Yet he has a look of utter defeat. "Don't worry!" I say again, my voice muffled in the mist and gloom. "We're going to find the road. I promise."

Danny raises his face, looks at me. His eyes are hollow, his mouth slack. "What road?"

A shiver passes through my heart. I shake my head, squeezing his hand a little tighter. "The road out of this place. Back to our world."

"What are you talking about?" He tilts his head to one side. "There is no way out. This is . . . endless."

"Don't talk like that!" I yank on his arm, dragging him after me. Slowly, slowly he lifts one leg from deep water and slogs forward. It's as though all the strength left in his body went into that one step. "Come on, Danny!" I urge. "We're not done yet!"

He looks up at me. Meets my eye.

Takes another step.

Then, suddenly, he falls. In a huge splash, he flounders up to his chest, his chin. With a cry, I reach out to him, but my feet are stuck. Mud seems to have fastened hold of my ankles, and I cannot escape. Screaming, I fight against it, which only makes it worse. I stretch out my hand. "Danny! Danny, grab hold of me!"

He sinks deeper. Water up over his mouth, his nose. I can see nothing but his eyes, wide and staring. He lifts one arm, straining. Our fingertips touch. Then he's gone. Water closes over his head, making barely a ripple in that space where he had been.

"*Danny!*" I scream and scream and scream again. Suddenly, horribly, my feet are free. I pull myself out of the pool and stretch my body across a little hummock of grass, reaching into the mud where Danny had been. I expect to find deep water, to touch the top of his head, to feel his hand.

But it's no more than an inch or two deep. A puddle. Nothing more. I scrabble desperately, pushing my fingers in as far as they will go, my hands sinking in mud up to the wrist. He's not there.

He never was.

"Danny! *Danny!*" I'm choking, sobbing, heaving. My voice echoes to the heavy gray sky, rolls across the endless emptiness of the fen. No one hears. No one cares. I'm alone.

At last, still sobbing, I pick myself up. I'm soaked through, my shift plastered to my body, hair clinging to my face and shoulders. Cold knifes through me as I wrap my arms around my middle, staring down into that shallow puddle. My own reflection looks up at me, muddy, indistinct. This can't be real. Danny was here; he was just here!

Only he wasn't. This whole time I believed I was trying to save him. And it was all a dream. A foolish, vain, pathetic dream.

"Danny," I whisper, my voice breaking. Mud and tears streak together down my cheeks. "Danny, please. Please." Tossing my head back, I drag in a ragged, shuddering breath.

That's when I see him. Standing in a pool, just a few yards away from me.

A young man wearing the tattered remains of a uniform.

17

I KNOW HIM.

His ragged uniform, once bright blue, is now faded, worn away at the elbows, knees, and cuffs. He wears a hat with a broken plume. Fringed epaulettes gild his shoulders, and bright silver buttons line his chest, many of them missing. His scabbard is empty as it hangs from his belt. I know it all.

I know his face too, though I've never seen it before. The last time I met him, I . . . I . . . in an inexplicable way, I *was* him. I rode inside him, looked through his eyes, experienced his story as he himself did. I'm familiar with that dark little mustache framing his upper lip, which took him months to grow. I'm familiar with the delicate scar beneath his eye from when his mother's lapdog bit him as a child.

And I remember how it felt to walk in his shoes. To be

responsible for the lives of fifty men, most of them much older and far more experienced. To know they are looking to him—me—for leadership, and I have let them down.

I stare at him. And he stares back at me. There's nothing predatory in his gaze. He doesn't look dangerous or angry or even afraid.

He's dead. I can see that now as I couldn't before, when I viewed this world through his eyes. His hand is pressed against a terrible gut wound. Blood and entrails spill out through his fingers. He's not in pain, however. His attitude is more like that of a boy trying to hold up a pair of baggy trousers without a belt. Whatever agonies he experienced in his passing, they are over now and done with.

I drag my eyes back to his face. It's a nice face. Curly brown hair, cut a bit ragged around his ears as though shorn by a blunt instrument, frames his delicate features. When he tilts his head, however, just the slightest movement, I see a flash of gaunt cheeks and hollow, empty eye sockets. But it's no more than a flash. Then he's back to normal, staring at me with wide blue eyes.

"It's you," I whisper.

He blinks. I glimpse those hollow sockets again in the lowering of his eyelids. "Is it?" he asks. His voice is gentle.

"I . . . I remember you."

"Have we met?"

"Um. Not really."

"Ah." He doesn't question further. He merely stands there, holding his gaping wound. Watching me.

I lick my dry lips. "I . . . I suppose you never made it across. In the story, that is."

"Made it across what?"

"The fen. You were trying to get your men to the far side. To meet with reinforcements."

"Ah." He's silent for a long moment. Then, at last, "There is no other side. There is nothing else. This is all there is. Forever and ever, even beyond the horizon."

Technically he's right. Maybe not wholly right, but certainly not wrong. Because he's not real. He's a creature born of the words used to create this world. Though he may possess memories of a past life, even those memories were merely the invention of whoever wrote this pathetic tale. All of his existence is bound up within Dulmier Fen.

"Um." I consider my next words carefully. "Do you know where my friend went?"

"What friend?"

"The man I was just with. A moment ago. Do you know what happened to him?"

"Ah." The young man slowly lifts his head back up. The balance is off, however, and it tips to the other side. Dark curls fall across his pale forehead. "He is here. They are all here."

"Where?"

He extends an arm, the one not holding his guts in place, waving vaguely at the mist, the marsh, the heavy sky. "Here."

My stomach tightens. "And where is . . . where is Old Guntor?"

It's a name I remember from the original story.

The young man blinks at me again, his eyes vanishing into those rotten hollows before reappearing. "Guntor died. They amputated his leg, and he died three days later." A tear escapes through his lashes and races down his dead gray cheek. "But he is here too."

"Can you see them?"

"I cannot. We lost each other. And then we were always lost. And we were always here."

I remember too well what happened the last time I encountered this place. It was my first attempt at writing a fresh binding. I took it slow, penning one word at a time, trying not to let myself become caught up in the grim narrative. But it caught me and dragged me under. I remember black water closing over my head. If the Prince hadn't grabbed me by the hair and dragged me back into our own world, I don't know what might have happened. Possibly I would have been trapped here too, along with the other sorry ghosts.

I didn't read to the end of the spell. I never learned the whole story of this young officer and his men. But I can guess.

"I'm sorry," I say softly.

He seems to consider this, the lines of his brow wrinkling. Finally, he answers, "Me too."

"I don't belong here," I continue. A little breeze blows through the grasses, cutting through the thin wet fabric of my shift. I wrap my arms around myself a little tighter. "Neither does my friend."

He blinks again, uncomprehending. I need to find a way to make him understand. There must be a place somewhere in this story where the veil between this world and my own is . . . I don't know. *Thinner* perhaps. But when I look around, the fen seems to go on forever without alteration. "Is there anywhere that's different?" I ask. "Anywhere that's . . . that's not just . . ." I don't know how to finish my question. I've never been caught in a spell like this and have no idea what the protocol might be.

But I'm in luck. The young officer nods. "There is a tree."

"A tree?" There are no trees anywhere within sight. But maybe that's a good thing. If I can find a place where the landscape changes even just a little, I might be able to push through realities. Or perhaps someone on the other side might reach in after me. If anyone's looking. Either way, it's better than standing here freezing to death. "Can you take me there?"

The ghost doesn't answer. He merely turns and walks slowly, ponderously through the sludge. I pick up the hem of my sodden shift and struggle after him, one muddy footstep after another. It's painful to walk away from the pool into which Danny disappeared. I feel as though I'm abandoning him. But there's no chance I can save Danny if I don't find my way out of this place first. If I can just reenter the waking world, perhaps I can use my powers of pen and paper and come back in after him. Meanwhile, I just have to believe he's alive in here. Somewhere. If not . . . no. I won't even consider that.

I follow the ghost for what feels like hours. Along the way I catch glimpses of other solitary figures on the edges of my vision. They stand in pools of stagnant water, never close to us or each other. They do not call out or try to reach us, and when I turn to look at any of them directly, they vanish. But I know they are there. I can *feel* their loneliness. The pain of their wounds. The anguish of their lost souls.

Finally, I see a tree up ahead. It seems to appear from nowhere through the parting mist. My heart gives a little thrilling jump at the sight, and I speed up, stepping too quickly. My foot slips, and I sink all the way up to my chest. Gasping, floundering, I try to recover my balance. But mud has gripped me in a tight hold. I pull against it, but it sucks me deeper, deeper. Now the water is up to my neck, my chin, my mouth.

"Help!" I cry.

The ghost is several paces away from me. Though we seem to be in the same muddy pool, he stands only a few inches deep. Slowly he turns and looks back.

"Please!" I say, holding out a desperate hand. "Please, help me!"

"I could never help," he says. "They all died. Because of me. One after another. Dead."

Even as I struggle to keep my head above water, my heart breaks a little. His despair is so absolute. "But I'm not dead," I say. Muddy water flows into my mouth, down my throat. I choke and sputter. "You can still help me! Please!"

He considers this. Then he lurches toward me, wincing as though each footstep aggravates his wound. Blood oozes, fresh and red through his fingers. But he makes his way back to me and kneels. After a moment, he holds out his other hand.

With the last of my strength, I lunge to take hold. For a terrible moment, I fear my fingers will pass right through his. Then, miraculously, his immaterial substance solidifies. He grasps my wrist and, with unexpected strength, hauls me out of the water. I stagger free, then hunch over, coughing up mud and long streams of spittle. My body shudders and quakes with cold, with fear, with relief, with horror, with far too many things all at once.

When the worst of the shaking has passed, I manage to lift my head, to look at the ghost. "Thank you!" I gasp, wiping the back of my hand across my mouth.

"You're wel—" he begins but breaks off with a cry. Suddenly, he's not a ghost anymore. He's solid, real, with a flush to his cheeks. He gasps with pain, staggers once, then collapses to his knees, gagging and sobbing.

I stare at him, horror-struck. I did this to him. In my need, I brought him back to physical life. I've made him reexperience the pain of his death. "I'm sorry!" I cry, rushing to him, kneeling, wrapping my arms around his shoulders. He weeps uncontrollably, his voice ragged in his throat. I pull him to me, rest his head on my shoulder, and rock him back and forth.

Eventually, his wild sobs subside into small gulping gasps. "It was my fault," he shudders, his mouth muffled against my breast. "I led them wrong. They obeyed my orders. And they died."

And then he'd died. Alone.

I remember it all, living out his story. I never finished it, but it's there in my mind, nonetheless. Tears stream freely down my cheeks, drop into his hair.

"I wish I'd never left home," he sighs. "I wish I'd never left Amelia. I wish . . . I wish . . . I wish I could have saved them."

"But you saved me." I kiss the top of his head and stroke my muddy fingers through his curls. "You pulled me out of the mire. You didn't fail me. You saved me, do you hear?"

He twists in my arms, tipping his face up to me. He's dying, nearly dead. But in that moment, a spark of life glimmers in his eye. "I . . . saved you . . ." He blinks slowly, almost as though he's sleepy and fighting it. With an effort he manages to raise his eyelids again. "Will you kiss me?"

"What?"

"One kiss." His lips pull to the side in an awful smile. "Please, Amelia. I might die, you know. Then you'll wish you'd kissed me before I left."

Oh. This is part of the story. The backstory for this young officer. Perhaps later on in the narrative he thought of her, his sweetheart. Amelia. I never read that far, never learned about her. But she's as real to him as any memory, as much a part of his tale as his violent death.

I shudder. Every instinct tells me to flee. Yes, he is pathetic and sad and dying. But he is also a Noswraith. How can I kiss something so dreadful?

But when I gaze down at his poor, sad, hopeful face . . . how can I not?

Slowly I bend my head. He closes his eyes. I find his lips with mine, and they are cold. He's already dead, I think. Succumbed to that terrible wound all over again. But I kiss him anyway. Softly, tenderly.

Suddenly, his lips aren't dead and cold. They're very warm, very alive. A hand reaches up, cups my cheek, and when I try to draw back, slips behind my head and holds me in place. A thrill of fear races through me. I yank back, staring down at my ghost.

But he is no ghost. He's Danny.

With a yelp of surprise, I push him away from me before grabbing his shoulders and pulling him back into my embrace. "What happened?" I cry. "Where were you? I saw you go under!"

He puts his arms around me, crushing me against him. "I don't know." His voice is small and thin. He buries his face in the crook of my neck. "I don't remember anything. Something wrapped around my ankle, pulled me under. Water closed over my head, and I was sure I was a dead man. Then . . . then . . ." He draws back, looking at me. And he's so alive, so real, so solid that I'm almost overwhelmed at the sight of him. "How am I here? Did you pull me out again?"

I don't answer. I get to my feet and turn in place, searching for some sign of my ghost. He's not here. Only bleak fen as far as the eye can see, save for that tree standing close by.

I bite my lower lip, blink back swelling tears. "Thank you," I whisper. I hope he heard me. I hope he knows.

Hastily I turn back to Danny. "Come on," I say, helping him to his feet. Staggering and stumbling, leaning against one another, we make our way to the tree. There, just as I'd hoped, I find it: a thin place in reality. It looks like a little rotten hole in the twisted trunk, but when I put my hand into it, it grows, spreads. Becomes an entire door. A door leading into a chamber vault full of books, in the center of which stands a pedestal.

"We're here!" I cry, towing Danny after me through the opening. "We've made it!" He doesn't say anything, merely stares around the space, utterly unbelieving. Ignoring him, I haul the door shut. We're not safe yet. The churning shadows overlying everything tell me we're still in the Nightmare. But our spirits are now back in the same room as our bodies, which means . . .

I climb the pedestal to where the open grimoire lies. "We're here!" I cry. "Get us out! Get us—"

A flash of blinding light.

Danny and I fall over backwards, landing hard on our backs in the middle of the vault floor. I'm stunned, dizzy. The ceiling above me spins wildly, and I blink hard in an effort to make it stabilize once more. Well before I've succeeded, two faces come blearily into view.

"By all the seven gods!" Mixael exclaims. "They're still alive!"

"WHAT WERE YOU THINKING?"

The senior librarian's voice rings against the stone walls and echoes painfully inside my head. I close my eyes. My body feels as though it's lying on a little raft tossed by a stormy sea. I'm still not entirely convinced I'm here and alive. Part of my brain still believes I'm clad in nothing but a soaking-wet shift and covered in mud from head to toe. But when I manage to pry my eyes open again and look down, I find I'm wearing my regular day dress. I hold my quivering hands up, studying them. All the familiar ink spatters, but no mud.

Mixael's voice still rattles somewhere in the back of my awareness, but I cannot pay attention to him just now. Groaning, I roll my head to one side. Danny is here, blinking up at the ceiling. Looking as dull and stupid as I feel. But he's here. I got him out. I got him out in time.

"Miss Darlington?" Andreas's voice, gentle by contrast to Mixael's ranting, breaks through the fog in my head. His eyes swim into focus, peering down at me from behind his spectacles. He holds out a hand. "We thought for sure you were a goner."

I let him help me into a seated position. "How long was I out?" I ask.

"Hours, Miss Darlington," Mixael replies. "Hours! Just wait until the Prince hears about this. He thinks so highly of your abilities, but I've warned him he's pushing you too fast. You're foolhardy! Survive a couple of close calls, and you think you're the stuff of legends. Let me tell you, it takes more than luck to make a librarian! And even then, even with all the skill in the world, sometimes it's . . . it's not . . ."

It's not enough. He doesn't have to finish. I can see the truth in his eyes: the death of his parents. Brave, powerful mages each, who knew the risks, knew the wraiths, knew the library like the backs of their hands. Who died brutal, untimely deaths.

How close had I just come to meeting a similar fate? But I can't regret my choice. When I look down at Danny, still lying on the floor, still gathering his wits and his strength, I feel nothing but satisfaction. He did not deserve the dark end he would have met in the Nightmare Realm.

"Did you encounter the Eight-Crowned Queen?" Andreas asks as he helps me to my feet.

"No, but there were others. Lots of others." I catch my balance, wait a moment for the room to stop spinning, then turn and offer Danny my hand. He's only just sitting up, his face deathly pale, his eyes sunken. He stares unseeing at my fingers. As his vision slowly clarifies, he tilts his head, looks up at me.

"I've got to go back," he says.

"What?" The word bursts from Mixael's lips like a shot fired.

"I came here for a purpose." Danny shakes his head and rubs a hand through his hair so that it stands on end. "I'm to fetch the bloodgem necklace of the Eight-Crowned Queen. I cannot leave without it."

"And why in the seven heavens of all seven gods would you want a hellish thing like that?"

Danny blinks up at Mixael as though only just becoming aware of his presence. "To free Clara," he says as though the answer is painfully obvious. "From her Obligation."

Mixael stares at him, his face drained of color save for stark freckles across his cheekbones. "You mean, you actually intend to go back in there?"

"It's the only way. If I don't, I won't break the Obligation, and then—"

"And then you belong to me."

I whirl, my pulse jumping at the sound of that voice I know all too well. Estrilde stands in the doorway of the vault. Magnificently tall, deadly, beautiful. In this dark space, she glows like a dawn star, and the gauzy swaths of her gown are like drifting clouds parting in the wake of her glory.

She steps daintily over a book with a broken spine as if it were a rotting carcass and casts a sweeping look around the chamber, at the tumbled bookshelf dragged to one side, and the many books spread and sprawled across the floor. Her lip curls in a sneer. As her eye passes briefly over me, my heart seems to stop. But she does not linger. I am too far beneath her to be worth more than the most glancing notice.

Then her gaze lands on Danny. She smiles.

"Come, pretty boy," she says, holding out a hand. "I did warn you, did I not? The cost of breaking another's Obligation is often too high. But come. There's no need to be downhearted. You will find me a fair and loving mistress. Take my hand now."

I turn to Danny, protests dying on my lips before I can speak them. I see his jaw clench, see his ashen face turn red with strain. A cord stands out across his forehead. I know that look. I know all too well the pain that accompanies resistance to an Obligation. Which means . . . Oh, gods on high! Which means he's already signed the agreement with Estrilde, already bound himself to her.

"No." I step into the space between the princess and Danny, my hands clenched into fists. "No! You cannot take him."

"Can I not?" Estrilde addresses herself to the space above my head, her voice mild, faintly amused.

I snarl up at her, foolish as a little lapdog facing down a wolf. "You don't even own my Obligation anymore! How can you possibly take him? It's not fair, it's not right, it's not—"

"You forget, Darling. My dear cousin retained Breaker's Rights when she and I made the transaction."

The sound of the Prince's voice shoots like branches of lightning through every nerve of my body. I whirl and freeze, stricken in place. Mixael and Andreas both let out yelps, and Danny recoils. Even Estrilde stiffens ever so slightly. She draws herself together and turns slowly, clearing my line of sight to the vault doorway.

The Prince stands in the opening, leaning casually, his arms crossed, one knee bent. I haven't seen him since our last encounter on the stair. It seems an age ago, but in reality it's been no more than a few days. My heart relearns to beat in a painful rush of fluttering in my throat. Blood rushes to my cheeks and then drains away, leaving me dizzy.

"Well," he says, surveying the group of us with idle curiosity. "This is quite the interesting tableau. Come a-calling at last, Estrilde? I generally serve tea in the parlor, but I'm sure I can ring for the butler if you prefer the atmosphere down here."

"Castien." Estrilde's face melts into a viper's smile. "I hoped I should meet you. I have an invitation to extend."

"An invitation, dear cousin?" The Prince's answering smile is equally poisonous.

"Indeed. To my betrothal ball." She tosses a lock of golden hair over one shoulder. "My uncle is opening his gates to all the worlds in celebration of my betrothal to Lord Ivor Illithor, heir apparent to the throne of Aurelis."

My fluttering heart freezes, then makes a sickening dive into my gut. For a moment I step back into a memory of Lord Ivor himself, gazing deep into my eyes. *"I've not giving up, Clara,"* he told me then. *"I'll never give up. Not until I can bring you safely home. To me."*

He meant it. I'm sure of it. Or almost sure. It goes against everything I've been taught to believe about the fae. They do not love us, not even when they are at their most ardent. Their idea of love is mere illusion and trickery, a glamour as powerful as the beauty spells they weave around their faces and forms. But looking into Ivor's eyes, I had thought . . . I believed . . .

Is this jealousy? This bitterness roiling in my heart? It feels painfully like it. Does this mean I'm in love with Ivor despite every possible effort not to fall for him? It's been days now since I so much as thought of his beautiful face, his eyes so full of longing, hope, and pain. I've hardly had a spare moment. But now, at the sound of his name, to have such feelings stoked to life . . .

I shake my head, close my eyes tight. I won't give in. I won't surrender to these emotions. I've fought this long, this hard. I am still mistress of my own heart.

The Prince's eyes are fixed upon me. I feel it. I know I must meet his gaze, offering absolutely nothing in return. No revelation of the turmoil in my breast, of the pain or confusion. So that is what I do. I fix a bland, nothing of a smile on my lips, raise my head, and look directly at him.

He narrows his eyes. Then, smooth as silk, he addresses himself to Estrilde. "So. You have gained a crown at last." He tilts his head. "Is this to be the fruition of all your deeply cherished dreams?"

For the barest fraction of an instant, she looks as though he's struck her in the gut. The instant passes, however, and she answers calmly, "I will be Queen of Aurelis. Wed to the man I love. What more could I ask?"

"You could demand the Rite of the Thorn," the Prince answers. "Take your crown in a contest of blood like any self-respecting murderous fae contender."

"And why should I fight to the death with the man to whom I have given my heart?" Estrilde draws herself straight, her chin set and proud. "I am glad, nay, *proud* to become Ivor's wife."

"Ivor's wife." The words drip from the Prince's lips like an insult. *"Queen consort."*

One wouldn't need magic senses to feel the power and wrath swelling from Estrilde's soul. I take a step back, bracing myself protectively in front of Danny. But when the princess speaks at last, she says only, "The ball will be held on Spring Summit Night. Let me know if you will attend. You may bring a guest. That pretty Ilusine, perhaps." With that, she turns from the Prince and fixes her gaze on Danny. "Now, we shall be going."

"Wait!" I protest again, finding my voice in a gulping rush. I spread my arms, as though I have any hope of preventing Estrilde from taking whatever she wishes whenever she wishes it. My eyes seek the Prince, desperate. "Surely there's something that can be done!"

"Indeed, Estrilde," the Prince says blandly, "perhaps we might take this little discussion out of the vaults and leave my librarians to their work."

"There is nothing to discuss. This human attempted to fulfill the Mighty Deed I set before him according to our bargain. He has failed. By the Laws of Obligation, he belongs to me, now and for the next fifteen years."

Fifteen years? *Fifteen years?* That's the same as my own Obligation sentence. Only Danny now stands at the very beginning of his. And what will become of Kitty during that time, bereft of her brother's protection and support? And Oscar. Oscar, all alone in the world, without either his sister or his friend to turn to. What chance does he have of survival?

"Please," I whisper, reaching out and clutching Danny's hand even as Estrilde's grip lands on his shoulder. "Don't do this. Don't take him."

Estrilde looks at me for the first time. In the depths of her eyes I see absolute hatred. Hatred I've known was there for some time now, but which I've tried very hard to deny and ignore. The selfsame hatred that drove her to sell my Obligation in the first place, dooming me to serve in the Doomed City.

"Unhand my Obligate," she says. And though she no longer holds me in her thrall, though I am no longer her creature, I release Danny's hand and step back as though struck.

A ragged gasp chokes in Danny's throat. He has no choice but to obey when the princess commands him to march. He staggers forward like a drunken man, his arm gripped by her pale hand. Though he is tall by human standards, Estrilde towers over him in all her fearful fae might.

The Prince steps back, making room for her to pull her victim out of the vault and into the dark passage. With a little cry, I race to the doorway after them. "You must do something!" I urge the Prince, catching hold of his sleeve.

"Must I?" The Prince looks down at me, his face cold and distant. "It seems to me your handsome doctor has dug his own grave."

Biting back a curse, I push past him into the dark passage. "Darling!" he calls after me, but I ignore him, pelting after the retreating form of the princess. Once more, I grab Danny's hand, squeezing hard. "I'm going to help you," I say, pouring all the force of conviction I can muster into the words. "I'm going to figure something out. I swear it."

Danny casts me a last desperate look. Then he's yanked out of my grasp, dragged behind Estrilde into the darkness and shadows. I'm left standing in that cold dark space, watching them disappear.

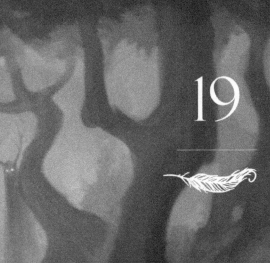

19

THE LIBRARIANS GATHER AT THE MAIN DRAFTING table on the first floor. I slump into a seat, my head dizzy, my body still shaking with the aftermath of horror. I find myself strangely aware both of the great vaulting sky above me, just on the far side of the crystal dome, and the plunging darkness down the citadel center, like a well to the bottom of the world. And here I am, caught between the two extremes. Balanced on a knife's edge.

I bury my face in my hands. Danny is gone. I've lost him. What will happen now? Will Kitty sit in her front-room window late into the night, watching every shadow that passes in the street below? Will she don her bonnet and venture out to Westbend Charity Hospital, asking who has seen her brother? How long before she suspects the truth?

How long before she blames me?

I should have done more. Rather than focusing so intently on getting us out, I should have tried to help. Perhaps together we could have navigated the treacherous ways of the Nightmare, found the Eight-Crowned Queen, and taken whatever object it was Estrilde wanted from her.

But what if we had? What if we succeeded? My Obligation would have been broken. And would I have returned to my own world? Never to think of Vespre again?

A sudden scraping sound startles me from the depths of my thoughts. I yank my head upright to look across the table. The Prince is there. He drags a chair across the floor, then lounges into it, feet propped on the table, fingers laced. "Well, that's done," he says in a deceptively easy tone. "The princess is off to her own world, her doting swains fawning in her wake. Couldn't be persuaded to stay for supper, despite all my pleadings. The promise of troldish culinary delights was not enough to sway her from her purpose."

Mixael and Andreas offer no response. They're both slumped in their seats, shoulders bowed, defeat in their eyes. They cast each other quick glances but cannot bring themselves to look my way. It's Mixael who finally breaks the uncomfortable silence. "So. How did it go in the human world? Any luck finding us a new librarian?"

The Prince tips his chair back on two legs. "Unfortunately, the lead went cold. My search for new recruits goes on."

My stomach turns over. Amid all the other concerns weighing on my mind, I'd almost forgotten my fear that Oscar was the object of the Prince's sudden interest. Does this mean he visited my brother and found him in a bad way? Or was it some other human with potential magic who had drawn his attention? Peering at the Prince through my lashes, I can read nothing in his face. And I cannot bear to ask outright.

Mixael utters a curse and throws up his hands. "What are we going to do? We need a new librarian. Now. Not later."

"Come, Silveri." The Prince undoes the topmost button of his jacket and loosens his collar, exposing his throat and collarbone. "You know very well this life isn't suited to just anyone. Especially if one's powers are not yet—and may never be—up to the task."

"Any help would be better than no help at all."

"Oh, in that opinion we must differ, my friend. An underqualified librarian left unchecked can cause far more damage than even the most ravenous Noswraith."

No one looks at me, but I am painfully aware that all attention is suddenly fixed my way. I cringe. Has Mixael filled the Prince in on the events of today already? I'm not sure if he's had a chance. Or has the Prince simply guessed at my rash decision to plunge into the Nightmare, alone and unaided?

No one speaks for several moments. Eventually, Andreas says quietly, "There must be something that can be done. There must be some way to . . . to conscript candidates, perhaps."

The Prince raises an eyebrow. "Mortal mages don't grow on trees, you know. Innate magical talent is required, not to mention the sanity with which to hone that talent into proper skill. Most who possess the talent do not possess the requisite sanity . . . as in the case of this particular inquiry."

"Surely you can find a moderately sane fellow with some talent, and we can train him up to the level we need," Mixael presses.

"Oh, are you advocating for the kidnapping of humans?" The Prince's mouth curves mirthlessly. "Because without proper cause—without a violation of the Pledge to serve as justification—that's what it would amount to. Darling, here, is the last known human mage to break the Pledge with a powerful act of human magic."

"Then what are we to do?" Mixael groans. "It's hopeless. Andreas and I are working inhuman hours, and Miss Darlington is constantly pushed to perform feats beyond her skill or training."

"Yes," the Prince says, shooting me a swift look. "I am well aware how Darling is extending herself beyond the reach of her powers."

A shadow passes over my soul. I hold his gaze for a long moment, then blink slowly. Offering nothing. No guilt. No remorse. Nothing.

Mixael tugs tufts of red hair at his temples so they stand out like wild flames. "Perhaps there's a solution we haven't thought of yet?" he says, his habitually optimistic voice heavy with doubt. "Some way to intensify the binding spells as we're writing them or . . . or . . . I don't know. Something."

"Perhaps we could use soulstones to augment our magic," Andreas suggests.

"We certainly could," the Prince replies. "If we don't mind giving our souls over to dark forces piece by ragged piece."

Andreas shrugs. "If we don't secure the library, we'll be giving our souls over to Noswraiths soon enough. First, we'll go mad like Vervaine. Then we'll be devoured. Like Soran. Like Nelle."

Mixael looks sick at the mention of his parents' names. He turns to the Prince, shaking his head. "I don't mean any disrespect, but . . ."

"But you're about to be disrespectful. Yes. I understand." The Prince sighs and rubs his hands down his face, pulling at the skin under his eyes before shaking his head. His hair ripples behind him, a gleaming waterfall of black silk. "I understand, Silveri. This is *my* job. *My* responsibility. I was given Vespre to protect, and I've been doing a pretty poor job of it lately. We've lost three librarians in two years alone, with no replacements to be had, for human magic is not what it once was. At the rate things are going . . ."

"The gate will have to be broken," Andreas says softly. "Vespre will be set adrift."

Deathly quiet descends on the table like a heavy shroud fallen across our souls. I've known for some time now about the failsafe set in place by Lodírhal. Should the Noswraiths escape their bindings and overrun the city, they will be a threat to all Eledria. The only choice is to cut the island free from this reality, to send it hurtling into the unknown void, carrying its nightmares with it, along with all the denizens of the city. And what of us librarians? Will we abandon the people we claim to serve? Will we make good our getaway and think no more of those sorry lives lost forever to the Hinter Realm?

We none of us speak for a long time. What is there to say? We face a grim future which we have all known was coming, but which is suddenly imminent and dire.

Then, suddenly, my lips are moving: "What if we didn't need mortal mages?"

The other three turn, looking at me. Andreas's expression is blank, Mixael's dismissive. The Prince's face I cannot read, but he says, "Don't imagine we've never thought of it. Fae magic does no good against Noswraiths. Any fae mages who have tried to take control of or bind a Noswraith have died gruesomely. It's the same for all—elves and dwarves, naiads and nixies, ettins and hobs. None understand the intricacies of written magic. Noswraiths can only be controlled by humans or those with enough human blood to work magic as humans do."

"What about troll magic?"

Three open-mouthed stares are my answer. I look around the table, searching for some hint of understanding. There is none. When my gaze lands on Mixael, he snorts and leans back, folding his arms. "Trolls don't have magic. At least, not magic that anyone understands. They're all about rocks and stone and their *Vagungad* cycle. And they certainly don't have any form of written language. How could they ever hope to contend with beings born of the written word?"

My lips part, the word *gubdagog* right on the tip of my tongue. But looking at the three of them again, I pause. After all, I'm still not entirely certain of what I glimpsed in the Temple of the Deeper

Dark. Perhaps I misunderstood the magic I sensed in that tangle of knots and threads. Besides, the low priestesswouldn't thank me for drawing the Prince's attention her way unnecessarily. No, best to wait. Bide my time, gather more information.

So rather than speak, I shrug my shoulders up to my ears. The Prince's gaze is a little too sharp for comfort, but he doesn't press me. Instead he addresses himself to Mixael once more. "For the time being, we must return to our regular duties. Maintain the library as best we can. Off with you now, men. I will come find you anon and receive your reports. For now . . ." His eyes return to me. "For now, I would speak to our junior librarian. Alone."

My fellow librarians cast me meaningful looks. Mixael is more than a little vindictive, while Andreas looks concerned. Refusing to meet either of their gazes, I simply sit there across from the Prince, my chin high, my expression blank. They slip away and vanish down the winding stairs, pursuing their own tasks. I feel more than a little like a maiden left chained to a pillar at the mouth of a dragon's den.

The Prince slides his feet off the table and lets the front legs of his chair hit the ground with a loud *thunk*. He leans forward, rests his elbows on the tabletop, steeples his fingers, and props his chin. "All right, Darling. It's just you and me now. Report."

Gone is that softness I sensed the last time we were alone together. Gone is that almost-but-not-quite-vulnerable look in his eye, that glimmering of hope, of fear. Nothing lies between us but the same old contention, antagonism, and suspicion from the earliest days of our acquaintance. Looking across the table at him, I see once more the face of that cold, cruel, disdainful Prince who took my Obligation and dragged me across worlds to this dark and terrible place without a moment's concern for my wishes or wellbeing.

How easy it is to forget sometimes that these people—these beings—are not our friends. They never were. They never will be. The first three rules I was taught upon my arrival in Eledria are as important now as they've ever been: *Never anger the fae. Never trust the fae. Never love the fae.*

I sit very straight in my seat, my hands folded before me. "The last few days have been quiet enough," I answer simply, my voice a perfect match for the blankness of my expression.

"Quiet enough, until your handsome doctor broke into my vaults and made merry with one of the most dangerous grimoires in this whole gods-doomed library."

I tuck my chin ever so slightly. An apology rises in my throat, but I swallow it back, forcing a lump of bitter bile down to my stomach. Instead I say only, "I did my best to dissuade him from making the attempt on my Obligation."

"Your *best* was not enough, apparently." The Prince drops one hand to the table, his fingers curling into a fist. "I suppose his love for you blinded him to all reason. Tell me, Darling, do you enjoy keeping men on a string, or is it all entirely accidental?"

Fire flares in my breast, but I keep my voice level when I answer. "My relationship with Daniel Gale is none of your concern."

"I beg to differ. It became my concern the minute that relationship compromised the safety of my entire city."

I snort. "Now you're exaggerating."

"Am I? And what exactly do you think will happen to Vespre if you go and get yourself killed?"

"Vespre is not my primary concern."

"And what about those children of yours? Those little creatures you claim to love?"

A terrible stillness comes over me. My heart, which a moment before had felt on fire, is suddenly hard as stone. I'm not sure it's even beating anymore.

"I care for their wellbeing," I answer softly. "Very much so. Even as I care for the wellbeing of this library and all its folk." I draw a long breath, hold it. Then, letting it out slowly, I add, "But if forced, I will always, *always* choose Oscar."

"Ah! There it is." The Prince sits back in his chair, arms crossed, eyes narrow. "It all comes down to the boy. And what of young Doctor Gale? How does he figure into things?" He shakes his head slowly. "You don't love him at all. Your concern for him is tied up in your concern for your brother."

"I do love Danny." I take those words and hurl them at him like stones. "I always have, and I always will. I love him more than a creature like you could ever understand." Dropping my voice, I speak the last words in an earnest whisper. "I would die for him."

The blood slowly drains from the Prince's cheeks. He looks as pale as he did when he lay on my hearth, his arms suspended above bowls, his human lifeforce dripping from his veins in red rivulets. Slowly, he stands. His hands knotted tight, he rests them heavily on the tabletop, his shoulders bowed, his head low and heavy. "Watch yourself. I've never yet enforced your Obligation. But if you drive me too far—"

"You'll what? Forbid me to care about those who mean more to me in this life than anything?"

His lip curls, flashing a single tooth. "Don't push me, Darling."

I rise abruptly, sliding my chair back with a harsh scrape. Leaning into the table, I match his stare with one of equal force. "When it comes to my loved ones, I'll push to the very limits of my strength. And I defy you—and all the forces of this world or any other—to stop me."

The air seems to have been sucked from the room. My pulse thunders in my ears, a steady, driving beat. I stare across that table, watching my own ferocious reflection doubled in the Prince's wide black pupils. Abruptly, he pushes back his chair and stands. Without a word, he turns on his heel and marches away, leaving me at the table. I watch him march to the nearest stairwell and vanish down the curving stairs to the lower floors.

My knees buckle. A sob bubbling in my throat, I sink into my chair, obliged to grab the edge of the table to keep from toppling to the floor. I remain there, shuddering, shaking. Pain throbs in my head, just behind my right eye. I bend over, press the heel of my hand into the eye socket, and blink back the tears trying desperately to escape.

M Y BLANKETS ARE SLOWLY CRUSHING ME.

Growling, I thrash my legs and flail my arms, almost surprised to find I'm not weighed down under iron sheets. The silken bedding simply flops off and lands in a puddle on the floor, leaving me exposed, my nightgown bunched up to my thighs. Now I'm too cold. Much too cold. I couldn't possibly sleep like this.

I turn over, bury my face in my pillow. I *will* fall asleep. I *will.* Why, oh, why am I still tossing and turning at this hour? When I fell into bed soon after twelve bells, I was so exhausted, I expected to be asleep before my head touched the pillow. That was ages ago now. And I'm still here. Still weary to my very bones. Still awake.

Somewhere far off, the bells toll three dolorous tones. I groan, squeezing my eyes a little tighter. But that's no use.

It only brings the images in my mind into clearer focus. The crawling beetles eating away at a red rose tucked into coiled, glossy hair. The hollow-eyed face gazing down at me from the gatehouse window, jaw gaping in a silent scream. The head-bobbing lizard-like chicken thing . . . the hanging man . . . the wafting phantom . . . the vast tentacled monstrosity in the sky revealed in flashes of lightning . . . all the nightmares, all crowded together, experienced again in quick succession.

Gods on high! It's a wonder I didn't go stark raving mad.

I sit up, my pillow clutched to my stomach. A shudder ripples down my spine, and I turn to stare around my room, expecting to see crawling things in the corners, on the walls. It's empty. I didn't dim the lanterns as much as usual before retiring to bed, not quite able to bear the dark. Which might very well be contributing to my lack of sleep. But at least I can see and know for certain that I'm not sharing the room with an unwelcome guest.

Slipping out of bed, I pad barefoot to the washroom. A silver mirror dominates one wall, framed in ornate curlicues. The glass is so pure, I'm quite certain it's wearing several layers of glamour. Beneath it is a silver basin of similar curlicue design, over which a spigot shaped like a water dragon arches. I turn a knob, and clear water flows from the dragon's open mouth into my hands. Though it's icy cold, I splash my face, then splash it again, gasping a little at each shocking contact of droplets against my skin. Then I fill my hands and press my face fully into the water. If only I could wash straight down into my brain, cleanse some of the darkness and dread. Then perhaps I would be able to sleep.

I lean over the basin. Droplets fall from my nose and chin and strands of hair. I watch the water swirl and race away down the drain. Slowly, I grip the knob, turn off the flow. Then, holding onto the edges of the basin, I push upright and face myself in the mirror glass.

A cry bursts from my lips as I stagger back three paces.

That face. For a moment—just a moment, no longer than the catch of a breath—it wasn't my face. Or rather, perhaps it was, but altered horribly. Pale. Gaunt. Almost dead, but not quite. And one eye gone. Nothing but an empty red socket and fresh blood pouring down cheek and chin.

The image is gone now. I see only myself. My cheeks are full and healthy. My eyes—both brown and blinking—stare at me from the glass. Wet hair clings to my forehead and around my ears, and my skin is flushed pink from the splashes of icy water. I look tired. Worn out. But no worse.

I stand there, breathing hard. There's a dull ache in my head, located just behind my right eye. It's nothing, though. Just a headache. Brought on by exhaustion.

"Get a grip on yourself," I whisper. My reflection scowls back at me sternly. Turning away, I stagger from the washroom and douse the light as I go. I return to my bed, bundle the blankets back onto the mattress, smooth them out, and fold the corner invitingly. Then I crawl back in and rest my head on the pillow.

And stare up at the spiderweb canopy over my head as the

hours cycle slowly by.

Over the next week, my fellow librarians and I are so overwhelmed with work, I scarcely have a chance to think of Danny, Oscar, or anything else. Working in sixteen-hour shifts with just eight hours in between to sleep, eat, and care for any personal needs, we exist in a constant state of reaffirming bindings, writing fresh spells, and inspecting the stacks for any books on the verge of breakdown. An outbreak of spellrot on the seventh floor keeps all of us hard at it for forty-eight hours straight. Once we have it under control, we're so close to dropping, the Prince sends us to catch a few precious hours of sleep while he watches the library on his own.

This, in and of itself, is dangerous. The Prince's human blood has not yet regenerated following his bleeding. Several times I've caught him in the act of opening a spellbook, his forehead furrowed as his eyes scan the page. Invariably he growls, slams the cover shut, and pushes the volume away. The written words contained within are nothing more than random squiggles and lines to his eyes, devoid of all meaning. Still, he supports us to the best of his ability.

As for he and I? Well, we've avoided each other since our last altercation. I can count on one hand the words he's spoken directly to me: "See to it," and "At once." That's it. In seven days.

Not that I'm complaining. I have no desire to interact with him more than absolutely necessary.

Throughout the week, I've scarcely seen the children and am more dependent than ever on Lir's help and support. Whenever I finish my shift, I make a point to see how they're getting on before crawling into bed. Apparently, Captain Khas has taken Har, Dig, and Calx in hand, determined that if they're going to be part of the palace household, they must contribute. She's training them as house guards, and I don't think they could be happier with the prospect.

Sis, however, has refused to join, preferring to spend her time scampering about the palace corridors, eluding Lir at every turn, and gathering random detritus for her most recent *gubdagog*.

"I'm going to throw the lot of them to the *Hrorark!*" Lir tells me passionately after one particularly exhausting day. But I can tell she's getting attached to the little trollings despite herself.

So the days creep by. And when five-bells rings out on the morning of the eighth day since the Prince's return, I find myself lying in my bed, staring up at my canopy, momentarily unable to summon the will to move. Ordinarily, Lir would be dragging me out from under the covers about now. But today is different. Today is my day off.

Groaning, I rub my hands down my tired face. Maybe I should just stay in bed. Take the day for much-needed sleep. I spent my last shift entirely on a single binding for a Noswraith known as the *Skull Crusher*. Sixteen hours of slow, meticulous, utterly exhausting work. The grimoire from which I was making my copy was so broken down that the ink had faded almost beyond legibility. I was obliged to use a magnifying lens to discern each individual word at a time while copying the spell into a fresh volume, all the while trying to keep the Skull Crusher from sticking an arm up out of the page and grasping my entire head in its horrible bony hand. I managed it in the long run and saw the new binding safely shelved. But the task took absolutely everything in me.

Which means I deserve an extra rest. Right?

"No," I mutter, and clamber out of bed. Shivering and stumbling, I put on my simplest, most unobtrusive gown, tie my hair in a modest knot at the nape of my neck, and wrap my cloak around my shoulders. Exiting my room, I take care to close the door quietly behind me, then flit down the hall like a shadow, making for the front entrance. I meet no one, not even one of Khas's guards. But last night I'd sent a message to the coachman, and I expect the morleth carriage to be waiting for me when I step out onto the front porch.

There is no carriage, however. I'm early, I suppose. Heaving a blustery sigh, I pick my way partway down the gigantic porch steps and take a seat. I'd hoped to make an early getaway, to avoid even the slightest chance of meeting anyone. I'd even skipped breakfast in my haste; a choice I will probably regret soon enough.

Perching on a stone step, my feet dangling, I look out across the city spread below me. Vespre is built around the central palace, which looms like a mountain peak above the streets and rooftops. The lower city disappears under stone and rock, but there are streets aplenty within my range of view. A purpling sky arches overhead. I never would have imagined upon first arriving in Vespre that I'd get used to a world without sunlight. But now? Truth be told, I've come to appreciate the beauty of this realm. Even the stars above are growing more and more familiar, constellations like friendly faces I've come to care for more than I like to admit.

"Off to see your brother, are you?"

My spine stiffens. Carefully I compose my face into a pleasant smile and demure lines before turning and blinking mildly over my shoulder.

The Prince stands just outside the doorway, his jacket open, his shirt loose, his hands deep in his trouser pockets. Upon seeing my smile, his brow creases. He saunters down the steps, moving so easily that one wouldn't even notice how very outsized they are for a man of his height, having been intended for beings much larger. When he's reached the step just above where I sit, he plunks down, his feet resting beside me, and leans his elbow heavily on one knee. For a moment, he holds his tongue, merely gazes out at the cityscape below us.

"Not your brother then," he says at last.

I won't answer. It's my free day. He cannot make me answer. I clasp my hands in my lap and face straight ahead, hoping his sharp fae ears don't catch the sudden tightness of my breath.

"Aurelis is warm at this turn of the cycle," the Prince continues. "You won't be needing this." He reaches out and plucks at the fabric of my cloak, pinching a fold just above my shoulder. I shrug away from him, then quickly straighten my shoulders once more. He retracts his hand and thoughtfully rubs his chin. "Now I wonder *why* exactly you would choose to waste the precious hours of your freedom on a jaunt into the very realm inhabited by my cousin, your former mistress and tormentor."

He knows why. I bite my tongue, determined not to be baited. At last, however, despite my best efforts, I turn sharply to him. "It's not his fault, you know. He truly believed he could rescue me. He didn't realize how cruel Estrilde can be. He expects others to be as noble as himself."

The Prince snorts. "I will beg your leave to withhold comment."

"When you say it like that, you're hardly *withholding* anything."

"Perhaps." He stretches a leg out in front of him and leans his weight back on one hand. "Have you not yet realized, Darling, that your doctor fellow made his own choices? You stated your position clearly. If he ignored your wishes and warnings and got himself entangled with the likes of Estrilde, that was his own fool fault."

He's right, of course. Blast and blight him. "It doesn't matter," I say with more conviction than I feel. "I may not bear all responsibility, but I do bear some. Besides, I just want to make certain he's . . . he's . . ."

"You want to make certain he's enjoying his servitude?" The Prince shakes his head, a mocking smile tilting his lips. "What's the point? Your time would be put to better use visiting that wastrel brother of yours. There, at least, you may do a little good."

I flash a sharp look at him from beneath my lashes. "What do you have against Doctor Gale anyway? Need I remind you that he saved your life?"

"Oh, I need no reminding. Nor need I remind you that, were it not for your own efforts, the noble physician would gladly have let me wither away and die right there on your kitchen floor. You'll pardon me for not falling over myself to extend the man extra charity."

"You don't know him."

"Perhaps not. But I know you. Can he say the same?"

As though caught by an invisible hook, my head turns, my eyes seeking his. I'm surprised to find him leaning in closer than I'd realized, his face mere inches from my own. I've not been this near him in days. During that time, the physical distance between us has only been intensified by the gulf between our souls. Yet in this moment that gulf seems to have been swept away. Nothing lies between him and me but a few inches of thin air.

I stare into his eyes, so dark the violet irises seem to have deepened to indigo. My own image is caught there, reflected back at me. For half an instant, I almost think I glimpse the unsettling image of a wounded face, a missing eye, and dripping blood. He blinks, however, and the image is gone, leaving only me there. Me as he sees me: stern, determined. Stubborn as a mule. Infuriating and intriguing in equal measure. Frightening.

Alluring.

What is this? What are these thoughts, these feelings? Are they his? Mine? Or is it all part of some dangerous fae glamour? The air is charged with energy akin to magic. I feel I could draw that charge into myself, set my blood boiling, my skin burning with light, with fire. It would be so easy. I need only lean forward a little bit. Close that space. Let the contact of our lips ignite the spark.

His hand moves. I don't see it, for my eyes are still caught in his, but I feel it, the warmth of his fingers slipping over mine. Tightening. His mouth opens. Warm breath touches my cold cheeks, as he breathes a single word: "Darling—"

In that moment, the sound of cloven hooves striking stone erupts down below. Yanked back into the present, I pull away and stand, wrapping my cloak tight around me. The black carriage pulls into the driveway below. The enormous troll coachman draws on the reins, dragging the morleth to a halt, then turns to me and tips his top hat.

My pulse beats wildly. I press a hand to my heart beneath the folds of my cloak. Aware that the Prince has already risen to his feet and stands on the step above me, I clear my throat. "It is my free day," I declare coldly without turning to face him. "I will use it as I see fit. I will return at eight bells this evening, as per the requirements of my Obligation."

I do not wait for his answer. I'm not obliged to, so I don't. I hasten down the huge steps, climb into the carriage, and speed on my way.

The Between Gate, used to travel from this world to others, stands on the shore of Noxaur, high on a cliff of black rock. The gate itself is huge, circular, and much weathered by the elements it has withstood for countless centuries. It's tall enough for a small giant to pass through comfortably. I feel like a tiny, insignificant doll in its shadow.

The heavy dial is still set to lead back into my world. Only with great difficulty do I manage to reset it for Aurelis. For a moment I fear I won't have the strength. Then the dial turns abruptly, spinning wildly in a complete cycle. The magic beneath the gate arch ripples, flares. I let out a yelp and fling up a hand to shield my eyes. But then the dial stops. The magic settles. When I look, I'm pleased to find it's selected Aurelis as I intended.

The view through the arch extends across the open sea, all the way to the hazy horizon where Vespre lies shrouded in mist. I find my gaze drawn that way. It's all too easy to imagine the Prince standing across from me, still on the front porch steps. His gaze crossing leagues to meet mine, to hold me fast in place.

I grind my teeth. I refuse to let him stop me. I have a purpose to fulfill. Gathering folds of my cloak in both hands, I take a single step toward the gate.

Before I take a second, however, a bone-chilling howl fills the air. I start, then whirl in place to see the dark landscape now spread before me—Noxaur, the Realm of Night. While twilight shrouds Vespre in perpetual gloom, this is a realm of true darkness alleviated only by a delicate crescent moon.

Another howl echoes eerily on the wind, and this time it is answered by a ghostly horn. I shudder. Everyone knows Noxaur is a wild, dangerous world into which few dare venture. The practices of the Noxaurian fae have provided fuel for many a dark and twisted tale throughout history. But this gate stands on neutral territory, or so I've been assured. The librarians of Vespre are free to come and go, so long as we are not foolish enough to venture inland. Not a temptation, I assure you.

Pulling my cloak tight around me, I hasten through the gate.

Stepping between realities is never a pleasure. One doesn't grow accustomed to the awful experience of having one's very matter and marrow broken apart, streamlined, and spread across multiple realities before finally coalescing back into a single place several worlds over. As a result, when my body re-forms, I stagger, stumble, and fall to my knees, dragging ragged gasps of air into my lungs. It takes several moments of blinking before I'm able to see that the world around me is bathed in soft morning-glow gold. I've left behind the darkness of Noxaur and returned to the Realm of Dawn.

"Breeehaww!"

Still kneeling, I turn and offer a somewhat shaky smile to the somber horned figure who stands before a stone dial very like the one I've just left. "Hullo, Lyklor. Did you miss me?"

The gatekeeper blinks his yellow eyes and shows big square teeth in what I believe is a smile. He even offers a—for want of a better word—*hand* and assists me to my feet. "Thank you," I say, and slip the cloak from my shoulders. It is, as the Prince warned, quite warm in Aurelis at this season. "Would you mind keeping this until my return? I shan't be long."

The gatekeeper bleats pleasantly, takes my cloak, and bundles it under his own dark robes. He nods at my enquiries after his health but offers no comment . . . which is fine, considering I don't understand a word he says. I like to think he appreciates the effort, at least.

There's nothing for it now but to face the city-palace.

Aurelis looms before me beyond a magnificent stretch of garden. The golden seat of King Lodírhal's kingdom is even more lofty and glorious than I remembered, the very picture of heaven as I once imagined it as a child. I even spy winged figures circling above the highest turrets.

The city itself, however, is far from heavenly. Rife with intrigue, danger, and subtle murderous poison, it is no different from any other court of Eledria. I survived my five years serving here only because I was stationed in the palace library. The fae have no interest in books and generally leave librarians to our own devices.

I set off along the garden paths, my steps quick and light. I wonder if Danny is working in the library now? It would make sense. Estrilde wouldn't have much other use for him, so she probably sent him to old Thaddeus Creakle. Not the worst fate when all's said and done.

Ducking into a shadowed arbor, I hasten down the path. Now that I'm here, I'm both eager and terrified at the prospect of seeing

Danny again. What has he experienced in this last week? Has he found the fae world terrible beyond imagining? Or have its beauties and glamours intoxicated him, lulling him into submission and complacency? I can only wonder and worry until I am with him again. Picking up my pace, I turn a corner—

And slam square into a broad, muscular frame.

Hands grip my shoulders, just preventing me from rebounding and tumbling in an ungraceful heap in the path. I gasp for breath, my senses addled as an overwhelming aura of beauty, light, goodness, and lust fills my senses. Dragging my head back, I blink up into the glow of Ivor Illithor's face.

"Clara!" he cries.

MY HEAD WHIRLS AS THOUGH I'VE BEEN DEPRIVED of air. How long have I stood here staring up at him, frozen in place while his fingers dig into my shoulders? I've lost all sense of time, all equilibrium. My mind floods with memories—so many memories of moments spent in dangerously close proximity with this glorious being. Memories of him gazing at me with those blood-burning eyes.

Like he's gazing at me now.

"Lord Ivor!" I gasp. Then I shake my head, desperate to shake some coherence back into place. "I hope you're well!" The words burst from my lips, tremulous and ridiculous and the only gods-blighted thing I can think to say in the moment. As if I were sitting at tea in Kitty's parlor, exchanging pleasantries with a passing acquaintance.

Ivor's brow constricts. "Why, yes. I am. And you?" He looks at me curiously. "Are you well? How does life in Vespre find you?"

"Oh, I'm well. I . . . I . . ." What can I possibly say? That I'm getting more used to my daily battles with living nightmares? That I'm discovering I have a natural aptitude for combating the worst horrors ever unleashed upon Eledria? That even when I'm utterly exhausted, overwhelmed to the point of despair, there's nowhere else I want to be?

"I am well. Thank you."

His eyes search my face, no doubt reading more than I like to reveal. "I've not seen you since my visit."

Such an obvious statement. Stupid even. And also . . . untrue? I frown suddenly as another memory plucks at my awareness: the night of the *hugagog* moth flight, when the fae Lords and Ladies from Solira danced in Vespre Palace, lighting up the gloom with their brilliance. Beautiful men and women had whirled before my eyes, but through the throng, I thought I caught a glimpse of a familiar face.

No, you imagined it. You were overwhelmed by the Soliran fae. Dazzled. Confused.

Is that a glamour? I blink and try to draw back. My magic senses have amplified significantly during my time in Vespre. What I might easily have overlooked before now touches my awareness like the faint hum of a mosquito. Is Ivor emitting an influence over me?

He wouldn't. He's not like that. He's different from the others.

Is he?

"Yes," I manage with an effort. "It has been some time." Another utterly pointless statement. But it works. It gets my tongue moving. When I speak again, my voice is firmer. "I understand I am to congratulate you on your betrothal to Princess Estrilde."

"Ah! You heard about that?"

He releases his hold on me. It's so abrupt, I stagger a little to reclaim my balance. Now that we're no longer physically connected, the faint awareness, the droning whine, vanishes. Is that a good thing? Does that mean he's ceased his attempts to glamour me? I pull myself a little straighter and offer a bland smile. "Indeed. Princess Estrilde extended an invitation to the Prince of Vespre. For the betrothal ball. She is . . . Well, naturally we are all delighted for her. And for you. You must be very happy."

"Must I?" Ivor takes a quick step. Startled, I retreat two paces, determined not to let the space between us shrink. But his eyes catch mine, flashing and sharp. "Nothing is settled," he says. "I've made no promise, spoken no vow. Estrilde and I have an . . . arrangement. But unless certain conditions are seen to, I am not committed."

I can't tear my gaze away. A voice deep down in my mind is urging, *Run, run, run!* But I can't move.

Those eyes of his. They're mesmerizing.

He reaches out, takes my hand. Immediately, the drone of glamour hums just within the range of my awareness. It's hard to concentrate on such things when I'm so alive to the warmth of his fingers pressing mine, the heat simmering in his gaze.

"You know I wanted things to be different." He lowers his head, cutting off the glow of sunlight above him, casting me into shadow. It doesn't matter. His golden eyes are like two dawning suns, lighting up my whole world. "I still do."

I bite my lip. More than anything, I want to stand on my toes and catch his lips with mine. Give in to that dangerous impulse, which has only grown harder to ignore with each passing second. After all, why should I not? He cares about me. I know he does. So what if he's using a glamour? It wouldn't be so effective if it were based on a lie. Would it? My mouth is dry. My throat is tight. My gaze drifts from his eyes down to his mouth. Those full lips, gently parted. So near to my own.

"What would have happened if you'd bought my Obligation from the Prince?"

Ivor pulls back. "What?"

I'm not sure where those words came from. But they're spoken now. Cold as a wall of ice between us. I press further. "Would you have set me free? Would you have . . . ?" The unfinished question hangs between us. We both know what I'm asking: *Would you have married me? Made me your queen?*

Because that is the promise Ivor had not *made* but strongly *implied*. That he wanted me for his bride. Me. Not Estrilde, not the beautiful, powerful, well-matched fae princess, a being of his own kind, of equal might and bearing. Me. Clara Darlington of Clamor Street.

But why? If there's any truth to the implication, *why?* King

Lodírhal took a human wife, but in the end it only caused him pain. His half-blood son is considered ineligible for the throne. His own life was cut short for being linked to his frail human bride. I've heard how devoted Lodírhal was to Dasyra, but would he have chosen such a wife if not for their Fatebond?

And there is no Fatebond here. Though my attraction to Ivor is powerful, though the force with which we seem to be drawn together is almost otherworldly, I know perfectly well this is no gods-ordained binding. In fact, when I'm free of his presence, I experience nothing but relief. When I'm in his atmosphere, he is both addicting and suffocating. I cannot breathe properly unless I am beyond his reach.

I stand there, holding his beautiful gaze, my unasked question burning between us. He cannot lie to me. And perhaps if he speaks the truth, I will finally have what I need to break his hold over me entirely.

"What do you think I want from you, Clara?" he asks softly. "What have I always wanted, from the moment I set eyes on you?"

The heartbreak in his face cuts me to the core. Am I wrong to harbor such suspicions? And what am I suspecting exactly?

He draws closer. The scent of him is so strong, so lusty, so delicious. "I want to be near you," he says. "I want you with me, by my side. Is that so much to ask? Just that you would be here. With me, always with me. Mine, both heart and soul."

He's not answered my question. Or has he? I'm not sure anymore. His scent is so powerful. This isn't a glamour, it can't be. This is real, and he is real, and he is so close, so beautiful, so powerful. Desire burns in his eyes, and that is real too.

And me? What do I feel? I'm not sure, but . . . but right now, I want to . . . I want to know what it would be like. To let myself be caught in his arms. To fall deeper and deeper under his spell.

"You're ensorcelled," Danny had said.

Maybe he was right. Maybe I don't care—

"Lord Ivor!"

A gasp on my lips, I pull away. It feels as if something in me rips away in ragged strands of flesh and blood and shattered bone. But the pain is brief, and once it passes I stand free and firm, three steps away from the golden fae lord.

A human stands on the garden path beyond us. I recognize her— Winifred, one of Estrilde's Obligates. She's been in the princess's service since before I came to Aurelis. We've never exchanged more than a few words, but in that moment, I'm happier to see her than I ever would have thought possible.

She twists her hands nervously, her eyes very wide. "Lord Ivor, the princess requires your company in her salon. At once."

Ivor draws a ragged breath, his nostrils flaring. His gaze flashes to meet mine. "I must go. I cannot keep her waiting. You'll not leave Aurelis again without seeing me, will you?"

He's trying to make me promise. I answer carefully: "My business here will take me much of the day, my lord."

His face is immobile, but something in his eye tells me he noticed my avoidance. Thankfully, he doesn't press the issue.

Instead, in a movement too quick for me to elude, he takes and kisses my hand. Heat flares through my skin at the contact of his lips. My stomach flutters, and my knees threaten to buckle even as the droning of glamour sings irritatingly in the back of my head.

The next moment, he's gone. Disappeared into the greenery behind the scurrying form of Winifred. Leaving me behind.

Thaddeus Creakle happens to be working at the front desk of Aurelis Library when I enter. He looks up, his face deeply lined in a standard librarian's scowl. At sight of me, however, those lines soften into something almost resembling a grin.

"Miss Darlington!" He hastens around the desk to grip my hands. "I did not expect to see you again! Are you returned from Vespre City?"

"Not for long," I admit. "It's my free day."

"And you took your precious hours to come see your old friends at the library? How thoughtful! But really, you shouldn't have."

Oh dear. I bite the inside of my cheek. It had never once occurred to me to pay a call on Thaddeus and the others since leaving Aurelis. Guilt bubbles in my gut, and I force myself to set aside more pressing questions to inquire after my former fellows. Thaddeus is uncharacteristically garrulous, and I feel the moments slipping through my hands like water. At last, I can bear no more.

"I must confess, Mister Creakle, I did not return solely for a pleasure visit."

"Indeed?" His smile fades. "Did the Prince send you?"

"Oh, no. This is my own errand." I pull in both lips and bite down hard. But now I've come this far, I can't very well stop. "Princess Estrilde acquired a new Obligate. This was about a week ago? He was trying to break my Obligation and . . ."

"Ah, yes!" Thaddeus nods and, with a last pat of my hand, returns to his place behind the desk. "I remember the new Obligate. A young fellow, yes? And handsome. I have the records here. I will tell you, Miss Darlington, no one has seen hide nor hair of him since."

My stomach tightens. "They've not? He's not working here in the library?"

Thaddeus shakes his head even as he pulls a large, heavy ledger out from one of the cubbies under the desk. All Obligate names and pertinent information are stored therein for easy reference. He opens the cover, licks his thumb, turns pages. He's so painstaking, I fear I might go mad. It doesn't make any sense—why would Estrilde not place Danny here? Perhaps she prefers to keep him close so she might enjoy his pretty face and figure. I shudder. I don't like to think of Danny in the role of Estrilde's footman.

"Here we are." Thaddeus pauses over a page, running his finger down the list of closely written names. All of those poor souls like me, who inadvertently broke the Pledge and found themselves sworn into service for crimes they never intended to commit. Thaddeus reaches the end of the row, the final name.

His brow tightens. His mustache twitches to one side. "Hmmm," he grunts, and flashes a quick glance at me over the rim of his spectacles. "What did you say the young man's name was?"

I hadn't said. "Gale. Daniel Gale."

"I'm sorry to hear it." Thaddeus closes the book and folds his hands. "I regret to inform you, Miss Darlington, that Daniel Gale has been sent Under."

THE CITY OF DAWN, LIKE MOST CITIES IN THE KNOWN worlds, is built atop various social strata. As Estrilde's Obligate, I spent the entirety of my time in the uppermost levels, where all is golden and beautiful, full of music, flowers, and song. It's too easy to believe this *is* Aurelis—the only Aurelis, the whole of Aurelis.

But this city has other levels. There is Under—down beneath all cellars and basements, down in the dark and the cold. Down where only the brave, the vicious, and the desperate dare venture. It is a realm of pixies and toadmongs, shadelings and peglers. Beautiful winged dearg drue and gruesome nuckelavee shelter in the deepest shadows, driven from their natural haunts in the darker realms. All these fall under the broad term "fae." But not all fae are the lofty highborn elfkin who rule the courts of Eledria.

Which isn't to say you won't find elfkin in Under as well. Indeed, it is commonly known that, for a lark or a dare, they will saunter into the city's bowels, there to indulge in unspeakable debaucheries.

"Please, Miss Darlington, let me urge you to leave well enough alone." Old Thaddeus comes out from behind the desk again, his wrinkled face puckered with concern. "Under is no place for you."

I nod. I hear him. But . . . but how can I abandon Danny? I got him into this mess. I've got to find him, got to know what's become of him. "Do you . . ." I clear my throat, not sure I want an answer. "Do you know what Estrilde has him doing? Down there?"

He doesn't meet my eye. "It's unsuitable for a lady's ears."

"I'm not a lady." I take a step closer to him, grab his sleeve. "I'm a librarian. I've both seen and committed my fair share of dark deeds. Don't try to shield my maidenly delicacy. Just tell me."

Thaddeus tries to pull away, but I tighten my grip. He casts me a last look, at war with himself. "I'm sorry, Miss Darlington. If I know anything about the princess's interests in the doings of Under . . . well, in all likelihood, she's entered him in the Games."

My stomach knots. I don't like the sound of that. Not one bit.

A lumpish young human sits on a stool with his back to the wall, one leg extended in front of the open doorway. If he's guardian of this gate, he's not exactly intimidating. "Give us the password then," he says as I approach down the damp, narrow passage.

He's not even bothered to open his eyes. His arms are crossed over his sagging chest, his head resting—I can only imagine uncomfortably—against the wall.

"Felaadar," I respond at once. I have no idea if it's right, but I remember the Prince uttering the same strange word at the entrance to the Den of Vipers.

It works surprisingly well. Not only does the young man drag his foot back from across the opening, he actually pries both eyes open and sits up a little straighter on his stool. Upon seeing me standing there, his brow knots with some confusion. He nonetheless nods toward the door and mutters a not altogether ungracious, "Fair endeavors to you, lady."

I step past him through the darkened door and find myself at the top of a stairway leading almost straight down through an ill-lit cavern. It's dark, gloomy, with only a few lanterns lit at odd intervals. The steps are uneven, all different heights and widths, and I'm obliged to grip the rail tightly to keep my balance. Strange figures waft past me on their way back up—all cloaked and hooded and covert. Members of Lodírhal's court? Possibly, but I cannot see their faces to recognize them.

When I reach the bottom of the stair, there's another door. No gatekeeper though; apparently the folk of Under trust the lout upstairs to guard their secrets. That, or their secrets simply aren't worth guarding.

I step through.

I'm immediately plunged into a bustling crowd, all elbowing, shoving, sometimes biting in their efforts to navigate the numerous streets and stalls. The space is far greater than I dreamed it would be, vast catacombs supported by lofty columns in the Aurelian style. The sunburst insignia of Lodírhal is emblazoned everywhere I look, shockingly out of place in this close, murky, fetid, furtive, ferocious atmosphere.

Lucky for me, the folk here are all rather too busy to take note of one lowly human Obligate in their midst. In addition, the aura of my Obligation provides protection; most fae would know better than to bother me for fear of insulting my master.

So I fight my way through the jostling flow, finally managing to find a clear space on the far side of what I must call a *street*. There, I grip hold of a signpost to keep myself anchored. Thaddeus gave me directions, and I search desperately above the heads of the hurrying crowd for some glimpse of the landmarks he mentioned. There—up the way and a little to my right. The sign of the Headless Swan.

Like a swimmer drawing breath, I brace myself and plunge into the throng again. By some miracle, I resurface close to the sign and take a left into the much narrower street behind it. There are a great many food sellers here. Food sellers and hungry folk . . . not a great combination. I neither trust the fae food enough to eat it nor trust the hungry fae folk not to try to eat me. A dearg drue lurking between two stalls offers me an alluring toothy smile, but judging by blood around her full, pouty lips, she's recently feasted. Even so, that smile of hers is almost enough to pull me off course, straight into her waiting arms.

Shuddering, I push on to the end of the street. It opens up, but only into a greater crowd than before. This crowd is more energetic than those I left behind. Every few minutes, they erupt in a raucous cheer complete with fist pounding and feet stomping and even some wild, warlike ululations. Every time their hands are upraised, I take the opportunity to duck, dodge, and weave my way a little deeper.

At last, I find myself pressed up against a wooden rail. Below me, ringing lanternlight illuminates a gaming pit. A game is well underway. A battle, rather—for there seem to be no rules to this game, only blood and brute force and brawling bodies. A hideous nuckelavee—its skinless body made up of pure corded muscle and sinew, its demonic double heads both flame-eyed and slavering—hurls itself at an armored warrior. She is six feet tall if she's an inch but nonetheless dwarfed by the towering demon-horse. Her only weapon is a silver lasso, which she twirls above her head. The nuckelavee charges her, four legs pounding, human torso twisting back to hurl a bone spear straight between her eyes.

The warrior dodges at the last instant. In the same rolling movement, she lets her lasso fly. It catches the nuckelavee by one hind hoof and sends the monster crashing to the ground. With a triumphant cry, she springs over her fallen foe and ties three of its four lashing hooves together before looping a noose around the neck of the human head.

The crowd goes wild. She stands, arms above her head, receiving cheers and boos in equal measure. Flowers and trash alike rain down from above, and she blows kisses and makes obscene gestures by turn, even as shadowy figures hasten into the pit to hustle her away and to drag off the bound nuckelavee.

"Never expect the *human* women to amount to much," someone mutters behind me. I cast a glance over my shoulder to see a hooded elf leaning close to whisper to his companion. "But gods above, when they do, it's worth a see!"

I shudder and turn back to the pit. A scurrying fat figure in brilliant pink ruffles makes its way to the center. He holds out all four arms, feathery antenna flicking from the top of his head as he smiles up at the crowd. He begins to speak in a chittering language that I don't know, but it serves to invigorate the already animated crowd. There's so much eager bloodlust in the air, it makes my stomach turn.

But then I hear the little pink creature speak a familiar word: *"Gale!"*

All the whooping and taunting and roaring fades away to nothing. I stand there, pressed awkwardly up against the rail, my heart thundering in my ears, my gaze fixed upon that terrible ring. Upon that doorway that has just opened and through which a familiar figure is unceremoniously tossed.

Danny.

He's shirtless. Bruised. His hair hangs in tatters over his forehead. His bare feet scrabble in the dirt for balance, but when he finds it, he pulls himself up with dignity. Hands clenched into fists, he marches to the center of the pit, towering over the creature in pink.

The crowd around me is chanting now: *"Gale! Gale! Gale!"* I cannot tell whether they're cheering or mocking him. Perhaps both. Either way, when a door on the opposite end of the pit opens and a satyr springs through, pumping his fists in the air, the onlookers go wild, stamping their feet, clapping their hands, hooting and hollering for the fight to begin.

And begin it does. The little pink creature spreads its wings and flies out of the way just in time, for the satyr throws himself straight at Danny without preamble. His powerful goat legs propel him forward, his huge, curling horns aimed straight at Danny's chest. A blow like that could crush a man's breastbone, pulverize his heart.

"*No!*" I shout, grabbing the rail.

But Danny nimbly ducks out of the way, eluding the blow. The quick-footed satyr regroups and lashes out with a kick that catches Danny in the back of his knee. Danny goes down again but keeps moving, keeps rolling, and avoids a stomping cloven hoof to the ear by inches. He kicks, aiming straight between the satyr's furry legs. The blow lands.

The crowd explodes with laughter and furious protests alike as the satyr lets out a pathetic bleat, goes cross-eyed, and doubles over. Danny scrambles to his feet and backs away, hands upraised. This elicits a storm of boos, and somewhere someone starts up a chant: "*Kill! Kill! Kill! Kill!*"

Danny shakes his head, teeth bared. Then he cries out and grabs his temples, pressing hard with both hands. I know that look. I know what's happening. He's in pain. He's fighting his Obligation. His

Obligation, which forces him to be here, forces him to fight. The laws of Obligation are supposed to protect us from forced violence . . . but you can trust the fae to figure out workarounds to anything.

The satyr shakes his horns and bleats again, stamping his hooves, digging grooves in the dirt. He pounds his chest, raises his fists, and waggles his goat tail, goading the crowd. Then he pivots abruptly and charges Danny again, horns down.

Danny is a man of peace. I've never known him to raise his hand in violence, only in defense, only to protect those more vulnerable than himself. He is a nurturer and caretaker, a healer.

It is like seeing a Nightmare version of the man I know when I watch him dodge the satyr, catch him around the neck, and squeeze. He braces his arm with the opposite elbow, his face twisted in a violent, concentrated grimace. With one foot, he effectively kicks the weirdly bowed knees of his opponent. They both tumble to the ground, but Danny's grip never lets up. He drives the satyr's face into the dirt, applying still more pressure.

Is he going to kill the creature? Am I about to watch my childhood friend, the gentlest person I know, commit murder right before my eyes and the eyes of this cheering, jeering throng? I grip the rail, pressed up against it by eager onlookers, hardly able to breathe.

At last, the satyr, on the verge of unconsciousness, taps Danny's elbow. It must be a signal, for Danny releases him, scrambles to his feet, and steps back. Panting hard, the satyr remains on the ground even as the mocking hoots and growls of the crowd roll like thunder overhead. Danny's bare chest heaves, but that horrible expression has left his face. His brow puckers with concern as he steps to the satyr's side, kneels, and offers his hand. With a vicious bleat, the satyr launches himself at Danny, its long-fingered hands closing around his throat. I scream, my voice lost to the eruption of laughter all around me.

A blast of purplish light sears my vision. Flinching away, I fling up both hands to shield my eyes. When the afterglow lessens, I stare blinkingly back down into the pit.

The satyr lies in crumpled ruin. His body blackened, smoking.

Danny utters a wordless roar. He crouches over his fallen foe, turns the creature over, and presses an ear to its chest. Before he can take further action, shadowy beings in hoods rush out, grab his arms, and drag him away, deaf to his protests and screams.

"There's always at least one idiot. Every time," someone behind me says with a chuckle. "Someone who thinks they're above the rules."

"Eh, the rules are daft anyway," his companion answers. "Why not let them kill each other? It's more fun that way."

"It's those cursed Obligation laws. If they die by accident, no harm. But there must be some measure of protection."

Protection? I watch the body of the satyr being carried off, still smoking. I can't tell if it's dead or not. Apparently attacking his opponent after conceding defeat violated some law, the punishment for which was swift and horrible. I strain my head, trying to catch a last glimpse of Danny as he disappears into the dark doorway. But the door slams, and he's gone.

ON THE FAR SIDE OF THE GAMING PIT IS A LITTLE village of shacks. There are few guards, for the denizens of this village are Obligated to remain. What further force is necessary?

It's quieter over here, away from the action, the brutal entertainment. When a scurrying bunyi passes close by, I manage to catch hold of his sleeve and ask, "Where might I find Princess Estrilde's Obligate?"

The bunyi gives me a look, then shrugs and points down a particular row of shacks. I hasten that way, my eyes sharp, searching for a familiar figure. The shacks are barely more than lean-tos: a roof, three walls, and no front. Hunched figures lounge on low beds, all in attitudes of defeat. None of them look my way, but I can tell from their various and strange shapes that they are not the man I seek.

Finally, at the very end of the row, I find him. He's lying on his back, one arm over his face. Still shirtless. Still sweaty and dirty from his brawl.

"Danny!"

At the sound of my voice, he sits bolt upright, his eyes wide as saucers. At the sight of me standing before him, he springs to his feet. "Clara! Is that really you?" He takes a step toward me, then stops. His hands move awkwardly, as though he doesn't know what to do with them. Hastily, I step forward and catch both his hands in mine, pressing them hard. But he shakes his head, his brow creased, and tries to pull away. "You shouldn't be here."

I only grip him harder. "What has happened, Danny? What has she done to you?"

As though all remaining strength has fled his body, he sinks onto the hard benchlike bed. "You warned me," he says softly. "You tried to, anyway. I should have listened. I should have—"

His voice breaks. Tears stream down his cheeks. I hesitate, uncertain what to say, what to do. Unwilling to relinquish his hands, I sit beside him, then slip an arm around his bare shoulder and pull him to me. He rests his head against mine, and the moment is both so intimate and so strange, I hardly know what I'm feeling, what I ought to be feeling. "What happened to the satyr?" I ask.

"He's dead." Danny stiffens in my arms and draws away. "Of course, he's dead. He violated the rules of the game—attacked me

306

when the bout was over. And they killed him for it." He slumps over and buries his face in his hands. "I could have saved him. I'm sure I could have gotten his heart going again if they'd let me. I could save so many of them! But they hold me back, they make me watch. They make me fight and then they make me watch while others fight and bleed and die. All for their sport."

This is so much worse than anything I'd imagined this past week in the few spare moments I'd thought of Danny and his Obligation. It's cruel. So cruel, it can't be anything but intentional. Estrilde has no reason to punish Danny. She means this to hurt *me*.

She could not have picked a more effective vengeance.

"I owe you an apology." Danny looks sidelong at me. "I never dreamed it would be anything like this. The task set for me to break your Obligation . . ." He clenches his jaw, breathes out a long sigh. "I thought my love for you would carry me through any trial, any tribulation. I thought the gods would give me strength, would guide my footsteps. But once I started reading that book . . ."

A cold shiver rolls down my spine. Even I, with the experiences I've accumulated over the last many weeks, wasn't prepared for the horrors of the Nightmare Realm. How much worse must it have been for Danny, sent in totally ignorant and woefully unprepared?

I must say something. Everything I can think of sounds lame, but I have to fill this silence. "It wasn't your fault."

Danny laughs bitterly. "Don't try to make it better, Clara. I know the truth. This is entirely my fault. You did everything you could to spare me. And now?" He rubs a hand down his face. "When I think of Kitty! And Oscar. And all my patients back at Westbend Charity. There was a little girl, you know. She had grey fever. I was trying the new protocol on her against Doctor Moore's orders. I swear, she was beginning to improve! But if I'm not there, who will continue the dosage? Old Thick-skull Moore will poison her in his efforts to knock the fever out. Another innocent life lost. All because I didn't heed your warnings. All because I wouldn't listen to you."

Tears fall, blazing hot trails down my cheeks. I dash them away harshly. Then I stand suddenly, looking down at Danny. "I'm going to get you out of this."

"What?" For an instant, hope lights his face. Then his eyes darken. "No, Clara. Don't give me false hope."

"I wouldn't!" I kneel before him and take his hands again, my face upturned to his. "There must be a way. Estrilde would not have made this bargain with you for no reason. She wants something. She wants . . . What was it you said she sent you after?"

"The bloodgem necklace."

"Yes. That. And I'll get it for her."

"No." Danny tries to pull his hands away again. "Don't do it. Don't go back into that world. Not for my sake, Clara. Please, I couldn't bear it!"

I hold his gaze firmly. "It's not for your sake. It's for Kitty's. For Oscar's. For that little girl suffering from grey fever, for all your patients both now and later. For all those people who need you whole and present and alive. Not torn apart, always thinking about something you cannot have, about someone . . ."

I stop. The heartbreak in his eyes is too much. I don't want to hurt him more than I already must, to emphasize all over again that we will never be able to be together. His love for me is all too evident, and the truth is . . . well, the truth is, part of me will always love him too.

I get to my feet, clenching my hands into fists at my sides. "I'm going to save you, Danny. Don't lose hope. Hold on just a little longer. Please."

He stands as well, looking down at me. Battered, bruised, half naked. And so dear, so very dear to me. He takes one of my hands, brings it to his lips. Then he presses my palm to his cheek, and I don't have the heart to pull away. "Please, Clara. You are not the fault here. You are the reason . . . you are *my* reason. For everything. Even now, when I close my eyes, I dream of the day I'll wake to find my Obligation ended. When we can return to our world. Together. It's the only thing that gives me hope, gives me breath. If something happened to you . . . if I had to face the rest of these long years and the rest of my sorry life without you . . ."

I back away, one slow step after the other. How is it that he still cannot understand? Nothing I say seems to make any difference! Resentment stabs my heart. Because I love him. But I will not marry him. I will not share a lifetime with him. And I need him to understand.

Only maybe . . . not yet. Maybe it's better to let him have something to hold onto. Just until I can get him out of this hellish situation.

"I must go." I back away another step. "My free day is almost done."

"Will you promise not to do anything foolish?"

"I promise only that I will help you."

"Clara, no—"

Before he can finish his protest, I duck out of his little shed and back into the dark streets of Under.

24

THE PALACE BELLS TOLL EIGHT DEEP TONES AS THE morleth carriage pulls to a halt at the base of the front steps. I push open the door and spring free before the coachman has a chance to climb down from his seat and offer me a hand. Holding my skirts away from my feet, I climb the steep steps, slip into the palace, and run all the way to the library. By the time I reach the doors, I'm breathless and more than a little windswept. I hastily smooth my hair, wait a few moments until my chest stops heaving, then push the doors open and step inside.

Mixael is at his desk. Hearing my footsteps, he pushes back his chair and greets me with a hollow-eyed ghost of a smile. "And how was your day, Miss Darlington?"

"Where is the Prince?" My own rudeness makes me cringe, but I haven't a moment to spare.

Mixael frowns. "He's down on the ninth floor, checking on a possible case of spine-brittle. Is everything quite all right?"

I toss back a "Yes, thank you, Mister Silveri!" as I'm already on my way to the nearest book lift. The pulley and chains creak, and the whole lift rocks unnervingly as I work levers and descend the floors. Part of me wishes I'd just taken the stairs, but I'm already winded, and I need at least some breath left for what I'm about to do.

By the time the lift finally screeches to a halt at the ninth floor, I'm positively bursting with impatience. I fling the gate open with a clatter and race along the curving shelves. None of this is good library protocol. The Noswraiths bound within those volumes are much too easily excited, like a dog seeing a rabbit dart by and unable to resist the instinct to chase. I hear the pages whispering, the leather covers groaning, and force myself to adjust my pace as I pass the arched entrances to various side corridors leading off from the main floor. Empty, empty, empty . . . did the Prince finish his inspection already? Has he moved on to one of the other floors? Blight it, I should have asked Mixael more specifics. Which series was showing signs of spine-brittle? I might have saved myself a vast deal of trouble, and I—

Ah. There he is.

I stand at the entrance to corridor six. Down near the far end, the tall figure of the Prince stands illuminated by moonfire glow. He's got a trolley with him, and his jacket is draped across the handle. Several jars of grease are collected on the topmost rack. Sleeves rolled to his elbows, he's hard at work rubbing grease into the spine of a growling grimoire.

The sight arrests me. Seeing the Prince—master of this city, of this whole doomed island—engaged in grunt work intended for junior librarians does something to my innards. For one thing, it reinforces in an all new and visceral way just how desperately understaffed we've become. For another, it's a sign of the Prince's reduced powers, his current inability to read or write or participate in any of the more dangerous tasks of a Vespre librarian.

It's also . . . well, in truth, it's not what I would have expected of him. Of the arrogant, condescending, conceited Prince I've come to know.

I stand there under the arch, my tongue suddenly cleaved to the roof of my mouth. I could still duck out of here; he seems unaware of my presence, after all. Now that I'm here, I'm not sure I have the courage to follow through on my purpose.

I've just taken a backwards step, of half a mind to slip away around the bend, when the Prince looks up. One eyebrow slides up his forehead, but he continues greasing the spine without pause. "Well, Darling?" he says. "Feeling an urge to get your hands dirty?"

Something about the way he says this . . . I can't quite pinpoint how, but I'm almost certain latent innuendo laces every word. That insouciant tone. That butter-won't-melt expression. Even the way his fingers work that grease into the leather. My skin prickles, and my stomach makes a strange little plunge. Quickly I brace myself, arms crossed defensively, knees locked. I will not let him win this fight before it's even begun.

"I'm going to break Danny's Obligation."

The Prince's hand stills. Just for a moment. Just long enough for those violet eyes of his to blink three times. Then he continues, massaging firmly. His other hand, the one holding the book steady, tightens, its knuckles standing out. The book growls a little louder than before, as though surprised by sudden pressure. "Are you?" he says at last.

I raise my chin a fraction. "If I fulfill the task Estrilde set for him, she will necessarily have to free him, correct?"

His lips purse slightly, the slightly fuller lower lip protruding just enough to draw my eye. He shrugs one shoulder. "Theoretically, yes. Practically speaking, no. If a breaker attempts and fails to break the Obligation, that's usually the end of things. An Obligate's master is hardly going to give his Obligate permission to go curse-breaking in turn, so it's a moot point."

I draw a careful breath. It takes all the courage I possess to speak the next words. But I cannot retreat now. I owe it to Danny. "You won't stop me."

His eyes flash, then narrow.

"You won't stop me," I repeat, "because you're Obligated to me in turn."

He sets the grimoire down on the trolley, takes up a rag, and begins meticulously wiping each finger, paying close attention to his nails. "That does put a new spin on the situation."

"Estrilde required Danny to bring her the bloodgem necklace belonging to the Eight-Crowned Queen." I take a step through the arch, into the passage. Into the same sphere of moonfire glow in which the Prince stands. "Is this possible? Can one take something from a Noswraith and bring it into this world?"

He picks at his cuticles. "Estrilde could not make a Breaker's Bargain that was impossible to fulfill. The Obligation would not hold under such a circumstance."

I take another step, then another, until nothing but the trolley separates us. "So I could do it. I could take the bloodgem necklace."

"Hardly." The Prince selects another volume from the shelf, turning the spine up to the light for inspection. "Anyone who tried to take anything from Idreloth would soon find himself devoured in a couple of quick bites. Either by the queen herself or one of her many husbands."

I shudder. I'm not exactly familiar with the Eight-Crowned Queen, though I recall her name from my lessons with Andreas. All I know for certain is that as a Greater Noswraith, she is far more dangerous than any of those beings I encountered on my recent jaunt into the Nightmare Realm.

"There must be some way to do it," I murmur, then tilt my head slightly, peering up at the Prince's illuminated face. "And you know how it could be done."

He turns his back sharply, snaps the book shut, and places it on the shelf. It rumbles threateningly and nearly wriggles its way off, but he firmly pushes it between two other volumes and gives it a warning tap with one finger. It settles down, and the Prince's finger trails on to the next book over. "You're going to get yourself killed,

Darling," he says without looking my way. "A shameful waste of a good librarian. And just when I find myself rather shorthanded. I'm afraid I cannot let you go running off on these fool's errands."

"Really?" I grip the trolley's sides, leaning over the pots of grease. "Are you going to Oblige me to give it up?"

He turns sharply, his gaze locked with mine. "Don't tempt me."

I push harder, rolling the trolley toward him so that it butts against his hip. "Weren't you the one urging me to be brave? Urging me to stop hiding, to own my power?"

"I meant that more in a save-the-worlds-from-ultimate-disaster sense, not a throw-your-life-away-for-the-sake-of-a-lover sense."

"Danny is not my lover."

I wish I could kick myself for speaking so quickly. No sooner do the words left my mouth than the Prince rounds on me, grabs his side of the trolley, and leans over, his face close to mine. "Indeed? Because from the way I see it, that brother of yours, those children you claim to love, the whole city of Vespre . . . all of them cease to matter in the face of one handsome young mortal for whom you feel an unwarranted burden of responsibility. You'd risk your life—thus risking all of theirs—for *his* sake."

My breath tightens in my chest. "How can I just go about my business, knowing he's suffering? I can't. It would eat me alive."

"Learn to live with it."

I shake my head. "Besides, it's not just about Danny. There's his sister . . . my brother . . . they both depend on him."

"Time for them to strap on their boots and fend for themselves like the rest of us."

I hate him. In that moment, I hate him more than I ever thought it possible to hate a living soul. More than I ever dreamed of hating my father. More than I ever managed to hate Estrilde or Lodírhal. I hate him for standing there, for speaking such callous words. I won't hear it. I won't! I won't let him twist me, persuade me, push me from my chosen course.

Letting go of the trolley, I back up three steps and draw myself as straight as I can, refusing to break his gaze. "It's not just Kitty and Oscar. It's the children. All of the children at Westbend Charity. Danny makes a difference there."

"And you—you, yourself, Clara Darlington—are responsible for all of them."

It's the first time he's used my proper name. Until this moment, I wasn't convinced he knew it. He's always acted as though I don't matter enough to bother remembering such a paltry detail. The shock of those two words falling from his lips is enough to stop me cold.

But I recover and force an answer between tense lips. "I am responsible for what has happened to Danny."

"You are not. You told him not to come after you. It was his choice to ignore you."

"I . . . I've . . ." How can I go on? Shame floods my face, and it's all I can do to not turn away and hide from his gaze. I don't want to explain. I don't want to admit how I've led Danny on all these years. How, afraid of causing hurt, I've gone on letting him hope.

Because I needed him. I needed him to watch over Oscar. Because he and Kitty were my only two connections in that world.

A small part of my brain tries to whisper: *You're not seeing rightly.* Maybe not. But I don't care.

"I won't explain myself to you." I face the Prince, my voice clear and firm. "I will help my friend in whatever way I can. And so . . ." I hesitate, licking my lips. But I've come this far; I must push on. "And so I would be much obliged if you would tell me how I might successfully retrieve the bloodgem necklace from the Eight-Crowned Queen."

The magic summoned to life at those simple words shocks through my being. It lashes out like a whip between me and the Prince. I can almost see the sparking energy wrap around his throat, squeezing tight. I've never been on this end of the Obligation before. It's thrilling in a way I cannot possibly describe. Thrilling, and sickening. I'm horror-struck to realize the power I have over the will of another sentient being, a power which the fae indulge with such ease, but which my very soul finds repugnant. Part of me wants to take it back. To break the Obligation, to apologize, to retreat.

But I hold the Prince's gaze. "Well? What is your answer?"

He still clings to the trolley. But he no longer looks as though he will spring right over it in a single bound. The tension in his arms and shoulders is different now, as though he's fighting with everything he has to keep himself upright. I know that battle. I've fought it myself. The resistance to Obligation can be excruciating, particularly when your Obliege is looking straight into your eyes.

Finally, he shakes his head and stands upright, breathing out a long sigh. All resistance has melted away; I can feel it right through that magical connection between us. He's given in.

Part of me wishes he hadn't. Part of me wishes he'd fought harder.

"You shouldn't try to steal the bloodgem." His voice is cold, distant. "You can never hope to succeed that way. Instead you must bargain for it. You must offer Idreloth something she wants more."

"Such as?"

"Such as her missing head."

"Her head?" My stomach clenches. "What . . . ?" I'm not certain what I'm asking. "She's headless?"

"Hardly. The Eight-Crowned Queen requires heads enough for all those crowns. But she lost one a while back."

"How?"

His jaw hardens. But the Obligation has him in full compliance now. "It was one of the more disastrous invasions on Vespre Library. One Lord Vokarum of Noxaur was convinced he'd landed on a way to accomplish what no fae mage in the long history of Eledria has ever managed before: controlling a Noswraith. It was . . ." He hesitates, his expression turning bitter. "It was a particularly repulsive spell. To work it, Vokarum journeyed to every court of Eledria, and in each new location found a maiden. Pure and virginal, of course, every one of them. He convinced them to marry him, bed him, and then kill themselves for his sake, thus breaking the marriage bond."

Shock hits me like a kick to the gut. "Why would he do something like that?"

"To create a powerful talisman—a spell of unbinding. Magic of the very blackest variety. The deaths of his wives were many and varied. The more pain involved, the greater the power in their spilled blood." The Prince passes a hand over his face. Part of me hopes he won't go on. But the Obligation stands, so he must. "Vokarum collected a drop of blood from each dead wife and placed them into a black crystal. This he set in a necklace of black chain, which he brought with him when he infiltrated my library.

"We were understaffed then—as we so often are—and my resources were stretched too thin. As a result, Vokarum made it to the vaults unimpeded. I don't know whether the Eight-Crowned Queen was his intended victim, or if he selected her at random. All I know for sure is that he entered the Nightmare Realm. Vokarum was, as you may have guessed, *ibrildian*: part human. Not a great part, but enough that he could read the grimoires and venture into the worlds contained therein.

"We did as was our practice. Upon discovering him standing over the spellbook, we locked the door and waited. Soon enough, we guessed, he would simply fall over dead. Then we'd clear out the corpse, reaffirm the binding, and go about our business.

"Instead some twelve hours after discovering the break-in, there was a terrible pounding on the door from the inside. When we looked, Vokarum, was there. He had one of the Eight-Crowned Queen's heads in his hands. He begged to be let out, and one of my librarians—a kindhearted but foolish fellow by the name of Fonroy—did just that. The Noxaurian lord fell out of the chamber.

"Fonroy was promptly impaled through the heart by the claws of one of the Queen's husbands, escaped from the Nightmare. The surviving librarians and I were hard pressed to contain both Idreloth and her dearly beloved horde. Her binding spell was well and truly broken. When the dust finally settled, and those of us who had survived had the wherewithal to look around, Vokarum had already fled. Along with Idreloth's head.

"We pieced together the story over time. Apparently the fool intended to use that cursed bloodgem to break the Noswraith's binding and set her free. Somehow, he thought she would, in gratitude, devote herself to him, even as he'd convinced all his poor sad wives to do.

"In a twist of fate, however, Idreloth accepted the gift and then turned her husbands upon the giver. Vokarum was only just fast enough to cut off one of her heads. He held it aloft, still screaming, and warded off her husbands long enough to escape back to this world with his prize."

"But how could he?" I ask, puzzled. "How could he take part of a Noswraith out of the Nightmare? I thought it was impossible."

"It should be, yes. The only explanation I have is that the gift of the bloodgem required a sacrifice of some sort. While Idreloth was unwilling to offer her love and devotion, she had to give something in order to possess it. Though I doubt it was a willing exchange. In fact, I'm sure she'd give the necklace up in a trice to reclaim her lost head." The Prince folds his arms and leans against the shelf, ignoring the grumbling grimoires as they recoil from him. "So there you have it, Darling. If you want that necklace, you must bargain for it, and the only bargain that will suffice is the original bargain that caused all this mess in the first place. A head for the necklace; a necklace for the head. Are you satisfied?"

"Yes."

I realize my mistake the moment the word leaves my mouth. If I had said no and pushed harder, I may have continued leaning into the Obligation. As it is, that power between us dissipates almost at once, vanishing like sparks in the night. I gape at the Prince, dumbfounded and stupid.

He smiles slowly. "Now the tables are turned. You cannot Oblige me again until I have enforced my will upon yours." He pushes up from the shelf and moves toward me, sidestepping the trolley. Soon he stands within a pace of me and bows his head until his eyes are level with mine. "And I won't." With that, he straightens and continues on his way out of the passage, leaving his trolley, his grease pots, and the books behind.

And I stand frozen in place, my heart pounding, my stomach twisting, wondering what in the names of all the good gods I've just done.

25

I SIT AT MY DESK THE FOLLOWING DAY, STARING AT THE
pile of grimoires gathered from the book lift. They all need
rebinding. Some of them stir dangerously, and I can feel the
containment spells disintegrating. None of the nightmares
trapped within are particularly dangerous, however. So I merely
tap the covers smartly with the handle of my quill blade and bid
them be still. I need to think. And think and think some more.

There are no two ways around it. I know what I must do:
convince the Prince to help me. Which he won't do without an
obligation. Which I cannot oblige unless he enforces his obligation
first. Which he has staunchly refused to do.

But what if . . .?

I trail the plume of my pen beneath my nose, my upper lips
twisting with thought. What if I force his hand? After all, he can't

even make me stay and work at the library day after day unless he enacts my Obligation. I could just leave.

I rub a hand across my face. Why did I have to think that thought? I can't leave. I can't! Obligation or no Obligation, I have responsibilities here.

Responsibilities that were thrust upon you, a traitorous voice whispers in the back of my mind. *Not your choice. Not your will.*

Oscar is waiting for me back home. Alone. Suffering. *He* is my responsibility. And if the Prince isn't going to make me stay on at Vespre, I ought to return to my brother. It's the only thing that makes sense. Only, can I bear to go and leave Danny behind? No. I must at least attempt to free him. Which means, I must convince the Prince to help me. Which means . . .

Growling suddenly, I grab the topmost grimoire on my stack, pull it to me, and get to work. For the rest of the day and late into the evening, I apply myself to my usual exhausting array of library tasks: bindings, reshelving, strengthening of spines, scouring of bookwyrms, and more. I inspect the shelves on the west side of the sixth floor and find several potentially compromised volumes that I lug back to my desk and secure as well.

These tasks complete, I venture in search of Andreas. He's just making his way down to the lower vaults to work on one of the Greater Noswraith spells. At my offer to assist him, he gives me a suspicious look through his round spectacles but ultimately agrees. Working together, we rebind a wretched nightmare known as The Haggard, securing its spell in record time.

"Thank you, Miss Darlington," Andreas says when we exit the vault and he turns the heavy lock. "I wasn't looking forward to that particular encounter. It went much better than I anticipated."

"Happy to help," I answer with a smile. We make our way back to the book lift, our footsteps illuminated by the lantern Andreas carries. "You're on night shift tonight, is that not so?"

He grunts.

"Unless I'm mistaken, it's your third time in five nights."

"That's the way of it when we're short-staffed like this." Andreas shrugs and opens the lift gate for me to step in ahead of him. Leaving his lantern behind, he enters after me, shuts the gate, and turns the lever. We begin our slow, creaking ascension. "We all must do our part."

I seize my opportunity. "Let me take your shift tonight, Mister Cornil."

He blinks at me again, the light of passing lanterns glinting off his spectacles. "Why?"

"I want to do my part. I'm quite capable of managing a shift on my own you know. You and Mister Silveri seem to think you must cover the entire library yourselves, but my training is practically complete. I know all the Greater Noswraith names by now, and most of the minor. Even those I don't know, I should have skill enough to temporarily bind at need." He looks ready to resist, but I press on. "Please, Mister Cornil. The stacks have been quieter than usual lately. Now is as good a time as any for me to prove myself. Let me take your shift, and you can take mine tomorrow."

Andreas chews the inside of his cheek. He doesn't answer until the lift has creaked and groaned its way almost to the top floor. Finally, he says, "If it's all right with Mister Silveri, it's all right with me."

We find Mixael at his desk, as harried and exhausted as ever. He casts us a bewildered look when we present our plan to him. In the end, however, he merely waves an ink-stained hand and utters a hurried, "Fine! Sure! Whatever you like! Just play havoc with my careful schedule and see if I notice!"

He bows back over his work without another word. Andreas and I take that as a "yes," and he retires for the night soon after. Two hours later, Mixael wanders over to my desk. "Are you certain you're all right, Miss Darlington?"

"Yes, quite." I smile and indicate my mostly clear desktop. "I've finished all the most immediate bindings and intend to spend my night walking the stacks from fifth through ninth floor. Is that acceptable to you?"

He's reluctant, but I can see in his eyes the desire to trust me, to lean on me. To know that he and Andreas have at least one more fully equipped ally in this hopeless battle they wage. They won't know for sure until they try me, though. I hold my chin high, meet his gaze with clear confidence. At last, he nods, wishes me a good night, and staggers off to his own rooms somewhere in the palace, hopefully for a restful sleep.

The library settles into a deeper quiet. Subdued, but subtly menacing. Like a tiger twitching as it dozes in the sun.

I take my satchel, book, and quill with me, along with a moonfire lantern as I walk the stacks. It's a tedious job. One's attention might all too easily drift away, missing a potentially compromised volume. If you want to survive in Vespre Library, you must remain alert, especially those nights when you're on your own as I am now.

Only two small books give me trouble. The first one I find trying to eat its way into the back of the bookshelf and escape through the wall—a hopeless task, if it only knew it, for nothing but layer upon layer of stone lies on the other side of the wooden slats. I pull it from the shelf, read through the binding, and seal it with its name on the final page. The book grumbles, its leather cover rippling like skin under my hand as I push it back into place. But it won't try that particular trick again anytime soon.

One floor down, another book has a go at me. It hides behind two larger volumes as I walk past, then springs from the shelf, lands in a heap of pages, and rises in the form of an awful flaky-skinned white monster on four legs. Thankfully I heard the initial *thunk*. In a trice, I whirl around, whip out my quill, and have a new binding scrawled out before the spindly nightmare can gather its ungainly limbs for a spring. Thank the gods I knew its name.

I fetch the now quiet volume and place it back on its shelf along with the new binding I've just written. I'm still checking to make certain the series is in proper order when a voice speaks behind me: "Well done."

I turn, my hand resting on grimoire spines. Swallowing against the tightness in my throat, I toss hair out of my eyes and force a smile. "It was simple enough. That wraith was not well formed."

The Prince approaches, one hand resting on the curved rail around the open center of the citadel. He steps into the glow of the nearest lantern, which reveals him rather more clothed than usual. His collar is tied, his double-breasted jacket buttoned to his throat. He looks a proper gentleman for once in his life. He might even be received in Kitty's front parlor if he behaved himself.

Standing across from me, he leans back against the rail and crosses his arms. The rail itself scarcely comes up as high as his waist, and if he leaned just a little too far, he'd surely go tumbling into the darkness waiting below. "Your skills have greatly improved in the last week," he says after a long, silent regard.

I mirror his stance, crossing my own arms and leaning my shoulder against a narrow panel separating two bookshelves. "You were right. Once my memory returned, everything got . . . easier." And harder. But I don't want to admit that. I don't want to admit how images of my father's gruesome end haunt me in the small hours of the night. I don't want to admit how the memory sends jolts of power burning through my veins, itching for escape at my fingertips. I don't want to admit any of it. Not to him. So I merely hold his gaze.

He tips his head back slightly, looking at me from beneath dark lashes. "Andreas was listed on the night-shift schedule."

"We traded," I reply to the unspoken question.

"Why?"

"He looked tired. More tired than usual." I hesitate before adding, "And I am not."

His expression is disbelieving. "I hope you're not planning to do something particularly foolish."

"I hope I'm not either." With that, I push away from the wall, adjust the set of my satchel strap, and continue to walk the floor. There is little point in pursuing this conversation. My path is set, my course decided. It remains to be seen how he will respond once he realizes my intentions.

"Wait."

The single word reaches out to grab me from behind, like fingers pinching my elbow. I stop, draw a breath. Then turn back to face him. "What?"

"By now, you know the truth. You can't ignore it, no matter how you pretend to." He uncrosses his arms and approaches me, one slow step after another, but stops several paces away. He's left the light of the nearest lantern, and his face is hidden in shadows. "Why do you stay, Darling?"

"I . . ." I stop, lick my lips. "I don't know what you're asking."

"Why do you stay here? In Vespre? You must have realized long ago that you could leave whenever you wished. Initially I thought I would use the Obligation to keep you here. But as time has passed, I've become more certain that I never could." He steps closer still, into the lantern light, which plays across the sharp planes of his face and lights up the depths of his eyes. "How could I enforce my will over a spirit like yours? To do so would be to crush that which is brightest and most beautiful."

I should go. I should pivot where I stand and run from here.

But I don't.

"I never thought I would say this," he continues. His steps are so fluid, so graceful, bringing him ever nearer, inexorable as the tide. "I never thought I would be glad to fall under Obligation to you. To find myself in your thrall. But I prefer this."

He stops. Only a single step separates us now. How easily he could reach out, how easily he could fold me in his arms, crush me against him. Instead he merely lifts his hand and rests a crooked finger beneath my chin, tilting my reluctant gaze up to his. "So tell me, Darling: why? Why do you stay on at the library? Most would run the moment they realized they could. Is it the children?"

My lips move soundlessly for a moment before I can push out the words: "Of course."

"I don't think so."

"No, it is. I love them. Truly."

"But you know they're better off with their own kind. That's why you've worked so hard to establish a connection with the low priestess. Don't think I haven't noticed. You may love them and they you, but you hardly see them. Your day-to-day duties take you away from them. So no." He shakes his head slowly. "I believe you care for them. But now that you've seen them settled in my house, you could wash your hands of the whole situation and walk away with a clear conscience."

"That just goes to show what little you know of love."

"Oh? You think I know little of love, do you?" His hand drops from my face. His fingers find mine in the shadows between us, drawing my hand up, pressing it against his breast. "Why don't you try me?" he whispers, his breath warm against my forehead. "Command me to do something, Darling. Anything."

"I can't." The words emerge in a whisper. "It's your turn."

"But I've already told you I won't force my will on you. Go ahead. Command me. See what I will do for you."

"Fine." I lift my eyes from the sight of my own pale hand pressed against his blue jacket. My gaze locks hard with his. "Help me save Danny."

Fire snaps in the depths of his pupils. His grip on my hand tightens almost to the point of pain. "I won't help you get yourself killed."

"Then get out of my way."

For a moment, he does not move. Not a breath stirs the air between us as we stare into each other's eyes, each waiting for the other to break.

Finally, he takes a step back. "I wish you a pleasant night, Darling. Don't hesitate to ring the bell if the nightmares nipping at your heels prove more than you can manage on your own."

With that, he turns and strides away. I watch him retreat around the curve, stepping from lanternlight into shadow and back again. At last I hear the ring of footsteps on metal as he climbs the spiral stair, leaving me alone among the grimoires. I let out a breath, close my eyes.

And try not to think just how close I'd come to commanding him to kiss me.

When six bells rings at last, signaling the end of the night shift, Andreas returns, looking refreshed. He finds me on the seventh floor, walking the stacks, and thanks me. "How did you fare last night?"

"Oh, it was uneventful." I refuse to think of the Prince's intense violet eyes gleaming at me by lanternlight.

Mixael arrives soon after, barely managing more than a grunt of greeting before he dives into the labor that all too easily overwhelms him. I stand in the library entrance, looking back at him slumped over his desk. Guilt pricks my conscience. What I'm about to do will certainly not help either Mixael or Andreas in their efforts. But I don't have a choice.

I return to my rooms directly. Though I want more than anything to lie down on my bed, at least for a little while, I don't dare. I could too easily sleep the hours away. I must try to accomplish my purpose before my next shift at the library begins.

So instead I change my gown, make certain I have both my quill and a fresh blank book stored in my satchel, then make my way across the hall to the children's room. Har, Dig, and Calx have already gone to their day's training with Khas, but Lir and Sis are both present. Sis is hard at work on a delicate *gubdagog*, small enough to suspend from her own four fingers and thumb. Lir is grumbling and straightening and tidying. Both turn immediately to greet me when I enter, Sis with a smile, Lir with a scowl. Sis tosses her tangle of threads aside without a second thought and throws herself at me with open arms.

"And how are we doing today?" I ask.

"Well enough," Lir responds with a sigh. "This one cannot be made to stop with the tangles! It's enough to drive me mad."

"Don't stop her," I answer quickly, smiling down at the child, who has wrapped herself around my knees and seeks to knock me over. I've learned to brace myself against Sis's more aggressive affections, however, and hold my ground. "Let her make as many tangles as she likes. It keeps her happy." I haven't yet told Lir my suspicions about the *gubdagogs* and their meaning. Best to keep it to myself until I know more. "I'll be leaving Vespre for the day," I say instead.

"What?" Lir frowns. "Didn't you just have a day off?"

"This is something else. A mission I must accomplish. I hope it won't take more than a few hours. But if it does, will you please keep an eye on the children? Tell the boys I said goodbye and . . . and will be home soon."

Lir looks suspicious, but I paint a carefully blank smile in place, projecting ease and confidence. At last, she heaves a sigh and agrees.

Sis, however, takes more persuading. "No! No, no go!" she cries, clinging to my legs. Lir has to pry her off me and hold her tight while I escape the room. "I'll be back soon, I promise!" I tell her even as I pull the door shut behind me. I can still hear her wailing on the other side. The sound follows as I escape down the hall. Tears prick my eyes, threatening to spill over, but I blink them back firmly, grip my satchel, and stride on.

I've learned to navigate the twisting passages of this labyrinthine palace better than I would have believed possible a few short weeks ago. When I first arrived in Vespre, I'd required an escort just to safely journey from one wing to the next. How different things are now, with my power once more ascendant, my magical skills honed. I no longer fear the deeper shadows of this gloomy world.

I hasten through the twists and turns until I reach the door I seek. It's nearly hidden in the wall, but I've learned to see it and don't hesitate before knocking. A few moments pass. I knock again.

Finally the door opens. The Prince stands in the opening. He wears no shoes or stockings, and his breeches are loose around the knees. Naturally, he hasn't got a shirt on, only a robe of burgundy silk, belted at the waist. The front hangs open to reveal his chiseled physique. He's still more fae than human now, so everything about him is infuriatingly exaggerated and beautiful.

His eyes widen with surprise. "Darling?"

I don't allow myself a second glance. Keeping my chin high, I hold his gaze. "I'm going to Noxaur," I say.

"You're *what?*"

"I'm going to pay a call upon Lord Vokarum. I will bargain with him and claim the head of the Eight-Crowned Queen. As you suggested."

A muscle in his jaw ticks. "You're mad."

"Perhaps. But I won't leave Danny to suffer at the hands of Estrilde. I won't leave his soul to be chipped away to nothing but a battered stump. I'm going to save him. Or I'm going to die trying."

"Do you realize how selfish you're being?"

I blink three times. But that's all the reaction I will permit myself. "Perhaps it's time I was selfish," I answer. "Perhaps it's time I stopped letting other people determine the shape of my life." I take a step back, my shoulders straight, my spine firm. "Will you help me?"

For a moment, I think he's going to lunge from that doorway and grab me by the arms. I almost hope he will. Instead he says only, "I will not."

"Then will you forbid me to go?"

His eyes narrow. I see the moment when he recognizes the trap I've set. I make myself wait, holding my breath, counting away the seconds. "Darling—" he begins.

I turn on my heel and march away. My ears strain, eager to hear some barked command, even an imperative, "Wait!"

But it doesn't come.

I reach the end of the passage, slip around the corner, and leave the Prince behind.

26

I SEND FOR THE MORLETH CARRIAGE TO BE BROUGHT around. The whole while I stand on the front porch awaiting its arrival, I expect the Prince to come bursting out, shouting commands, ordering me to stop.

But he doesn't. The carriage rolls up. I descend the steps. The troll coachman helps me inside and shuts the door. I sit forward on the bench, pull back the curtain, and peer out the window up to the open doors above. Empty. Dark.

He's calling my bluff.

The carriage lurches into motion, jostling me back into my seat. I grip the upholstery with tense fingers, my jaw clenched tight. The joke's on him, of course. Because I'm not bluffing. I'm going to do this. One way or another.

A sudden stabbing pain in my head makes me grimace and press a hand against my right eye. Why does it hurt so? Like someone's jabbed a red-hot needle straight through into my brain. I groan and curl into a little ball of misery on the bench, waiting for the pain to pass. All the while, a voice whispers in my head:

You're not seeing rightly.

I'll teach you to see as I do.

He really loves you . . . you know . . .

I squeeze my eyes tighter. In the darkness behind my eyelids, I see Danny's face again. So broken. So defeated. I know too well how many Obligates never survive to the ends of their Obligations. The Law of Obligation forbids masters and mistresses from directly causing their Obligates harm. But though the fae are dangerously law-abiding, they are all too adept at finding workarounds. They may not harm their Obligates, so they simply allow them to fall into situations that will ultimately break them down, driving them to harm themselves. Like Mary West. Like countless others.

The terms of Obligation are not intended to favor the Obligates.

By the time the carriage touches down, the pain in my head has reduced to a murmur. I unfold my body, and when the coachman opens the door, I'm ready to take his hand and step down onto the long pier leading to the Noxaur shore. The Between Gate stands on the cliffs not far away.

"Excuse me," I say, turning suddenly to the coachman. "Do you know the way to Lord Vokarum's domain?"

The troll's rocky brow crinkles like a tectonic shift. "Lord Vokarum?" He points with a big square hand. "*Hirak!* That be

Vokarum's domain you see, *gruaka* girl." His huge head shakes heavily on his big broad shoulders. "But a little'un like you no ought go there. Is bad."

A shudder creeps its way up my spine. All this time, we've lived adjacent to this wife-killing maniac? I suppose the denizens of the Doomed City are hardened to all the horrors Eledria has to offer. But there's something weirdly *safe* about Noswraiths. They cannot help themselves. They did not create themselves but simply are what their makers called into being. If they are savage and bloodthirsty, chaotic and destructive, at least they are not malicious. To be malicious, one must have the capacity for good and choose otherwise. That is true evil.

I grip the strap of my satchel, facing down the pier. For a moment, my courage nearly fails me. It takes everything I have to not climb back into that carriage and bid the driver take me home. "Will you wait?" I say instead.

"*Korkor, gruaka* girl."

The coachman gives me a moonfire lantern. And a good thing too. Though I've grown used to the gloom of Vespre, perpetual twilight could not prepare me for the true depths of Night. Once I've marched to the end of the pier, stepped onto the rocky beach, and climbed up to higher, firmer soil, the sky overhead abruptly darkens. It's so stark that when I look up, I'm almost certain I can see a line above me where the purple ends and the deep blue indigo begins. Were it not for the lantern, I'm not certain I'd have the courage to continue.

As it is, I have no excuse. I trudge into the dark realm, leaving the beach, the pier, and the ocean behind. I toss the Between Gate only one longing glance. I must fight the urge to run to it, to turn the dial to my own world, to step through into my home kitchen. But that is not my path. Not yet.

Putting my head down, I march on into the Night Realm. The landscape beyond the beach is flat and open. Seeing numerous tall, twisted trees with trunks like thick vines all wound together and heavy branches shrouded in waxy-looking leaves the size of dinner plates, I give them wide berth. I don't know what they are, but they give off a subtle impression of sentience. And menace. Best not to take chances.

I need to find a road. That's the first goal. Noxaur is, as I recall, a realm broken into numerous fiefdoms, with only a few major cities. But Lord Vokarum must have a seat of power—a fortress or a citadel, a palace even. Something to which a road will lead. If I can find one.

For the moment, there's nothing but wide, empty, rolling landscape. I feel terribly exposed under the starry sky. Maybe I ought to douse my light. It does feel a bit like a swinging signal, alerting every dangerous, crawling, shadowy thing hidden within this apparently barren landscape to my presence. But what if I can't get it going again? What if I end up trapped in this world, alone in the dark? I've never been particularly afraid of the dark. But I've also never before taken a stroll through a world of perpetual night.

A family of waddling fat creatures scuttles across the path of light cast from my lantern. They hiss, eyes flashing in the glow, before hurrying on, dragging bristling tails behind them. I freeze in place, heart pounding. Whatever they were, they don't seem to crave the flesh of a human maid. Not at the moment, at least.

When the sound of scurrying feet fades, I continue climbing the slope of a small hill. From its crown I gaze down into a little valley. Ah! There's the path I've been seeking. Not a broad road, but a narrow dirt trail. Still, it's distinct enough that I believe it was made on purpose, not by chance. It must lead somewhere. Maybe not to the doorstep of a powerful Noxaurian lord. But somewhere.

I pick up my pace. My lantern light reflects off pale hides, and swift shapes that look rather like pint-sized deer spring away. Noxaur has not yet proven anywhere near as dangerous as I've always imagined. Nothing bloodthirsty or savage as far as the eye can see . . . which, granted, isn't all that far. But my eyes are slowly adjusting, and soon even the stars seem brighter than before.

No sooner does the thought pass through my head than I hear the first long, lonely howl.

It doesn't sound like a wolf. At least, not how I imagine a wolf would sound. I'm a city girl, so I haven't much experience to draw from. Nonetheless, I can't help the shuddering idea that it sounds more like someone pretending to be a wolf.

I swing my lantern toward the sound. But there's nothing to be seen. Whatever it was—whoever it was—is nowhere near. Best to mind my own business.

With some relief, I reach the path and follow it further

inland. Another lonely howl sounds, still far off. Shivers ripple along the back of my neck, but I give my head a quick shake and hurry onward. The sound of running water tickles my ears just before a broad river comes into sight. The path leads straight to a white bridge, beautifully crafted with a strange, angular design to the rails and treads. It arches over the river, and on the far side I can see that the path widens into a proper road complete with paving stones.

Something about this doesn't feel right. Why would a dirt track lead to a bridge this well constructed? It's almost as though . . . as though it knows what I'm looking for. As though it lies in wait. For me. My footsteps slow, slow. Stop. I don't know why, but I'm almost certain something lurks beneath that bridge. Something bad. And hungry.

I back up, biting my lower lip. There's no way in the nine hells I'm crossing that bridge. I look downriver, to my left. A gloomy forest stands there. Not the unsettling waxy-leafed trees I'd seen closer to the ocean. These seem to be coniferous, with spindly needles standing out in stark silhouette against the starlight. At ground level, the wood is dark and gloomy, and another one of those lonely howls echoes from within its depths.

Shaking my head, I turn the other way, upriver, toward a field of tall grass shining with pale flowers. They seem to glitter gently, radiating their own inner light. I can just hear a faint hum, like insects but more musical. A far more appealing prospect, and maybe I could find another way across the river if I go far enough.

I take a step. And stop.

What are you thinking, Clara? You've read enough stories to know better!

The safer way is *always* a trap. Something lurks in those tall grasses, beneath those gently waving flowers. Or perhaps the flowers themselves are the peril, and once I'm in among them, they'll lull me into an enchanted sleep and feast upon my sleeping body. No, no, I can't go that way. I certainly can't cross the bridge. And I can't go back, not when I've barely started.

It's the dark and dreadful forest for me. Huzzah.

I take the plunge into the trees, determined to stay as close to the river as possible. Maybe I'll find a fallen log that will serve as a bridge? Or a narrow place where I can contrive a way across? Either way, it feels safer somehow to stay close to the water. It makes me feel as though I know what I'm doing, as though there's some purpose in my wandering.

Another howl. This time answered almost immediately by a second.

I stop in my tracks, heart thudding. Those voices were closer this time. Have I made a mistake? Maybe I should have risked that flower-strewn meadow or that incongruous bridge. Maybe . . . maybe . . . "Blight it!" I turn sharply.

The river. It's gone. It was there just a moment ago, and now it's not. Did I inadvertently wander away from it? Or was the river never really there at all?

"Blight it, blight it," I mutter, as close to proper cursing as I'll allow myself. I draw a steadying breath, let it out slowly, then begin to turn, intending to retrace my steps. But no, that's a mistake as well. After all, without proper landmarks, how will I be able to tell if I've turned all the way? It's probably better to just keep going. To see if I can't find the river again, or at least a far side to this forest.

Gripping my lantern hard, I forge on three paces. I haven't taken a fourth before smoke begins creeping in. It's silent, coiling, curling, and faintly green in the moonfire glow. There's a subtle stench, a little sweet, a little sour. Is it some sort of incense? I wave a hand before my face, trying to clear my view. The air is so thick now, my lanternlight cannot penetrate it. I can't see the trees surrounding me anymore. There's a strange sense of *space* all around, just on the other side of the smoke screen. I'm afraid to move, afraid I might step over the edge of something, plummet, and fall.

Another howl. Echoing. Lusty. Answered soon after by a second and a third. Then a fourth and a fifth, a whole chorus of howling. By now I'm quite certain those aren't wolves. The tone and timbre are wrong. Those aren't animal voices at all.

I start to run. I can't help myself. Blind instinct takes over, and I race into the smoke, feet thumping, heart pounding, lantern swinging. The green coils snake around my limbs, into my nostrils, my panting mouth. It tastes of sugary icing and honey and death. My eyes burn, tears streaming, and my head swims.

A branch catches my foot. With a gasp and a grunt, I hit the ground hard. My lantern globe shatters. Moonfire flashes and goes out. I lie in pitch darkness.

Gritting my teeth, I push myself upright. I won't give in so easily! Staggering forward, I walk right into a tree. With a gasp, I wrap my arms around it for support. Only to realize it's not a tree.

I look up.

Two blazing red eyes gaze down at me. The smoke draws back like a veil, revealing a half mask of white bone set with cruel, curved horns. Full lips part in a smile, revealing dagger-sharp teeth.

"Well, well, well." The voice purrs, the language unknown but transformed via enchantment the moment it touches my ear. "Look, my friends! Look what we've smoked out."

Choking on a cry, I unwrap my arms and stagger back, only to fall into another pair of waiting arms. I scream and struggle, kicking, elbowing, flailing. "What a prize!" a voice over my head crows. "Our lord will be delighted."

I'm flung forward, staggering, to land in another pair of arms. Pushing back, I lash out with one hand only to have my wrist caught in a viselike grip. "Don't scratch, little kitten," a woman's voice croons. "You need to save your strength. Sleep now."

A hand wraps around my face, covering my mouth and nose. I struggle harder, try to bite, to scream, any resistance I can manage. But it's useless. Shadows close in. The last thing I remember is the hand falling away, a sack coming down over my head, and the stomach-plunging sensation of being lifted off my feet.

Then my ears are full of howls. Followed by oblivion.

THE PRINCE

THERE'S A PILE OF WORK WAITING ON MY DESK. Small tasks, none of them a strain on the human magic which I dare not use. Covers in need of oiling, spines in need of stitching. New volumes to be bound and pressed and made ready for the spells they will contain. More than enough to keep me busy for hours.

Yet it all lies untouched as I pace my office. From the window to the door and back again.

She's gone. She's gone, fool girl, on her fool's errand.

I know what she's trying to do. I know how she intends to provoke me. But I'm not in the habit of letting myself be manipulated by human women. If she must go, then let her! And let her discover her own error. Does she truly think she can meet with a monster like Vokarum? Does she truly think she can beg, barter, or cajole him?

He'll kill her. He'll kill her, and he'll laugh as he does it.

I pass a hand over my face. My breath is labored, ratcheting in my throat.

She cannot help herself. It's not in her nature to give up on those for whom she cares. It's not in her nature to flinch in the face of fear or personal danger. She would rather suffer than let one she loves suffer.

Though she'll leave me suffering agonies without a second thought.

"Gods damn and blight her," I growl, coming to a halt in front of my office door. Did I really think she cared about me? Did I really think I counted in the number of those she considers worth the sacrifice of her own self? I'm not so vain. I know she despises me. Sometimes I think . . . hope . . . But that's just damned idiocy. I am her master. Her enslaver. I bought her and dragged her away to this world against her will, forcing her to fight in this ancient, hopeless war. And I'll admit, I took pleasure in doing so. In watching her flail.

How she surprised me, though. At every turn of this little dance, she's surprised me. With her courage, her tenacity. Her stubborn will to master secret arts which have bested far greater mages than she over the centuries. She has fought by my side with that same reckless courage which everything in my being even now decries.

What would I do? Would I change her if I could? Force her into some more manageable shape? Something I could control, something I could protect. Something I could keep by my side forever.

No. For to do so would be destroy everything in her that draws me with such irresistible force.

With a snarl, I turn and march back to the window. Leaning over the sill I gaze out across the city. The magicked view of Aurelis has long since faded, and I never bothered to replace it. Instead the hazy dark shore of Noxaur lies on the far horizon under its blanket of eternal night.

She cannot survive what she's walking into it. I know what awaits her. The fear, the horror. The slaughter.

"Damn," I whisper. The barest breath of a sound.

Then I turn to my desk, reaching first for quill and book. But no. No, such weapons will do me no good. Not cursed as I am. I need something sharper.

I tear my sword down from its mount on the wall.

CLARA

27

I COME RELUCTANTLY TO MY SENSES, AWARE OF multiple discomforts all at once. First, there's still smoke in my nostrils, only it no longer smells sweet. Second, I'm lying on wooden bars that dig painfully into my flesh.

Third, it's growing more uncomfortably hot by the moment. In fact, the skin of my right hand is starting to hurt.

I open my eyes. It doesn't help, for my head is still covered in scratchy sackcloth. I yank back my hand only to realize it's dangling between the thin bars on which I lie. Hastily, I draw it back through, pull it close to my body. My satchel! A little scrabbling, and I find the strap still slung over my shoulder and across my torso, the familiar weight near my hip. That's a mercy, at least. However useless they might be in this world, I still feel better, knowing I haven't lost my book and quill.

I try to push upright. The world sways sickeningly. Unsettling creaks fill my ears, and that terrible heat still rises from below. Hands shaking, I grab at the sack over my head and yank it off. My eyes are momentarily dazzled by light and spinning shadows. Blinking in mute confusion, I stare around, struggling to make sense of my surroundings.

The scene slowly comes into focus. I see almost as though I'm standing a little apart, viewing from above. As if it's a play or a story, and I'm merely a distant observer. It's the only way I can grapple with the reality in that moment: the reality of a cage woven of thin branches and lashed together with vines. Suspended and swinging some twenty feet above a pit of dancing flames.

My stomach fills with writhing, frenzied snakes. I scramble, terror driving me to clamber at the bars, frantic for some means of escape. The cage sways wildly, stopping my heart. For a moment, I'm convinced I'm tumbling, plunging into that fire.

Laughter punctuates the air. I lift my gaze to the dark figures standing just beyond the light cast from the pit. Tall, powerful figures. At first glance, my fear-addled brain thinks they're skeletons. But no, they're clad in bone armor. Skull masks cover their faces, gleaming in the firelight. Some of those masks are horned, some boast enormous, sagging jaws. Some have upper rows of long teeth, like demonic grins.

Have I fallen back into the Nightmare? No, for that would be too good to be true. In the Nightmare I have power. Here, I have none.

One of the figures steps into the ring of light. First, a huge foot with great black talon-like toenails that curve so far, they cut into the soil. A brawny leg follows, naked to the waist. He wears a loose, skin loincloth, and I don't want to speculate as to what kind of skin it's fashioned from. It doesn't look like animal hide. Skulls swing from his belt, some of them certainly human. He wears a breastplate formed of rib bones, and flat shoulder blades jut like epaulettes from his shoulders. Enormous twelve-point antlers arch from his brow, a magnificent crown. The lower half of his face is visible beneath a mask of pale bone. He's square-jawed, handsome. But when he smiles, his lips pull back to reveal file-sharpened, blood-stained teeth.

He approaches the edge of the pit, drawing near to my swinging cage. Light gleams on glossy locks of midnight hair flowing over his shoulders and illuminates the dusky color of his skin. Only now do I realize the antlers aren't part of his mask at all. They emerge from his forehead, which bulges with the extra bone necessary to support such weight. His eyes level with mine, he tilts his head, his thick, muscular neck straining slightly.

"At last." His voice rolls like distant thunder. "The goddess has heard my prayer." Yellow eyes glint, reflecting fire. He reaches out, pokes a finger through the wicker weaving. A talon nail twirls a lock of my hair. With a single twist, the razor edge cuts the lock free. It falls to the flames below. A little puff of smoke, and it is gone. Engulfed.

I scream, scrambling to the back of the cage. It tilts and sways sickeningly. I grab the bars while laughter erupts around me.

The tall fae smiles even more broadly than before. "Come!" he says, spreading his arms and looking around at his fellows. "Come closer and see the gift our goddess has bestowed upon us."

The strange figures close in, thirteen of them in total, men and women alike. Some are short, some towering. The firelight dancing across their features illuminates all different skin tones—some purple and dusky like their leader, some crimson, some blue. A few have scales, and at least one is covered in inky black fur. They draw as near as they can to the edge of the pit, their eager faces leering at me from behind their masks. I can't escape them. There's nowhere to hide from their stares, from their leers, from their long fingers reaching out to poke and prod me.

At length, however, the antlered leader speaks a word of command. His people obey at once, retreating into the darkness. Their glinting eyes reflect the firelight all around me, their gazes full of hunger. I grip my satchel hard with one hand, my other hand grasping the upper part of my cage as I face the leader.

"Human maid." The antlered one speaks in my own language now, not in fae tongue glamoured to make itself comprehensible. This is much worse. He sounds incongruously cultured and elegant, with an accent such as one would hear only in the highest-born houses of my world. "You are most fortunate among mortals," he says, "blessed by the goddess Tanyl herself and sent to me in my need and despair. Thanks to you, the Wild Hunt shall ride again!"

Howls erupt in the night. At last I know the source of those lonely voices I'd heard before. I was right: not wolves. Much worse than wolves.

The leader holds up his hands, and his people fall silent. He addresses me again, still smiling that same blood-stained smile. "The Hunt is an ancient tradition from before the dawn of time, holy and sacred to Tanyl herself. Yet we, her faithful, have been thwarted in our desire to honor her name for the last many turns of the cycle. Until tonight! Tonight, the sea breeze carried the scent of human blood across rivers and vales, awakening the senses of all those born to chase, to catch, to rend, to feast. Tonight, the grace of the goddess comes to her people once again through you, most blessed and beloved of maidens."

The heat and smoke rising from the pit is nearly unbearable. My skirts provide some protection, but I can feel my skin beginning to blister. "Please," I croak, forcing words out through the thickness of terror. "There's been some mistake. I seek Lord Vokarum."

The antlered man tilts his head. "I am Lord Vokarum. You have sought and found me. Does this not prove the truth of my words? The ways of the goddess are mysterious, for when I look upon you, I think, *She is small, pathetic, weak as a mewling kitten.* But then I think as well, *My goddess has sent her. Which means she must be worthy prey.* Tell me truthfully, little human. You are gifted with magic beyond the dreams of fae, are you not? Perhaps you are a warrior."

"No!" I answer desperately. "No, I'm no warrior. I'm a librarian."

"Ah." He licks his lips hungrily, looking round at his people. "But that is better still. Have we not heard of the power of mortal librarians? Those mighty mages who dwell across the water on the haunted isle? Long have we desired to pluck one of their number from their mysterious realm of books and letters. Long have we desired to test our skill against such power." His people murmur and mutter. Excitement mounts, churning in the atmosphere.

I try to draw myself up straight, which is difficult to accomplish in a swaying basket cage. "I will not participate in any hunt." I say, desperately trying not to let my voice quaver. "I am an Obligate of the Prince of Vespre. You threaten my life at your own peril."

"Indeed?' Vokarum's brow cannot pucker because of the bone plating, but he does look mildly perplexed for a moment. "And was it the Prince who sent you thither?"

"Yes," I answer at once, with conviction.

It's not good enough. The fae lord's smile slices across his face once more, red teeth gleaming dangerously. "An example of the human power of deceit. How delightful! Unfortunately for you, I long ago learned to scent falsehood on the lips of mortals. It is not by your Prince's will that you are here, but your own. Which means, Obligate, you have stepped beyond the protections of your Obligation."

I shake my head wildly, my courage slipping fast. "I won't do it. I won't let you hunt me."

"Indeed? Would you prefer to die now?"

With a heart-stopping creak, the basket lowers suddenly, dropping a good foot closer to the flames. A scream rips from my throat as the heat intensifies. I grip the upper bars of the cage, trying to physically climb higher, however useless it might be.

"What do you say, mortal?" Vokarum cries above the wild hyena laughter of his people. "Will you agree to the terms of our hunt?"

"Yes!" I shriek. In that moment I would have agreed to anything, positively anything, no matter how base or dreadful. The sheer relief of the cage being lifted, of the heat retreating from my trembling flesh, was worth any promise. I shudder, sweat pouring down my body and soaking through my garments as I face the sparking eyes of my captor.

He takes a step nearer, his clawed toes curling over the very lip of the pit. Leaning forward, he speaks in a low, gleeful tone. "You will flee across the Valley of Bones. One hour will be yours, no more. When the moon reaches the zenith of the sky, my sisters, my brothers, and I will set upon you with horse and spear, with arrow and blade. If you reach the Mercy Stones before we catch you, you will be declared Queen of the Hunt and showered with jewels beyond measure."

"I . . . I don't want jewels." The words rasp painfully from my throat. But I haven't fully forgotten my mission. "I want to name my prize."

Vokarum chuckles. "Very well, little mortal. Should you survive, name it you will. So long as it be within my power to grant, you shall have whatever you desire. Agreed?"

I nod. Suddenly, the cage swings to one side. I scream again, convinced it's falling. Instead it angles me over solid ground. The bottom drops out from under me, and I fall in a heap, landing hard on top of my satchel and book. The hunters laugh as I scramble to my feet and back away from the pit. My head swivels, my wild eyes struggling to see all of the dreadful figures simultaneously as they close in around me.

"That way," Vokarum says, swinging his arm to my right. I look where he indicates. We stand at the top of a steep ravine. Below is a valley full of dark patches of forest, bare rock, and a rushing silver river, bright beneath the starlight. "The Valley of Bones awaits. And there"—he raises his arm, pointing now to a series of stark black stones on the hilltop on the far side of the valley. A pale moon rises, gleaming between them, transforming their silhouettes to gigantic, jagged teeth. "Your hope, your safety, your freedom."

He smiles down at me, a voracious, lust-fueled smile that makes me stagger back three paces. His red tongue flicks out, dances across the front of his sharp teeth. "Run, little mortal. Run for your life."

I turn in place, take in the gleaming eyes of the hungry folk around me. They stamp their feet, pawing like eager horses ready to begin the race. Light from the firepit glows on the white of their bone masks. Several of them feint at me, weapons flashing, but at a bark from Vokarum they back down.

The seconds are ticking by. Each one precious, each one the difference between life and death. I stagger, stumble, catch my balance. Back away from the fire, away from those eyes, away from that still-swinging cage.

Then I turn and flee into the dark.

28

I DON'T MANAGE MORE THAN FIVE PACES BEFORE I SLIP,
fall, and tumble down the steep incline. There's nothing I can
do but fling my arms over my head, hoping I don't hit a stone
and brain myself, thus bringing this Wild Hunt to an abrupt and
ignominious end.

When I stop at last, I lie on my back, breathing hard for some
moments. My pulse thunders, nearly drowning out the echoing
laughter of the hunters above. When I peer up, I see their
silhouettes lining the ridge. Their horned heads look demonic by
the light of the red pit fire.

Gathering my limbs under me, I rise. Nothing is broken, at
least. I try to turn, to run, but for the moment, can't bring myself
to tear my gaze away from those awful figures. Will they truly
give me a full hour start? It seems too much. Surely the moment

my back is turned they'll descend upon me in a ravenous horde, driving spears through my throat, my chest, my spine.

But they don't move. They stand still as statues, their laughter faded now, their gazes intent. The whole world seems to have fallen down a deep well of silence. The only sound to be heard is the echoing thud of my own frantic heartbeat.

I wrench myself away. The fae cannot lie. I must remember that. If Vokarum said I would have an hour, an hour I must have. It's as simple as that, or so I tell myself over and over again as I pick my way down the ravine.

At first, it's too dark to see anything clearly. I'm nearly blind and convinced that one false step will send me plummeting for a second time, this time possibly never to stop. As I go, however, my eyes begin to adjust. The starlight here is much brighter than in Vespre. I can pick out details of color that should be impossible to discern. Such as the spiky flowers sprouting from between boulders and through cracks in the ravine wall. They're red. Bloodred. A color which should not be visible by starlight but which fairly pulses with vivid life before my addled gaze.

I shudder and continue, using my hands as much as my feet as I pick my way down into the valley. When I finally reach the bottom, I peer back up. The figures of the Wild Hunt still stand above me. Their eyes are fiery pinpoints. I wish I hadn't looked.

Gripping my satchel strap with both hands, I stride into the valley. At least I'd had the forethought to don a stout pair of walking shoes before setting out on this mad quest and I'm not trying to outrun the huntsmen while wearing delicate library slippers. By now, the moon has risen above the standing stones on the opposite ridge and casts its light into the valley. It's so bright, it feels almost like a blue-cast day.

I pick up my pace. Now is the time to run! All too soon, however, I come upon a great tangle of briar. I manage to slow in time not to run directly into it. Frantically, I turn first to the right, then to the left, but the briar extends far on both sides. I hate wasting precious seconds trying to figure out a way around.

Gritting my teeth, I plunge into the tangled branches. Vicious thorns tear at my flesh. I try to tell myself it'll be worse to be torn up by the Wild Hunts' blades, but it's no use. Shuddering with pain, bleeding from innumerable small cuts, I pull back again. I have no choice but to try to go around.

On pure whim alone, I turn right and start running, searching for a thin place, an opening. A clear wailing note blares out across the sky, rolls across the valley. I utter a little bleat of surprise and whirl about to stare back up the ridge. The huntsmen are still there. One stands apart from the rest, his arm upraised, an ivory horn held to his lips. Is he signaling the quarter hour? Gods spare me, surely it took no more than a handful of minutes for me to make my way down that ridge! But . . . My gaze travels back up the steep descent. A worm of dread writhes in my stomach. It probably took much longer than I'd realized.

Choking on a sob, I plunge straight into the briars. I keep my arms up to protect my face from lashing thorns, ignoring all the cuts, ignoring the pain. I have no time to waste in searching for a less painful way through that may not exist.

Maybe the gods are with me, for I find a thin place and, with a little ducking and several loud rips, emerge at last on the far side. Before me lies a stretch of open country. Long grass ripples like wind-tossed waves in the moonlight. No time to stop and wonder what danger might lurk in that grass. I run. As hard and fast as I can, my satchel slapping against my hipbone with each footfall. The laces of one shoe come undone, and I don't stop to tie them. I just keep running. The shoe flies off. I take several more running steps before, with a growl, I turn, race back, and search for it in the grass. I can't leave such an obvious token behind for the Hunt, can I? Although, I realize rather stupidly even as my hand closes around the shoe, that trail of bent and broken grass blades is already painfully clear.

Clutching the shoe to my chest, I limp-run the rest of the way across the field. A stand of trees awaits me; I plunge gratefully into their shadows. I'm obliged to slow down at once, however, for here I have only dapples of moonlight by which to navigate. Otherwise, I'm back to running blind. I pause, lean my back against a tree, and shove my foot into my shoe. My fingers shake so hard, I can't get a proper grip on the laces.

The horn sounds again. Long and low. Half an hour gone—half my time.

With a little squealing curse, I knot the laces in a snarl, shove the ends down inside the upper lip of my shoe, and stagger on.

Branches slap at my face, lash at my already thorn-torn skin. The worst of it is, I've lost sight of the distant Mercy Stones. I've only the faintest idea in which direction my destination lies. I should stop. Regroup. Make certain I don't wander too far in the wrong direction. I feel the minutes passing all too swiftly. My life could end up hanging on the threads of mere seconds.

An outcropping of stone catches my eye through the trees. Though it's to the left of my current route, I change course and hasten to it, glad of a more immediate goal. It's taller than I first realized, a great mound of rough stone, limned in moonlight. It will take me precious minutes to climb, all for the chance of a view over the treetops. It's a chance I'll have to take.

I climb swiftly. One would think my time spent in Vespre Library bowed over books would have atrophied my muscles, but in fact I've grown stronger. What with carting all those volumes up and down all those stairs, not to mention the mad sprints required when fleeing hungry Noswraiths, I'm in far better condition now than ever before in my life. Which isn't saying much, to be sure. Yet somehow I manage to reach the top of that pile of rock without breaking anything.

I dare not stand upright at the summit for fear of making myself an obvious target. Instead, clinging to the higher stones, I keep low and look around. There! The Mercy Stones on their ridge high above. Gods spare me, I was heading off in the wrong direction entirely.

A river cuts through the forest not far from me. Is it the same river I encountered earlier, before meeting Vokarum and his hunters?

It doesn't matter. What matters is that it flows in a winding track across the valley, toward the stones. If I can make my way to the river now, I can use it as a guide through this forest.

It's as good a plan as any. Though, I realize as I climb back down, it's likely the same plan used by many runners before me. How many of them successfully eluded the Wild Hunt and ended up showered with jewels? Not many, I would hazard.

I have no opportunity to devise another plan, however. By the time I shimmy back down the rocks, the third horn is sounding. My hour is almost up.

Choking back the sob rising in my throat, I stumble blindly through the trees in the direction I believe the river lies. When I finally catch the sound of running water, it's the most beautiful melody I've ever heard. I press on until the murmur becomes a roar. Suddenly I'm standing above a rushing torrent that cuts its way through rock and earth, racing in wild abandon down from the mountains above. Light radiating from the climbing moon gleams bright off pale boulders and white froth.

I can't go as fast as I would like, for the terrain is rough and uneven. At any second I expect to hear the final horn sound. I keep thinking now, now, *now*. But it doesn't sound. And it goes on not sounding. Instead, after what feels like both an age and mere minutes, a cold, clear, vibrating howl rips across the sky.

My heart stops. I turn in place, staring upriver. That sounded much closer than I would like. So close that . . . Oh gods! Gods above, spare me! They didn't sound the final horn. They didn't give me warning. Now they're on my trail and have been for I don't know how long.

A whimper burbles in my throat. I scamper too quickly for safety down a steep pile of rocks beside the waterfall. At the base of the falls, the river pools before continuing its flow. My rolling, desperate eye spies a shadowy cave on the far side of the rushing curtain of water. An overwhelming urge comes over me to duck behind the falls. To crouch in those shadows. To cover my head and take shelter until the Wild Hunt passes by. In the moment, it seems almost reasonable. Why would I not? It would give me a chance to find my breath, to cool my blistered feet, to soothe the cuts on my arms, legs, neck, and face. I could catch droplets from the falls, quench my thirst. Dredge up reserves of strength hidden deep down beneath my fear.

I sidle closer, inching my way closer to the falls. My foot reaches the edge of the pool. I hesitate. I may have to swim to get behind the water and into the cave. I'm not a good swimmer, and I—

Two slimy green hands lurch from the foam-churning water, latch hold of my foot, and pull.

THE PRINCE

M Y MORLETH EATS UP THE SKY, HOOVES TEARING through darkness as it gallops across the stretch of water dividing Vespre from the far dark shore. I do not drive it to land when we pass from the Twilit Realm into the Kingdom of Night, but keep to the air. The beast snorts sulfur, displeased by the moonlight. I dig in my heels, drive him on faster, harder.

Somewhere in the distance, a horn sounds. Long and lonely, like a lost soul howling for mercy. My gut clenches. I know that horn. Vokarum and his Wild Hunt are on the prowl. I don't have to guess who has become their prey.

The Valley of Bones yawns below me. I guide my morleth down into it. I'm familiar with the pattern of the horned lord's hunts, how he drives his victims. Clara is down there. Somewhere. And she's still alive. I would know it if she wasn't, surely.

Movement below. My gaze sharpens, my fae sight quick and keen by moonlight. I see masks. Horns. Spears. The Wild Hunt is on the prowl, eager and ravenous. I lift my gaze to the distant circle of stones on the far side of the valley. Clara's destination. But I cannot go to meet her there. I must find her now, before Vokarum and his hunters do.

I reach out along the thread that connects us—that delicate filament of soul which always seems to lead me back to her. It's too thin; I can scarcely feel it. All the grievance between us, all the hard words and hurt and frustration have strained it nearly to the point of breaking. Though still present, it cannot guide me.

A rocky promontory draws my gaze, pale among the dark trees. I circle my morleth. A figure climbs the side of it, all long and spidery limbs, hooded and cloaked in animal pelt, a set of spears strapped to its back.

With a vicious *"Jah!"* I draw my sword and urge my mount lower. The hunter sees me coming, pulls itself up onto the top of the promontory, and brandishes one of its spears. Drawing back its muscular arm, it sends the spear whistling through the air. Its aim is straight and true. It pierces my mount's chest, shattering bone, tearing flesh and sinew.

With a scream, my morleth evaporates in a puff of smoke, gone from this realm back to its own shadowy dimension. Leaving me to plummet through the air. I angle my body, control my descent, trusting to my fae grace and agility. In the blink of an eye, I turn my fall into an attack. My blade sings as it meets a deflecting spear shaft. Landing lightly, I drop, roll, avoiding the bone spearhead as the hunter seeks to skewer me.

The hunter roars, angered at its near miss. An answering roar rises in my throat as I rise and hurl myself at my enemy. All my rage, all my fear, all the terrible storm of my soul powers my arm as I hack and slice, driving that fiend to the brink of the outcropping. Mad red eyes gleam at me through the sockets of that skull mask.

I press in close, my blade poised against the monster's throat. "You're on her trail," I snarl. "Which way did she go?"

The hunter's mouth twists in a terrible leer. A purple tongue flicks out, licking hungry lips. "You're too late, lover boy. She's as good as dead!"

"Tell me, or I'll slit you from throat to groin and spill your intestines for your brothers to feast upon."

With a wild howl, the hunter hurls me off, stronger than I expect. It swipes a knife from a sheath at its thigh and lunges, the blade aimed for my face. I avoid the blow and thrust my sword arm straight and true. My weapon pierces the hunter's side, through his abdomen, and emerges out the far side.

A terrible, gurgling cry. Blood spills over the hunter's teeth. He reaches out one shaking hand, tries to wrench my grip from the sword hilt. The red light flickering in depths of those skull sockets fades, vanishes.

I yank the blade back ruthlessly and watch my enemy fall, tumbling into the trees below. Then, panting hard, I turn to survey the forest around me. The hunter must have detected her somehow. A scent, a taste on the wind, something even my senses cannot detect. She's close though. I can feel it. She's close, and if I can just—

A scream. Piercing and high.

Human.

Spitting curses through my teeth, I hurl myself over the edge of the promontory.

CLARA

I SCREAM.

I know I shouldn't. All I've done is let the Wild Hunt know exactly where I am. But I can't help it. The sound rips from my lungs as I fall backwards.

I have no chance to recover. The hands clutching my foot are attached to spindly little arms, but whoever is on the other end of them has all the leverage now. They yank me halfway into the water before my flailing hands manage to grab the rough edge of a boulder. I scream again, despite every effort to bite back the sound. My legs kick up a storm of froth and bubbles.

Then, quite suddenly, my shoe pops off.

The next moment, I'm scrambling and scrabbling away from the water's edge, crawling into the trees. Shudders rack my body. Half sobbing with terror, I press my back against the nearest trunk, pull up my knees, and wrap my arms around my soaked skirts. My one bare foot stands out white against the dark ground. It was the shoe I'd kicked off in the field. The one I'd hastily pushed back on, not bothering to tie the laces. Lucky for me I hadn't.

Another howl erupts in the night, followed by a second, a third. A whole pack of howling, echoing and reechoing through the trees, across the valley. They've found my trail. They're going to be on me in moments.

Still sobbing, I get to my feet and run. No time to feel the pain shooting through my bare foot. No time to worry if I'm going the right direction anymore, if I'm not sticking close enough to the river, if I'm too close, if I'm leaving too obvious a trail. I simply run. My satchel swings behind me, my arms pump the air, my hair flows in limp strands down my neck and shoulders.

I don't know what instinct makes me stop suddenly. Perhaps the goddess Tanyl doesn't want to make things too easy for her dreadful followers. Whatever the reason may be, I stop short just on the edge of the trees. Before me lies a stretch of bare, stony country, all ragged and savage, with only a few lonely trees rising here and there to lift skeletal arms to the sky. Ahead, the valley begins to rise again, climbing to the ridge where the Mercy Stones wait.

But much nearer—no more than twenty yards from where I stand—is one of the hunters.

It's a woman. Naked save for a sparse loincloth and a terrible breastplate of hand bones covering her bosom. Her horns twist to delicate points above her long blade-like ears. In the moonlight her skin gleams lavender, smeared with red handprint patterns that might be paint but might just as easily be blood. She stands poised on a stony outcropping, one leg bent. As I watch, her broad chest expands. Her clear yellow eyes spark as she searches along the tree line.

I duck back before those eyes sweep across my position. A mistake—the movement draws her gaze flicking sharply my direction. She stands a moment in frozen interest, ears pricked forward. Then she crouches, springs, and lands gracefully on uneven terrain below the outcropping.

The next moment, she's loping straight toward me.

I have no choice. Though the Mercy Stones are up ahead, I put my back to them and flee into the forest. Every step is an agony. Whatever feeble shreds of hope I'd tried to cling to now disintegrate through my fingers.

I retrace my footsteps, following the trail I've just broken through the forest. Soon the river's roar draws me back. Any moment, I expect to feel the spine-splitting pierce of a spearhead tearing through my body. But it doesn't come. I can't even hear footsteps pursuing me. Is the huntress on my tail or not?

I stagger to a halt. The waterfall lies before me. And the pool. And the cave. Once again, the urge to hide is almost overwhelming. This time, however, I recognize it for what it is: a glamour. Probably put forth by the nixie in the pool. An effective lure for unsuspecting prey.

I take a step to change course and flee into the deeper trees. Then I stop and look back at the pool, frowning.

On impulse, I yank my second shoe off my foot. Wincing with pain, I creep down to the pool, stretch out my arm as far as it will go, and drop the shoe right there, right on the edge. I scramble back up the rocks to the top of the waterfall, flatten myself there, and wait, peering down into the little grotto below.

The huntress appears like a phantom, melting out of the trees. She sinks into a crouch, and though I cannot hear anything, I can see the way her head dips and bobs as she sniffs the air through slitted nostrils. She creeps forward, knees bent, arms extended for support, sometimes dropping her head right to the ground. Smelling out my path, no doubt. Perhaps she does not see well in the dark. Or perhaps she simply prefers to be guided by her nose.

I hold my breath. If I stir even a hair, I'll give away my position. Those big ears of hers will pick up the barest sound. Then she'll make a single spring with those powerful haunches, catch me by the back of the head, and rip out my throat with her teeth. I can see it all, much too vividly. So I don't breathe. Blood throbs in my ears, and my lungs burn for lack of air. And still I don't breathe.

The huntress sniffs closer to the pool's edge. Her twitching ears prick forward as her attention focuses on my shoe. Still crouching, she ambles nearer, drops her head to sniff it.

Green hands shoot out from the water, catch hold of her ears, yank her off her balance, and right into the pool.

I'm up like a shot. I won't wait to find out who wins the

ensuing battle. With splashes and water-logged cries bursting in my ears, I clamber down the stones and back into the forest. The trail I've made is easy enough to follow, especially now that my eyes have adjusted.

More howling echoes through the trees around me. The Wild Hunt is closing in. Is this why I'm not dead? Why the huntswoman didn't chase me down and kill me with ease, as I'm sure she could have? She was simply making certain I didn't get past her, didn't have a clear route to the Mercy Stones. It was her job to drive me back into the forest.

I reach the edge of the trees and burst out into the moonlight. My bare feet leap from rock to rock, leaving bloody footprints in my wake. Shadows move in my peripheral vision . . . long, loping shadows. Horses? Wolves? Some combination of the two? I neither know nor care. Their riders are horned and howling, waving wild spears over their heads. They close in on my right, giving me no choice but to veer left and duck among the lower rocks of the rising valley slope.

The howling redoubles. I force myself to clamber a little higher, knocking loose stones free as I go. The Wild Hunt urge their mounts up the steepest slopes. They're before me, behind me, on either side. I have nowhere to hide, nowhere to flee.

I come to a halt beneath the shining moonlight, my gaze uplifted to the Mercy Stones far overhead. The foremost of the riders lets out a joyful yip and spurs his beast straight toward me, his spear poised overhead.

Suddenly, a shadow blocks out the moon.

I whirl. My eyes widen. A massive figure now stands before me. Vaguely man shaped, but in the same way that a child might form a doll out of mud and sticks, poking its finger into the topmost lump to make rude eyes and a lumpish mouth. Unlike a mud doll, which disintegrates at the slightest touch, this being stomps one great foot, and the whole valley seems to shake.

The riders slow their beasts. The hunter nearest me lowers his spear. His glittering eyes widen behind the bone mask. Then, with a wild whoop, he charges and flings his weapon. It hits its mark, directly between the two misshapen eyes of the rock giant. There it sticks, shaft vibrating.

The giant lets out a long, slow roar. Lifting one mighty fist, it yanks the spear away. Then it takes a leisurely, lumbering stride, swings a great arm, and knocks the hunter right off the back of his leaping mount. The hunter hits the ground with a sickening crunch. His body lies bent at a grotesque angle.

In that moment, an enormous mud-and-rock foot plants on the ground right in front of me. I stare at it, shocked by the sudden impulse that's come over me. Then, with a little shrug, I leap, land on that foot, and wrap my arms around a huge stone ankle.

The giant doesn't notice—as more of the Wild Hunt closes in, its attention is fully focused on stomping, pounding, crushing, and pulverizing. A cacophony of shrieks, howls, and growls explodes through my senses. I close my eyes, concentrating on nothing more than holding on as hard as I can. Death surrounds me. But then, I've grown rather used to walking with death lately. Perhaps I've developed a knack for it.

Finally, the foot comes down in a jarring step that knocks me loose. I roll, land on the ground, and keep rolling, trying to get clear of that foot before it stomps again. A shadow passes over me, then I'm bathed in moonlight once more. I draw a breath, count my limbs—all four present and accounted for—then spring upright.

The giant is a little farther down the slope. He clutches a horned man in one hand and a horned woman in the other. As I watch, he smacks them together like two dolls. I don't wait to see more. For the moment, the Wild Hunt is distracted. This is my chance.

Though pain courses through every jarred and aching bone in my body, I turn and race up the slope. I don't know where I find the strength. I know only that I must take any advantage offered to me and worry about thankful offerings later. The Mercy Stones are not far now. I see them—five jagged pillars shaped by ancient hands during long-ago cycles, before this age of the worlds. They seem both ancient and new to my eyes, brilliant and beautiful and so, so close.

Then a figure steps out from among the stones. Great antlers arc over his head, and his yellow eyes flash catlike with triumph.

I stop. It's too sudden, and I cannot keep my balance. My body tips forward. I land hard on my knees.

"Well done, little librarian," Vokarum says. "You were better prey than I could have hoped for. I will thank the goddess for both your life and your death and vow to drink a toast in your honor from your skull before I mount it on my wall."

He steps toward me, one deliberate pace after another. Then he stops. Braces himself. Raises his bristling spear up to shoulder height. Teeth flashing, he throws back his head to utter a ululating howl of triumph that rings out across the valley.

He doesn't see what my hands are doing.

He doesn't see how I've drawn my satchel onto my lap and pulled the book from inside.

He doesn't see the quill in my hand.

I never break his gaze. I hold those two yellow eyes of his with mine. Let him see what he wants to see. The cornered prey. Defeated. Despairing. Down on her knees.

He doesn't see my pen flick, quick and sure, forming the four simple letters of a single word: *Emma*.

"Gods forgive me," I whisper.

Vokarum's eyes narrow, the black pupils narrowing to slits. He tilts his head questioningly.

And then the red mist rolls in.

30

IT MOVES IN SLOW, UNDULATING COILS. LAZY. UNHURRIED. Like giant red serpents sliding between the stones, roiling down the slope. The color is brilliant even under moonlight, a red so bright, so glaring, it's almost painful to look upon. It reaches Vokarum where he stands, parts around his feet, and continues on, straight toward me.

Vokarum gives a little start of surprise, lowering his spear. He stares down at the mist, his lips curled in a snarl. He steps from one side to another, but the mist continues to wrap around his feet, clinging. He curses and stamps. Then suddenly, his whole body stiffens. I hear him draw a sharp breath just before he whirls and stares up at the Mercy Stones.

I look too. I don't want to. I know what I'll see there. But it's too late to stop it. So I will look. I will see what I've done.

A slight, pale figure stands among the stones in the center of a broad, flat, sacrificial slab. Her dark hair hangs over her face. Her white nightgown floats about her body, stirred gently by the mountain breeze. Moonlight shines all around her but seems to miss her, leaving her shrouded in a dark aura but nonetheless clearly visible down to the last exquisite detail. The delicate stitching of her hem. The cracked and broken nails of her bare feet. The tiny silver needle and trailing black thread pinched between the middle finger and thumb of her right hand.

She lifts her head. Hair falls away from her face, revealing the raw black stitches closing up her eyes. She smiles beatifically.

He's really most kind, she says. *You don't even know how kind he can be.*

"Noswraith!" Vokarum utters, followed by a harsh word that can only be a curse. He draws back his spear, takes aim, hurls it with all the might in his powerful arm. It speeds straight and true, pierces the little woman straight through the heart, and passes through her like she's nothing more than a dream. For that's all she is.

The spearhead strikes the stone slab behind her and shatters. The shaft falls, clatters to the ground, and rolls to a stop. The Eyeless Woman does not react. She lifts one bony foot, steps down from the altar stone. Toe to heel. Firm, but unrushed. She takes another step and another. Her red mist flows out and around her like an avalanche gathering and growing as it tumbles down the mountainside.

Vokarum screams, a high, wild, purely animal sound. He turns, kicking up clouds of red mist as he flees, but unable to get free of it.

The onslaught continues rolling after him. I hear him shout warnings to his people down below, hear answering shouts and howls.

Then the mist swallows me whole.

It's not like the last time I was caught. Then, my vision was obscured, and the pain began almost immediately, the pulverizing of my mind and body from some unseen force. This time, it's as though I kneel in a little pocket of safety, surrounded by some invisible shield. The mist rolls over me and around me, but where I sit, my book and quill in my lap, I am untouched.

Wondering, I get to my feet, still holding the book open, my quill poised. The mist obscures even the sky overhead, cutting me off from the world. I turn in place, seeking some thin place I might dart through to safety.

That's when the screams begin.

I know those screams. They're familiar. Like old friends. I've heard them many times before. Desperate and pleading. Angry and howling. Murderous and blubbering and broken. I've heard them all before, even as I hear them now. Muffled, distant, but unmistakable.

And it's my fault. I've done this.

I press my hands over my ears. I've dropped the book and quill, but it doesn't matter. All that matters is blocking out those horrible screams, blocking out the knowledge of what I've done. It's no use. I feel the deaths, the destruction. The lives of those horned hunters being ripped apart. This isn't some spindly-limbed water nixie pulling someone in for a dunking. This isn't some rock giant rudely awakened from slumber and lashing out in groggy rage.

This is a Noswraith. Pure, chaotic devastation. Born of my mind. Summoned by my pen.

And I've turned it loose on beings who have no means of defending themselves.

Something makes me look up. I don't know what, for there is no sound other than the distant screams. But somehow I open my eyes, lift my head. There! The mist has cleared. Just a little, just enough to create a path between me and the Mercy Stones. This is my chance.

I run. I don't think about it. I don't consider whether or not this might be a trap. It wouldn't matter anyway. Now I've seen the way, all I can do is run, run, run, promising myself that when I stand among those stones, when I reach that central slab, I will be safe, safe, safe.

I leap in among the stones and collapse against the altar. My hands are white and stark against that dark rock and the bloodstains of ancient days. Painful breaths heave in and out of my lungs, tearing up my throat. But I've made it. I've survived the Wild Hunt. I've reached the Mercy Stones, and now I'm owed my prize. I can get that head. I can save Danny, and—

I whirl around.

The Eyeless Woman stands before me, not even a full step between us. Her face is close to mine, her horrible stitched-up eyes twitching as though she's trying to raise her eyelids. Choking on a cry, I leap back, my hips pressed up against the stone slab. Suddenly, warm wetness pours down the right side of my face, and a stabbing pain explodes in my eye. I put up a hand only to find the socket is empty. Blood gushes, pouring freely.

The Eyeless Woman tilts her head to one side. The black threads binding her eyes dangle against her cheekbones, down her long, thin neck. *You're not seeing rightly.* Her lips twist back in a beaming, joyful smile. *I'll teach you to see as I do.*

Her hand catches me by the throat, drives me onto my back. I'm pinned to the stone altar. Only it's not an altar anymore. It's a rickety wooden table beneath the low rafters of a dark little kitchen. The kettle whistles cheerfully on the stovetop, and the cellar door stands open, red mist and gruesome screams billowing up from below. I writhe, twist, grapple to get hold of the edge of the table, to find some leverage. But the Eyeless Woman holds me fast, smiling down at me.

She holds up her needle and thread. *This won't hurt a bit,* she says and drives the needle into my cheek. More pain explodes in my head. I scream and kick and flail, helpless in her grasp. She bows over me, stitching, pulling. *It'll all be easier soon. And we can be happy. Together. Like we're meant to be.*

My single eye stares wildly up at her. Her grip on my throat is choking me, cutting off air. Darkness closes in and then . . .

And then the whistling tea kettle is flying through the air. It strikes her in the side of the head, warping her face.

She vanishes. I sit up partway, choking in a desperate gasp of air, then collapse back on the table. Slowly, the wooden boards beneath me melt back into ancient, bloodstained stone. Overhead, stars, not ceiling rafters, spin wildly as my vision cuts in and out.

I'm still struggling to catch my breath when a golden face appears in my line of view. "Darling, are you awake?"

I gurgle, blurt. Blink and shake my head. Oh gods! I have two eyes! Two eyes, both able to blink. My hands fly to my face, feeling all the little cuts and knicks from thorns but no gushing blood, no empty socket, no trailing threads. "I'm awake!" I gasp in a thin, choked voice.

Then hands gently help me to sit up, to swing my legs over the edge of the slab. I nearly fall, but strong arms catch and support me as I lean heavily into a warm, solid body and breathe in the scent of leather and ink and spice and *home*.

"Oh, gods!" I press my face into the Prince's chest. I can't believe he's here. I can't believe he came. I didn't think he would. His arms are around me, one hand rubbing little circles into my back.

"What have you done, Darling?" he says, his voice dark and deep. I whimper, unable to explain, unable even to try. He presses me a little closer. "Never mind. That's not important now. You have to bind her. Do you understand? *You* have to bind her. Where is your book?"

Shuddering, I pull back a little to look around us. The red mist still roils between the Mercy Stones and covers much of the ground. I spy an empty space where it avoids the book I dropped. My quill lies beside it.

When I point, the Prince springs to retrieve them, darting nimbly to elude the mist's curling fingers. He brings them back to me, presses them into my hands. "I wish I could do this for you," he says, gazing earnestly into my eyes. "My blood is not yet restored. I had just enough power to enter the Nightmare, to draw you out again. But I cannot bind her." He wraps his fingers over my hand, squeezing gently. "You can do it, Darling. I know you can."

"Yes." I grip the quill and meet his gaze. My brow tightens into a stern line. "Yes, I can. I will."

I bow over the book. For a moment, my hand hesitates. The page seems very blank and white, my pen very small and useless, my own mind turned to a puddle of terror. But all I must do is put words to the paper. Just that. The simplest thing in all the worlds. And the hardest.

I force my hand to move, press the nib into parchment. Shape that first word, then a second, a third. They come swiftly now, messy and rushed, spattering ink and leaving great gaps where there's nothing but the indentation of the pen pressed into the page. None of that matters. The magic is what counts. I take what's in my head and pour it out through my hand, transforming nothing into realities and worlds and wonders all captured in little squiggles of ink.

The Mercy Stones melt away. The night sky. The valley. Even the Prince. Once more, the listing walls of the little kitchen surround me, the rafters low overhead. The only thing that remains constant is the mist. It clings to the floor and piles up in the corners, belched from the open door of the coal cellar. Light from the stove fire illuminates it, reflecting against it until the whole room glows like the very pit of hell.

The Eyeless Woman stands in the open cellar door. She turns to face me. Her lips part, spread. Her smile is beautiful—it always was. Beautiful and strained and determined and terrified. She tips her face up, stretches out her hands, her palms extended as though to receive blessings from heaven.

Dearest, she says. Her sewn-up eyes twitch wildly, the stitches straining. *Dearest, come see for yourself. He really loves you, you—*

I drop to the floor and snatch up the spear shaft that doesn't belong in this world, but which lies beside the altar stone just one world over. Its broken head dangles from one end as I drive the butt straight into the Eyeless Woman's stomach.

Her voice chokes. Her smile shatters.

She lets out a pained gasp and staggers back a single step. A step that brings her right over the cellar stair, poised, off-balance.

"Sweet dreams, Emma," I growl and take another lunging step.

A gut-wrenching cry rips from her throat. Arms wheeling, she strives to catch herself as she tilts backwards into the waiting mist. I hear the thud of her body falling downstairs, her screams echoing, shattering, devastating.

Dropping the spear shaft, I leap forward. It takes all the courage I possess to reach through the open doorway into that writhing mist, to find the cellar door's handle, grasp it. Drag it shut.

Boom.

The house echoes like a cavernous tomb as the door settles in its frame. Beyond it, deep down below, the screaming never ends.

THE PRINCE

ER BODY CRUMPLES IN ON ITSELF LIKE A PIECE OF old parchment. The quill pen flutters from her fingertip, and the book tips from her lifeless hands.

She falls.

I catch her first, the book second. The cover burns as it hits my palms, magic bursting from its core. The spell is strong, but the ink is still drying. The Noswraith inside strains and twists against its bindings.

With a snap, I close the book. Slowly, the red mist around us begins to dissipate, coiling away into the darkness and gone. Soon there is nothing but barren rockface all around us. We are crouched under the stars, surrounded by that circle of stones.

I draw a long breath. Let it out slowly. Then, certain the binding will hold, I set the book down on the altar slab and turn my attention entirely to the girl in my arms. "Darling?" I breathe, stroking strands of hair back from her face.

She's so still, and her skin is so cold. A surge of panic wracks me. Gently I lay her down, then place my head against her chest. A prayer of gratitude slips from my lips. There's a heartbeat. Her strength is spent, but she's alive and whole. I can only hope her mind has not broken. I've seen it happen too many times, when a creator comes face-to-face with the monster born of her own dark soul. Vervain was not the first nor will she be the last to fall into insanity as the only source of escape from such horror.

But I won't let it happen to Clara. Not here. Not tonight.

"Darling?" I whisper, peering into her face. Her eyelids are not fully closed; I can just see the gleam of vacant eyes through her long lashes. "Darling, answer me. Answer me, gods damn it!"

She remains perfectly still.

I tip my head back, staring up at the heavens. Then I curse again, baring my teeth as I bow over her, press her to me, bury my face in her hair. "I thought I'd lost you. I thought you were gone where I could never reach you again. Why? Why must you do this? Why must you put yourself at such risk for those who do not deserve it?"

She does not answer. She does not move. There's wetness in her hair. Tears. Mine? I curse and shake my head viciously. I should hate her. I should loathe and despise her for putting me through such torture. But the truth is, I'd prefer this pain, this fear, this torment to any life I might live without her. Better to know the awful extent to which my heart may be wrung than to live with a heart untouched.

Eventually movement in the valley draws my gaze. Masked figures, eerie in the moonlight. All those hunters not torn to shreds by the Eyeless Woman. A grim smile pulls at my lips. Vokarum and his bloodthirsty hounds had no idea what sort of prey they'd chosen when they set upon my brave, my beautiful, my deadly librarian.

"You'd best wake up soon, Darling," I murmur as a tall figure stalks up the hillside, antlers gleaming in the moonlight. "We're not out of danger yet."

CLARA

I COME TO WITH A START.

My body jolts as though I'm pitching over a brink, plunging into darkness. I try to flail my arms, to catch myself, but my limbs won't obey me. It's like I'm bound, wrapped in iron coils, helpless.

Only . . . only no. These aren't iron coils holding me fast. They're arms. Strong arms, encircling my body. I'm not falling after all. I breathe in deeply, inhaling the scent of leather and subtle, strange spices. My head rests on a broad shoulder, my face tucked into the curve of a neck and cheek. I feel safe, but I don't want to. A groan vibrates in my throat, almost like a growl. But when I try again to move, I cannot find the strength.

"See!" barks a harsh voice. "The human lives." The words sound as though they're spoken through tremendous pain. I can't recall to whom that voice belongs, but it sends a blade of dread sliding through my heart. "Give her up, Prince. Her life is forfeit."

"I'm unclear how you've arrived at that conclusion," comes the answer, smooth as silk. "She reached the Mercy Stones before you caught her, did she not? If I'm remembering the rules of the Wild Hunt correctly, you owe her one shower of rare jewels."

With near superhuman effort, I manage to drag an eye open. A veil of inky hair falls across my vision, but I can just see a tall, indistinct form. His stance is odd. He lists heavily to one side, and his right arm dangles limp, appearing to be smashed, with bits of white bone sticking out through the flesh. His face is mangled, one eye swollen completely shut. Blue blood pours from his nose and lips, over his chin. The once proud antlers arching from his brow are broken with raw ragged edges.

But his one good eye flicks to meet mine. His swollen lips draw back, revealing bloodied gums and broken teeth. He points, his hand trembling with the effort required. "She summoned a Noswraith." Every word spits more blue blood. "She broke the Pledge. She killed my hunters, slaughtered them without mercy. What defense had they against such witchcraft?"

"Eh, serves them right." It's the Prince who answers. Of course, it is. Until this moment I've not quite been able to place the source of that calming scent, that sense of safety, of protection. Now, as my awareness slowly clarifies, I couldn't mistake him for anyone else. "Did no one ever warn you not to prey upon librarians? You must have known you were no match for her."

"We did not expect her to use her powers thusly!"

"Well, what did you expect her to do? Write you a late notice?" The Prince *tsks* severely. "You'd best not speak too loudly of Pledge-breaking, Vokarum. You know as well as I that the snaring of humans for the Wild Hunt is forbidden. If she has broken the Pledge, it was only in response to your initial breaking. Do you wish to take up the matter with King Maeral? We can venture to the Court of Night straight away, and—"

Vokarum utters a dreadful curse. His whole bloody, pulverized body lurches as though he wants to hurl himself straight at me, rip me from the Prince's arms, and tear me limb from limb. But his one good eye flashes from me to the Prince and stays there. Though the Prince is seated on the ground with one knee bent, holding me in his arms, something impends in the atmosphere around him—a tension of power that even I in my half-addled state cannot miss. Perhaps, were he not battered and bruised, the Noxaur lord would be willing to take the risk.

Instead he bares his broken teeth, spits another glob of blue blood. And backs off. Taking one lurching, agonized step after another, he retreats down the hillside, finally turning his back on us. I try to shake my head, try to shout. My body is too limp, nearly lifeless. All I can manage is a pathetic, mewling little, "I . . . I won the hunt . . ."

"Oh, that's right." The Prince lifts his head and calls after Vokarum's disappearing form, "What about that shower of jewels? She'd prefer diamonds and rubies, but emeralds are acceptable."

I try to force out more words, try to protest that I don't want jewels. I'm owed a request, whatever is in his power to grant. And I know exactly what I will ask for. But I cannot find the strength to speak.

Vokarum doesn't pause or break stride. He merely raises his hand in an obscene gesture and continues limping down the incline. Darkness envelops him, shielding him from my view.

"Well, Darling," the Prince says, resting his cheek atop my head once more, "you may have to wait to collect on your debt."

I let out a shuddering sigh. My eyelids fall. For now I can do nothing but lie still, encircled in the Prince's arms, listening to the sound of his heartbeat while he holds me beneath the watching eye of the moon.

I drift in and out of consciousness.

Sometimes I'm walking down an endless passage toward a round window gleaming with silver light. No matter how far I go, I never draw any nearer. The passage simply lengthens beneath my feet, the shadows stretching on forever, the light just out of reach. Open doorways line the walls on either side of me, leading into empty black chambers.

From those chambers a voice whispers: *He really loves you, you know. I'll teach you to see as I see.*

Other times, however, I regain awareness to find my head cradled on the Prince's shoulder, my body scooped in his arms and held against his chest. Wild terrain under starlight drifts in and out of my spinning vision. Open fields, dark forests, a bridge arching across a rushing river. Whatever stirs beneath the bridge goes still at the Prince's bark of: *"Felaadar."*

We cross unimpeded to the far side.

Not long after, the Prince halts. He lets out a long breath. "Well, Darling," he says into my hair, "though the ballads like to make out that a handsome hero may carry his ladylove indefinitely across all sorts of terrain, I've just about had it. Time for a breather, or we're both going to end up tumbled in a ditch."

Ladylove? I don't let the word linger in my mind as the Prince sets me down in a rather ignoble heap of limbs at the base of a large tree. The gnarled roots seem to curl welcomingly around me. Moss grows up the trunk like a natural cushion for my back and shoulders.

The Prince himself takes a seat on an arch of root partially upraised from the soil. He props his elbows on his knees and leans heavily forward, his hair falling in a black curtain over one shoulder. "Oaks are always friendly to humans," he says, tilting his gaze up to the branches interlaced above. "Tuck that tidbit away for future reference. If ever you find yourself traveling alone through the wilds of Eledria, always look for the oaks. They'll give you shelter. They don't care for fae much," he adds when the root on which he sits gives a sudden shiver and very nearly upends him. He slaps it sharply, like he might smack the rump of a recalcitrant horse. "Steady on!"

The tree rustles its leaves but otherwise goes quiet. It stands at the top of a rise overlooking the Valley of Bones on one side and the ocean on the other. From this position, I can see both the Mercy Stones and the Between Gate on its cliff in the not-so-far-off distance. Beyond the gate lies the pier where the morleth carriage waits to take me home.

Home . . . without Idreloth's head.

I hunch over, shivering suddenly, though the sea breeze caressing my face isn't cold. I plant my palms over my eyes, trying to press out the pain behind my right eyeball. For a long moment I can do nothing but sit in that attitude, not thinking, not feeling. Simply being. The Prince offers me silence; for that I am grateful.

At length, however, I feel his hand on my elbow. I shoot him a quick glance and find he's offering me a flask. "Drink," he says.

I accept, pleased to discover the flask contains pure water. Gods spare me, I am utterly parched! The relief of liquid rolling down my throat is like a sweet miracle.

When I'm done, I wipe my mouth with the back of my hand and offer the flask back to the Prince. He reaches to take it, his fingers closing around my own. A spark seems to shoot up my arm. I look up and meet his gaze. His expression is utterly unfathomable. I know he's furious. How could he not be? What I've done is so dangerous, almost lunatic.

I bite my lower lip. Then, though he has not asked, I say, "Emma was my mother."

For a moment he does not move. Then, very slowly, he blinks.

At a slight pressure from him, I release the flask, let him reclaim it. He tucks it inside the front of his jacket. I wrap my arms around my middle, waiting for questions I'm sure are coming. They don't. He continues to offer me silence.

But in that silence there's space waiting to be filled.

"She let our father hurt him," I say softly, turning from the Prince to look out across the open water beneath the starlit sky. "Oscar, I mean. My brother. She let our father hurt him. Me too, sometimes. Then she would find us and hold us. Comfort us. She would tell us it was going to be all right, reassure us over and over again. *He really loves you, you know,* she would say. *He's in pain,* she would say. *He was hurt when he was young. He doesn't know how to love properly. We have to help him. We have to teach him. We have to forgive him.*

"Then he would hurt us again. Mostly Oscar, because he was the boy and so much like Dad. So talented, so brilliant, so vulnerable. Dad used to boast of how proud he was of his 'boy genius.' But when we were home, when no one was around, he told Oscar he would never amount to anything. That he was useless, lazy. Too much like our mother. He would beat him, lock him in the cellar. Punish him for failing to measure up to his exacting standards.

"I was just a girl. I didn't matter as much. For the most part, Dad didn't bother with me. But when I tried to interfere for Oscar, then he would . . . he would . . ."

I can't finish. I don't want to. And the Prince sits there, his gaze never straying from my face. I feel it even if I dare not meet it.

Drawing a long breath, I tuck strands of hair behind my ear and continue. "Mama was always there to hold us when he was done. And we loved her for it. She was our angel. It wasn't until later— after she died, after she left us alone with him—that I started to wonder: Why didn't she save us? Why didn't she stop him? Why didn't she get us out?

"Instead she blinded herself. On purpose."

The old bitterness churns in my gut like poison. I lean into the oak tree, trying to draw comfort from its ancient strength. The smell of earth and moss and sea air fills my nostrils. But nothing can calm that burning in the pit of my soul.

"She blinded herself," I whisper, gazing up at the night sky through the branches and leaves. "And then she blinded us. We hated him, but we never questioned him. And we hated ourselves and our inability to please him, to be what he needed us to be. Worthy of his love. Worthy of his kindness rather than his wrath. Why could we never love him into loving us? Why?"

I rock side to side softly, trying to recall the way Mama would hold me and rock me when I cried onto her shoulder. I can almost feel her arms around me now, can almost hear her crooning voice: *He really loves you . . . he really loves you . . . he just doesn't know how to show it.*

"Dad loved me the most when he discovered that I was like him too. That I also wrote. I kept my secret stories hidden underneath the loose floorboard in my room. But he found them. And when he read the story I penned soon after Mama died . . . Oh! He was proud of me then. For the first time ever, he looked at me and said I was like him after all. He said, *'I always thought you were nothing more than a pale copy of that woman I married. But you've got more of me in you after all, don't you?'*

"It was like bathing in sunlight after a lifetime of darkness. I basked in his favor. I gloried in his praise. And when he told me he could take the story, make it better, that I could watch him do it and learn, I had never felt so . . . so valuable. Like I was the most important thing in the world. I thought, this is what it means to finally earn my father's regard.

"He took the story of the Eyeless Woman. He rewrote it in his style, smoothed out the rough patches. Made it shine. And when he sold and put his name on it, I never thought to protest. After all, why should I be credited? I was nothing but an extension of him, a tool for his use and benefit.

"Thus, he died. Executed for the monster I created."

A sob tears from my throat. I try to swallow it back, but it forces its way free, a painful, breaking sound. I stuff my knuckles into my mouth, desperate to smother a second and a third sob, but they refuse to be stilled. Tears spill down my cheeks as memories of that bloody end play in my head. All those memories I had blissfully lived without while under Estrilde's curse.

And still, the Prince sits by. Quiet. Waiting. Once, I see his hand stretch out as though he would touch me, but he stops himself and draws it back.

After a time, I find my voice again. "I wonder sometimes what

Mama would think if she knew I'd killed the man she loved. Maybe that's why she haunts me? Maybe it's her way of seeking vengeance." I drag my hand across my face, wiping away tears. Then I look up at the Prince, meet his steady gaze. "Well? Say something! I've gone and made a mess of it all. I've turned my Noswraith loose and killed again. I deserve to die. I deserve to be executed for my crimes, even as I should have been executed five years ago. So what are you going to do?"

This time when he reaches out, he takes my hand without hesitation. His fingers close around mine, and he doesn't seem to notice or mind how wet they are with tears and snot. Squeezing firmly, he draws my hand to his chest, presses it against his heart. I catch my breath, staring up at him, startled by the intensity of his gaze.

"You are strong, Clara Darlington," he says. "You are nothing like your father. That man was weak. The weakest man I've ever seen."

"He was a genius. It's a terrible burden to bear, the weight of genius."

"That sounds like the excuse of a weak man."

I bow my head, lowering my eyelashes.

"A strong man would never throw his daughter to the wolves in a bid to save his own skin. I saw him for what he was the moment I laid eyes on him." The Prince leans forward, his grip on my hand tightening. He touches my cheek with a gentle finger, wiping a stray tear away. Then he trails that finger down to my chin and tilts my face up, trying to catch my gaze. "I saw you as well."

It's a sweet sort of agony to look into his eyes. To see there what looks like . . . *wonder.* He shouldn't look at me that way. I don't deserve it. I never have. I never will.

"I'd never seen anything so magnificent," he whispers.

I shake my head. How can that be true? I remember too well kneeling before Lodírhal's terrible throne. I remember how I shuddered and wailed, how I made a fool of myself in my terror.

"I don't know what you thought you saw," I answer. "I don't know what you continue to think you see. But I'm not that. I'm not powerful. Even the Noswraith was the result of my father's efforts. Not mine."

"Edgar Darlington could never have brought such a fiend to life." The words are dark, edged with dangerous fire. "To create a Noswraith, one must live the very depths of human pain. Such pain can only be born from love. True love, bent and twisted and broken. Edgar Darlington never loved. He didn't know the meaning of the word. His heart was never broken because it was a stone. Thus, he was ultimately limited in his power.

"But you? You know how to love. Your heart has been broken, and from that heartbreak you created life. Dark, dreadful life, but life, nonetheless. Yours is a power far beyond your father's mean scope."

I pull away from his touch, pressing back against the oak. "So I am guilty. It is I who should have died that night, my head which should have rolled."

The Prince doesn't release his hold on my hand. "We are none of us innocent. But your darkness was not purposefully created. You did not choose to bring the Eyeless Woman to life. You did not even choose to share her story. That choice was taken from you.

Thus, you are absolved of that particular guilt."

I twist my head around, glaring up at him almost ferociously. "And how can *you* absolve me?"

"Perhaps I can't." He shakes his head slowly, his lips tilting in an agonizingly beautiful smile. "But I can forgive you."

"I killed your mother."

"I forgive you."

"I killed those monsters tonight. Unleashed horror and let them be battered to death."

"I forgive you."

"I placed you in danger. Imperiled the whole library."

"I forgive you."

I stare at him. Why do I sense he's not saying *I forgive you* at all? Those are his words, yes—three words, simply spoken yet deeply profound. But . . . another meaning underlies them. A deeper meaning. He speaks one set of words . . . but if I listen closely, it is three other words I hear.

"Why?" I ask at last, my voice little more than breath.

He smiles again. "That is for me to know and for you to discover."

Suddenly, I want to kiss him. The urge is so strong, it's nearly enough to overcome me. I want to lean forward, catch his face in both hands, and draw his lips to mine. To lay claim to the unspoken something that I both fear and hope he now offers, burning in the air between us.

But I can't. Because I don't deserve to claim such a gift. I never did. I never could.

Rising abruptly, I reclaim my hand from his, step over the oak's big roots, and pace swiftly away from its shelter. My footsteps carry me to the edge of the rise. There I stand, gazing out on the ocean, on the distant hazy horizon where Vespre lies.

"We should go," I whisper. I'm not sure the words carry back to where the Prince still sits behind me. Steeling my resolve, I lift my chin and speak again more firmly. "We should go."

After a moment, he rises. I listen to his footsteps approaching behind me, feel how near he stands at my back. My whole being prickles with the wish that he would reach out even now, wrap his arms around me, and draw me to him.

But all he says, in a voice so soft I can only just discern it over the sighing of the wind, is: "Your carriage awaits, Darling."

I'M NOT SURE HOW THE PRINCE MANAGED TO ARRIVE
in Noxaur just in time to rescue me. There isn't a second
morleth carriage waiting at the pier, after all. He must have
some other means of travel of which I'm unaware.

However it may be, he assists me into the waiting carriage and
proceeds to climb in after me. To my relief, he takes a seat on the
opposite bench and fixes his gaze firmly out the window. Offering
me privacy, of a sort. I am grateful.

The carriage lurches into motion, the Darksteppers soon
finding their stride as they carry us into the sky. I pull back a bit of
black curtain. My view through the window is made up entirely of
ocean and stars arching on to meet a seemingly endless horizon.
The sight makes me dizzy. Sighing, I let the curtain drop and lean
back against the seat cushions. My body is bruised and exhausted.

I long for nothing more than to sink into one of the scented baths Lir likes to draw for me. To let steam and sweet-smelling vapors carry away the stink of fear and horror and guilt.

But I cannot let myself relax. Not yet. I must stay sharp.

Opening my eyes, I find the Prince's gaze turned to me once more. The carriage feels suddenly too close and too dark for comfort. I shift awkwardly, twisting my hands in my lap. Then I draw a deep breath, pull my shoulders back, and fix a carefully blank expression in place.

"I will be returning to Noxaur tomorrow," I say as casually as though remarking on the weather.

"What?" The word snaps from his lips, sharp as a bite.

I neither flinch nor hesitate. "I bargained with Vokarum before the hunt began. We agreed that should I survive, I was to name my own prize. I intend to claim the head of the Eight-Crowned Queen."

The Prince's eyes flare in the shadows. "Don't be foolish. After the events of the day, there's no way Vokarum will honor such a bargain."

"He is fae. He will have to."

To my dismay, the Prince shakes his head. "Both sides of this particular bargain involved Pledge-breaking. You'll find it doesn't hold."

A stone sinks in my chest. All of that terror . . . all of that pain . . . all of that death and darkness . . . for nothing? No. It cannot be. But when I look into the Prince's eyes, I see no deceit there. He might be lying, of course. His human blood may have regenerated enough to allow for a lie. But I don't think so.

"Fine," I say coldly, refusing to let any disappointment color my tone. "I'll just have to make another bargain then."

Terrible stillness comes over the Prince. He may as well have turned to stone. I turn away, look out the window again. Watch the passing stars, the rushing waves. When I crane my neck, I can just discern the shores of Vespre. Soon we'll be flying over the city.

"What can you possibly be thinking, Darling? If, indeed, you're thinking at all."

I inhale slowly, hold my breath, count to ten. When I face the Prince again, I am as cool as a winter morning. "Vokarum won't try to hunt me again. He knows my power. He knows what I am willing to do. Now that we understand one another, I'm sure we can reach an equitable bargain."

"*Equitable* and *Vokarum* don't belong in the same sentence." The Prince narrows his eyes, his jaw twitching. "I'm beginning to doubt the word makes any sense relating to you either. The events of this insane day should have driven such notions from your head."

"On the contrary, I feel more confident than ever in my ability to get what I need. Why?" I tilt my head and offer a thin-lipped smile. "Don't you want me to try again?"

"That question merits no answer. You're being a fool."

"I am determined to do whatever I must to save Danny."

My words have affected him. I can almost see his soul writhing behind the mirrors of his eyes. He wants to forbid me. It's right there on the tip of his tongue. And when I refuse to hear reason, he'll take a step further. Because he must. If he wants to keep me safe, he must.

His lips part. I wait, my breath held. The injunction is coming, I'm sure of it.

"Soran Silveri once told me the true origins of his Noswraith."

I frown. The Prince's voice is musing, distant. This is not at all what I expected him to say.

He continues, however, his eyes a little distant, gazing off into some middle space over my shoulder: "He told me that the Thorn Maiden—Helenia, as is her true name—was inspired by a woman he once loved who betrayed him and broke his heart. He believed when he wrote the spell of her making that he recreated her. But in the end, he said, the Helenia born of his pen was nothing like his faithless lover. Rather, she was Soran. A twisted, dark, tangled thing born straight from his own heart. As much a part of him as his breath, his soul."

It takes everything I have to maintain the cold mask on my face. Fire pounds in my veins. I open my mouth, my lips curling back in snarl. "I am *nothing* like Emma."

"Aren't you?"

"Emma was passive. Frightened. Weak." I sit straighter, my hands gripping the edges of the seat. "I am nothing like her. I will do whatever it takes to save Danny, and, in so doing, I will save Oscar as well. I will take action. I will put myself at risk for their sakes. I won't just sit back and watch them suffer."

"And you think your mother did not risk her own life every day to stay with your father?"

"She was a coward. She never raised a finger to help us."

"No. Instead she sacrificed everything she loved on the altar of her chosen god." The Prince leans forward in his seat, drawing his face level with mine. "And what of you? What idol have you chosen? And what are you willing to sacrifice for its sake?"

I wrench away from him, dragging in a ragged gasp of breath. With everything I have in me, I throw up a wall of silence as impenetrable as any spell. I cannot bear him. I cannot bear to look at him, to speak to him, to hear him. Not now. He doesn't understand. He cannot understand. He doesn't know what it's like to watch a little brother beaten both physically and emotionally by his own father. To be helpless to do anything to prevent it. He doesn't know what it is to feel that one would give one's all to protect the innocent, to preserve what is true and beautiful and right. And, when that chance is lost, to reclaim whatever good still remains.

You're not seeing rightly . . .

The voice whispers in the back of my head, just behind the throbbing in my right eye socket. Something hot and wet trickles down my cheek, but when I put up my hand to touch it, my fingers come away unstained.

You're not seeing rightly . . . you're not seeing rightly . . .

I am not the one struggling to see. It's him. It's the Prince. He doesn't see, he doesn't understand. But I'll show him. I'll show him what it means to truly love. To risk everything for the sake of the one beloved.

The morleth pass over the twilit city of Vespre, touching down at last before the palace steps. The carriage driver climbs down from his seat and opens the door, extending a stone hand to me. I don't move to take it. I remain where I am, drawing long steadying breaths. I know what I must do. And I'm not afraid to do it. I merely need a moment to compose myself. That is all.

Then I lift my gaze and catch the Prince's eyes.

"Tomorrow, I will return to Noxaur. I will find Lord Vokarum. I will have my bargain."

His skin has drained of all color, leaving him pale and a bit sunken around the eyes. He looks not unlike he did when the curse had him in its clutches. "You are determined to make this mistake."

"I am determined to save Danny."

His jaw clenches. "Very well." He leans forward, drawing his tense face near to my own. "You have pushed me to the brink, Darling. What choice do I have?" He looks as though he will be sick. "Your labor is owed to the library. I forbid you to abandon that labor for any other venture. Until your Obligation is complete, you will honor your duties as a Vespre librarian."

I've won.

It was as easy as that in the end. I feel the stranglehold of Obligation pouring out from him, wrapping around me. But I don't resist. Why would I? This is exactly what I hoped for.

"Very well, Prince," I answer with a smile. "I will honor my Obligation as I must. Until my next free day. And then . . ." I lean toward him, bring my nose within an inch of his, our lips a mere breath apart. With only the slightest tilt forward, I could close that space between us.

I drop my voice to a whisper, "And then I will exact your Obligation in turn."

ENSLAVED

SHE'S WILLING TO GIVE UP EVERYTHING.

**HE'S WILLING TO GIVE UP EVERYTHING...
EXCEPT FOR HER.**

The time has come. Clara will command the Prince of the Doomed City himself to aid her in her quest. Together, they must travel into the various courts of Eledria, facing foes and monsters, each more deadly than the last. But each new bargain tangles her in a web of intrigue far more dangerous than she ever imagined.

Worse still, she finds herself becoming irresistibly drawn to the enigmatic Prince . . .

Return to wander through the dangerous realms of the fae with Clara and her Prince. Fair warning: this book will break your heart!

ALSO BY SYLVIA MERCEDES

This arranged marriage romance about a human princess forced to wed a dark and desperate Shadow King is sure to entice!

BRIDE OF THE SHADOW KING TRILOGY

Though she is the oldest daughter, Princess Faraine lives in the background, shunned from court and kept out of sight. Her chronic illness makes her a liability to the crown, and she has learned to give place to her beautiful, favored younger sister in all things.

When the handsome and enigmatic Shadow King comes seeking a bride, Faraine is not surprised that her sister is his choice.

Though not eager to take a human bride, King Vor is willing to do what is necessary for the sake of his people. When he meets the lively Princess Ilsevel, he agrees to a marriage.

So why can't he get the haunting eyes of her older sister out of his head?

The first book in a new fantasy romance series, this sweeping tale of love and betrayal is perfect for readers looking for a touch of spice to go with the sweet in their next swoony, slow-burn romance.

ABOUT THE AUTHOR

SYLVIA MERCEDES makes her home in the idyllic North Carolina countryside with her handsome husband, numerous small children, and the feline duo affectionately known as the Fluffy Brothers. When she's not writing she's . . . okay, let's be honest. When she's not writing, she's running around after her kids, cleaning up glitter, trying to plan healthy-ish meals, and wondering where she left her phone. In between, she reads a steady diet of fantasy novels.

But mostly she's writing.

After a short career in Traditional Publishing (under a different name), Sylvia decided to take the plunge into the Indie Publishing World and is enjoying every minute of it. She's the author of the acclaimed Venatrix Chronicles, as well as The Scarred Mage of Roseward trilogy, and the romantic fantasy series, Of Candlelight and Shadows.